TO LOVE A HERO

Also by Suzanne Goodwin

FLOODTIDE
SISTERS
COUSINS
DAUGHTERS
LOVERS

TO LOVE A HERO

SUZANNE GOODWIN

Michael Joseph
LONDON

MICHAEL JOSEPH LTD

Published by the Penguin Group
27 Wrights Lane, London W8 5TZ, England
Viking Penguin Inc., 40 West 23rd Street, New York, New York 10010, USA
Penguin Books Australia Ltd, Ringwood, Victoria, Australia
Penguin Books Canada Ltd, 2801 John Street, Markham, Ontario, Canada L3R 1B4
Penguin Books (NZ) Ltd. 182–190 Wairau Road, Auckland 10, New Zealand

Penguin Books Ltd, Registered Offices: Harmondsworth, Middlesex, England

First published 1989

Typeset in Linotron 11/12½pt Ehrhardt by Wilmaset, Wirral
Printed and bound in Great Britain by
Richard Clay (The Chaucer Press) Ltd, Bungary, Suffolk

A CIP catalogue record for this book
is available from the British Library

ISBN 0 7181 3195 9

Library of Congress catalog number 89-84726

PART ONE

1

It was a time of sudden death and people were practical. The news was broken to Sorrel Scott by a Wren officer who, after a word of sympathy, granted her compassionate leave and gave her a railway pass. Sorrel had to fill in a fresh form. She had no next of kin.

Lilian Scott was killed on a winter night, when a hit-and-run bomber flew over London. The real blitz had ended in 1941, and now at the start of 1942 any bombing of the capital was rare and almost haphazard. Londoners could stay in their homes at night instead of trekking to the Underground with thick coats, blankets, baskets of food. Cockney jokes and sing-songs, shrouded figures in bunks, no longer altered the stations into modern catacombs. Sometimes the sirens did wail and people sighed, 'Oh, not *again*!' Then a few random bombs were dropped, and the enemy escaped or was shot down in flames. It was nothing to worry about.

On a bitter night at the end of January a German bomber came buzzing over the great blacked-out city, and an old fashioned block of flats near Kensington Gardens was directly hit. It vanished in clouds of dust.

Margaret Reilly was Sorrel's only close Wren friend, and when she heard the news she thought, well, people get killed all the time. Will Graham, a flight lieutenant who had flirted with her last week, had been lost two days ago over the North Sea. He was scarcely mentioned now. And besides, thought Margaret, Sorrel had once confessed that she and her mother were not close. She'd said an odd thing:

'I'm not sure we actually love each other. How does one know?'

'Oh. One knows all right.'

Sorrel had looked at her.

'Then I suppose I don't.'

Margaret remembered this when Sorrel, white in the face, returned from seeing the commanding officer. Margaret murmured a few words of sympathy and after that, though kind, was matter-of-fact. Sorrel behaved well. But she was thoughtful.

Snow had fallen at the start of the year and had not melted. It lay on the frozen fields near the sea, like icing sugar sprinkled on a dark plum cake. The girls should have been stationed in a Wrennery: austere naval quarters would at least have been warmish and dry. But there was no room for them at the Fleet Air Arm base, and a dozen or so Wrens had to live in what were called landladies' digs. Margaret and Sorrel shared a bedroom of penetrating cold. It was damp, too. When they took clean clothes from the chest of drawers and draped them in front of the sputtering gas fire, the clothes steamed.

Margaret Reilly was good-tempered and good-looking in a striking goddess-like way. Her family came from Dublin and she had the Irish charm. She was a tall, dimpled, confident girl with a pretty pitch of voice; she laughed easily. She was also philosophical, called the icy weather 'a bit sharp', and when rain beat down observed that in Ireland it would scarcely be noticed. She was cheerful and it was a duty to be so.

Sorrel was not as remarkable-looking as her friend, nor Irish dark. Her thick brown hair was naturally curly, her hazel eyes swam, making her look half-asleep. Men thought that sexy, but it was an accident of birth inherited from a forgotten grandmother. Belying the swimming expression of her eyes, she was impulsive. Margaret's common sense rarely stopped her from doing rash things.

Until her mother's death it had been Sorrel who was rather a star among the Wren ratings. She was the first to sit up late at night altering her badly cut uniform to make it fit. She invented a way to wear the hideously unbecoming gabardine uniform hat, rolling up the brim and tugging the hat down at an angle. And when the station commander during a lecture announced that one girl might go on a flight in a Fairy Seal, Sorrel volunteered so fast that the other girls hadn't time to open their mouths.

The approaching flight was the talk of the Wrens' Mess, and an impressed silence fell when a large naval rating came to fetch her.

He accompanied Sorrel across the airstrip. A strongish wind was blowing. She knew, didn't she, he asked, that she was going to fly in an open cockpit? He gave her a leg-up into the small plane which was waiting, and fastened her in by what he called the monkey chain.

'If there's an airpocket and the plane drops down, we don't want you left up in the air, now, do we? Ho ho.'

He told her to fix on her parachute.

'Ever parachuted? Don't worry, you only pull the cord. Flown before, have you?'

'Never.'

'Know what to do if your pilot says jump?'

'I jump.'

'That's the ticket. And if you're sick, you can pay me two bob and I'll clean up after you.'

Sorrel returned from the flight weak in the knees, and crimson in the face from excitement. Margaret Reilly couldn't help a stab of envy – she and Sorrel were often rivals in their work. Both were quick, and both liked to excel. She wished she had been as fast as Sorrel at volunteering to fly.

Margaret was fond of Sorrel. Belonging to a large family, she couldn't imagine what it would be like to be an only child. In the way of life in the services, Margaret needed her. The Wrens were a mixture of different characters, disparate backgrounds. There was a mousey girl who had been a brilliant history scholar at Cambridge, two shop assistants from John Lewis's, a sexy-looking girl called Moyra who could take a car to pieces and put it together again. And many others. Sorrel suited Margaret, and they got on well until Lilian Scott was killed.

Convinced that sympathy was weakening, if not actually dangerous, Margaret's manner to her friend during the days that followed the tragedy was careful. Never too sympathetic. Sometimes rather brisk. Sorrel ignored that. Life was uncomfortable, concentrated, intensely busy. The girls were allowed little time to think and less time off. Sorrel and Margaret were on a photographic course, and were working hard. In the free hours between lectures, they sometimes took a bus into Littleport.

In peacetime and summertime, the Sussex town had been a happy place. Bathers had hired the rows of painted bathing huts, and emerged from them in swimsuits to hobble down the shingle. In windy weather, families camped inside the huts, brewing tea and eating cup cakes. When the tide was out it revealed enormous stretches of ribbed sand where the children spent hours making sandcastles and digging lakes. Then back came the tide, leaving the sand flat all over again, ready for more pies and turrets and pools for crabs and emerald-coloured seaweed.

The town was dreary now. It was shabby and nearly deserted, the wind blew down the streets and in the distance the winter sea made a dull steady roar.

Soon after their arrival at Littleport, the two friends had found a refuge for their time off – a teashop in a side street. It was called The Blue Parrot, was gratefully warm and chintzy, and was owned by a birdlike woman, more sparrow than parrot, who admired everybody in uniform. She gave Sorrel and Margaret extra slices of her victory sponge, made from a Ministry of Food recipe with potatoes and breadcrumbs, and charged them for only one slice.

On a bitter afternoon three weeks after Lilian Scott was killed, the two friends were nursing teacups in The Blue Parrot. Margaret, thought Sorrel with rare irony, has stopped behaving like a nurse coming into the ward to check on a patient emerging from the anaesthetic. Thank heaven for that.

Sorrel perfectly understood why Margaret had been behaving the way she had. She knew her friend had been doing what she was convinced was right. She had mutely said to Sorrel, don't let go. Hang on. Keep a stiff upper lip, you *need* to do that.

Margaret was perfectly right; to crack up under sorrow and an uneasy conscience was out of the question. One shouldn't and didn't. But Margaret still got on her nerves. Particularly a recent trick of not answering if it looked as if Sorrel were going to talk about the past. Is she afraid that even mentioning my mother will make me start to cry? wondered Sorrel. There had been, in consequence of Margaret's good intentions and Sorrel's grief, an impasse between the friends. Margaret's nervous carefulness meant that Sorrel hadn't been able to tell her just how horrible it had been when she'd gone to London.

Her mother's flat was in a quiet part of Kensington near the park; the taxi driver had stopped at the far end of the street.

'Sorry, Miss, can't go no further after last night's raid.'

Sorrel waited until he had driven away, then ducked under a rope stretched across the road with a 'No Entry' sign hastily erected beside it.

She walked towards her home. As she came nearer she began to shiver. Coniston Mansions was an old-fashioned, pleasant brick building of the 1890s, comfortable and rather stately, with lofty windows and a pair of large glass-fronted doors. Picking her way with difficulty across fallen timbers and mounds of broken bricks and shattered glass, the girl came to the edge of a crater. It was like looking down into an open mine. It was deep and black and charred by fire. Death lay there. As she stood looking down, a few flakes of snow fluttered through the air like torn paper, landing on the burnt bricks and decorating them.

The rest of the day was an organised nightmare. She reported to the police who sent her to the Civil Defence. At a large defence post somebody told the ashen-faced girl as much as was known. The time of the bomb. When the fire services and rescuers had arrived. The fact that nothing could be done, there were no survivors – as if Sorrel, having seen the crater, needed to know that. Kind people, and the great dirty city was full of them, made her mugs of strong tea. After a long wait at the defence post, she saw a man approaching. He was carrying a cardboard box. It contained the only things which had been found in the ruins. A shoe. Some half-burnt books. A broken string of blue beads. A broken tortoiseshell cigarette case. Some uniform buttons and a cap with a Royal Artillery badge. There was a remnant from a black velvet dress. And a mesh handbag.

When she saw it, Sorrel felt sick. She recognised it, although the silver mesh was quite black.

'That's my mother's.'

'I thought it might be. There's a powder compact with L.S. on the lid,' said the man kindly. 'Perhaps you'd like to look at what's inside.'

Accustomed to his work, gentle, compassionate, he put the blackened object into her hands.

Sorrel tipped the contents into her lap. The compact was of blue enamel, the initials in marcasite; it had been a present from her father to her mother years ago. There was a lipstick, worn down at one side, and a handkerchief. A tiny purse containing a pound note. The keys of the flat on a ring with a miniature champagne cork which Lilian had won in a raffle. Right at the bottom of the handbag, folded small, was a letter.

Sorrel signed for the bag, gave her naval address and went out into the dying afternoon, passing an old woman selling snowdrops. She bought two bunches for fourpence. Walking back to the crater and standing by it in the gathering dark, she undid the raffia round the stalks and threw the flowers, thin blossom by thin blossom, on to the rubble.

Returning to the base, she was quiet and sensible, did not go to the medical officer for something to make her sleep, didn't even take aspirins. She sat among the other Wrens, working to the roar of planes outside on the airfield, flying round, landing, then taking off and doing the whole thing again. The noisy training was called circuits and bumps. Her companions were kind to her. Margaret continued to be brisk.

In the last two years tragedy had become a commonplace. Emerging from air raid shelters in the dawn, people walked back to find their homes blown to pieces. Families lost their sons at Dunkirk, their husbands in the Atlantic. And now, in February 1942, the calamities were making Britain reel; the fall of Singapore was the worst disaster ever to happen to the British army. What had happened to Sorrel, thought Margaret, shrank into nothing when you looked at what was happening in the world.

Not to Sorrel, though. She'd had no time to prepare for the cruel exit and her head was filled, night and day, with terrible questions. Had her mother been alone when the bomb fell? Or with friends, sitting down to one of those boring games of bridge. She played bridge with Mrs Greenway who lived on the floor below, which might explain the keys in the handbag. But why the pound note? Perhaps it was there from the last time Lilian had gone out to dinner. My God, thought Sorrel, what does it matter? She was probably with Maud Greenway and her husband, having a sherry and smiling at his facetious jokes. They had heard the warning and taken no notice. The people in Coniston Mansions had remained in their own flats through the blitz, proudly saying, 'These old blocks are solid; none of the modern rubbish.' The sound had wailed across London. Then had come the bee-buzz overhead. And the next minute – eternity.

It shocked Sorrel, as she picked up her own life, to discover that she did not grieve enough for the mother who had been wiped out as if somebody had trodden on a pale soft moth. Lilian Scott had resembled such a creature. She had clouded grey hair, a thin delicate face, her voice was soft, her movements fluttery. She was reserved and, in a way, she was cold. Sorrel knew Lilian had worried over money but she would never talk about it. Sometimes when she was on leave, Sorrel came into the drawing room to find her at the desk going through her papers. Seeing her daughter, she always covered up what she was doing with a blotter and asked Sorrel to 'leave her in peace'. Now, thought Sorrel, there was nothing to do for her poor mother but that.

The emotion known to the young when their parents die came strongly to Sorrel. She should have asked more, coaxed more, listened more to learn about the reserved stranger she'd known, and not known, all her life. It was my fault, she thought, I could have done something to get through to her. But in her heart she knew that wasn't true. Lilian did not wish Sorrel to probe. She kept her away. And with the remorse at her own lack of daughterly love Sorrel was filled with uncomfortable curiosity.

She had shown Margaret Reilly the letter she had found in the handbag. It had mystified both girls, who had talked it over a number of times. The letter was written on expensive paper, the handwriting strong and slanting, the engraved address a mere: 'Evendon Priory, Hampshire'. It was dated three weeks before Lilian's death.

My dear Lilian,

I received your letter and I must tell you that since you have already been paid your usual monthly cheque, and indeed only recently I added an extra £100 at your request, I'm afraid I cannot see my way to send any more at present.

I realise you have expenses and that your daughter, serving her country, needs an allowance. But I must admit I think the amount you give her seems excessive. I hope you will not be too upset and think me harsh, but the fact is that now we must all learn to live within our incomes. The usual amount will, in due course, be sent to your account. But *not* in advance, and *not* more than the customary sum.

Surely, with a little thought, you can manage very well. Grace joins me in sending her regards. Now why don't you come and visit us at the Priory? You would enjoy the Hampshire air and we can feed you up with Grace's farm eggs and milk.

Just drop us a line if you would like to come.

As ever,
George

Sitting in The Blue Parrot, warm for the first time that day, Sorrel fished the letter out once again from the webbing gas mask case which girls in the three services used as handbags, their hoarded make-up jogging against the celluloid eyepiece of the mask.

Rereading the letter for the twentieth time, Sorrel rubbed her chin. Margaret said, 'I wish you'd listen to me about all this.'

Sorrel didn't answer, but continued to look at the letter. 'Fascinating to find out who he actually *is*,' she said, after a pause.

'Sorrel, wouldn't it be wiser to let the whole thing drop?'

'What thing?' Sorrel asked impatiently. They had had this conversation before. 'What do I know about Mother's money? Nothing. As I told you, all the bank did was post me the awful overdraft. Apparently there is no family solicitor, and everything she – and I – owned is kaput.'

'Oh, I know.' Margaret sighed.

Sorrel did not give her a very friendly look. She knew Margaret had a horror of the effect of pity or self-pity or both. She was treating Sorrel as she herself would prefer to be treated in time of tragedy.

But Sorrel, finishing off some crumbs of the victory sponge, found herself resenting Margaret's well-meant principles and behaviour. Would Margaret have been different, she wondered, if Sorrel had belonged to a large and loving family like the Reillys? Sorrel had remembered, once or twice, the fact that she'd confessed to Margaret that she did not exactly love her mother.

Margaret's life brimmed with love. The Reillys lived in Chichester, a home full, six children, parents, visiting aunts and grandparents, all devoted, admiring each other, talking at the same time, keeping in touch when the war parted them. Margaret had a brother in the navy, sisters and brothers still at school. Family feeling was strong. They telephoned each other, wrote and received family letters, and when parted knitted scarves and pullovers for each other. They were a united clan, and proud of their Irishry. It was as if all the year round they wore bunches of shamrock pinned to their lapels. Possibly to escape Margaret's stern attitude just now, Sorrel had decided upon a wild goose chase.

'I shall find out who this George is', she said, folding up the letter.

'Honestly, I don't know what good that will do.'

No, you don't, do you? thought Sorrel. You're not miserable and penniless, with a dead mother about whom you feel guilty all the time. But she could not say any of that. Her friend's face was kind. That was the devil of it.

'Of course, poor Sorrel, there's no insurance,' remarked Margaret, after a moment. 'War counts as an act of God.'

'Don't rub it in.'

'But I'm not!' exclaimed Margaret, somewhat horrified, 'I was only – '

'Oh, I know. Sorry. I'm jumpy at present. It's probably those bank statements,' she added, preferring to talk about something concrete. 'There's still this month's payment from George, whoever he is. But of course the allowance is sure to stop.'

'You mean they'll inform him?'

'Yes. They'll have to.'

The girls were silent for a moment.

'But *why* did he pay her any money at all?' said Sorrel. The question was one she'd repeated over and over. To Margaret. To herself.

'You don't know for certain that he did.'

'Oh, don't be silly, Margaret, his letter says so.' Sorrel irritably stuffed the letter back in her gas mask case.

'It would be much easier for me just to shut up,' said Margaret, her handsome face serious. 'But what's the use of a friend who doesn't say what she thinks? I really do feel you shouldn't go haring off to try and find that man. Suppose you actually succeeded. All you'd ask would be about the money, which is – well – a bit crude, isn't it? Whatever he did for your mother, Sorrel, he's scarcely likely to do it for you.'

'You mean he was her lover, ages ago.'

Margaret looked down her nose; Sorrel had offended her prudery.

'Anyway,' continued Sorrel, 'what else can I do with my weekend leave?'

'I hope you're not going to tell him you've taken an entire weekend to hunt him out, whoever he is, supposing you *do* find him. Then he'll be certain you're only turning up because of the money.'

'Of course I won't tell him. I'll say I'm on my way to friends and just called in on the off-chance.'

'As far as I'm concerned, I wish you were staying with friends. Us,' said Margaret. 'But it's obvious you've made up your mind.'

Glad of distraction, Sorrel went to the library on her half-day pass and found a guidebook on Hampshire. 'Evendon Priory. Fine stone house, 1650 to 1675, on ruins of medieval priory. Fishpond and tithe barn.' She studied the map. She'd take a train to Portsmouth, then try for one on a branch line. From Evendon station she would get a lift from some kindly intentioned person. Sorrel had all the confidence of a girl in uniform who had travelled once in a Rolls and many times in army lorries and bakers' vans.

She was early at the station which in the usual wartime way was crowded; nobody appeared to be heeding a large poster which asked 'Is Your Journey Really Necessary?' When the train arrived Sorrel managed to get a seat, given her by a gallant elderly civilian. But she had to make her thin self thinner, for there were soon nineteen people in the carriage, not counting a baby wrapped in a shawl, who slept for most of the journey. When he did wake, his mother fed him with a bottle which he loudly sucked, his little glittering eyes fixed upon it, daring his mother to take it away.

The train started half an hour late. The stations at which it stopped had no identification, for the names of every railway station, every signpost, town and village had been removed all over the British Isles at the time of the expected invasion in September 1940. Since then to travel anywhere was a journey in limbo. It took ingenuity and the fortunate presence of local people in a train for a traveller to discover where the devil he happened to be.

Hours crawled as slowly as the train, which did not only halt at mysterious stations but in tunnels, when there was a good deal of clicking cigarette lighters and striking matches, since the compartment lights didn't work. And many times the train simply came to a stop in a waste of snow-locked fields where, across the country and in misty woods, an uncanny silence brooded. People were squashed together. They were cold and their breath was a smoke. At midday they produced packets of sandwiches and there was some good-natured swapping, Spam for cheese and pickle.

The morning wore into afternoon and the train began to empty. By the time Sorrel arrived at a tiny unmarked and deserted station which two women assured her was Evendon, many of the travellers were gone.

'Are you sure this is it?' asked Sorrel, letting down the window.

'It's Evendon all right. We should know, shouldn't we?' The women nudged each other and giggled, as if the very platform held sexy memories.

As Sorrel emerged from the train, the cold struck her in the face. The compartment had been unheated but human beings had partly warmed it, and outside the air was biting. At the barrier she asked an aged porter if he happened to know Evendon Priory.

'Yes, Miss, 'course I do,' said the old man who, like the rest of the country, admired girls in uniform. 'Jack Bishop's going that way. He delivers of a Friday. Jack – want to give a young lady a lift?'

Sorrel found herself in a bone-rattling van in the company of a man who looked like an ostler. He had a wind-reddened face, his cheeks a network of broken veins, a thin sharp nose and one or two missing teeth. The van was piled with boxes of groceries and smelled of biscuits. The smell of a village shop. He hunched over the wheel, whistling to himself as the sheets of ice jagged across the road.

'You a relative of his lordship's, Miss?'

'I'm sorry?'

'You related to Lord Martyn at the Priory. That's where you're going, isn't it?'

'Yes. I'm sorry, I was looking at the ice, you're driving so well and there's no grit on the road,' said Sorrel, rather quickly. 'No, I'm not a relative. Just a friend of the family.'

'They'll be glad to see you I daresay. Oo-er! Look at that.'

He swerved away from a lake of ice.

So it's *Lord* Martyn, thought Sorrel. Can that be George? Perhaps his lordship is ninety and George is the son. Margaret's going to be right, damn it. Coming here will be difficult and extremely embarrassing. I wish I hadn't done it. No, that's not true . . . and she stared at the road between snow-scattered woods, the road leading towards the end of the mystery.

Bishop was more relaxed now, there was less ice about; it only shone silver in the ditches. She asked casually if he knew Lord Martyn well.

'I could say I know him pretty well, Miss. I'll tell you what he is. A benefactor. Guess how much petrol I'm allowed for this van every month? Five blessed gallons. When that's all gone, I have to deliver on me bike. But his lordship finds me a gallon or two now and again, God bless him. It's the same in the parish. My missus never gets a no from Lord and Lady Martyn for her stall at the bazaar.'

The van rounded a corner and slowed down by some open gates of impressive, elaborate wrought iron. There was a wide drive edged with chestnut trees. Clumps of snowdrops. And in the icy distance a very large, very old stone house.

'Here we are. Fine old place, isn't it? And hasn't been requisitioned like Hayden Court, *that's* crawling with soldiers now. Well, I daresay his lordship's got pull,' said Jack Bishop, switching off the engine and opening the door of the van for her. 'They say he's a friend of Lord Beaverbrook. Chaps like that. I'm going round the back to deliver so I'll say goodbye.'

'Thanks for the lift, Mr Bishop.'

'Do anything for the Wrens.'

The van trundled off towards a further gate leading to scattered outbuildings.

As she walked down the drive, Sorrel looked at the house spread out in front of her. Frosty lawns ebbed round it, and at the far end of the lawns were two magnificent cedar trees.

Beyond the house was a jumble of outbuildings towards which Jack Bishop's van was now making its way.

Sorrel's heart began to beat in expectation. She went up to the front door supported, under a portico, by wooden posts as grey as the house itself. There was a bell. She pressed it, and heard it pealing somewhere in the house.

Silence.

Then the sound of light footsteps.

2

A middle-aged woman opened the door. She was dressed entirely in grey, blouse, cardigan, skirt, thick stockings. Her manner was neither warm nor cold but had a faint air of harassment.

'Yes?'

'Lady Martyn?' enquired Sorrel experimentally.

The woman looked very surprised.

'I am the housekeeper. Do you wish to see Lady Martyn? She is not at home.'

'It is Lord Martyn I have called to see,' said Sorrel, deciding on a bold approach. 'Is he in, by any lucky chance? My name is Scott.'

For one daring moment she toyed with the idea of adding, 'And is his first name George?' She decided against it.

The housekeeper said she would see if his lordship was 'available', and invited Sorrel into the house, leaving her in a broad quarry-tiled entrance hall. Sorrel sat down near a fire of logs which were nearly green and running with sap. Although they gave out almost no heat, she held out her hands. She wondered if her mother used to come sometimes to this house. What were these people to her mother? Acquaintances? Never-mentioned friends? Lilian Scott had told her nothing about them, and listen as she might, all Sorrel could hear was the silence which the dead leave behind.

Five minutes went by. Ten. A grandfather clock chimed somewhere. She was feeling hungry. He isn't going to see me, she thought, so I shall never know any of the answers. How Margaret is going to crow.

There was the sound of footsteps and she turned, expecting the housekeeper. A stocky man came round the corner, looking enquiring.

'Surely it can't be – of course it is. You're Lilian's daughter. How very delightful!'

He seized her hand and pumped it up and down, like a member of parliament meeting a prospective voter. He was the soul of welcome and it was clear he had no idea that her mother was dead. It seemed cruel to wipe the smile off that confident face. Before she could speak he went on.

'And how is your dear mother? It's far too long since we've seen her, can't you persuade her to come and stay with us?'

She blurted out, 'My mother's dead, Lord Martyn. She was killed in a London raid a few weeks ago.'

'Oh my God.'

He started forward and to her dismay she saw his eyes brim with tears.

'My dear child. My dear child. What a terrible thing.' He felt for a handkerchief. Sorrel stood by respectfully thinking, in surprise, that he was fond of her mother. She didn't know why she hadn't expected that.

'You must tell me everything,' he said, putting away the handkerchief. 'Come in. Tell me exactly what happened. What a terrible thing,' he added, almost to himself.

He took her arm, and they walked down a long passage to a room which was full of space and pale silk-covered furniture. At its far end was a line of windows overlooking the back of the house, spreading frosty lawns and bare trees. In a stone fireplace a fire was burning, brighter and larger than the green logs in the hall. The room was stylish, there were vases of winter leaves, a high, old-fashioned screen of the kind seen in Boucher paintings, a beautiful antique clock on the marble chimney piece. Settling her by the fire, he rang for tea. It was brought by the housekeeper.

'Drink your tea before we talk,' he said, pouring out and offering Sorrel toast from under a silver cover. She saw that the emotion was gone from his face; he was as calm as she. During the meal he asked her questions, nodding in sympathy at her replies, refilling the silver teapot, glancing up with a kindly smile. His movements were finicky. His face, while he was listening, set into hard, grave lines. Middle age had given him jowls which blurred the good lines of his jaw, but he was still handsome. He gave an impression of power, his neck thick, his shoulders heavy. When he was serious, he looked ill-tempered. He had strangely coloured hair, black overlaid with silver, like a steel helmet. It was combed back in a style of the 1930s and had been greased.

'It was so good of you to come here to break the news in person,' he said quietly. 'A very brave thing to do. Where are you stationed, Sorrel? May I call you that?'

'Of course. I am in Sussex, just outside Littleport. At the naval base there.'

'That's a goodish way. Was the journey difficult?'

'It wasn't too bad.'

'It was more than kind of you to come. You should have telephoned or written and I would have sent a car.'

She said nothing, thinking with a saving gleam of amusement that since she hadn't known his surname, and the exchange wouldn't give her the Priory number, she could have done no such thing. He sat looking into the flames.

'I can't get used to your mother being gone. Sadly, we haven't seen Lilian for a long time. Too long. Since your father's funeral. That was when we lived in Surrey, not far from your family. I do remember you as a tiny child. . .'

He fell into a muse. Sorrel was silent. Finally he looked up and said in an altered, slightly probing voice, 'Your mother talked about us, of course.'

'I'm afraid she didn't. There were a lot of things she didn't talk about to me.'

He nodded. He said it was a sad fact of life that parents often did not share the past with their children. Sorrel had an impression – was it imagined? – that he was relieved. He said something about her mother having been proud of her joining the Wrens.

Sorrel let the cliché go. She undid her gas mask case and took out the letter which, by now, was thumbed and grubby.

'I've been wondering about this, Lord Martyn.'

He felt for his glasses, put them on, and took the dog-eared piece of paper.

'Where did you get my letter, Sorrel?'

'From the Civil Defence. It was in her handbag. After the bomb. It was the only thing of hers they did find.'

He shuddered.

It seemed the time to speak out.

'Lord Martyn – I'm afraid I didn't come here to break the news. I would have, if I'd known about you, but as I said, Mother never even told me you were a friend. I didn't know your surname until I arrived at Evendon and a man gave me a lift in his van. The letter is what brought me. I keep wondering if maybe you're our family trustee.'

He gave a slight laugh but before he could answer the door opened and a woman came into the room. He stood up.

'Grace. This is Lilian's daughter Sorrel Scott. She has brought tragic news. Poor Lilian was killed in a raid last month.'

Lady Martyn gave a violent start, pressing her hand to her bosom. Her eyes filled with tears, as his had done. She said in a choked voice, 'I must sit down.' Murmuring comforting words, 'I know, I know,' as if it was she and not Sorrel who had been bereaved, he led her to an armchair and stood by her, chafing one of her hands.

Grace Martyn must have weighed more than fourteen stone. Her size was commanding; like a ship with many sails she billowed as she moved. Her face was large and shaped like a plate, her chin pointed as a cat's and she had dark eyes, as George Martyn had. She wore ancient tweeds and ribbed stockings. When she had recovered, she managed a tremulous smile.

In the half hour that followed Lady Martyn rang for fresh tea and aspirins, recovered while Sorrel watched, and asked the visitor questions, listening to Sorrel's answers with a nod, as if she herself were a high-up Wren of commissioned rank. She had a curious habit of larding her talk with patriotism; Sorrel was unused to hearing about Dear Old England, and Albion, and Our Shores.

'It is wonderful to see you girls in uniform. Admirals all for England's sake. Honour be yours and fame. I only wish I could join you. But – '

'My wife has taken over the Priory farm,' explained George Martyn. 'I keep telling her that what she is doing is the best war effort of the lot.'

'Chamberlain did say that the war depends as much on producing more food at home as on the exploits of our fighting men,' agreed Lady Martyn. 'But one hankers, you know. One hankers. For the *comfort* of uniform.'

Sorrel nodded politely, thinking it so much rot. She wished the lady had not come in and interrupted her talk with Lord Martyn. She wished she would go.

'My wife is turning over all our land to agriculture,' George Martyn continued, still in a placating, admiring voice which, Sorrel thought, if it were addressed to her would make her feel quite violent. 'She is a countrywoman to her finger-ends. She can make the oats grow and the hens lay.'

After the tea, Lady Martyn sat in a chair well drawn up to the fire and began to reminisce about Sorrel's mother and their shared past. Forgetting her frustration Sorrel listened, hearing of times before she was born, of the 1900s, the early 1920s. For all her patriotism, and Grace Martyn apparently knew some of Churchill's speeches by heart, she scarcely touched upon the Great War. She spoke instead of a countryfied life in Surrey where the Martyns and the Scotts appeared to have enjoyed a kind of unending tennis party. Names drifted in.

'Bunny Sinclair was a friend of both families.'

'He must be getting on, he was older than us.'

'Tommy Layton had a pash on your mother, Sorrel. He once gave her three pairs of gloves!'

Grace spoke as if Lilian had been her most intimate friend and Sorrel found it odd that these close companions hadn't met for more than fifteen years. Yet George Martyn had paid her mother an allowance. Why?

The light began to fade, the day was over. Lord Martyn stood up and went round the room, switching on table lamps which made pools of light on glossy laurel leaves and silver-framed photographs. Grace patted a mongrel dog who had trotted in. He put his black seal-like head worshipfully on her knee. I suppose I ought to go, thought Sorrel. It was going to be difficult to get a lift in the dark. Perhaps they'll help me to get to the station. Why did he laugh when I asked if he was our trustee?

Her mother came into her thoughts just then. Sorrel saw her clearly, the aureole of clouded hair, the thin face shadowed with worry, the snappy impatient manner with herself. 'Sorrel, do stop hanging round me. Haven't you anything to do?' It was like being haunted. The ghost wouldn't go away. She wondered if that was because the Martyns were also thinking of her.

George Martyn was pulling each curtain carefully to shut out the daylight and hide the lights in the room from outside. The curtains were lined with black satin, and there were a good many windows.

'Why are you doing that, George? Evie does it perfectly well. Ring for her.'

'Women have no idea how to pull curtains. They need to be set properly.'

He twitched a fold, then returned to the fire.

'It's freezing hard. Well, Sorrel? You don't intend to go just yet, do you? I take it you are on leave. And of course you must stay the night.'

'Of course,' agreed Grace, with less enthusiasm, tugging the dog's ears. He squealed a little.

Glad not to be going out into the dark, Sorrel trotted out her thanks and the prepared explanation of 'friends I'm staying with over the weekend'.

'At least you'll be our guest tonight,' he said. 'Our son is also on leave just now. So you'll meet him.'

Grace stood up, with more spring than seemed possible for so monumental a figure, and asked if Sorrel would excuse her.'There's a lot to do on the farm, even in winter.'

Sorrel remained by the fire while George Martyn, having asked her permission, lit his pipe. A short time ago her mother had haunted her; now the spicy smell of the tobacco reminded her of her father who had smoked something similar. She thought, I'm an orphan. It sounded rather absurd.

'Did you know my parents well, Lord Martyn?'

'Of course. Your father was a colleague of mine for years. A clever chap, a clever chap,' he said.

She took it at a run.

'I've been wondering if you are our family trustee.'

He pulled at the pipe, took it from his mouth. 'Yes, you asked me that before my wife came in. I'm afraid, Sorrel, the answer is no.' He paused and said, with a slight smile, 'Why did you think I might be?'

'Because you sent my mother money,' she blurted out, blunt and young, and found herself hastily adding, 'She was lucky to have such a friend.'

The compliment appeared to please him.

'Well, I think I can flatter myself I was a friend of hers, although we scarcely ever saw each other. But I'm not your trustee, my dear, and I very much doubt if there is one.' The girl looked at him solemnly – it was obvious what she was thinking. 'You are wondering why I paid Lilian that money, aren't you? The fact is, my dear, your mother and I were distantly related. Some kind of third cousins. We used to joke about it.'

He had already begun to use the special, slightly religious tone reserved for speaking of the dead.

'When your poor father died suddenly, I thought it only right to step into the breach.'

Sorrel had a stab of disappointment, but couldn't pretend to herself that she was surprised. It would have been unbelievable luck if this stranger had turned out to be a trustee, whatever that meant; rather like discovering she had a new elderly relative, an uncle perhaps. Instead she had simply met a philanthropist. For a moment, looking at him, she forgot that all she would have in the future was her Wren pay, a princely fifteen shillings a week.

Lord Martyn talked commonplaces for a while, then rang for the housekeeper to show Sorrel to her room.

Evie took her up a staircase, down a corridor and then another. How large the house was. All over Britain now, houses of this size had been requisitioned. The government had ruled that great houses must be used for the war effort. Some had been taken over by the Admiralty. Others by the army or the RAF, who had built Nissen huts in eighteenth-century parks, and seen to it that the precious treasures of the past were all removed, stowed away in attics and cellars, while empty rooms thundered to the noise of heavy boots. Sometimes, more fortunately for the owners of mansions and manors, officers were billeted on the family. Further down the scale were big houses now invaded by evacuees and their attendant problems.

Here all Sorrel saw were open doors to empty rooms. Everywhere was spacious and polished and empty.

The room to which Evie eventually led her was comfortable with a royal blue carpet and a double bed covered in flower-patterned blue and white chintz. On the wall was a Victorian print called *Blind Man's Buff*, in which everybody, from grandfather to children to collie dog, was smiling. By the empty fireplace was a large antique oil stove. The housekeeper knelt beside it as if in prayer, turning the knob and studying the flame closely.

'It has to turn blue all the way round or there will be smuts floating about. It's very temperamental. I used to have it in my nursery.'

'It's lovely to be really warm,' said Sorrel as the housekeeper stood up again. 'I almost never am. At our digs we simply freeze.'

'Oh, you poor things! That's not right when you're in the services.' The elderly woman became less shy, and when she smiled she was charming. Her nose was as snub as a clown's and her chin had a dimple in the middle.

'The bathroom's here, Miss Scott, it's your own, and I've put some towels for you. There's heaps of hot water. Dinner is in an hour.'

Alone, Sorrel peered into the chaste white bathroom to admire large towels embroidered with an 'M'. She wandered round the bedroom, opening an inlaid box on the windowsill. It had been for needlework a hundred years ago; the lid was of buttoned satin split with the years, the cotton reels were made of ivory. There were even some rusty pins. On the dressing table was a cut-glass vase of snowdrops. She stood looking at them. Remembering a bomb crater.

These people are rich, she thought, when later she was enjoying a hot bath. The only titled people Sorrel had met had been a Sir John and Lady Palmer at an Eastbourne hotel where she and her mother had lived for a while before the war. Lilian had said they were poor as church mice and added, significantly, 'He drank it all away.' Lord Martyn apparently drank nothing away. But Sorrel wondered about the Priory. Apart from its lack of officers or soldiers or evacuees. She knew the house was very old; the guidebook had said so. It was rambling and beautiful, its walls thick, its windowsills very broad. It was itself. And yet it didn't seem to contain things which had grown with it. Once in 1938 Sorrel had been taken to a grand charity ball at a Sussex mansion by a boyfriend of hers. She remembered a place crammed with objects. Paintings and marbles, bronzes and rare carpets, tapestries, miniatures, fans and signed photographs of royalty. And a wondrous amount of junk. Bad watercolours which must have been painted years before by relatives. Stones collected and forgotten, and rusted swords or guns which looked as if they'd been hung on the wall centuries ago. The Priory was too neat. It wasn't a paradox to say it was too new.

She was intrigued by the place to which her adventurous spirit had brought her. She enjoyed a feeling of guilt. Where had the war gone? Nobody here was cold or shabby or bombed out – or dead. She fished a clean uniform shirt from her small canvas holdall, buttoned it and sat down to make up her face and do her hair.

The only flaw in the luxurious evening ahead was her sense of anticlimax. The letter in her mother's handbag had occupied her thoughts, served to keep away by its enigmas the hollow feeling of loss. It had been something to think about instead of wondering over her mother's last awful moments. The truth turned out to be dull. Lord Martyn had given money to her mother because of a distant blood tie. And because he was generous. That was all there was.

The pre-war sound of a gong reverberated from somewhere downstairs. I bet that's Evie, thought Sorrel. She probably does the cooking as well.

With a final look at herself in the glass she opened the door. And stepped straight into the arms of a man in army uniform. He saved her from tripping by catching her.

'I say, I am sorry, you opened that door rather suddenly,' he exclaimed. 'I heard a Wren was nesting at the Priory, I wasn't expecting her in full flight. I'm Ronald Martyn. Called Toby.'

He held out his hand.

'And you're the daughter of my father's old friends. I'm afraid I never met your family – to be exact, I must have done when we were all rather small, but I don't remember them. I'm glad to meet you.'

They shook hands. 'Shall we go down?' he said, falling into step beside her. Sorrel's feeling of flatness disappeared. She liked the look of her new acquaintance very much. He was a major, and wore the purple and white ribbon of the MC. He could have been any age from the mid-twenties to thirty, and was both handsome and ugly. He had thick, fawn-coloured English hair cut very short, showing a well-shaped head. He had a thin, beaky, eagle-ish face and a strong prominent nose. His manner was bustling.

'Rumour has it,' he remarked as they turned the corner of the corridor, 'that my father's got hold of some black market gin to welcome the fighting forces.'

'I thought it was only the navy who preferred gin.'

'Pink gins in the cabin. Red-rimmed eyes on deck?'

'You mustn't attack the senior service, Major.'

'I daresay I shall.'

He took her down into a kind of large hall in the centre of the house, apparently used as a sitting room although an imposing staircase ascended from its far end. It was furnished with leather chairs, a sofa, the walls were partly panelled and a large fire filled the air with the bitter smell of woodsmoke. The hearth was open and surrounded on three sides by a leather-topped bench.

'One can sit with one's feet practically in the fire,' said Toby, demonstrating. 'Toast your toes while I forage for gin.'

He went across to a long table by the staircase, returning with two glasses and remarking that he hoped the drink would be all right. 'I've been mingy with the angostura. Cheers.' He lifted his glass.

Murmuring a reply, she took a sip and practically choked; it was almost neat gin. Concentrating on trying not to cough until she was purple in the face, she hastily put down the glass and looked around the room – straight at a portrait of her companion. It was an oil painting, large and heavily framed; lit from below it commanded attention. Toby was painted in uniform, the MC ribbon on his breast. Behind him was a small landscape done in a sort of pastiche of Renaissance paintings, with a winding river, chestnut trees and a house which she supposed was the Priory. In the way of painted eyes, he stared straight from the canvas.

Toby Martyn gave a loud sigh.

'You've noticed it already. I wish Mother hadn't decided to light up the thing. It makes it so much worse.'

He sat down on the bench beside her.

'Don't you like it?'

'Well, of course, she can paint. Used to do quite a lot of portraits before the war; she had a studio upstairs. She's given all that up now, she's only interested in the farm. But she decided to do my picture after Dunkirk when I was on leave. Can't say I approve of it. My CO said it looks like Errol Flynn.'

'I think it's very like you.'

His laugh was sudden and loud, something like the rattle of machine-gun fire.

'I'm like Errol Flynn, am I, Miss Scott? I say, I like your first name – Evie told me it's Sorrel. Were you called after the stuff that grows in meadows?'

'No, the stuff that pops up in the gardens,' she said, smiling.

'It has a white and purple flower. It was my father's idea, it grew near the house where I was born.'

'Very poetic.' He sounded like a boy.

He stared at his feet in glittering army shoes, placed close to the low-heeled Wren shoes Sorrel had to wear and detested.

'Fun having you here. The first time in living memory my father has produced an acquaintance who's young and beautiful. Pop goes in for the grizzled elderly. MPs. Cabinet ministers occasionally. Businessmen. Beaverbrook dropped in on one of his trips around the country, rousing up the manufacturers. You can just imagine the sort of chaps my father knows.'

'Actually, I only met Lord Martyn for the first time today, Major.'

'Please call me Toby.'

'I'd like to,' Sorrel said. Then, to get it over, 'I came here to tell your father that my mother had been killed.'

She did not know why she was so blunt, coarse even. She was immediately ashamed of using death in conversation with a stranger. Had she expected to change his manner to her? He looked into his glass and nodded.

'My father told me. A bloody hit and runner.'

He sounded like Margaret Reilly.

'One can see you know how to take it,' he added and looked up at her. Sorrel wanted to deserve the look; it was full of silent admiration. For a moment she actually longed to be in a state of noble, hidden grief. The feeling was not new, she had spoken about it to Margaret, saying that the Victorians knew how to behave, *they* wore black and paid death its terrible due. Margaret had said an odd thing.

'There's always going to be time for sorrow. Don't wish for it before it comes.'

In the pause which followed Toby's steady look, his parents came down the staircase. They made an unlikely couple, George Martyn handsome in a dinner jacket, his silver helmet of hair shining like steel, his wife's enormous bulk wrapped in plum-coloured velvet with diamond buttons.

'I don't think we will have a drink before dinner, Toby,' said

Grace Martyn, in answer to her son's offer. 'We mustn't upset Evie.'

The quartet trooped out of the hall.

If the rest of the Priory lacked the clutter and mixtures of an aristocratic past, the dining room did try to live up to tradition, thought Sorrel. The furniture was old and elaborate, candles in silver candlesticks shone on a table like a rich treacle-coloured lake. Everybody sat in carved chairs. For the second time in an hour Sorrel wondered what had happened to the war. They were waited upon by an elderly maid in cap and apron, ate guinea fowl and drank champagne. The meal finished with a caramel pudding and real cream. George Martyn carved the fowl and Evie hovered; now and then Toby made flirtatious remarks to her and succeeded in getting a laugh and an embarrassed blush.

When Evie and the maid left at the end of the meal, after Evie had switched off the lights, leaving the family in candle-light, Grace Martyn said in a silvery voice, 'Toby, I do wish you'd leave poor Evie alone. You know how she is about you.'

'I only muttered in her shell-like ear.'

'Something improper, I suppose.'

'Mother, how can you think such a thing?'

They both laughed. George Martyn poured more champagne.

'I notice neither of you has happened to mention Singapore,' said Toby, turning from one parent to the other. They looked back at him, wearing the same expression of attention, almost of respect. Toby began to talk.

Sorrel listened with a growing astonishment. Wearing the ribbon of the Military Cross, the young man launched into an attack on the progress of the war, the actions of the government and the records of all three services. Sorrel had never heard such sedition.

'Look at the mess we're in. The situation is ghastly. Ghastly,' he said, buttering a biscuit on which he balanced a square of white Stilton cheese.

'Just let's consider Singapore last week. Yes, I know you're both avoiding the subject because you aren't partial to bad news. But what do you think of the *British* surrendering to the *Japs*?'

'It was because the High Command was convinced the attack would come from the sea – ' began his father but Toby interrupted.

'Oh yes, they were certain, weren't they? Barrages of gunfire all planned to resist non-existent enemy ships. Nobody could possibly get through the jungle, that's what the thickheads said. And just what the Japs did. They got through and what's more they did it on foot – no, I forgot, some of them used bicycles! And they captured our whole damned garrison. What did the army do? Held up their hands and gave in. Those little yellow fellows took thousands upon thousands of prisoners. It makes one weep.'

'The papers said less than 50,000.'

'My dear parent, you are the only person left in the country, well, Mother makes the second, who believes the bad news turned on its head to make it look acceptable. The number of prisoners must be three times more than that. We're dished out tripe because the government daren't tell us the truth. Singapore was a fortress. A garrisoned fortress. And what happened was a defeat which shows us up as cowards as well as fools. No, we can't win this war. It's the enemy who is winning. The Japs. And, of course, the Germans, magnificent fighters, efficient, obedient, with guts and ideals. It is no good looking at me in that startled way,' he added, turning to grin at Sorrel. 'What have you to say in defence of your own service? The little matter of the *Scharnhorst* and the *Gneisenau*. Let alone the *Prinz Eugen*?'

I ought to have known they'd come steaming into the conversation, thought Sorrel. In the last ten days, the names of the three German battleships had been repeated in every home in the British Isles, and shuddered at in every British ship at sea. The Germans had pulled off a brilliant coup – their ships were in French Biscay ports and they'd made a dash through the Channel to get back home, under heavy air escort. And succeeded.

'The navy and the RAF were caught with their pants down,'

said Toby. 'They launched torpedo aircraft, bombers, motor torpedo boats. They even attacked a destroyer.'

'*Gneisenau* hit a mine,' said George Martyn.

'*Scharnhorst* hit two,' added Grace.

'And both ships got back to base,' said Toby pityingly. '*The Times* called it the most mortifying episode in English naval history.'

While Sorrel listened in silence, now and then Toby looked across the table at her. Once it was she who glanced at him, and when he caught her eyes, she had to look away. It was a silent kind of flirtation.

Toby's father lit a cigar; he had a very faint air of satisfaction.

'There's one thing you appear to have forgotten, my dear boy, a little matter of the Dutch in 1667 sailing right up the Thames as far as Chatham. They set fire to our warships, and there was even talk of abandoning the Tower of London. Now – you can scarcely compare *that* to a few German ships racing home.'

Toby was ready for the Dutch. He trotted out answers so glibly that Sorrel knew he had used them before.

That disgrace had been entirely different, he said, the English sailors were mutinying, the dockyards left unguarded, how could one say that was worse than German ships sailing up *our* Channel which one was told was protected – no, commanded – by *our* warships not to mention our air force? It was ludicrous.

Evie and the antique maid had long since left the room and now that Toby had polished off the services, he aimed his gun at a new target, the lower classes. Finishing the champagne, he declared it was his firm belief that the lower classes were responsible for getting us into this war.

'Popular feeling, going to the rescue of gallant Poland? If we'd had the sense we'd have kept out of the mess altogether. Let Hitler tidy up Europe, which he was doing very nicely. But oh no, the people started waving flags. The Germans know how to cope with the hoi polloi, they shove 'em into uniform and make them jump to attention.'

'But isn't that just what is happening here?'

'My poor Mother, you can't draw a parallel between the British lower classes and the Germans. Why, in this country they only do as they're told if they agree with you. Well, Sorrel? I'm talking too much but you haven't been sticking up for the navy, I notice.'

'Because she can't get a word in edgeways, my dear boy, but she's disapproving of you. She is not used to revolution at the dinner table,' said George Martyn smiling at the girl.

'And I think it's time we left you to your port and more attacks on this sceptred isle,' said Grace, standing up. As the two women left the room, Sorrel heard Toby mutter something about the army. His father burst into a hearty, flattering laugh.

Coffee was waiting by the fire in the hall. Grace sat down, spreading her velvet skirts, and indicated the fireside bench to Sorrel. The mongrel trotted in from somewhere, sidled up to his mistress and laid his head on her knee. Grace poured coffee, and began to stroke the dog who shut his eyes in ecstasy.

'Toby is the limit,' she said after a moment. 'He only does it to annoy because he knows it teases. One would think he was a ghastly pro-Nazi, the way he goes on.'

She sipped her coffee with the daintiness of the very stout.

Sorrel was in a quandary. She half believed Toby had meant what he said. She loved physical courage and the haggard excited man seemed to embody that virtue. But she was confused.

'He was the same as a child,' said Grace. 'Getting hold of cranky ideas, loves and hates. Bees in his bonnet. His older brother Edmund and he used to fight like wildcats whenever Toby began to carry on. I remember Edmund throwing Toby right down the stairs, shouting: "Our school motto is Conquer Little Things and that's what I'm doing" – Toby was smaller than Edmund then. He had bruises all over,' she added with a chuckle.

'I didn't know you have another son, Lady Martyn.'

The older woman carefully put down her cup.

'Edmund was killed at Dunkirk. You must forgive me if I

don't talk about him. We don't, really. It's just when I think about them as children that somehow . . . shall we change the subject?'

She turned brightly sharp-smiling eyes towards Sorrel and enquired if she knew many army people. No? A pity. There was a note of condescension. Edmund and Toby had both been to Sandhurst, they'd sat for the examinations before the war and 'done brilliantly'. Lady Martyn enjoyed talking as much as her son did; easy and voluble, she began a long description of Toby's first weeks at Sandhurst.

'Of course, Edmund had to put up with all the same things, but it was Toby who described them so graphically. Conscripts today just don't know they're born, do you know, they actually imagine the training is hard! Toby was never a milksop, but he did find, after public school, that Sandhurst was a facer. They had to be up at half past six every morning, then drill, cleaning, more drill and on parade at the stroke of seven. When the senior officer had kit parade, he wouldn't be satisfied with the most shining equipment. Oh no. He had to see the whites of his own eyes in their bayonet blades. *And* be able to comb his hair in the reflection of their scabbards.'

Grace laughed. Her expression changed and became solemn. 'Of course the training is long and hard. It's what a soldier needs. And it forms the character.'

She brightened again. 'I wonder if you know my favourite army story. It summarises the services for me. An officer found a Scots Guards sergeant lying in the desert gasping "water, water". Thinking the poor fellow was dying of thirst, he fell on his knees beside him and brought out his water bottle. "Thank heaven," said the sergeant. "Now I can Blanco my equipment!" '

'My *dear* Mother,' said a voice from the door, 'you're not telling that old chestnut. It's been going the rounds since the Crimea.'

Toby came across the hall carrying a balloon glass of brandy, followed by his father similarly armed. Grace smiled at them, half closing her eyes.

Sorrel imagined the Martyns would remain by the fire and

Toby start to rant again, he looked very cheerful. But the older people stayed less than twenty minutes before George said they really must go to bed.

'You'll have to forgive us old fogeys. We need our sleep,' he said. 'Grace has her farm and her livestock to cope with. She gets up at the crack, and needs all her energy.'

'One does one's best,' said Grace. 'We have to remember that every endeavour must be made to grow the greatest volume of food of which this fertile land is capable.'

It sounded Churchillian. Surely it was?

'Yes. Well. I am an early riser too, I leave for London before eight. Which reminds me, Sorrel, could I persuade you to breakfast with me? Grace will be with her Guernseys and Toby takes the chance on leave to have a lie-in.'

Sorrel said she'd very much like to have breakfast with him.

'Good. And when you decide on a train – Evie will telephone the station to find one – we'll send you in the car.'

She thanked him. He looked at her kindly.

'Come again soon now you know where we live. And next time, remember now, no arrangements to stay with other friends. Goodnight to you both.'

'Don't stay up too late, Toby,' added Grace.

The Martyns went up the staircase in conversation, and disappeared along the first landing. As their voices began to die away, Toby looked at Sorrel and winked.

'Tired?'

'Not a bit.'

'Nor I. Parents waste the best part of the day. Shall we dance? They can't hear the gramophone, their room's at the other end of the house.'

He went to a table, wound up a gramophone and chose a record from a pile in their paper envelopes. A haunting, wailing tune began. A man sang, 'I've flown around the world in a plane, Settled revolutions in Spain.' He added that he was broken-hearted – 'still I can't get started with you.'

Toby stretched out his arms and she went towards him. She found him very attractive; he was so filled with nervous energy, slightly excited and exciting, his face was lined for a man who was still young. He wasn't relaxed as the naval officers she knew seemed to be. He was strung up and affected her with a sense of urgency, something unknown, dangerous even. He held her close and they began to dance.

I've been consulted by Franklin D.
And Greta Garbo asked me to tea,
Still I'm broken-hearted
'Cos I can't get started with you.

Toby danced out of time but Sorrel didn't care. When the record ended, he put it on again. He played it four times, pressing her close. She melted into his arms, her senses almost swimming. The record ended for the fourth time, and ignoring the scraping noise as it circled and circled he bent and gave her a long kiss. Shutting her eyes, clutching the muscular man who held her, she returned the embrace, opening her lips, letting him enter and explore her mouth, feeling desire take hold of her in the most intimate parts of her body, knowing pleasure and longing for the taste of him.

'Darling. Darling,' was all he said. And went on kissing her.

When they separated he looked as she felt. Slightly dazed. He turned off the gramophone and then switched off standard lamps and table lamps. The room was dark except for the last glow of the dying fire. She stood adrift.

Returning, he picked her up in his arms as if she weighed nothing, carried her to the sofa, and lay down beside her.

3

The housekeeper woke Sorrel from the deep sleep of the young at quarter past seven, bringing tea. Sorrel took the hint, rose, bathed and hurriedly dressed in her uniform. Evie returned at five to eight, to accompany her to the breakfast room.

'I'm afraid you'd never find it by yourself.'

She was right, for the Priory was larger and rambled more than Sorrel had imagined. She was taken down passages and round corners, now and again up half flights of stairs. The old house was wonderfully clean and in perfect repair. Once they went down a corridor with low church-like windows, and Sorrel saw a stone crucifix set right into the wall; its figure was worn, its outlines softened by the centuries. Then they passed a row of closed doors.

'That's where we store the Sir Jacob Croxley Collection,' said Evie. 'It was sent down from London. Lord Martyn has agreed to keep all the stuff here safely for the duration. There were packing cases galore – paintings and miniatures and tapestries and some statues, and glass cases full of old coins. You never saw so much. Lady Martyn says we're a sort of museum, really. Except everything's covered up and sewn into canvas.'

Sorrel now understood why the Priory had not been requisitioned, and why there were no troops billeted there.

Evie finally took her to a small panelled room at the far end of the house where there was the smell of coffee, and a gas fire burned comfortably. In the greyish light reflecting the snow-scattered ground outside, George Martyn looked older and tougher. His steel helmet of hair shone, his city suit was black with a grey silk tie. He half rose, told Evie they would serve themselves, and poured Sorrel's coffee. Then, giving her the *Daily Mail*, he disappeared behind *The Times*. Sorrel enjoyed the breakfast – the coffee wasn't the same acorn-flavoured drink served at the landladies' digs, and the marmalade tasted of oranges. But she did wonder why she had been invited to this speechless meal. Eventually he folded the newspaper, poured some more coffee and said he hoped his son had not kept her up too late. He gave a smile which had considerable charm, and which showed his certainty that he could capture people.

'It's a pity you can't stay and keep Toby company. There's a local shortage of pretty girls. However, I know we will see you again. The reason I selfishly asked you to get up early, Sorrel, is that I wanted a word with you alone.'

She looked at him, her slightly slanting, swimming eyes interested yet still dreamy. She was an appealing young thing, he thought. He liked her appearance, the way she carried her dark head, her voice, her confident friendly manner, her courage at her sad loss. A pity Grace had never had a daughter; he had a weakness for youth and good looks and would have enjoyed spoiling a young girl.

'It's about your mother's finances.'

He did not miss her blush.

'I take it Lilian had an overdraft.'

'Yes. The bank sent the statements to me.'

The overdraft had alarmed her. It had even worried Margaret Reilly. Sorrel had gone to her commanding officer, a short brisk young woman who told her that as a member of the services, Sorrel's responsibility for the debt would be put into abeyance.

'We'll write to the bank manager if you prefer it,' said the officer. 'Of course I make no doubt you will pay it back, little by little, when peace breaks out. But who knows? You might marry money, Scott.'

She had laughed at her own joke.

Seeing the blush, George Martyn nodded.

'You mustn't be upset, Sorrel, your mother did her best but she was not the world's cleverest manager of her money affairs as I had reason to tell her now and then. I daresay you thought my letter pretty harsh.'

'Of course I didn't.'

'I regret it all the same. It's dreadful how one regrets some perfectly normal action after an unexpected death. I can't bear to think that, for a few pounds I could easily have afforded, I upset your poor mother. I don't forgive myself.'

'But you were so generous to her.'

'Thank you. That's kind but not quite true. But you must stop worrying about the overdraft, I shall telephone the manager this morning, get the thing cleared up and settle the account. Please don't thank me, it's the least I can do.'

'But I do thank you! I am so grateful!'

He looked at her oddly. 'My dear child, I don't deserve that. I wish I did. Now let me tell you something a little more interesting. I intend to reduce my monthly cheque, of course, since sadly there is now only one Scott to help and not two. But I shall tell the bank manager to open an account in your name. And – you won't find me ungenerous.'

She was staggered. 'But you can't possibly . . . I never expected . . .'

'I certainly can. And will.'

He was unused to such a reaction. Grace had been wrong last night when sitting up in bed she declared the girl had come here on the scrounge. He liked the gratitude and even more the unworldliness; he felt as if he were writing a cheque for a wartime charity.

'You must look on me as an older member of your family, Sorrel. I am glad to help, my dear child, just as I was with your mother. Is it in order to give me a kiss?'

She sprang up and pressed her lips to the elderly olive-skinned face.

'How kind you are. I don't know what to say or how to thank you.'

'By coming to see us again.'

Evie put her head round the door.

'The car has arrived, Sir.'

'Thank you, Evie.'

Bidding Sorrel goodbye, he left the room; and left her in the starry state of pauper elevated to sudden wealth. When she'd finished her breakfast, Evie appeared again to say that the Major was still asleep.

'What a pity. I'll miss him.'

'Lord Martyn has ordered the car to take you to the station to catch the 12.15. Is that convenient?'

'Thank you. It's perfect.'

'The Major will be up long before that,' said Evie who had decided to march into his room and give him a good shake. She'd been his nanny once upon a time. She asked the young Wren if she would like to walk round the farm, or would she prefer to stay indoors? The fire was lit in the hall and it was comfortable there. Sorrel, glowing with good news, asked if there were any Wellington boots.

'Dozens.'

Evie took her down a passage leading to one of many back doors. Boots in regiments were lined under pegs for raincoats. Sorrel, standing on one leg, pushed her foot into a number of clammy mud-splashed boots and finally chose a pair which more or less fitted. She went out of doors.

There was a thin, uncertain winter sun, and still the remainder of the snow. The cold burned her cheeks as she walked away from the house, past an ancient wall against which pear trees had been trained; leafless and closely pruned, they were like the knotted veins in elderly hands. She scarcely noticed the trees, the wall, the fading snow. She was trying to take in the astounding fact that Lord Martyn had given her an allowance – it was something she had simply not even considered. Margaret, for the first time in her life, was going to be speechless.

Walking past a great beamed and thatched barn she heard the sound of whistling. Someone was whistling the same tune she and Toby had danced to last night. 'Still I can't get started with you.' The little sound amused her, and – the barn door was ajar - she went inside.

How old it was. High-ceilinged, beams crossing and re-crossing overhead, a smell of grain and dust. At its far and shadowy end lit by a small window thick with cobwebs a man was whitewashing a wall. He turned, to see a thin girl in dark uniform framed against the winter light.

'Hello,' she said.

'Good morning.' He gave the wall a brush-sweep and stood back to study the effect. Sorrel walked across a floor scattered with wheat husks and straw.

'You've got a long job there. Are you going to do the entire barn?'

'Oh no. Only this bit. We're installing new grain bins and I might as well stack 'em up against a clean wall while we're about it. The bins are arriving today with any luck because I can't spare much longer.'

'The farm means a lot of work, I suppose.'

The remark made him grin.

'It also means a lot of clerking.'

'Such as?' enquired Sorrel, who rather liked the young man. He was both tall and large, taller than Toby and giving a greater impression of physical strength. His shoulders were broad, his forearms, whitewashed, thick as young trees. He looked hard and relaxed, where Toby was wiry and nervous. He had a roundish face, beautiful large grey eyes and fair hair also spattered with whitewash.

He seemed perfectly willing to chat.

'I discovered this morning, by sheer chance, that we're in trouble for selling our potatoes retail,' he said. 'Now I shall have to write to some office or other and get another form for yet another licence. It's like Kafka. At present we are dealing with nineteen.'

'Forms?'

'Licences.'

Untidy, dusty, he had a kind of authority.

She looked about.

'How enormous this barn is. I suppose it's very old – Tudor, even.'

'Older than that. 1325. It's a tithe barn. The peasants came here every year after the harvest, trotted up to give their proportion – sheaves of corn, eggs, hams. The recorders were the monks from the Priory, of course. They sat at a table writing it all down. "Twixton. Last year you brought the Abbot 47 sheaves. This year it is 32. Why is that? Explain yourself." '

His manner was comic. Monk and schoolmaster.

'Are there any ghosts?' asked Sorrel hopefully.

'Of course.'

He put down his brush.

'I'm not sure I can paint with an audience. I'm not the world's expert with whitewash, in any case. Tell me what a Wren is doing in this army stronghold?'

'Oh. Just a friend.'

'But I haven't seen you before.'

'No. My first visit,' said Sorrel, deliberately vague. Adding curiously, 'How did you know about the barn and the monks and things?'

'Lots of people do.'

'Are you an historian, then?'

'Not exactly.' He was teasing her.

'And do you know about the Priory, too?'

'Quite a bit.'

'I'd love to hear about it. It's a marvellous house.'

'Perhaps I'll tell you sometime. Now it's my turn. What is it like being a Wren?'

'Fine.'

'You surprise me.'

'Are you one of those who think women shouldn't be in uniform?' asked Sorrel, disappointed and piqued. And why wasn't he in uniform himself, come to that.

'Let's say I consider that nobody should be in uniform,' was the unexpected and shocking reply. She was just going to burst out when there was a shadow in the doorway at the far end of the barn.

'There you are,' called Toby. 'Evie said you'd be somewhere

round the farm. Come along. I want you to see The Chief. He's my charger.'

Ignoring the presence of the young man, he simply stood waiting for her to join him. Muttering goodbye, she walked over to Toby and they left the barn together.

Toby was in uniform, his appearance, buttons glinting, in absurd contrast to the man with the paintbrush. He led her out into the bright morning. They walked in the silence of people who have kissed a good deal.

'I like to start the day saying hello to my horse,' he said, after a pause. 'I've brought him an apple; it's only a windfall, Evie is very mean with apples at this time of year. The Chief won't mind it being bruised. He loves apples.'

'Is he in the stables, Toby?'

'There's nobody there to look after the dear chap. He's in the field with the farm horses. He has to work, too, I'm sorry to say. He pulls the milk float. Poor man. But not today. So let's see where he's got to.'

They went to the edge of a large field and stood looking over the gate.

'Must be in the barn. God, it's cold.'

At the edge of the field was a workmanlike building with a corrugated iron roof. Toby opened the door.

'Chief? Chief? Where are you, boy?'

There was a whinny and a tall nut-brown horse shining as silk came trotting up. Toby gave him the apple, which the horse loudly crunched. Toby patted him, felt his legs and then, putting out his arms, hugged the beautiful creature round the shoulders, leaning his head against the horse's neck. The Chief snorted gently and nuzzled against him.

'He thinks he'll find another apple. He knows which pocket I keep them in. Sorry, Chief, that's your ration for today.'

With a long sigh and a final pat, Toby left the horse, who watched them go.

'I always like to see him first,' Toby said. 'It isn't until I've said hello to The Chief that I'm ready for the day.'

They were walking into the icy bareness of what had been a garden. Part of it had been ploughed, part was still set with rose bushes. Toby squeezed her arm against his side. His voice was almost as tender as when he had talked to the horse.

'It's a good thing my commanding officer can't see me arm in arm with a little Wren in uniform.'

'I know. Very improper.' Her voice was tender, too.

'If we meet in town, Sorrel, you'll have to wear civvies. I shall like that. I can imagine you in a ballgown.'

Sorrel, who owned nothing in the world but uniform and one skirt and jersey, said, 'I shall look wonderful.'

'You do anyway.'

He stopped walking and turned to look at her, his seamed soldier's face gentle. For a second she thought he was going to kiss her but his eyes went over her shoulder towards the many-windowed house.

'God, it's cold,' he repeated. 'Let's walk as far as the fountain and then go indoors and have coffee.'

Now and then slithering on the frozen surface of the brick path, they went across the rose garden and beyond it to other gardens, all of which had been ploughed up. In the distance was a haze of winter trees, a haze of winter mist. It was very silent until somewhere far off there was a splitting, cracking noise. Toby grimaced.

'I hate that sound. It's the branch of a tree.'

The fountain, a circular stone basin, was filled with opaque greenish ice; in the centre was the bronze figure of a naked girl, her long hair falling over her shoulders.

'Poor poppet, she needs a winter vest. Come along now – right turn, quick march.'

They wheeled about and returned to the house. Plumes of smoke were rising in the still air.

'That was an odd sort of man I met in your barn. Who was he?' asked Sorrel as they went indoors.

'A farmworker.'

He might have been speaking of a stray cat.

'He seemed rather clever. Does he run your farm?'

'Good grief, no. Mother does it all. Come and get warm. I don't want to send you back to base with pneumonia.'

The hall fire smouldered in masses of fragrant ash lit on the bed of last night's blaze. Evie appeared with coffee, her clown's face soft when she looked at Toby. When Sorrel and he were alone, sitting talking idly, she kept thinking – oh why did I lie and say I must go? I could have stayed all weekend. She looked covertly at her watch . . . time was going so quickly.

'You'll soon be on your way,' he suddenly snapped.

The voice was positively unpleasant and Sorrel was very taken aback. She looked up at him in dismay.

'B-but I wasn't wondering about the time because I want to go!'

'Why, then?'

He seemed really annoyed and she exclaimed before she could stop herself, 'Because I wish it could last longer!'

His expression completely altered. For a moment she'd seen a different man. He had looked like iron. Why? Was he somebody who couldn't bear the slightest flick against his self-esteem? She didn't know the answer, but was only glad tenderness had returned. This time he risked kissing her, knowing nobody was about. He drew her to him, opened her lips with his tongue, held her shoulders in a grip so strong that he hurt her. She felt again the disturbed sexual longing of last night.

'Sorrel, Sorrel, I wish it could last, too. Now. Now.'

When he stopped kissing her she drew a sobbing breath. He stood looking at her.

'I want to ask you something.'

'Anything.'

'Suppose I ask something you won't want to do.'

'Anything,' she passionately repeated.

He looked down at the hand he had taken hold of; it was pale with youth.

'I want you to write to me.'

Such a simple request.

'Of course. I want to. But *you* must too.'

'My letters are rubbish. Mother says so – she writes wonderful stuff. I can't manage anything worth reading.'

'Whatever you write, I'll like it.'

'Will you? Will you?'

They stared at each other. Their words were so lame. It was Toby, then, who looked at his watch.

'Six minutes.'

'That's a long time, isn't it?'

But soon Evie appeared to say the car had arrived. He pulled Sorrel to her feet and they walked through to the stone-floored entrance hall where she had waited yesterday to meet a man she did not know. There was a large black car by the open front door; an elderly chauffeur in grey uniform.

Sorrel climbed into the car. She looked small in a motor meant for businessmen or the enormous figure of Lady Martyn. Toby leaned into the car.

'Don't be too nice to my rivals in the navy.'

He saluted as the car moved away.

Sitting on a bulging kit bag belonging to one of the soldiers filling the train corridor, greatcoated figures with rifles, Sorrel listened to the train's monotonous song. She was returning richer than she had left. She had met people who'd asked her to treat them as her family. And she had met Toby Martyn. She thought about the hours they had spent on the sofa by the dying fire, until it had grown so dark they could scarcely see each other. They had not made love. Everything else but not the right true end. She had wanted him, and she knew he'd fiercely wanted her too, but he was a man who would never force the pace. Sorrel and Margaret had both spent time with men who kept no such gentlemanly rule. The girls at various times had had to bear angry scenes and sexual struggles. They had managed, as Sorrel once put it, 'to get back home without actually being raped'.

'I wish you wouldn't be so crude,' Margaret had said, after describing by what she omitted her trouble with a naval lieutenant on a previous evening.

'That's what they have in mind. Probably plan it all beforehand,' Sorrel said.

'They're men,' said Margaret. As a Catholic, lust surprised her.

It had not been like that with Toby who was exciting and

sexy and passionate and who'd known how much she wanted him to take her. But he had never touched her in the most intimate part of her body except through her clothes, pressing his hand there until she thought she must die of blissful frustration. Her thoughts were full of sex. But she had always believed that girls who went to bed with men the first time they met them were beyond the pale. They were, Sorrel thought with pious morality, scarcely better than prostitutes. Sex was about love, not taking off your underclothes. She did not even use the word knickers or pants in her mind; she wanted love to be romantic. Yes, sex must be a part of love, and the affair she'd had the previous year had been a miserable failure. A few months before she had volunteered for the Wrens she'd given her virginity to Tom Langton, an RAF pilot, dark, romantic and nervous, who had been madly in love with her. She had thought she had felt the same, particularly for the most modern of heroes, a boy with wings. Sex had not been a success; he was too strung up and sometimes his lovemaking had not worked at all which had horribly upset him. Sorrel comforted him, telling him as women had done at such times since the beginning of the world that it did not matter, when they both knew how desperately it did. The RAF were carrying out bombing raids on North Germany then; Tom was posted to Yorkshire. Sorrel never heard from him again. She often wondered if he had been killed but was too faint-hearted to find out. It was better to think he had got over her and found another girl.

She had loved him a little, but it had been mostly a desire to be in love, and curiosity, and half-awake desire. And he was a pilot. But she'd never felt for Tom, not once, the passion that had frightened her last night with Toby. He wasn't a man she understood. He seemed dangerous. It excited her to think that.

She had to change trains at Portsmouth, spent a shivering hour in an unheated waiting room with more troops and one or two women muffled up in scarves like refugees. At last the local train for Littleport arrived. As it crawled through Portsmouth in the dusk, she stared out at the bombed buildings propped up with great wooden supports as if crippled. They were dark with winter rains and had begun to seem like the ruins of an older civilisation. The train made its slow way through the suburbs where every shop and house was plunged in the fading twilight. Not a gleam anywhere. The hoardings were the only cheerful things, saying merrily that 'Careless Talk Costs Lives' and 'It's Your Britain, Fight for it Now!' On one stretch of railway wall there was a large poster of a man; he had a faint resemblance to Toby.

'Think of the Wounded! Give all you can to the Red Cross.' cried the poster before the last of the daylight blotted it out.

Leaning back against the compartment door and staring into the dark Sorrel thought of Toby, and the beautiful old house, and George Martyn's kindness, and the large, faintly hostile figure of Toby's mother. She remembered the way one put one's feet in the fender. Toby's Errol Flynn portrait, its painted eyes watching her. And then she thought of a young man spattered with whitewash, and grimaced. He had been the second young man in twenty-four hours to talk sedition. Toby had given a startling performance during supper last night, praising the enemy and sneering at his own country. Then this morning a farmworker actually said people should not be in uniform. Had he meant we should not fight, and wasn't that treachery? she wondered.

During her love affair with Tom Langton she had met a friend of his, a pilot who had been shot down in flames. He'd just returned from a fourth long stay in hospital, but his face was still nothing but livid scar tissue, his nose an invented lump of flesh. He had been matter-of-fact, making jokes, daring people to insult him with pity. To try and recover from such things was terrible – there were mental as well as physical burns. Had it been like that with the man on the farm, had he been badly wounded or had his plane crashed? What had happened to make him hate everything to do with war? But he hadn't the unhealthy pinched look of a man who has been ill; he looked strong and healthy. Of course farming was a reserved occupation but what man with guts chose such a thing?

Forgetting him, her heart flew back to Toby. How difficult it was going to be to see him again. Why, it would be almost impossible. I suppose last night was what people call a wartime romance. They are so beautiful and they cannot last. Everybody says so.

4

Margaret was deeply interested when she heard the news. Sorrel glowingly described Evendon Priory and the Martyns, and had the satisfaction of seeing that her friend was fascinated. Margaret was also generous enough to admit that Sorrel, after all, had been right to go.

When she heard about the money Margaret exclaimed, 'Congratulations!', rather as if Sorrel had won first prize in a raffle. The person whom Sorrel only mentioned casually was Toby. For some reason she didn't want to talk about him. But she thought about him a great deal.

The days after her return to Sussex were like planes taking off every hour, each trip planned in advance and logged. In the Wrens, time was like that. From the moment you put on a scratchy uniform, you became a debtor, owing your life and loyalty, your obedience and long hours of work to the great invisible despot. The navy was hungry to be served, and never satisfied.

The petty officers who gave lectures for the course taught the girls various aspects of photography; there was the job of photographing new recruits, a dull enough task resulting in pictures for reference as bad as those taken for police records. Even the handsomest man or woman looked, thought Sorrel, like an old lag. More difficult was accurately photographing faulty pieces of aircraft engines which were brought in, so that enlargements could be studied by naval engineers. The cameras used by the Wrens were clumsy, weighing over twelve pounds, and the girls learned to develop and print their own work. Easily the most interesting job was taking photographs from a plane. Lying on her stomach, her camera set into the belly of the Fairy Seal aircraft, Sorrel had to photograph service camps scattered in various parts of the southern counties. When the pictures were enlarged they clearly showed all the camps and their camouflage – or to be exact which parts of the camps could be seen from the air and which, successfully, could not. 'If I can see it, then the camouflage's no good,' said an officer, stabbing at one of Sorrel's photographs. 'And that one sticks out like a sore thumb.'

A few days after Sorrel's return to base she was handed a letter. The Wren officer in charge of the post, nicknamed by the ratings 'Heartbreak Hannah', noticed that Wren Scott blushed the colour of a beetroot. The officer hid a smile. Young Scott, an object of much sympathy, seemed to be in better shape. A blush could mean a man.

Like a bird thrown a crust and not daring to peck it until safely alone, Sorrel took her letter to the darkroom. The handwriting on the envelope had a soldierly quality about it. She opened it with a feeling of expectancy. It began with an endearment she'd never seen or heard before. Toby wrote:

> Darlingest.
>
> It looks as if I'll get a 24 hour next month, and I hope to wheedle some petrol from my father. If I do, I could drive over to Littleport. Could you get away for an hour or two if that happens?
>
> It would mean so much to me.
>
> Toby

When the afternoon lecture was over, Sorrel and Margaret had a break and there was time to tramp into town for tea at The Blue Parrot. The snow had finally gone, the day was sunny and smelled of the sea. In identical navy blue greatcoats, dark figures with pink cheeks, the girls swung along in silence. Both were preoccupied. Margaret was thinking about a Canadian called Les. He was very handsome, very smitten, very passionate, and there were the usual difficulties. Margaret wanted to confide in Sorrel but was too vain to confess she needed advice. Besides, Sorrel was two years younger than she was and Margaret remained convinced that nothing Sorrel might suggest would be of the least use. I have nobody to turn to, she thought gloomily. How could she tell her mother? She shuddered at the idea. Mrs Reilly was a deeply devout Irish Catholic. There was almost a kind of innocence about her; she had never even told her eldest daughter the facts of life. And Margaret was bothered. Last night she had only just managed to remain a virgin. Les had been so strong, so male, so urgent – and so attractive. They had been locked in each other's arms in the back of a car parked in a country lane. Margaret was roused. That was the worst part, that *she* had wanted *him*. She no longer felt in control of her heart and body. It was like driving a car with broken brakes.

At first Sorrel was not aware of the quality of her friend's silence, she was too absorbed by Toby's letter and the sentence, 'it would mean so much to me'. It moved her. They arrived at the cheerful teashop, were welcomed by its sparrow owner and sat down at a table near the gas fire. Sorrel ordered tea and flapjacks.

'They're only stodge,' said Margaret, her beautiful face dour.

The café's owner had trotted cheerfully away.

'Flour and potato but hot and filling,' said Sorrel.

Emerging from selfish happiness, she finally noticed her friend's expression and added that Margaret looked as if she needed a plateful of flapjacks. There was no reply.

When the tea arrived, Margaret always poured out, offering whatever they had ordered as if she were the hostess, although each girl paid for herself down to the last halfpenny. It was part of her queenliness; it was gracefully done and it amused Sorrel, who did not mind.

'Toby Martyn may be able to drive over to the base. If I can wangle an hour or two. Do you think I could?'

'I expect so,' said Margaret absently.

Sorrel gave a blissful sigh.

'What fun . . . seeing him again.'

Coming out of her reverie, Margaret looked rather solemnly at her. 'You've only met Major Martyn once. Shouldn't you think things out first?'

'Oh, I have! I've thought of nothing else!'

'I don't think you should be so lighthearted about it.'

Sorrel couldn't help laughing. 'You mean lighthearted about sex? Is that it?'

'It's no good sounding like that, Sorrel. You must have realised by now how difficult it is for girls. Things aren't the way they used to be. We're away from home. On our own. And feelings get so strong even when one tries to stop them.'

'Perhaps we should let them rip.'

'We can't. We mustn't. It's wrong.'

Margaret's face was tense, she looked almost anguished and Sorrel felt a rare moment of pity. Silence fell for a while. Sorrel cradled her cup in her hands and returned to thoughts of Toby, her face dreamy. Margaret said:

'Your attitude worries me.'

'You think I shall be too keen.'

'One can't let the man win.'

'Oh dear, is it a battle, then?'

'Don't be so – you know perfectly well what I mean. It's us, the women, who have everything to lose.'

Sorrel had the grace to stop looking pleased with herself. Her friend didn't know that Sorrel's pearl of great price, her virginity, had been lost two years ago. It was true that Margaret sometimes glanced at her rather suspiciously when giving one of her sermons on being chaste. But as Sorrel always agreed with every word, Margaret felt she could relax. She did now.

But she told herself that Sorrel's attitudes still worried her.

After a further letter from Toby, Sorrel did manage to be given four hours' leave on the right day. She wrote to him hurriedly at his army camp. 'I'm being let out. Can you really manage to get here? It's such a way and your father's petrol must be so precious!'

He telephoned the next morning.

'I'll be at the sentry gate at 4.15.'

A pause.
'I can't wait.'
'Nor me.'

The bomb which killed Lilian Scott had left in the dust of its wake many poisonous things: misery and shock, self-accusation and at times a wave of intense loneliness. Sorrel hadn't realised that by losing her mother she lost her own past; there was nobody left to whom the same things had happened, on whom the same sun and rain fallen. Nobody left who had sat in deck chairs in a Sussex garden, moving the chair across the lawn to chase the afternoon's creeping sunlight. Nobody who knew the same weak family jokes or had watched the same sea. And nobody had eaten, from a paper bag bought by Sorrel's father, the yellow juicy William pears of August while sitting on a shingle beach.

Once Lilian had made a dress for her daughter when Sorrel was about five years old: her mother's only attempt at dressmaking. Pale brown satin with bands of rosebuds round the hem. That dress had also blown away in the dust.

But the falling bomb had brought with it one curious blessing. Sorrel had been stripped of every single thing she owned except her uniform, a shabby jersey and skirt, and a few photographs. And in return been given a new kind of life. There was a peculiar simplicity about literally having nothing. Meeting Toby, however, posed a new problem – he was an officer and couldn't be seen in public with a mere Wren rating. Sorrel would have to beg or borrow some civilian clothes. She consulted Margaret who would have been delighted to lend any of her dresses, but her hips were too broad and her figure too ample for the slender Sorrel. A friendly redheaded Wren, Moyra Thompson, heard of the dilemma and knocked at the door of Sorrel and Margaret's cabin, as the damp bedroom was called.

She strolled in, a cigarette between her lips, a rakish young woman popular with every man at the base.

'I hear there's a boyfriend on the horizon and you haven't a thing to wear. Can I help? There's my heather suit which might fit. What about shoes?'

'Fives,' breathed Sorrel, unable to believe her luck. Moyra had fascinating clothes.

'Good,' said Moyra, producing something she had been hiding behind her back. 'How's about these?'

The shoes, with thick wedge soles, were of burgundy suede with bands of snakeskin, straps and large buckles, and were recognisably designed by America's most famous shoemaker – Joyce. His shoes, advertised in *Vogue*, were coveted by every girl in England.

'Moyra, are you sure?'

'Of course. Try them on. See? A perfect fit. They're my lucky shoes. Don't be surprised at anything that happens to you when you wear Joyce shoes,' said Moyra with a lecherous wink.

Margaret bit her lip. She did not approve of Moyra and was sorry that Sorrel was accepting anything from her.

But Sorrel was enchanted by a suit, a lilac-coloured silk blouse and, above all, by the shoes. When she was dressed she admired her reflection in the oval mirror on the inside of the wardrobe. Then went to the guard room to wait – still looking down now and again to admire her fashionable feet. Two naval ratings came into the guard room; one gave a wink more suggestive than Moyra's.

The sergeant on duty offered Sorrel a kitchen chair and some tea. He was busy answering the never-silent telephone, wore a pencil behind his ear and now and again used it to stir his tea. Sorrel looked at the clock. Perhaps Toby wouldn't come. His leave had been cancelled. The petrol hadn't materialised. Her thoughts fluttered from one disappointment to another. She finally settled for the fact that with army efficiency he would certainly telephone to let her know he wasn't coming.

Her thoughts started to flutter again. Suppose he did arrive – they would be disappointed in each other. They had only met once and this meeting a second time would be a mistake. A stupid miserable mistake.

Five minutes before the time, a rating looked through the door of the office.

'Visitor for Wren Scott, Sergeant.'

'Right. Wren on her way,' was the short reply.

Sorrel hurried down the drive towards the gates. It had been fine and dry all day and a little pale sunshine still lingered, but in a clean sky the moon was visible. At the gates was a long low-slung car, a pre-war SS. Toby jumped out. All he said was 'Hello', and for a moment she thought they were going to shake hands. Then, more loudly, he called, 'Thank you'. The rating at the gate saluted and Toby acknowledged it.

Sorrel climbed into the car and they set off in the direction of the sea. Here, along the front once bright with striped red and white deck chairs, were enormous rolls of rusting barbed wire. All the beaches were mined and forbidden to civilians, and one section of the front was lined with concrete tank blocks. Toby stopped the car between two of these, facing a sea which was flat, calm and shining. She looked at him, wishing she didn't feel shy. She was afraid to speak. He switched off the engine and turned round. How could she have imagined she would be disappointed? He was so much more than she remembered, his face, his voice, the look he gave her, the way he smiled, the parallel lines on his forehead.

'I love your get-up,' he said. 'One's always surprised. Seeing a girl out of uniform.'

She didn't say the clothes were borrowed. She didn't say the shoes were lucky.

'Cigarette?'

'No. No, thank you.'

'Are you sure?'

'Yes, but do smoke if you want to.' It sounded awkward and it was.

'Not now. Not yet.'

And she was in his arms.

They kissed like lovers whom the brutal war had dragged apart for years. They murmured and drew away only to kiss again, opening their mouths as if dying of thirst. They turned into one human, not two, pressing their cheeks against each other, winding their arms round each other's necks, almost sobbing. When at last they broke apart, they were breathless. And as her breath and heart slowed down she heard for the first time the waves dragging on the shingle.

'Shall we go to my hotel and talk?'

'Your hotel!'

'I've booked in at the the Royal Arundel for tonight.'

'But Toby, I've only got four hours.'

'I know. Back at the base by eight. I shall spend the night at the hotel and drive back very early. I might leave about five, it's good, driving at that time. Don't expect too much from the old Royal. It's a miracle it's open and I'm sure the meal will be disgusting. But I can promise a good bottle of Bollinger. I went down to the cellars.'

'Toby!'

He laughed at her reaction, backed and turned the car, saying that Dunkirk had taught him to forage and now it was second nature. Had he told her about the meal he'd had at Rouen during the 'spot of bother'? Snails and fresh trout and duckling and the most astonishing burgundy, 1925. 'But Jerry bombed the place just before we started on the strawberries and cream.'

The old hotel set back from the sea front faced expanses of unkempt grass which had been lawns in peacetime. The building had a certain early Victorian charm, white pillars, lines of pleasantly proportioned windows; it was of painted stucco. But wind and weather and war had been busy. It looked dirty now. In the dying light of evening the rows of windows were nothing but blinded eyes.

Through swing doors Toby lifted a heavy plush curtain which hung there to exclude the faintest chink of light. They entered a hall which had seen better days. The chandelier was lit with only two bulbs, and the laurel-wreathed carpet had not been swept. As Toby and Sorrel passed the open doors of the dining room, they saw seas of empty tables, hopefully laid with white cloths.

The old man in porter's uniform gave Toby a key and called him Major. Toby was genial.

'Don't forget, Marchant. Your very best table for my guest.'

'How on earth do you know his name?' whispered Sorrel as they went up the stairs. The lift was out of order.

'Practice. One must remember the names of all the chaps in the regiment. It's the same thing.'

'I'm impressed.'

'Oh good,' said Toby heartily.

Sorrel did not feel in the least hearty. Nothing had been said as to why they ascended the dim stair, or walked down a corridor which had the air of not having seen a man or woman for a hundred years.

Toby had said, 'We can talk.' She wondered if that was what they were going to do.

The silence was like being deaf.

She was so nervous that once or twice she felt faint. She glanced at him as he was fitting the key, attached to an outsized numbered brass label, into the lock of the door. He opened the door and stepped back for her to go in first. It was nearly dark now but the room glowed.

'I left on the fire. Wait a second. I'd better do the blackout.'

He pulled and tugged at the curtains and then switched on a bedside light. The gas fire was the only comfortable thing in the bare, ugly room. A double bed was covered with dark red sateen. The dressing-table was large enough for a giantess, and the wardrobe nine feet tall. The down-at-heel oversized anonymity increased her shivering expectancy. She was here alone with a man who since he had first kissed her had come like an invader into her thoughts. She had sometimes half tried to escape him because every thought was sexual, but he wouldn't let her. Toby locked the door. He stood at a distance from her.

'*Oh darlingest. Will you?*'

She ran to him.

They undressed with their backs to each other. The room was suddenly darkened, he had switched off the light. She finished taking off her clothes, knickers, suspender belt and precious silk stockings, in the dull glow of the fire. She had no chance to see him naked, he clasped her from behind, hugging her, and she felt how cold his hands were. He pressed hard against her, and she could feel how much he wanted her. Turning her round, he picked her up in his arms.

He made love to her in complete silence, fiercely and strongly and deeply, his body so taut that he trembled. Sorrel abandoned herself to him, to the penetrating body which somehow seemed to plunge into her soul. She lay lost, possessed, and when his climax came she somehow followed him although with Tom Langton she had never had one and always wondered how.

Now they were a single being, moist with sweat and love-making. He separated from her, giving a long, shuddering sigh. They lay still until she leaned forward to pull the eiderdown over them, for the room was very cold. She turned to look at him in the dim light – she could just make out the thin face, a pool of shadows under the cheekbones, his closed eyes. He breathed regularly, he was asleep. Sorrel didn't sleep. She simply lay in joy beside this hard stranger. She wanted to know everything about him. Who was he? What had been his life, his fighting life? What had happened to him in the two years of the war? What kind of man was this who now owned her body, who had entered her and mastered her. She turned again very slowly, so as not to wake him, and stared at the jutting line of his nose, the strong line of his jaw. She did not even know how old this lover of hers might be. A hunger for knowlege, the bewitching thought of all she was going to learn, came to her. It was beautiful to be so ignorant, and to feel so strongly.

She had been told that you could wake people if you looked at them intensely enough. Now he did open his eyes. He said slowly, 'Kiss me.'

They exchanged a long loving kiss.

'You taste good.'

'So do you.'

'We're a marvellous couple, wouldn't you say?'

'Oh yes.'

He sat up and yawned.

'I feel like Juliet,' Sorrel said, running her hand down his spine. How thin his back was.

'Why is that?'

'I bet you've never seen the play.'

'No,' he spoke in a tender rallying tone. 'Tell me about it.'

'Not now. It's sad. But after they've made love she doesn't want the time to go and pretends it hasn't. That's how I feel. Toby?'

'Darlingest?'

'How long have I got?'

'Mind if I switch on the light?'

'Yes. But do.'

He lit the lamp, looked at his watch and said there were two and a quarter hours left.

Outside in the dark were the secrets of war. The sea washed against the shingle and against the barbed wire which it rusted with its salt. On the beaches, hidden under sand where children had made their castles, the mines were buried. And above among the stars the raiders might come tonight or tomorrow and young men fly up to fight them and perhaps die in flames. The war brought death, sorrow, privation and terror like an excruciating weight upon the heart. But among the horrors were strange gifts. Sharp and piercing sweetness of small fragments of time. To Sorrel and Toby, naked in the deserted hotel by the dangerous sea, the war turned two hours into a treasure so exquisite they could scarcely believe it was theirs.

They climbed out of bed, draped blankets round their shoulders and crouched by the fire. They decided it would be mad to waste a precious hour eating dinner.

'We can eat in half an hour.'

'Twenty minutes,' said Toby. 'But I must tell Marchant.'

'Can't you ring reception?'

'My dear girl, that telephone's dead for the duration.'

He dressed and left the room. She sat staring at the glowing bars of clay. He was back soon, looking pleased.

'All fixed. We eat at 7.50 and I'll drive you back at 8.10. Marchant knows the form. I told him to put our Bollinger on ice. I don't think he's ever done such a thing before; he was in the Royal Engineers until he was forty, and never did civilian work until he came to this place as a commissionaire. Now,' he squatted beside her, 'what shall we talk about?'

'You.'

'No we won't.'

'Please.'

'What is there to say?'

'Dunkirk.'

'It's been talked into the ground.'

'Not in the navy. Of course we heard all about the ships going over, anything that could float, even old Channel steamers and yachts and dinghies, and the navy's very proud of their bit. But I don't know about what really happened in France, except what we heard on the wireless or read in the papers.'

'Oh, them.'

'Don't start on your hobby horse,' she said teasingly. 'I want to hear about you, not about the government telling us lies and the Germans being so much better than us.'

'I never said better. Just better at the job in hand.'

She leaned against him.

'Tell.'

'I'd much rather hear about you.'

'Toby. Do tell me.'

He was unused to being asked such a thing by a woman. Even his mother never intruded on his other life. She simply listened in admiring silence if he chose to talk, she never asked him to do so. But he thought this girl a wonder. Her radiant English looks moved him, he was stirred by her thin, long-legged yet womanly body, by the slanting eyes which swam when she looked at him. He loved to hear her pretty, laughing voice. He was drunk with her physical presence, her passion, her very smell. He had scarcely dared to hope he would possess her and when he decided to take a room at the hotel realised he was risking a refusal from her, which he would loathe and had not known until now. Toby had had many women. He was nervously highly sexed and they found the tough reserved man irresistible.

Girls wanted to catch him because he would not be caught. Other sorts of women wanted him in bed, pursued him and had been a damned nuisance afterwards. Sorrel wasn't like that. When they had been at Evendon and she had returned his kisses, when they had been by the sea an hour ago, he had believed – perhaps only hoped – she'd let him make love to her.

And it had happened.

Gratefulness and astonishment filled him, and when she asked him about the fighting in France he was glad to answer. Nothing she wanted could offend him. Nothing she did was wrong or out of joint.

She asked him first why he became a regular soldier.

'What a question. To see the world without having to pay, I suppose.'

'But your father is rich.'

'He's not badly off, but that isn't how it goes. I didn't want to squeeze money out of him, he's so generous. And I did want to see the world. There were other reasons too.'

'What were those?'

He laughed shyly. 'I suppose I liked the idea of dealing with men instead of adding machines in an office and all that.'

'Toby, what on earth would you be doing in an office! You could have stayed at the Priory and ridden The Chief and been a country gentleman.'

'No, darlingest. I couldn't.'

'Why not? It sounds just your kind of life.'

'Father is a businessman. He would never have allowed ny brother or me to live off his money. He works hard and expected us to do the same.'

'But he's a lord.'

'You're very sweet,' he said, laughing. 'Did you think it was an inherited title? Father has cotton mills and factories near Manchester. He was given the title in the last war for the work he did . . . huge supplies to Mesopotamia and Palestine.'

Sorrel was interested and disappointed. She rearranged her ideas about aristocrats living at the Priory.

He tightened his arm about her naked waist, soothed by her femininity, her nearness and, when she turned to look at him, by her swimming eyes. He began hesitatingly to talk about himself. He found he wanted to tell her something very private, the reason he'd longed to be in charge of soldiers under his command. He wanted to care for them, he said, and to serve them as well as to serve with them. He wanted to understand them – their characters, their interests and faults, to know of their families and difficulties. He wanted it so much. He said a touching thing. The day he had sat for his Sandurst examination he had won £50 'on a jolly little horse at Goodwood called Comrade.' It seemed an omen.

His time at Sandhurst sounded to Sorrel like a kind of dream; she had not forgotten Grace's description of the officer combing his hair in the reflection of the cadets' polished swords. What Toby described was very different, a picture of pageantry, of drums rolling, battalions parading before the King, the noise of commands, the click of obedient feet. She heard in his voice the tones of love and it was not the same voice which had flayed his country and admired the enemy.

And then he began to tell her about France in 1940. His regiment had been posted south of Lille before the Germans invaded. The countryside was bare and depressing, the weather bitter, the people of northern France dour and unfriendly. Once an army shell had made a hole in a farmhouse roof during an exercise. 'The farmer and his wife behaved like mad people. It was as if they hated us. They rushed out, shouting and swearing, and the man threw a rake at my sergeant and hit him in the stomach. It was appalling to deal with people who felt like that.'

But there had been one Frenchman who was a real friend. A Monsieur Courbeville living in the house where Toby was billeted.

'Imagine it, Sorrel, he'd been one of the top instructors at the French army's fencing school in Paris. A little man, walked like a cat, very delicate and pernickety. We got on like a house on fire, and he asked if I'd like some fencing lessons.'

'What possible use could they be?'

He couldn't help laughing.

'A good deal. We were taught at Sandhurst although I was never any good. Fencing trains the eye and the hand. Gives you balance and teaches you to move fast. It is invaluable.'

She thought that so much nonsense but still liked the incongruous picture of her lover in France in 1940, fencing with a distinguished if elderly Frenchman.

'Courbeville was an artist,' he said. 'He could knock a foil out of my hand in ten seconds flat as easily as lighting a match. It was a pleasure to be worsted by him. He taught me the *attaque au flanc* and the *parade de tierce* and all kinds of other things. After a fortnight's hard grind he said I had improved. I felt it too.'

Toby described the hideous cold of the first wartime winter, and the conditions in which his men had lived. They had washed in water with two inches of ice upon it, they were issued with only three thin blankets each and the barns and stables where they slept were swept by draughts like sharpened knives. Even work could not keep the men warm. They had the job of widening a ditch, turning it into a stream against oncoming tanks. They were up to their knees in water in the blinding rain. When he spoke of his men, Sorrel heard the deep affection. He cared for them, would have died for them. There was something troubling in that protective love and she was jealous of his soldiers.

'We were in a foreign country trying to talk a foreign language. We were cold, we slept badly, we were always in intense discomfort. You could call it misery. We were given scarcely any leave. But there was no crime among my chaps. They simply bore it, got on with it, joked about it.'

Now and again he mentioned his brother, a year his senior, who had also been to Sandhurst and had joined the same regiment. When he talked of Edmund he was casual. There wasn't any sadness in his voice. She knew this was a part of his life she wasn't allowed to ask about yet. But she couldn't help asking about his MC. Toby shrugged.

'It just happened to be me. It could have been any of the others. But it looked as if my lot were going to be cut off. We were damned nearly surrounded, and my chaps just fought their way out.'

'*You* led them.'

'Did I? I suppose so.' He glanced at his watch. 'God!

Dinner's in five minutes. Hurry, Sorrel! Make yourself respectable.'

Sorrel dressed in desperate haste, pulling on the pretty suit, pushing her feet into her American shoes. She was combing her hair in the giant looking-glass while Toby fastened his Sam Browne, looping the strap over his right shoulder. In what seemed a minute he was changed, point device, in control. He glanced about and found her handkerchief.

'Ready?'

'Yes.'

'Then off we go.'

He turned out the fire and they left the room, going in silence down the ill-lit corridor.

Behind them the emotions they had shared, the excitement and sexual joy, floated for a while. Then burst like an iridescent bubble in the cold air.

He had never said he loved her; and he didn't in his short letters which she read over and over. Perhaps he hadn't fallen in love. But Sorrel knew she had, and it came to her as a most extraordinary fact. When had it happened? When they had been by the fire at Evendon, or when she'd sat with him in the car by the sea, and suddenly felt so happy she could scarcely bear it? Or was it when they lay down and he first entered her body and her soul? She had never been in love until now and had often said, as people do who haven't known the lunacy, that she was probably incapable of it. But here was a man whose whole personality possessed her. She could think of nothing, nothing but him.

His body was muscular and hard to the touch. Bone and muscle formed the face which was set and wary. There were hidden things in him. She did not understand them. Was he like the unicorn, the wild creature only a virgin could tame? Remembering her own lost virginity, she had a pang of the heart. Perhaps if she'd been still untouched, Toby, like the beautiful fabled creature, would have been conquered. But the unicorn was tragic, and she could discern nothing tragic in Toby who was born, she thought, to be the victor . . .

She slept badly, woke early. She made up fantasies in which they had an hour of leave and returned to the bedroom at the end of the deserted corridor, and made love until they were half-dead with exhaustion.

Margaret was interested – perhaps a little envious.

'Did you have a good time?'

'We had a wonderful supper at the Royal Arundel.'

'That's odd, Sorrel. My parents said the food is quite awful.'

But Margaret was more cheerful, for her own problem, to go to bed or not to go to bed, had been solved. Canadian Les had been posted to Norfolk. She missed him very much. But without the temptations of her own hot Irish blood and a sexually aroused man, she was now at ease with her Catholic conscience again. How infinitely easier to concentrate on work when there was no man in one's mind.

One evening some weeks after Toby's visit, the girls were going to bed in their cabin. The landlady had given them one of her usual disgusting suppers, and when they were alone Margaret produced a cardboard box sent by her mother. It contained biscuits and a precious bar of chocolate. Always generous, she divided the spoils exactly into two. Handsome and virginal in camel-hair dressing gown, her face and teeth washed, her black hair brushed hard and shining, she sat on the bed eating a biscuit.

Sorrel licked a final smear of chocolate off her finger.

'Sorrel,' said Margaret suddenly, 'it's time you pulled yourself together.'

'Got undressed and into bed, you mean? I'm in a hanging about mood.'

'And have been for weeks. You're not nearly as interested in the job as you used to be. It's Major Martyn,' added Margaret, accusing her friend of her own previous sins. 'Your mind's on him.'

Sorrel looked self-conscious and said nothing.

'For the love of Mike keep at it,' admonished Margaret. 'We haven't got long before we go to Greenwich and we need good reports. You do still want a commission, don't you? I know I do.'

Sorrel did want a commission. And it would be humiliating to be stuck in the ranks with her friend sailing off into glory.

She undressed and pulled on her nightdress.

'I suppose I am being rather a fool. Okay. You win.'

'Good,' said Margaret heartily. Feeling they were now united in virtue, she switched off the light.

Resentfully admitting to herself that her friend's criticisms were justified, Sorrel determined to concentrate on her work instead of Toby. When it was her turn to be flown over the camouflaged camps, she very well knew that although her photographs were good, sometimes excellent, what she had to do afterwards, to develop and cut and paste the photographs into a sequence to make a complete panorama, she did badly. She had never been clever with her hands, and Margaret was as neat-fingered as an artist. Flying had another disadvantage. Margaret had an iron stomach, Sorrel felt airsick. As she had to stare down at the coloured counties moving beneath her, the plane would shudder, drop into an airpocket or rise like a seagull.

'Whoops-a-daisy, here we go again,' the pilot would shout.

Sometimes she was too busy to notice the switchbacks until the last few minutes, but one afternoon when they landed in a very bumpy airstream, she emerged from the plane as green as grass. The mechanic on the airstrip shouted with laughter.

'You bin sick, then, Scott?'

'Certainly not.'

'Good-oh.'

He slapped her so hard on the back that she tripped and fell on her face.

April came. It was weeks since she had seen Toby and she was due for real leave, five whole days. Margaret again suggested she could go to Chichester and spend it with the Reillys.

'My brother Philip, we call him Flip, may be home on leave. You'll love him. And the rest of the family. The house is big enough for everybody, we play ping-pong on the dining room table and my father's wizard at racing demon. As for the family – Sheila's just the sort of girl you'll like, so pretty and clever and amusing, and there's Maeve and Kath and little Patrick. My brother may be at sea, but you'd like him too. Everybody's such fun. And Mum keeps asking when you're coming. You'll have a grand time.'

Sorrel was touched and grateful and, indeed, rather wanted to accept an invitation to what sounded like a non-stop Irish Ceili. But Toby's letters kept repeating that he'd be able to see her soon. Suppose she left for Chichester just when he got leave? She dared not risk it. Margaret was very disappointed when she explained.

At last, at the start of a sunny May, he wrote to ask her to come and stay at the Priory. 'It's my embarkation leave, actually! 'When she read that, Sorrel had a pang so sharp that it astonished her.

Moyra lounged into Sorrel's cabin one evening, smoking her inevitable cigarette. What was there about her that was so rakish? Her walk, perhaps. Or the look in her eye.

'Rumour has it you're due for some leave. Need any clothes?'

'Moyra, you are good!' Sorrel, thinking of Toby – and of her pathetic lack of civilian clothes – couldn't believe her luck.

'I wouldn't exactly say that,' said Moyra, laughing.

Margaret looked at her disapprovingly, but Moyra didn't notice and soon returned with arms full of dresses. Seeing Sorrel twisting this way and that in real silk, Margaret felt depressed. Sorrel was her friend. She was the one who should give her things, lend her things.

When Moyra had left, she said, 'Why don't you find out about Bundles for Britain? There's a place in London, I think it's near Berkeley Square, where people go if they've been bombed out. They get American clothes free. Somebody Sheila knew got some frocks from Hollywood.'

Sorrel couldn't help laughing.

'I'd rather go to Harrods and buy something new.'

'What about coupons?'

'Eight for a dress, six for silk stockings. Golly, I wish I could buy those too on the black m—' began Sorrel. 'Okay, okay, just joking.'

'I'm not sure I believe you.'

'I'm not sure I do either.'

Sun and blue skies made the cramped and crawling journey bearable. The train windows were open and, although smuts blew in, so did the spring. When Sorrel finally walked out of Evendon station and looked about for the Daimler – Toby had written that she would be met – she was startled to see the Martyns' chauffeur beside a pony and trap.

'Good afternoon, Miss. We'll have you home in a jiff.'

He settled her into the trap and chirruped to the horse. They set off into a changed countryside. Every tree seemed to have burst into blossom, every field was freshly green and the verges on either side of the road were massed with yellow dandelions like stars. When they turned through the Priory's open gates and trotted down the drive, there was the old house. And larches coming out, looking as if they were hung with lace.

The front door was opened by Evie, smiling as if Sorrel were one of the family. She took her bag. It made Sorrel shy to be waited on.

'Lord Martyn is in the drawing room,' said Evie, accompanying her down the long passage and opening the door for her.

All the windows at the far end of the room were wide, there was a crab apple in flower on a distant green bank. A smell of growing things seemed to be floating into the room.

George Martyn sprang up to kiss her on the cheek and ask her fatherly questions. He was sure she'd had no lunch, probably a cup of tea before she left Littleport. Would Evie be a dear and cut the visitor a sandwich? His welcome was so warm that Sorrel, meeting his dark eyes, had a feeling of sexy sinfulness. He doesn't know he is talking to Toby's mistress, she thought. The idea excited her. She asked herself for the hundredth time – how can we possibly make love here? How can we possibly not?

'My son tells me he managed to meet you in Sussex for a short time a couple of months ago.'

'Only because you were kind enough to give him some petrol, Lord Martyn.'

'I spoil the boy. Always did.'

'We had dinner at the local hotel,' said Sorrel in a friendly voice. He returned her innocent look with a penetrating one which business colleagues knew well. He hadn't made up his mind about this young woman.

'And what do you think of Toby?'

If it was meant to take her unawares, it did not succeed. She replied with engaging naturalness.

'I like him very much. Everybody must.'

'Except the enemy.'

She dutifully smiled.

'He's just come back from a gunnery course,' remarked his father. 'Very bronzed and full of talk about the regiment. His mother complained that he smelled of gun oil and I daresay he did. He's bursting with health. What he calls fighting fit.'

There was a not uncomfortable pause. Martyn had remained home at the Priory today deliberately to see this girl, at some inconvenience to himself. There were problems over the enormous numbers of uniforms needed from his Lancashire factories. The army was being difficult and Beaverbrook, who had heard about it, demanding and short-tempered. On the telephone for hours at a stretch, Martyn was tired. The trouble was not with production but with staff. No sooner had he got a good team together than some key man volunteered or was called up. The call-up was something he accepted like an act of God. But volunteers annoyed him. Appearing calm, George Martyn wore a mask. Beneath it, his own nature with its worship of success, detestation of failure and anger easily roused, seethed like a sea full of fish. Despite his warmth to the girl he was not in a good humour. He was also having trouble with Grace who could be insupportably tiresome.

Martyn admired his wife's culture, her good mind, her skill with the farm and her confidence when meeting his celebrated colleagues. She was excellent with cabinet ministers and industrialists. But he was repelled by her hardness. That was his prerogative. He liked his wife ample, sentimental, given to quoting patriotic poetry, amusing, clever, catty and maternal.

She had decided to dislike the girl Toby had invited to stay during his leave. Grace had been polite enough when Sorrel

Scott had called with the tragic news of Lilian's death. But now that her son – alas, her only son – was showing an interest in the girl, Grace had altered towards her. George Martyn studied his youthful visitor and saw how sexually attractive she was. In a curious way she was rather poised. Perhaps tragedy had done that, he had seen the armour worn by the young. Toby had protected himself in it when Edmund died. George had an idea that his boy might be serious about Lilian's daughter, which was why Grace had taken against her. It irked him. He never became used to Grace's public radiance and private claws. And she'd never liked Lilian.

Sorrel's first hours at the Priory took on the same pattern as those of her previous visit. George Martyn looked after her and Lady Martyn eventually appeared, grotesque this time in riding breeches, to ask if George had seen Scrap? She nodded briefly.

'Scrap is the mongrel my wife is much attached to,' explained George. 'I believe you met him last time you were here. No, my dear, I haven't set eyes on him since last night. Why?'

'He has disappeared.'

'Ask Dion Fulford to look.'

Grace was impatient.

'Fulford is out with the horses. Ploughing and pressing the six-acre field which, as I told you, we're sowing with oats. I can't have him wasting time looking for that fool of a dog. I'll have to do it myself.'

Later she peered round the door to say the dog had been found, shut in an empty stable.

Evie showed Sorrel up to the same bedroom she had been given on her first visit. Having made sure the visitor had all she needed, the housekeeper lingered. Her manner was warm.

'It must be lovely in the Wrens.'

'You sound as if you'd like to be in uniform.'

'Maybe once. But I'm too old. And besides . . .'

'Besides, they can't spare you.'

'I wouldn't say that.' Evie's pale face very slightly blushed. She asked Sorrel something of life as a Wren and Sorrel, seeing her interest, couldn't resist showing off about her trips in the Fairy Seal Fighter. Evie was a most satisfactory listener, far kinder and more flattering than Lilian had been.

'I hope you'll call me Evie,' she shyly said.

'I'd like to. And please call me Sorrel. You do have a pretty name, Evie, and isn't it a coincidence? Being so like the name of the house and the village.' Sorrel had meant to remark on this to Toby.

'Oh, but it isn't my real name. Edmund thought of it. I used to be nanny to both boys when we lived in Surrey, and they just called me Nanny then. But when we moved here and they were going to prep school Edmund nicknamed me Miss Evie of Evendon because he said I ordered them both about so much. They did think it was funny. After that they always used it and somehow it stuck, and Lord and Lady Martyn began to use it too. Now I forget my real name is Betty, except when I go home to my sister. Evie of Evendon . . . It was just like Edmund. He was the joker of the family.'

Her voice was like Toby's when he spoke of his dead brother. It had no undertones.

When she'd gone, Sorrel had a bath and put on Moyra's real silk dress, a dull corn colour. She felt a different person from the girl in blue serge. Embarkation leave, she thought. I've only just found you, now I shall lose you again . . . she started at a light knock on the door.

It was Toby. He came in, his finger to his lips, carefully shut the door, then flung out his arms. He pulled her to him so tightly that the buttons on his uniform hurt her breasts. They kissed and kissed.

'Oh darlingest. Oh poppet.'

He held her closer and closer against the bruising buttons, rocking and embracing. They were like the figure of the myth, the human creature once divided into two, and twining in desperate embrace to try and grow back into one again. At last they parted.

'Do your hair.'

'Is it a mess?'

'Yes. It is. Stop looking at me like that.'

'Like what?'

'See you in the hall in five minutes.'

'You do your hair too.'

'And wash my face in cold water. Good idea. Might make me sane again.'

He was gone.

She fell rather than sat down on the bed. How could they make love? Why had he invited her to stay here? It was going to drive them both mad. She went into the bathroom, filled the basin with cold water and plunged her face into it. It made her gasp.

When she came downstairs into the central hall she looked composed and lovely in the softly coloured dress. Toby and his parents were sitting there, drinking Toby's favourite pink gin.

'What a transformation,' said George Martyn. 'That's a very lovely dress, Sorrel. Isn't it, Grace?'

'Yes,' said Grace, adding rather quickly, 'fill up my glass, Toby, your father only gave me half rations.'

Dinner was not an intimate family meal, as Toby had invited two of his junior officers. David Strickland and Alec Watts were as young as Sorrel, David big and freckled, Alec short, thin and dark. Their manner was the same. It was attentive, graceful, and they were always ready to laugh.

Grace was serene with four men seated at her candlelit table. She paid no attention to Sorrel, who was simply glad to be in the same room with Toby and listen. The talk centred on the hectic days the young men had shared in the retreat to Dunkirk. It was the same story which Toby had partly confided to Sorrel at the Royal Arundel; but he had spoken of it to her as if it were a kind of secret. Now it was described in vivid detail, resembling one of the chaotic old-fashioned paintings of the Great War in the *Illustrated London News*, where the sky was lit with bursting shells.

The three men talked in turn, adding details or interrupting each other. All three spoke of what had happened in the same way, with the same tones of brisk reminiscence. The Mid-hamptonshires had been going towards Brussels under orders; when they reached the suburbs they saw a vast fire, 'the best they'd ever seen' – the enemy had just bombed a fuel storage tank. The roads were crammed with retreating Belgian troops and civilians. The Midhamptons fell over telephone cables, climbed the wreckages of cars, saw many bodies lying unheeded. They had the job of helping the Sappers to blow up a railway bridge and prevent the enemy advancing.

'Do you remember the French corporal, Sir?' said David.

Toby laughed, asking how he could forget him. A big fattish man in French uniform had appeared, quite alone and nothing to do with the shambling Belgian soldiers dragging down the roads. He was darkly suntanned; he looked extraordinary among all the white faces. He was from Provence, and had an almost incomprehensible accent. He had been with five men, they'd met some tanks and hidden in a wood, then gone in the wrong direction, having forgotten all their maps. Later his fellows were wiped out. He was now totally lost and begged to join *'les braves Anglais'*.

'He hadn't even kept his rifle,' said Toby, more in sorrow than in anger. 'But we found him a weapon belonging to one of our sergeants who'd been killed.'

'What happened to him?' asked Grace.

'Poor chap fell on the beaches.'

The trio then went on to describe blowing up the bridge. As mere infantry, they had had no idea how enjoyable the spectacle would be. When the moment came, the huge structure actually seemed to rise up very slowly in the air, without any smoke or noise, in the eeriest manner. Then there was a crack like the sound of doom.

'Damned great paving stones hailing down on us, and metal and heaven knows what. We burrowed down as deep as we could in our pits and just hoped for the best.'

The retreat across France was chaos. They marched three days and three nights, were lightheaded from lack of sleep; the halts they made only exaggerated the agonised exhaustion. Nobody had anything to eat for forty-eight hours, but at last they passed a factory occupied by the British, and a soldier ran out with sackfuls of tinned pears, shouting, 'That's all there is in the place.'

'We couldn't believe our luck,' said Toby.

Grace was incredulous. 'Belgian tinned pears! I recall them only too well in puddings when I was at my Brussels finishing school. They tasted of nothing at all. Just like talking to yourself.'

'They tasted like manna from heaven to us, Lady Martyn,' said David. 'We divided them between us. One tin for every three men. Out came the tin openers in less time than it takes to tell you, and we all just wolfed down those pears and positively swooshled up the juice.'

'And had the most fearful stomach rumbles later on,' put in Alec.

'That's putting it politely, it was worse than rumbles,' finished Toby and they all roared with laughter. They turned their hunger into a joke. Hardships sounded like adventures. Yet the story was full of death. They had been bombed when they tried to sleep, machine-gunned while they marched. They described the nightmare hurry at the end when they arrived at the port, all the beaches teeming with men, ships just leaving, and how they had waded out up to their necks and somehow been dragged on board a pleasure steamer. But a German plane had machine-gunned the ship, and some of the men who'd been through so much had died on the decks.

At last the talk ended, and Grace stood up, collecting Sorrel with a look and leading the way into the drawing room. It was quiet. Both women were silent, thinking the same. That Toby might have been killed. That his brother had been. They had been listening to a battle of life and death they would never, never share with the men who'd known its terrors.

Sorrel put the thought out of her mind and looked across at Grace Martyn; she knew Toby's mother disliked her. I wish I liked *her*, whatever she thinks of me, reflected the girl. But who can get themselves to like somebody and be disliked in return? It was impossible. She reminded herself that the elderly woman was a tragic figure. Somewhere in that big body must be a stricken heart. But Sorrel couldn't manage the unselfish vision. There they sat, Grace Martyn and herself, in this rich room, a pool of luxury in a dark country vowed to war, half-ruined, short of food and braced to die. And both women were at the mercy of the future.

Sorrel stirred uneasily, wondering if Toby's mother could hurt her in some way. She would like to be rid of me although she doesn't know what is going on. But what *is* going on? Oh God, I wish Toby would come.

'More coffee?'

'Please. It's marvellous coffee, the best I have ever tasted.'

'My husband brings it from the City,' said Grace, taking Sorrel's cup. She could have added that her husband brought a good many things from the City. Tins of butter, eiderdowns, cigars, extra blankets, hams, biscuits, wine and gin.

'You found Scrap, then,' remarked Sorrel.

One had to say something.

'The fool got himself shut in somehow. Probably one of the land-girls slammed the door. Incredibly stupid.'

Hunting for something else to say, Sorrel asked how many people worked on the farm. She was informed that there were four. Two land-girls and two men. Grace did not call them by their names. Longing for the others to come and rescue her, Sorrel then found herself asking how many acres were farmed at the Priory.

'We have a hundred. It doesn't sound much, but it takes a mort of work,' said Grace in the voice of teacher to idiot. 'We grow potatoes and hay, oats, rye and vetch for the silage and so on. There's our stock. We farm our land, rear our animals, and produce food of the highest quality, I'm glad to say.'

Sorrel nodded, her face set in an agonised look of stiff insincerity.

'Take grass,' continued Grace, pleased to talk even if it was only to her. 'Grass is grass to the uninitiated. To farmers it's valuable winter feed. We must study different varieties, choose scientifically to provide the best grazing. The land must be right. Its heart must be cared for.'

Without waiting for comments from the uninitiated she said, 'Is my son taking you to the Wings for Victory ball on Thursday?'

'Why, no. He hasn't mentioned it, Lady Martyn.'

'Really? I suppose he's decided not to go because he wants to be home as much as possible, as it's his embarkation leave. He told you he's off, I suppose?'

'Yes. He did.'

'Off to an unknown destination,' said Grace brightly. 'One can't ask where, of course. "Careless Talk Costs Lives." Serving our country, do you see, is all that matters.'

It sounded as if she, not Sorrel, were the Wren in uniform.

There was the rumble of male voices and the officers, followed by their host, trooped in. George Martyn suggested billiards and the young men eagerly agreed. In the billiard room the play went on for two hours. George Martyn won a game or two and Toby competed with him. Alec and David larked about, winning or losing with equal amusement. Sorrel had never held a cue in her hands, just as she'd never grasped the reins of a horse. She said she would not try to play, it would slow things down. Toby asked her to stand beside him.

'You'll be my mascot.'

'A gal to bring you luck,' said Alec, 'like at Monte Carlo. Chaps ask the prettiest gal in the room to hand them their counters.'

Toby explained the game.

'You see that coloured ball, that's my mother's and I intend to pot – her – firmly – like – that.'

Crack! The ball vanished down the pocket.

'Pig,' said Grace.

'He plays to win,' said George with approval.

'Good shot, Sir,' chorused the junior officers.

The lights shone down on the green baize, throwing harsh shadows on intent faces. Grace fat and catlike, George Martyn with his steel helmet of hair, the young men whose faces were as unmarked as flowers. And on Toby's eagle profile. He showed Sorrel how to play a shot.

'The important thing is to put your left hand on the table – so – and rest on the palm and splay out your fingers. Now. Place the cue in the little V between your forefinger and thumb. Good. Keep your hand quite still.'

When he touched her, she knew he knew she was trembling.

His expression did not alter from cool interest of instructor to tyro. Then she looked up and caught his mother watching her.

It was after midnight when Toby walked to the front door to see his friends off. An army staff car had come for them.

'Don't wait for Toby, he and the boys will be standing about talking for hours,' said Grace to Sorrel. George looked at the girl and shook his head.

'You're very pale. We've tired you out. Now go off to bed and get the roses back in those cheeks.'

There was nothing to do but say goodnight. Up in her room Sorrel slowly undressed and sat in front of the looking-glass brushing her hair. She was so tense that her back ached.

She heard the distant slam of a door somewhere. Then the old house, as if sighing, fell silent.

It was strange to hear so deep a quiet. Sorrel's digs with Margaret were in a terrace house in a street where, through the blackout, people walked by late at night talking and laughing. In the small hours army lorries thundered past. And always there was the noise of planes. But here a spell was falling on the house like black velvet.

She wandered into the bathroom and turned on the taps carefully, so that the water only trickled instead of making a noisy roar. When the bath was full at last, she took off her nightdress and slipped into the water, floating in its grateful warmth, trying to be calm and relaxed. Toby will be in his room, his friends must have gone by now. He will be undressing. Is he thinking of me? Is he the sort of person who goes to bed and falls asleep the moment his head touches the pillow? How can he? I never shall. She closed her eyes, the warm water lapping round her, and began to think of the moment earlier this evening when he'd come into her room. She tried to remember the kiss.

Opening her eyes, she looked across the bathroom.

He was there.

She gave a violent start. He had come in as quietly as a cat, and was standing looking down at her. He wore a white dressing gown; he was different from the soldier of her thoughts.

'Ssh,' he whispered before she could speak, 'I've been creeping about like a burglar. I think they're all asleep by now but I daren't risk making a noise and having some of the floorboards creak.' He stared down at her body in the water, her pointed breasts, her maidenhair.

'Why are you having a bath?'

'I don't know.'

She stood up, the water pouring from her like Venus. He undid the dressing gown, he was naked beneath it. He stepped into the bath with her.

'I've never made love in water before.'

He pushed her legs apart with his own and effortlessly entered her.

The next morning she couldn't remember how long they had made love in the bath or exactly what it had felt like, except at first the lapping warmth, and then it had all been excitement, and Toby thrusting deep inside her, and the water round them like sex itself. They had climbed out afterwards, dried each other, towelling backs and buttocks, kissing, and going into the bedroom had fallen on the bed and started all over again. She fell asleep exhausted in his arms and only woke because he shook her shoulder.

'It will soon be light.'

'Five more minutes . . . '

'Four . . . '

A pause.

'Sorrel. Don't you dare.'

And then he climbed out of bed, tied on his robe and went silently from the room. Sorrel slept until nine o'clock when the maid woke her, bringing a tray of breakfast. The old woman, despite a respectful good morning, wore a prunes and prisms face. She disapproves of me, thought Sorrel. She can't guess, can she? Why do I imagine such nonsense? But she avoided the old servant's eye and was glad when she was gone.

Too lazy to eat or drink, Sorrel lay in a helpless bliss. Sometime during the night, sometime between their lovemaking, they had talked of this being his last leave but even that knowledge did not hurt, it couldn't because her body had been used for delight so much that she was conscious of nothing else. When she finally got up and went into the bathroom it gave her a sexual thrill to see trampled towels and the soapdish on the floor where Toby had put it, saying it was sticking into his back. When she was dressed she looked at herself closely in the glass. All that lovemaking. Did it show? She saw complacently that there were violet-coloured shadows under her eyes.

Downstairs the sun was flooding into the old house, every window was wide. There was no sign of the family, although down a corridor she glimpsed the old maid. Sorrel couldn't stay indoors. She could hear comfortable farmyard noises, the lowing of cows, a cock's crow, and then far away in the woods somewhere the sweet melancholy sound of a cuckoo. For a moment she was wildly happy.

She walked out of the house, crossed by the stables and then, rounding a corner, stopped to stare. The cherry orchard was in flower. She hadn't even noticed that there was an orchard, her ignorant town-bred eyes hadn't marked it the last time she was at the Priory. It took her breath away. The trees were covered with flowering snow, they simply stood and blossomed. They were like brides. It was impossible to enjoy the beauty by herself and hearing footsteps she spun round, thinking it was Toby. A man was coming towards her, bent under a sack held across his shoulders. It was the farmworker she had met whitewashing the barn.

She smiled, longing to talk, still joyful.

'Hello.'

He hesitated, halted, rolled the sack to the ground and straightened up.

'Good morning.'

It was clear that he didn't want to stop or put down the sack, and unwilling politeness had forced him to do so. He bent to pick it up again.

'That looks as if it weighs a ton,' said Sorrel in a friendly voice, hoping to delay him.

'Half a hundredweight to be exact. Phosphates.'

She saw that he hadn't an idea who she was.

'You don't recognise me. I know *you*, though. You once told me the date of the medieval barn. 1325. And you described the priests getting nasty if the peasants hadn't brought them enough.'

'Good grief, you're not the Wren?'

'I suppose I look different out of uniform.'

'Yes. You do.'

He bent to take up his burden again. She was piqued. Despite shapeless clothes and dirty cracked hands he was attractive in a way.

'I remember you said you didn't like uniform.'

Again he straightened up.

'That's true.'

'All uniforms,' she asked teasingly.

'I dislike what they represent,' was the serious reply. She raised her eyebrows. How old was he? Twenty-five? More? He must have been called up ages ago. I suppose he decided to remain working on the farm, she thought. I can't understand a man who does that rather than fight.

'Uniform's not so bad,' she said easily 'I quite enjoy it. And it has a marvellous advantage.'

Her manner was engaging and he responded in a pleasanter voice, 'I can't imagine what that is.'

'I don't have to worry about what to wear. Day in, day out, on with the navy blue.'

That did make him laugh.

'I do remember you. You're a friend of Toby's.'

'You know him well?' It was snobbish of her to be surprised. He shrugged, saying he had known Toby and Edmund Martyn 'slightly' for years. She was still curious.

'My name's Scott,' she said , offering the information like a handshake, 'Sorrel Scott.'

'How do you do? I'm Dion Fulford and – sorry but I must go. This is our first spell of good weather and we're trying to recover lost time. There have been some non-stop gales. But now,' he added, with a note of satisfaction, 'the wheat is really starting.'

'And the cherries. I've been admiring the orchard.'

'Country people round here call it the cherry flourish,' he

said, looking up at the trees. 'Last year the late frosts killed most of the crop.'

'This time you'll get basketsful.'

'Not necessarily. The birds eat the tops off the blossom, let alone making feasts of the fruit.'

'I thought you farmers got children to make themselves useful. Couldn't they scare away the birds?'

'We do get the kids at harvest,' he said. 'But they'd scarcely be let out of school to sit for days clapping their hands and shouting. There's another problem. The war agricultural people haven't a machine to help pick the fruit. Look, there's one of the villains –' and he pointed up at a branch where a bird with a pink breast had alighted.

'How beautiful he is!'

'A bullfinch,' he said, clapping his hands. The bird vanished in a flash of white and grey.

'I'm sure you'll get tons of cherries,' said Sorrel, always one for the happy end, 'and people really long for fruit now.'

'We can live in hope,' he said dryly. 'It's as necessary as phosphates.' And this time he did shoulder the sack.

'We'll meet again,' said Sorrel.

'Somehow I don't think so. But I liked talking to you.' He walked away in the direction of the stables.

As Sorrel returned to the house she heard somebody call her name. It was Toby.

'I've been looking for you. Evie has made us some fresh coffee.'

'How delicious. I was in the orchard,' she said, taking his arm. Seeing him filled her with fresh joy. As they walked together towards the house they met a long procession of ducks, one following the other like soldiers in cream-coloured uniforms, most of them quacking or shaking their tails. She burst out laughing, turning to share her amusement.

'Aren't they funny, Toby?'

All he said, unsmilingly, was 'Sorrel.'

'Yes?'

'I saw you talking to that farmworker.'

She was too happy for a moment to take it in.

'Hasn't he got an odd name – Dion. Nearly as odd as mine.'
'I'd rather you didn't.'
'Waste his time? He's quite nice, and I only chatted for a minute or two, slave-driver.'
'That's not what I meant. I would rather you did not talk to him at all.'
'Toby. What do you mean?'
'What I say. Don't talk to him. He is a conscientious objector.'
She was staggered.
'I thought you would be shocked.'
'I am. How *extraordinary*. Does he really think – really feel – '
'I don't give a damn what he thinks or feels,' burst out Toby. 'He disgusts me. I can't bear to look at him. When I remember my men lost in France . . . come along. Let's enjoy the day and forget such creatures exist.'
And he turned to her, the iron melting into tenderness.

5

Embarkation leave. The words were never far from Sorrel's mind, but she was fiercely determined not to let them spoil this exquisite time given her like a blessing. Toby took her for long country walks in the sunshine. They went down overgrown green lanes, crossed meadows yellow with buttercups, or wandered by the fast river which ran under a bridge by an ancient mill, or chuckled past thatched cottages. All day long they never met a soul.

At night they dined with his parents, and Toby talked too much, returning to his sport of praising the Germans. Sorrel didn't care. When she was with the Martyns she was silent, a subdued young woman against whom it would be impossible to say a word. But now and then George Martyn looked curiously at her, making out nothing but her beauty and serenity. He was unused to a state of bliss, did not recognise it, and remarked later to his wife, 'The girl seems very quiet. I suppose the dear chap has told her his regiment is going East.'

'Of course he has,' said Grace sharply.

Her son's preoccupation with the Wren was getting on her nerves. She longed for a little of Toby's company, she was lonely for him. How could she betray anything as embarrassing as painful mother love? Since their mid-teens both her boys had always had girls around, pretty little creatures whose names Grace had forgotten. Preferring not to think about it, she supposed her sons were highly sexed: their father certainly was. One girl she did remember was a dark, glowing, very rich

South American called Inez. Edmund had been far too keen on Inez, and had invited her to be his partner at two of the Sandhurst balls. Remembering her elder son's flirtatious way with the Venezuelan heiress, thinking it such bad taste to show blatant interest in public in a member of the opposite sex, she almost forgot Edmund was dead. And now here was Toby spending every waking moment with that Wren. I never liked Lilian Scott, vapid woman, she thought. I can't understand why George bothered with her after her husband died. Her thoughts turned painfully back to Toby. She longed for a little time with him. For that sense of his affection, attention, admiration, knowing he was like herself and her soldier forebears. She was at home with him. She did not admit to herself that she loved him more than her husband, but it was true. And he was going away. Where? To what fate? She couldn't bear to think about that.

He was always with that girl now. They set off in the morning with sandwiches, going God knows where to look at God knows what. Churches or monuments, lakes or woods. She swerved away from imagining their embraces. And there was one day left and that was all.

Time was running away for Sorrel as swiftly as for Grace. The sand in the huge hour-glass, piled up richly when she had arrived at the Priory, had run in a thin unstopping stream through the tiny aperture and now the base of the glass was almost full, the top almost empty. Every night Toby crept into her room when the house was asleep, and they made love over and over again. He seemed to penetrate almost into her soul. He possessed her. Owned her. And then, blended and worn out with bliss, they rolled apart to lie with the curtains open, the windows wide, the moon shining straight on their faces.

'That's a bomber's moon,' Toby once said, and then grasped and squeezed her hand. 'Damn. Damn. Forgive me, darlingest, what a swine I am to forget.'

Sorrel kissed his hand. She could not say that there were whole days when her poor mother's ghost never came into her mind – the only person reigning there was himself. He had asked about Lilian, and she'd told him a little of her childhood and girlhood. She saw he wasn't very interested. Why, she fondly thought, should he be? What he gave her was silent sympathy for her mother's death which she did not deserve. He behaved as if she were brave.

One night he did talk about his brother, but not about when Edmund was killed, only about their life as boys at Evendon, the ponds they had fished, the rivers they had swum. In his descriptions, Edmund was the quickest, kindest, most daring, courageous. Sorrel could not match his words with the photograph of Edmund she had seen in the drawing room. But Toby had worked an oyster touch, perhaps, with the past and it shone like a pearl.

On another night towards dawn she was very quiet, so quiet that he thought she was asleep, but when he leaned on his elbow to look, her eyes were open.

'What is it? What are you thinking?'

She swallowed. She knew there was a question she had to ask him, and it frightened her. It had been somewhere in her mind ever since they'd first made love at the hotel, and it returned to hurt her when she least expected it. She had to know the answer. But it would be terrible if the answer wasn't right.

'Toby. Tell me something.'

'Anything.'

'Turn your back. Don't look at me.'

'Fool. Very well.'

With only the pale shape of his naked back to speak to she said in a low voice, 'Don't answer at once. Wait before you do.'

'Darlingest, what is this nonsense?'

'It isn't nonsense. No, don't turn round. Don't touch me. Just listen . . . were you very shocked when we first made love that time? You never asked if there'd been anybody else but of course you knew. That it wasn't the first time for me. Did you hate it? I don't know how men feel about that.'

He did not speak or move.

Oh God, she thought, he doesn't think I'm the right kind. His kind. I suppose he thinks I sleep with a lot of men. Why did I ask? I was mad.

She lay rigid.

And then he turned and pushed an arm under her and leaned down.

'I thought it was wonderful of you to let me. And because I *know* you, I know that whoever the man was, you must have loved him.'

'Yes. Yes. We were going to be married. He was in the RAF and he was killed.'

'Dear girl. I was sure it was something like that. You hid it from me because you're so courageous. I honour you for it.'

He kissed her.

Later they made love again and it was more violent and passionate, and the lie seemed very honourable. Scarcely remembering Tom Langton, she began to believe what she had said, even while she still knew it was not true. Yes. Tom had asked her to marry him, and he had been tragically killed in an air battle over France. His death had ennobled her. He flew out of her mind.

On the last of their May mornings, Toby decided to give Sorrel a riding lesson. He arranged to borrow a pony from a neighbouring farm, and Evie produced some jodhpurs which had been Toby's when he was a schoolboy. They fitted Sorrel surprisingly well but stank of mothballs. Evie also gave her a hard hat covered with velvet, with a peak. She and Toby laughed when Sorrel was ready.

'She looks just like a boy,' said Evie.

'No she doesn't,' said Toby.

Sorrel's pony was a mild little animal, pure white and inevitably called Snowball. Toby fetched The Chief who stood patiently, towering over Sorrel's small horse. Toby saddled both horses, while Sorrel watched in impressed silence. As he put on The Chief's bridle he said, 'You don't know much about horses, do you?'

'Not a thing. They are very beautiful.'

He was amused.

'When you begin to understand them you will love them as I do. A horse can be such a friend. He trusts you. He's bold but he's calm, and when he knows you he wants to please you. That's the great thing. He relies on you and you must never let him down. Now. First thing. How to mount. Face forwards, your left foot in the stirrup and – up!'

Sorrel found herself on Snowball's back.

Toby was a patient teacher. He explained how she must have a straight back but not a stiff one, she must be supple but not slack. She obeyed. If a horse wants to please a human, she thought, *I* want to please Toby. Sitting on the pony, she had a new view of the world. Toby adjusted her stirrups.

'Legs snug on either side. One mustn't see the daylight between them and the saddle. Now, don't grip so tightly with your legs or your muscles will tense and stiffen.'

They set off. Sorrel soon found her balance and grew accustomed to the feel of the walk.

'You're nice and straight,' he said.

It was a morning of all mornings to be riding. Summer had burst suddenly, every flower was opening, every leaf uncurling. Fresh green in the hedges hid the long black thorns and the ditches which had been filled with icy mud in winter now brimmed with buttercups. The birds sang as if they'd burst their hearts with joy.

'How The Chief loves to be out with us,' Toby said, patting the horse's glossy neck. 'My poor Chief is actually a hunter with all the right qualities for the job. He's bold but safe and he's keen as mustard. Now look at him. He has to pull the milk float, with the bottles making that filthy din. They've trained him to bear the shafts but he feels it, he feels it all the time, poor man. He's patient and dignified, but he minds, don't you, boy? When peace comes, I'll take you both hunting.' He looked at her. 'And now you can sit comfortably for the walk, shall we rise to the trot?'

She hadn't known it was so difficult. Such jarring and jolting. She was certain she was going to fall off. But Toby encouraged her and she learned how to rise and fall with the movement of the horse, finally discovering she could follow the pattern – she could actually do it. 'Good work!' said her teacher.

After a time Toby put his hand on the leading rein and gently turned Snowball's head; they began to trot homeward. He jumped down to open the gate and they walked the horses into the stable yard.

'Down you get and into the house for the hottest bath you can bear, or you'll ache like fury later. See you in half an hour.'

'Aye, aye, sir.'

'My good woman, I would remind you that I am not in the navy.'

'Sorry, Major, Sir!'

Sorrel saluted and he was shaking his fist at her when Dion Fulford appeared in the yard. Toby's face hardened, he turned and said in a harsh, insulting voice, 'Take this pony back to Butterbox.'

He held out the reins to Dion at arm's length, as if to keep him at the greatest possible distance.

Dion gave a sort of a smile.

'Afraid not. There's a gap in the lower field, and if I don't get a move on, the bull will get out. We wouldn't want that, would we?'

He looked mischievously at Toby.

Sorrel went scarlet. The two men faced each other like animals pausing before an onslaught. She did not doubt which animal would strike hardest, and cause bloodshed, and be victor.

'Do as I tell you.'

'Sorry.'

Dion looked as if the man in uniform amused him. 'I can't do what you ask. You'll have to take the pony back. I'm certainly not having our bull charging all over the shop, doing a lot of expensive damage, let alone the risk of him attacking somebody.'

'Yourself, you mean.'

'No, I don't but I'll do as well as the next man. Or girl. Bulls are dangerous and this one particularly as it's a dairy bull. Didn't your mother tell you about him? Sorry,' he repeated, his grey eyes slightly enlarged, 'I'm off.'

Before Toby could say another word he walked away.

Toby stood like a stone. He was so angry that he couldn't speak. Sorrel was angry for him. How dare Dion Fulford disobey him? How dare he smile as if Toby was funny. A man like that. A man afraid to fight, who wouldn't risk his life like everybody else in England – it was shameful. But while Toby still remained silently furious, she had a sudden image of a bull head down, charging at Dion. Or herself.

The little horse began to fidget.

'Shall we walk her to Butterbox?' suggested Sorrel, wanting to break the now deadly silence.

'Put her in the barn.' Toby spoke as if to an army servant. 'He shall take her later.'

The pony trotted meekly indoors, and Sorrel shut her in and returned to Toby. He pulled himself together with a shudder.

'I apologise,' he said in a more normal voice.

'Honestly, it doesn't matter.'

'Of course it does. I apologise for that man. Come along.'

He began walking towards the house very fast, and suddenly burst out, 'Conchies! How can my mother stand them?'

When Sorrel came downstairs after bathing and changing, she found Toby and Grace sitting by the open window. She saw that Toby had not recovered.

'I've told Mother she must get rid of him.'

Grace raised her eyes heavenward.

'My dear boy, I agree with every word you say. I consider that pacifists have no right to live in this land at all. Why should they travel in *our* trains, eat in *our* restaurants? They don't deserve to be citizens. They are pariahs.'

'Get rid of him.'

'I wish I could. But it's impossible.'

'Of course it isn't.'

'Toby, all I have are the two land-girls. Connie isn't so bad, although she doesn't work hard, but Ann gets filthy colds in the winter which infect us all, and last harvest, if you please, produced an attack of hay fever.'

'There's your cowman.'

'Syd? He does some cutting and carrying, he boils the swill and so on. He's got less brains than Scrap. He's a simpleton.

No, Toby, until your father uses his influence to get me another man, I shall have to *bear* that one. I find it difficult even to give him orders. I suppose the thing is worse because the Fulfords used to live in the village. One stupidly expects loyalty from one's own people.'

'Are they a local family, then?' Sorrel refused to be ignored any longer.

'They used to live in Evendon,' answered Grace, clearly not wishing to discuss anything with Sorrel, but forced to reply since Toby had fallen into a black silence. 'The father officiated at some tinpot local chapel at the other end of the village. Low church. He preached the most fearful sermons, I'm told. But he and his wife cleared out of England before the war. Typical. And the son's worse.'

Sorrel looked over at Toby who was staring at the ground. His face was vicious. This is going to ruin our last night, she thought, and I can't bear it. She spoke with a rush of feeling.

'I can't imagine a man refusing to fight.'

Then he did look up.

'That's because you're normal with the right healthy instincts, thank God.'

'Don't let's upset ourselves over that creature,' said Grace, her voice raised as if she were about to make a speech. 'What we must always keep in our minds is that production of food is all-important. It is the life-blood of these islands.'

It was Churchill again.

After luncheon Grace went up to her study, a small panelled room overlooking the glories of the cherry orchard and the rise of the fifty-acre field. She sighed as she sat down at the desk Evie never dared to tidy, heaped with papers, most of them printed forms in haphazard batches: Grace had no method. Week after week, she thought resentfully, the government added more burdens to the wartime farmer.

Dion Fulford had bicycled into town on the previous day to see Norman Fry, the man in charge of the local War Agricultural Committee who had, it seemed, been helpful. Grace never went to visit the committee herself. Quick and clever as she was, filling in forms made her nervous. She could not translate the rules and regulations into English she could understand. To Fulford they were as clear as crystal. As she began laboriously going through the papers now, she found a précis and a suggestion in Fulford's neat writing attached to every page.

She knew perfectly well she couldn't get rid of him, yet shared every one of Toby's feelings. Her beloved Edmund was buried in a ditch in France, and here was a strong healthy young man who had publicly stated that he was against the war. She saw him working on the farm, laughing with the land-girls, glowing with life. And hated him.

When she first learned that the authorities had allocated Fulford, a conscientious objecter, to the Priory she had wanted to vomit. George had been sympathetic at first. But when Grace had something on her mind she couldn't stop talking about it, and after the twentieth ranting speech he shouted, 'Sack him or keep him, but for God's sake shut up.' And marched out of the room.

Deeply offended, she avoided the subject with her husband after that. It was a spiteful relief to listen to Toby echoing her own sentiments.

But Grace, like the god Janus, had two faces. One was filled with loathing for the pacifist . . . and then she turned the other face. She had never worked before in her life and it was with Dion that she made things grow and ripen, living in harmony with the changing seasons. With him she knew the dramas and the ruined hopes, sometimes the deep satisfactions of a farm. Dion adapted, improved, extended, it was he who grew the cabbages in place of roses. He and Grace served the land and made it serve them; it was a primitive task and they were bound together in doing it.

George Martyn's attitude to the young man was one of indifference. He had disliked the father, a poverty-stricken minister who preached sermons which stirred up the working classes. To do that was a disgrace. But John Fulford had left the country before the war, had been replaced by a mild sort of fellow who gave no trouble, and the son did not interest him – neither his principles nor the young man himself. George's work for the war effort was enormous, and one pacifist was a grain of sand on the beach. But just occasionally he saw some of the Priory's official forms, or noticed the quality of the farming which his wife claimed as hers. And smiled.

Toby recovered his good humour during the afternoon, and suggested to Sorrel they should go for a stroll in 'Father's Walk', a stretch of the garden which was of no agricultural use, a narrow band of grass, almost a corridor, with high yew hedges on either side. It had been designed and planted in the 1780s, and still had a quaint formality. George Martyn gave express orders that the lawns there should remain cut and the hedges trimmed. He often went there to walk up and down while wrestling with business problems. In the spring and autumn, it was well sheltered from the wind.

Sorrel and Toby walked as far as an old freckled stone bench and sat down. They were so quiet that a fat thrush pecking nearby hopped almost on to Sorrel's foot – until Toby moved and it flew hastily away.

'Did you hear the tanks this morning?' he said, breaking the spell. 'I was back in my room and I heard them roaring by. I went down to the gate to watch. There must have been over fifty.'

'Where do you suppose they were going?'

'On exercises. My God, it's nothing but exercises. That's all we've done for months. Years. Since Dunkirk.'

There was frustration in his grating voice.

When he turned from lover to soldier, Sorrel was out of her depth and could only listen in respectful silence. He got to his feet and they began to walk back on the soft springing turf, the dark walls of yew on either side.

'Last month we had an entire division on the move,' he said. 'All round the country. Chaps are getting used to the new stuff, which is far better designed and more powerful than the lot we abandoned in France.'

He began to describe the equipment that the army had left behind when they somehow managed to get to the ships waiting for them at Dunkirk. Tanks and field artillery, mountains of rifles and ammunition, stores, even steel hats. 'I suppose the Germans will put it to some use,' he said, 'although our stuff isn't a patch on theirs.'

Sorrel wondered what to say that wasn't ignorant and naive, and finally came up with:

'Toby, didn't you say you'd show me your kit?'

He stopped frowning, and looked pleased.

'Would you really like to see it?'

Toby's bedroom was at the other end of the house from her own; she had never visited it. When they went in, he left the door wide open.

His uniform was neatly laid out on chests of drawers and chairs; it was no secret that the regiment was going East, and the battle blouses and trousers were made of palish khaki drill. There were two pairs of shorts, two thick flannel shirts. The only large pile consisted of khaki socks, there must have been two dozen pairs or more, all beautifully marked with name tapes by Evie.

'Aren't the shirts awful?' said Toby, picking one up. 'Thick as blankets. That's because we'll sweat like pigs and mustn't get chilled – the same principle as covering up a horse after hunting. Still, it is odd . . . you end up feeling like a wet rag and looking like one. We're only allowed to take essentials - nothing like mess kit so one can look decent. Not even any respectable luggage, only those canvas kit bags.'

His clothes upset her, separated her from him – their very texture meant for the desert. She turned away, and noticed a fencing foil hanging on thc wall by a leather thong.

'Did you fence with that?' For a moment she saw Toby as a figure in Dumas.

'Not any more. Actually, it's only a trophy, I won it at school for the Parker-Fawkes prize. Mother enjoyed watching me fence, she was so bloodthirsty. She told my fencing master she was sorry the foils were tipped!'

On a shelf were rows of silver cups cleaned to a high polish, and she picked them up, noticing that some were from his prep school, some from Sandhurst, some for shooting at Bisley. Among many photographs in leather frames were two of the

King inspecting rows of young men in uniform: they stood as straight as doorposts.

Sorrel knelt down to look at the books. Twenty volumes of the history of the Great War. A life of the Duke of Wellington. Books on tactics. A worn-looking Bible. And *Forty-One Years In India* by General Roberts.

On the top of the bookshelf was the largest photograph in the room, silver-framed. Sorrel recognised the man in the picture, there was a similar photograph downstairs in the drawing room. It was Edmund Martyn. He was like and unlike Toby. He had the same prominent nose, but it was less of a beak. His jaw was rounder, his mouth curled and he wore a smile which one might call a smirk. He had heavy-lidded eyes, and he was handsomer than Toby. Sorrel stood looking at the dead son his mother often invited to sit at her dinner table.

'You remember Edmund used to say – '

'Your brother didn't agree with you, Toby.'

Grace had once told Sorrel they did not talk about Edmund but that wasn't true – she did. Toby accepted his brother's presence in the conversation; he rarely mentioned him when he and Sorrel were alone.

While she stood looking at the picture, Toby came up and stood behind her. But, conscious of the open door, didn't touch her.

'Mother gave me that one so I have to put it on show, but Edmund couldn't stick it. Disliked it about as much as I do the portrait of me, poor Mother! I don't know how the photographer managed it, but he made the poor chap look like a film star. Pathetic. Two film stars in the family.'

'I think Edmund's rather beautiful.'

'I'd like to have seen his face if he'd heard that!'

When he began to laugh, so did she.

The day was full of gaiety. It was spirited and light-hearted; Toby and Sorrel seemed to laugh a good deal, to be happy all the time. They did not know that they were the victims of a curse, put on them by the gods who were about to make them suffer. Everything seemed brightened, more intense. The loud birdsong, the light of the afternoon, the smell of hay, the accidental touch of hands. They wandered down the lane and leaned on a gate; the grass had not yet been cut, it was tall and feathery.

Then there was a sweet high noise, and across the field trotted The Chief. He put his head over the gate, and Toby gently stroked his nose.

'Dear old boy, did you think I wouldn't come to see you again today?'

He put his hand into his pocket and brought out some lumps of sugar. The horse crunched loudly, blinking long eyelashes.

Toby kissed his velvet nose and said he'd come to say a proper goodbye tomorrow morning.

The Chief, hoping for more sugar, turned his noble head and watched them as they walked away.

'See that wood over there? Edmund and I used to go pigeon shooting there.'

'I hope you missed.'

'Never.'

'Did you eat them?'

'I suppose the staff did. Stop asking silly questions. Have I shown you the summerhouse?'

There had been a folly in the Priory gardens once; a tiny imitation Roman temple. But the years had rotted the wooden floor, and lichen and age had crumbled the stone. When he'd bought the house, George Martyn had the folly pulled down, and in its place was built a tiny octagonal place of pine, many-windowed and set upon a kind of wheel. The whole pretty thing could be pushed round to face the direction of the sun all day long. Before the war Grace used to read there, and Evie brought her tea.

'I'll shove it round. Watch. Then nobody can see us,' said Toby, setting the summerhouse creaking and shuddering as it slowly moved its windows away from the house.

Inside smelled of dust and potting compost. There were dead flies along the window ledge, and gardening tools stacked in corners, and two faded deck chairs. Toby came up to her and pressed her in his arms and gave her a long, sweet-tasting and exploring kiss.

'A few more hours and I'll be able to love you again.'

'Do you want to?'

'Oh darlingest.'

When they separated his face looked blurred.

He walked about restlessly, then sat on a rickety table and swung one leg. Since the encounter with Dion Fulford he'd changed out of uniform, and in mufti, as he called it, lost the heroic look, the worn ribbon of the MC purple and white, the glistening buttons which bruised her breasts. Yet how curiously a pair of dark trousers and white shirt became a uniform. It was something in the way he'd tied a white silk scarf at his neck; it was the fit and crease of his trousers, the shoes polished until they shone. He had rolled up his sleeves, they set perfectly. His sinewy arms were brown.

'I suppose you want to go, in a way,' she said suddenly. The idea had only just come to her.

'We all do. It's our job,' Toby answered. He swung his leg. 'Do you know how long it is since we saw active service? Two bloody years. We've slogged and slogged to get ourselves ready, starting in a small way, slowly getting into tougher training. New troops are pouring in, thank heaven, but they're raw as uncooked potatoes. We've trained 'em, *and* ourselves, until we can't wait for the word go. The fact is, Sorrel,' he continued, 'since we crawled ashore at Ramsgate in 1940 not a shot have we fired in anger. We want to get started. Since the German offensive in Libya, I can't listen to the wireless.'

'Perhaps that's where you'll be sent – to Libya.'

'Perhaps. Somebody's got to stop them and by God I'd like it to be us.'

When he talked of the army he used the plural; 'we' did not mean the generals, it meant his men. His fellow-fighters. She could hear in his voice, see in his face how he loved them. She was filled with appalled reverence.

He went on swinging his leg.

'Things have got to be changed,' he said. 'Look at the uniform.'

While he was talking Sorrel could scarcely listen. Happiness, longing and desire shot through her; she looked at the harsh angles of his face and wanted to touch him. She dragged herself back with an effort.

'What's wrong with the uniform, Toby?'

'Medically, it's insane,' he said. 'The whole design of battle dress is an abysmal mistake. Doctor Lavery was here the other day and he agrees. The MOs say the same thing. When men are fighting in the cold – it was icy in Normandy and the desert's freezing at night, the cold affects the unprotected stomach and kidneys.'

She did not know whether to laugh or cry, and thought, I suppose that's why I love him. It seemed an odd kind of reason.

'Why isn't something done about it?' he said. 'Another thing. Soldiers loathe those forage caps, they're ashamed to wear the things. Have you noticed how sloppy they look?'

'They do sort of cram them on.'

'Over one ear, like clowns. The guards wear their peaked caps with real smartness. Our line regiments are jealous of the way they look. A soldier isn't a good soldier unless he's proud of his appearance, arrogant in the way he holds himself. You can't dress a man like a roadsweeper and expect him to fight like a warrior. Take the Germans.'

Oh heaven, she thought, I wish he'd stop.

'They wear a small sword or a long knife in their belts,' he said, demonstrating, 'whenever they walk out. They're smart as paint and what's more, they're armed. Our chaps walk out in that pathetic battle dress – unarmed. They envy the navy. And the RAF although they call them rude names. They even envy the ARP. When a man in the army can put "Commando" or the wings of a parachute corps on his shoulders he sews on the flashes within half an hour. It gives him some self-respect for a change. Shall we go?' he finished very suddenly, and practically pulled her down the summerhouse steps and back into the garden.

Later they played tennis on a lawn which Grace, putting her head out of an upstairs window, shouted would soon be under the plough. 'So make the best of it while it's there.'

And the hot May evening began to draw to its close and tennis was over and they went indoors to change.

Sorrel put on the corn-coloured silk Toby liked the best, and finished the last drops of her Chanel No. 5 which her mother had given her two years ago. She came down the stairs, poised and pretty, and George Martyn looked her over with approval; he already saw a soldier's wife.

Grace was in flowing pre-war Liberty silk with good pearls. George wore a velvet smoking jacket – and Toby was back in uniform. The only mournful note in a festive atmosphere was the record Toby had put on the gramophone. The haunting *Warsaw Concerto*.

Dinner was, in a sense, like the afternoon just gone by, not forced but cheerful. Toby's stuttering machine-gun fire of laughter burst out, George served champagne, Grace presided, dreamily serene. At the end of the meal, Toby said, 'Mother, as it's my last night you've got to give us my favourite.'

Grace demurred.

'Please, Mother.'

'You don't want to hear that old thing again,' she said in a consenting voice.

'Of course I do and so does Father, and what about Sorrel? She's never had the chance to hear it at all.'

With more but weaker protestations, Grace agreed. The men leaned back, smoking and relaxed. Grace began to recite.

Her voice was well pitched and mellow, there was feeling in it and a certain sadness. It was like the voice of an actress who knows how to move her audience; which strings of the heart she can tug and make vibrate.

> 'There's a breathless hush in the close tonight –
> Ten to make and the match to win –
> A bumping pitch and a blinding light,
> An hour to play and the last man in.'

It was only at the final lines of the poem that her voice blurred:

> 'This they all with a joyful mind
> Bear through life like a torch in flame,
> And falling, fling to the host behind
> Play up, play up and play the game.'

She dabbed her eyes.

There was a pause.

'You always cry at that bit,' Toby said.

Grace did not call Sorrel with a look to leave the men to drink their port. Everybody left the table at the same time, Grace agreed to a glass of port brought to her in the drawing room and George poured Sorrel a doll-sized glass of crème de menthe.

Although the blackout curtains were pulled, the summer air came into the room. The family sat laughing and talking. Grace reminisced, speaking of school prizegivings and plays, of Sandhurst and the time Toby and Edmund had taken their parents on the lake, hiring a dinghy from the boatkeeper whom the cadets nicknamed 'Mrs Admiral'. She spoke of the great day immortalised in the photographs in Toby's room – the battalion parading before the King and, said Grace, 'the Adjutant on that magnificent charger.'

To Sorrel it was an England before the battle of Waterloo. Grace's husband and son listened, smiled, nodded – but then Sorrel found she couldn't listen any more. The happiness which had possessed her and Toby, breathing in their faces, was suddenly and unbearably gone. She felt like a poor prisoner stretched screaming upon a rack. At last, after an hour George stood up and said the longed-for 'we must turn in, Grace'.

As the Martyns left the room, Sorrel saw that Grace had not shut the door, it stood wide open. Toby said loudly, 'I daresay you're tired, Sorrel.'

'Yes, I am, rather. I'd better go to bed, too.'

'Good idea.'

They waited, hearing his mother's voice going into the distance until she and George Martyn turned the corner of the landing and the sound faded.

Sorrel looked at Toby.

'What time do you have to go?'

'Half past five.'

'Will it be dawn?'

'Just about.'

Silence.

'Sorrel, I don't want you to see me off.'

She gave a sharp intake of breath.

'No,' she said. 'I'd hate it. Come. Let's go up.'

As he always did, he left her before she reached her bedroom; she shut her door and undressed. All day the surge of desire had been flooding through her, ebbing, returning.

Now she knew that at last she was going to drown. She climbed naked into bed and waited for the door to open. And when it did she thought she would die of bliss.

All over the dark country, all over the dark world, lovers were locked together in a climax of passion created by the terrible presence of death. That terror made love so sharp it was as if the thrust could never end, the joy and pleasure never stop coming, sorrow kept back by the sheer sexual power of love. Toby made love to her all night long. Now and then they half slept, only to wake and begin all over again . . .

But when the first pale edge showed round the curtains he stirred, padded over to look out of the window and sniff the beginning of the day. He came back to fold her not in a sexy embrace, but to give her a long hard hug.

'My girl. You're my girl now and always.'

'Yes. I am.'

'I've worn you out.'

'Lovely. To be worn out by lovely you.'

His face was grey in the grey light.

'Now listen, I want to talk seriously. I couldn't yesterday, couldn't say anything about us – didn't I bore you with a lot of rot about the army? I bored you so.'

'Never. You couldn't. It's impossible.'

'Fool. Let's be practical. I think we should marry. God, girl, you jumped out of your skin! Of course we must marry, idiot woman, how else can we get through? The point is, I can't marry you now. But directly I get back, we buy the ring. Okay?'

He peered down at her face. She had said nothing.

'I see you agree. That was a funny kind of a proposal, wasn't it? My father proposed to Mother in a punt at Wargrave. Well, that's what she says. Now. I don't want to worry about you. So –

a question. Are you okay for money? I know that Wrens don't get much pay and now your mother's dead . . .'

'Darling Toby, didn't your father tell you?'

'Tell me what?'

'That he gave my mother an allowance and now gives me one? He said she was a sort of distant cousin, and he looked after her when she became a widow. Then she was killed, and he did the same for me. I was flabbergasted.'

'It's so like him,' said Toby in a satisfied voice. 'I didn't know we're related. What a lark. And I'm glad about the money, it makes you a bit official, doesn't it? Part of the family. Sure he gives you enough?'

'Of course he does and stop breaking my heart,' she said, laughing.

He traced the line of her nose with his finger.

'I wish I could marry you now. I'd like to pick you up and carry you to the church. I worship you.'

Silence.

'Sorrel?'

'My darling?'

'I meant it about not seeing me off. I'm going now. It's well after four. So this is goodbye. I forbid you even to get up. When I leave I want to know you're still lying here where I left you. In this bed. Do you understand?'

And then suddenly she violently wished he was gone, that he'd left the room, left the house, left her to the pain which was waiting for her.

6

Early that summer the Americans arrived. Sorrel and Margaret watched them driving along the roads leading to the town, stopping in Littleport to crowd into a favourite pub, the Norfolk Arms, which overnight became the haunt of blonde girls in bright clothes. The Wrens sniffily avoided the Norfolk which somebody nicknamed the 'Open Arms'. Margaret said it was incredible that 'so many tarty women have materialised out of nowhere.'

Soon the Sussex countryside was invaded. Everywhere you looked, thought Sorrel, were the GIs. They weren't like the rangy Hollywood gods women had imagined all Americans to be. Some of them were short, some stocky as miners, many were black-eyed and olive-skinned, Greek, Italian. Others were as fair as Swedes, with white eyelashes and brilliantly blue eyes. They had difficult names. Walewski. Fuentes. Boroviak. Perotti. But for all their worldwide mixture, they had a universal quality, their casualness. They walked easily, like cowboys. They preferred to sit rather than stand – on the ground, on a windowsill, on top of a wall. And they had a universal generosity to every child they set eyes on, using their wonderful currency of Mars Bars.

They poured into the cities and hung about the villages. They marched and mustered and thundered by in jeeps, they drank and sang, 'You made me love you, I didn't wanna do it.' When they took taxis, they spread out the left hand, palm covered with money and said, 'What's the damage, Buster? Take your pick.'

Margaret's disapproval of the tarty girls was intense and Sorrel began to wonder if her friend was jealous. The girls wore lipstick the colour of dark red roses and shoulder-length Rita Hayworth hair. GIs liked their women with a lot of hair; the Hollywood sirens had locks like mermaids. The fashionable wartime roll of hair worn round the head, formed by a stocking tied firmly with the hair tucked into it like a halo, was discarded. Curling hair now poured down feminine cheeks and shoulders and backs. Disliking the girls, Margaret was fascinated by the Yankee officers. Her Canadian admirer, long gone, had left a dent in her virgin heart as if he'd pressed his finger into it. She was drawn to the Americans, and they to her.

The mayor of Littleport and his wife gave a sherry party of welcome for 'Our Transatlantic Cousins', and Margaret managed to get an invitation for Sorrel and herself. They put on their civilian dresses. Sorrel borrowed a brown silk from Moyra, but Margaret wore Irish green taffeta the colour of her eyes. She had a whale of a time, was introduced to dozens of Americans of varying attractions and ranks and seemed to be enchanted with every one of them.

Perhaps because she couldn't help thinking about Toby, Sorrel did not seem to be very popular except with one fattish young man who was distinctly lecherous; she had to be rescued by a naval officer friend of hers. The American went straight to the bar and drank a good deal, glowering at her furiously from a distance.

After the party, Margaret was constantly telephoned, and when she had a weekend pass, she was collected by a jeep.

'Hop in, lady.'

She asked Sorrel to come with her on the succession of dates. When Sorrel politely refused, Margaret, who liked to share, was annoyed. She thought her friend was turning into a bore.

To Margaret all Americans spelled a fascinating foreign world. When she talked about them, the school marm in her disappeared, she laughed with affection. She spoke of places they had told her about – Providence, Midnight, Versailles and Delight. She grew prettier and softer. For the first time since Sorrel had known her, the goddess was stepping down from her pedestal.

She had that certain look, melting, possible, of a girl ready to fall into bed. But with whom? I wonder if it all started with Margaret because she guessed I did it, thought Sorrel. Perhaps making love is infectious, like catching the flu.

Toby had disappeared to take a long, long journey. The Straits of Gibraltar were British, the Union Jack flew upon the Rock, but the Mediterranean was so thick with mines that it was impossible for British ships to take the short route through the tideless sea. Italy had become a vast submarine base; if Allied ships weren't attacked by submarines or hit by Stukas from the air they could meet the submerged floating death of mines.

'Crossing the Med is like going into a school of sharks,' Toby once said to her.

Sorrel knew, all women whose men had gone towards the East knew, that troops bound for Egypt or further still for India and Burma, made the six weeks' journey by sea round the Cape.

She liked to think of her lover during those weeks of his voyage. She imagined him on board a ship which hugged the misty coastline of Africa. Once she had read a description by Conrad of the scent of Africa, a musky, mysterious, perfumed, unforgettable smell which drifted across the water. Toby would smell that when he stood on deck at night. Trying to imagine Toby so often, there were moments when Sorrel had the idea that her spirit could fly. That the waste of waters which lay between them could be made to vanish by the love in her. She was beside him, she could see him. Sometimes when she lay in her bunk in the dark, and Margaret had fallen asleep, Sorrel concentrated so intently that it felt like praying.

During the day there was nothing but work. Now it was Sorrel and not the perplexed Margaret who began to excel at the most difficult photography, winning from her instructor an occasional 'Well done, Scott'.

Two weeks after Toby had gone and long before she could hope for a letter, Sorrel received a parcel. The Wren officer on duty and in charge of the post enjoyed a joke.

'I hope, Scott, it's not something you lost at the Astor?'

She was quoting a favourite song the ratings sang.

> She had to go and lose it at the Astor,
> She didn't take her mother's good advice.
> There aren't so many girls today who've got one,
> And she wouldn't let it go at any price.

'A Cartier label, too, Scott. Tut-tut.'

Excited and puzzled, Sorrel took the parcel out into the dark-room where nobody was on duty. In the obscure bluish light she began to open it; it was far too well packed. She cut the string, undid many layers of paper, then tissue paper and finally found inside a white Cartier box. And in that, a black velvet jewel case. It contained a gold brooch. Toby's regimental crest. Two winged horses, a bear's paw grasping a javelin, the regimental motto in a scroll: *'Virtus semper viridias'*.

The crest was enamelled in scarlet, green and black. A neatly typed card said: 'Sent at the request of Major Ronald Martyn. We apologise for the delay.'

Sorrel took the brooch and kissed it. And from that day wore it on the front of her petticoat.

I wish I could be branded with Toby's name, she thought, and thrust the pin in so deep that it pierced her skin.

Summer was advancing. Near the sea the fields were high with shivering mauve-coloured grasses. Margaret's admirers took her to dances at the American HQ but Sorrel would not go with her. Margaret became still more annoyed; she had reasons for needing feminine company.

'Since Toby Martyn turned up in your life you've got the *cafard* all the time,' Margaret said, using a word she'd picked up in a favourite school book, the romantic *Beau Geste*. She spread out her best civilian dress, full-skirted and blue and white, with a sash. 'You're not the same girl who used to be fun.'

'I can't go out with a lot of Americans when Toby may be fighting for his life.'

'Don't be melodramatic. He's probably in Cairo by now, hobnobbing with the brass hats,' said Margaret, taking off her uniform shirt.

'He's in the infantry and for all I know he could be dead. Leave me alone.'

Sorrel walked out, slamming the door.

Margaret washed and dressed with care, brushing her curly hair with a hundred strokes and painting her large mouth with a new American lipstick. It was unpatriotic of Sorrel to say Toby Martyn might be dead. One didn't think, didn't say such things.

Margaret finished her make-up and left the digs with a swinging step, dark, glowing, ripe and Irish, ready for the party. She hummed 'Keep Smiling Thru'. Nobody sang marching songs.

Sorrel was glad to be by herself and to go to bed early. The news from North Africa had begun to alarm her. Bad in May, it seemed in June to be getting steadily worse. The Germans under their brilliant general Rommel were leaping forward, they had at last captured Tobruk and they'd taken thousands of prisoners. It looked as if the campaign in North Africa was going to be lost. Was he there? Among the prisoners? Among the dead? She unpinned her brooch and fastened it on her nightdress and lay down, hoping it would help her to sleep.

At last at the very end of July a letter came. He was in Egypt. Unlike thousands of letters received by girls all over the land, some letters so cut about they looked like doilies, all little holes where censored words had been removed, or in other cases blacked out with thick forbidding lines, there wasn't a sentence missing from Toby's letter.

He told her nothing the censor could object to. The journey had been fine, the regiment was in good form. David and Alec sent their best and 'hope you are behaving!' He described a dinner in a Cairo restaurant, 'A lot of rice, don't know how it was cooked, it looked pink but tasted first-rate, and some kind of meat David and I couldn't identify, spicy, and heaps of gaudy-looking vegetables.' He had seen a mosque by moonlight. Perhaps the moon had reminded him of something; he did end his letter, 'I think about you, darlingest. Think of me. Yours, Toby.'

Or was it 'Your Toby'? She looked closely. No she couldn't pretend that it was.

The photographic course ended at last, and both Margaret and Sorrel had the good reports which beforehand they had agonised over. There was news of their postings. For the first time since joining the Wrens they were to be parted, Margaret to East Anglia, Sorrel to Somerset. Both were to work as ratings in photographic departments.

When they knew they were leaving, Margaret became kinder. She changed towards Sorrel and forgave her for refusing the American dates. Hearing Sorrel had received a letter from Toby, she was genuinely pleased.

By a coincidence or a guess or the businessman's memory which files intervals of time, George Martyn telephoned Sorrel, asked her news, congratulated her on doing well and promptly invited her to stay.

'You must have some leave coming up. We'd be delighted to see you, my dear child.'

Sorrel could scarcely refuse, and managed to sound enthusiastic, which she was not. She had remained grateful and mystified as to why Toby's father gave her money. The outlandish idea that she was his illegitimate daughter had been dispelled the first time she'd seen the Martyns, since if there had been such a relationship, she would be half-sister to their son and George would certainly have prevented her from meeting Toby. It would have been easy enough to get rid of her on that first visit.

But. There seemed to be buts about both Toby's parents. She did not want to go to the Priory and she did not know why.

Martyn, exclaiming 'excellent!' when she accepted, said he would arrange for her to be met. They talked about trains.

Margaret declared that the invitation was a good sign.

'It's absolutely the best thing. Getting to know a guy's family. I only wish I could meet Byron Schlegel's folks.'

'Folks?'

Margaret giggled self-consciously. 'I can't help picking up the way they talk. Did I tell you Byron comes from New York?'

'You sure did.'

Sorrel was sorry to be leaving Littleport, to lose Margaret, to say goodbye to generous Moyra and other friends, and to the shabby seaside town and The Blue Parrot. She felt subdued when she took a bus to the station, carrying the canvas bag with her few possessions, and caught the train which would take her to Portsmouth on her way to Evendon. Pretty, too pale in her dark uniform, she was given a seat by a gallant elderly gentleman with a curling moustache, and a sandwich by a girl with a baby in her lap. The sun was hot, the dusty train windows were open, the countryside misty and green. Girls, not men, were working in the fields. When she finally arrived at the sleepy old station and came through the barrier where nobody took her ticket, there was the chauffeur standing by the pony trap. He greeted her respectfully. Perhaps Margaret's right, thought Sorrel.

The trap set off into the hot late afternoon. The wind which faintly blew was hot as well, and they went into shadows cast by high trees, then out into blazing sunshine, then into shadow again, shaded, dazzled, shaded. Sorrel thought, at least Toby will be glad to know I came. I am doing what he wants. And that will please him and make him happy when he thinks of home.

The more Toby took command of her imagination, the more she fell in love with him. Loved him and saw him as he was. She sometimes thought it was dangerous for him to be such a harsh and innocent romantic. Younger than he was, she still felt that. His hatred of the muddle and defeats of the past three years of war, the tragedies of Dunkirk and Singapore, the terrible price of the Atlantic convoys – had they made him different or had he always been so? He praised the enemy, he disdained the lower classes as he called them for not being the respected, respectful men and women of the past – he had his own vision of the world. He did not get it from his father, a worldly negotiator, she thought, and probably a cynic for all his generosity and charm. Tony had inherited from Grace the hymnbook patriotism which he laughed at and obeyed. But his ideals were all his own.

The prospect of being with his parents and without Toby was dismaying, mainly because of Grace who resembled an enormous ship bearing down and quite capable of cutting Sorrel's small craft in two.

The trap turned in through the gates. There lay the old house covered in yellow rambling roses, basking in the sun. The front door was wide open and Scrap slept on the warm stone, black face between black paws. Hearing footsteps he opened his eyes, bluish whites, brown centres. Then shut them again.

Walker tugged at the bell. Nobody came.

'Evie must be out, Miss Scott. And his lordship's in London.'

'Perhaps Lady Martyn's around?'

'I'm afraid not, she's with all those imps of kids.'

'Kids, Walker?'

'It's the harvest, Miss.'

She vaguely remembered Dion Fulford had said children helped sometimes around the farm.

'Couldn't do without them, really,' said the chauffeur, giving the bell another tug.

'What exactly do they do?' asked the London girl.

'Help in all kinds of ways,' said the old man with a slight smile. 'Turn the stooks so the sun and air can dry 'em from the rain and the dew. Carry the sheaves. Help load the trailer. Run errands. Fight each other,' he added, 'and get in the way. They're limbs of Satan but we need 'em and they know it.'

His eyes wandered and Sorrel took the hint.

'Please don't worry about me. I can look after myself. I'll pop upstairs and unpack.'

Looking relieved, he put down her canvas bag and led the pony and trap away.

Sorrel went indoors, up the staircase and towards what had been her room. The door was ajar and she saw it must be hers still, since there were yellow roses in a vase on the dressing table. And two of the enormous Martyn towels in the bathroom.

She stood listening to the noisy silence of the country. She looked at the bed covered, this time, in virginal white honeycomb. She went to the window and stared down at what had been the lawn where she and Toby had played tennis. Grace had been as good as her word, it was ploughed and planted with lines of potato plants starred with small white flowers.

Walker's description of the harvesting intrigued her; she very much wanted to find her way down to the field where it was going on. But Grace would be there, and so, for certain, would be Dion Fulford.

She was glad to shed the hot uniform and change into a new dress. A naval officer who had his eye on Sorrel had given her a present of some of his clothing coupons – she'd been a disappointment to him later but the gesture was gallant. Sorrel had ordered a dress from Harrods and a Wren friend on leave in London had collected it for her. It was of fine cotton in orange and white checks. Peeling off her black Wren stockings, she put on white ankle socks. None of the girls in the Wrens wore stockings with civilian clothes. The government had declared threateningly that if women did not wear socks this summer, there would be no stockings next winter.

Her legs were the colour of a fish's belly and she'd forgotten to buy any of the brown paint which Margaret had used with such effect.

Sorrel went slowly down the stairs. How empty the house was. Rich and ordered and empty. She looked into the drawing room. Flowers, and not a soul. In the big hall where she and Toby had sat with their feet on the fender she met Scrap again. He trotted up as if she was an important member of the family, and when she went into the garden, he followed.

The land baked in the heat as she and the dog crossed the rose garden where vegetables grew in rows, and went into the overgrown lane. She climbed a barred gate and sat on top of it, chewing a stem of grass. Scrap flopped in the shade nearby.

There was a jingling, chinking sound and down the lane came a man leading an enormous brown and white horse. It was Dion Fulford. Man and horse, as if united, walked at the same pace to the music of the harness. Watching him come nearer she was filled with dismay. She didn't want to see him, didn't want to talk to him.

He stopped. The great horse waited peacefully.

'It's that Wren again,' he said with a smile.

'Hello.'

'You can't be here to see Toby this time.'

'Major Martyn is overseas.'

'I know. He went at the end of May. I reckon he may be in Libya by now.'

'Nobody knows where he is.'

He stood looking at her thoughtfully.

He offended her. How dared he be relaxed and easy when so many were dead or doomed to die, sacrificing their lives to save the skins of people like him?

'I see,' he said.

'What do you mean – "I see". You don't know anything about him.'

'I meant that I could see by your manner Toby told you I am a pacifist.'

'Yes.'

'Which is why you are being rude.'

'I'm not in the least rude.'

'Of course you are. I don't blame you. Most people react like that. They don't exactly hound us as they did in the last war, handing out white feathers and even attacking pacifists in the street. But the feeling's there. There's a gap. We're on our own.'

'You chose to be.'

'Of course. We register. And go before a tribunal to put our cases.'

'About not wanting to fight.'

She fixed her mind on Toby, because of Fulford's quietness, a kind of male gentleness. You shouldn't like a pacifist and Toby hated him.

'You shove all conscientious objectors into one huge great bucket of tar, don't you? But there's no such thing as a typical pacifist. We all think differently. The only thing we have in common is being opposed to war.'

'A just war? A war for freedom?'

He looked at her almost helplessly.

'We can't discuss this now. I must get back to the harvest. I only came to collect Prince.'

'It doesn't matter.'

He embarrassed her. She ought to dislike him and he embarrassed her.

'Of course it matters. Look, I really must go but – '

He hesitated and something, in him or was it in herself, made her ashamed. She said self-consciously, 'How's the harvest going?'

'Okay. Most of my workers today are ten years old, and I've been teaching them the right way to stand up the sheaves, and keep pace with the reaping.'

He accepted her half apology, her half offer of peace between them.

'I'm keeping you,' Sorrel said, adding to her own surprise, 'I wish I could come and help with the harvest.'

He raised his eyebrows.

'I do too. But I don't think it would be very tactful, would it? Grace Martyn's there.'

Sorrel said nothing.

'I'm sure you'd like being part of it,' he said. 'Fields and fields of sheaf stooks. They're so satisfactory. Somebody called it the crown of the year.'

His hand still held the rein of the huge, gentle horse. He said suddenly, 'I've had an idea. Why can't we meet this evening?'

She was very taken aback.

'If you're thinking that I can't leave the harvest,' he said, misreading her expression, 'Grace Martyn's asked me to see a man from the Agricultural Committee. She's made a mess of one of our permits, and he's coming to the Priory. It'll only take ten minutes. I could make it for a drink after that before I dash back to the fields.'

'I don't think I can.'

'Why not?'

'I – '

Then he did get her meaning. 'You think the Martyns wouldn't like you to meet me? You're quite right. But they don't have dinner until after eight and my appointment is at seven. Surely you could slip down the back stair, nobody would see you. We could have a very quick drink at The Raven, that's our local pub. Do come.'

She didn't know what to say.

'Don't you think you owe it to me,' he said after a moment, 'at least to hear my side of the story? Otherwise if we meet, as we probably will occasionally round the farm, it'll never be right between us.'

She did not reply and he went on, 'The Raven's past the Priory on the left, just after the road turns. I'll wait at the corner.' He looked intently at her and said, 'Thanks,' before leading the horse away.

Evie greeted Sorrel on her return to the house with the concern of a woman who had found somebody fainting in the Sahara. She ushered Sorrel into the main hall, returning with tea and a home-made gooseberry tart, to stand near the table while she poured out and waited on her.

I wish she'd sit down, thought Sorrel, smiling up at her. I can't suggest it. This place is full of problems.

'How's the harvest going?' she asked; it seemed to be the question of the afternoon.

'Rather well I gather. Did you see them up in the forty-acre field? You ought to go and watch for a bit. It's quite a sight.'

'How many people are helping?'

'As many as we can get. Some local farmhands we've borrowed, their harvest is already in, and Connie and Ann, our land-girls. A pack of village children. The cowman, of course. I go and lend a hand in the evening when dinner's in the oven.'

'And there's Dion Fulford. I met him just now.'

A lock of Evie's soft hair had escaped from one of her slides. She fastened it back. Sorrel thought she looked somewhat pink as she said, 'He's a conchie.'

'I know. Toby told me.'

'I don't think you should talk to him really,' Evie said after a moment's hesitation. 'Of course I've known Dion since he was a child and I have a word with him sometimes. But not if Lady Martyn is about, it upsets her. I'm sure you know the Major can't stand him. No, better not talk to him, Sorrel.'

Sorrel did not exactly reply and Scrap interrupted, hoping for gooseberry tart.

After tea she went up to change for dinner, Evie having indicated that this was still the custom at the Priory. Sorrel was feeling nervous. What on earth had possessed her to agree to meet Dion Fulford? She'd started this afternoon by disliking him and within ten minutes had agreed to have a drink with him. She was mad. If she was spotted it would be very unpleasant – the Martyns might even write and tell Toby who would be angry and hurt. Sorrel could not bear to imagine that.

But as she was dressing, commonsense took over. Why shouldn't she go and talk to him? She wasn't the Martyns' property, and with Toby thousands of miles away she must make her own decisions. She wanted to hear what Dion had to say for himself; it was contemptible to take other people's opinions without question. It was bad enough having to obey in the Wrens, jump to it from morning until night and follow orders, some of which were pretty ludicrous. She wasn't going to behave like that in private life.

It was just after seven when she was dressed and ready. As Dion had foretold, the house was quiet and nobody was about. The servants' staircase was along a passage to the right and, walking carefully because the floorboards creaked, she arrived at the head of the stair, crept down on tiptoe and a minute or two later was safely in the garden. In five minutes she was walking slowly down the road. She was early.

It was a sweet time of summer evening, the shadows elongated, a thrush singing loudly somewhere. At the turn of the road she saw him sitting in the grass among the meadowsweet and ragged robin. He stood up and waved; he was still in his farm clothes but must have had a bath, his hair was wet.

'I knew you'd escape.'

'Nobody saw me,' said Sorrel, with a grin, annoyed with herself for feeling guilty.

'We've got a good quarter of an hour. George Martyn never gets back early, and Grace is safe up in the forty-acre bossing the kids. Here's The Raven. I'll go in and get us something to drink. We could have it in the back garden.'

'Shall I come in with you?'

She felt slightly shy.

'You don't want to stand around in that smelly old bar. The river's at the bottom of the garden. Shall we sit on the bank?'

He disappeared into the pub and Sorrel went round the outside of the house to the garden. Here there were trees which kept off most of the late sun, it was cool and shady. Two American GIs were sitting on a seat under a walnut tree. Sorrel went down to the river, which raced by under a rickety wooden bridge. She sat on the grass, and Dion came out of the French windows carrying two glasses. Watching him, she thought, he's handsome. And has no right to be.

He sat down beside her and he, too, stared at the river.

'Look,' he said, 'there's a water vole.'

'Oh, where?'

'That thing which looks like a piece of floating wood. It's swimming against the current.'

She looked eagerly, and saw that there was a small brown object which turned as it came closer into a small brown animal. It nipped swiftly into a hole just above the water line.

'I thought they were much bigger,' she said. 'I've only seen pictures in books.'

'Not a country girl then?'

'School in Eastbourne, home in London, I'm afraid.'

'One wouldn't think it.'

'I'm not sure if that's a compliment or not,' she said, smiling. She drank the cider and only politeness stopped her from making a face. It was disgustingly sour.

Dion leaned on his elbow. He thought how the clinging silk dress changed her. He detested seeing women in those hideous uniforms, versions of the same thing worn by men.

To him it seemed an indication that girls, too, were meant to fight – to throw their soft lovely bodies on to the barricades.

'Thank you for coming this evening,' he said. 'By the way, will you call me Dion? And your name's Sorrel, which is new to me.'

'My father was very fond of wood sorrel, though it's only a weed,' she said. 'He said the leaves were like shamrocks which are lucky. And he liked the white and purple flowers. He invented my name.'

'A delicate-looking plant but thrives almost anywhere, even in 100 mile-an-hour gales,' he said, teasing her. She smiled somewhat awkwardly and sipped the cider again.

'Revolting, isn't it?' he said, 'I should have bought you a rum and lime. Girls seem to like that. Do Wrens drink it?'

'Some of them. Sometimes.'

'I wish you wouldn't look so serious. Have I put you in a spot asking you here? We'll go if you prefer it.'

She spoke quickly. 'I'm glad I came. I didn't – don't – want to be prejudiced. I know it isn't against the law to be the way you are, but I can't understand it.'

He reflected for a moment or two, not looking at her but again at the hurrying river. One of the GIs made some kind of joke, and his friend burst out laughing.

'I suppose it might explain slightly if I told you what I said at my appeal at the tribunal. It does sound like the French Revolution, doesn't it? Or as if I'm in the dock. So I seem to be most of the time. Pacifists are always being judged, stuck up as Aunt Sallies. Some people go as far as to call us traitors. What I said officially was quite simple. Sorrel – ' he used her name as if he had known her a long time, 'I can't, I truly cannot go to war. For me military service would be taking lessons in murder. Of course I don't object to any kind of civil defence. And if the bombs started falling around, I'd put out the fires or dig people from buildings or whatever's needed. But I don't believe in war. And I don't think either side is right.'

'But Germany was the attacker! She invaded Czechoslovakia and Poland. Stole other people's countries. She's turning them into slaves.'

'I know. I know. It's hideously, criminally wrong. But for me killing Germans is also wrong. It's murder. I'm sorry.'

'No you're not.'

He raised his eyebrows.

'You're right. I am not sorry. You'll despise me for saying this, but my beliefs are a misery to me. Such a feeling of isolation. It's like having earache all the time and knowing it will not get better.'

She did not know what to say. She threw a leaf into the river, which swirled it away fast.

'I went to a church bazaar the other day,' he went on. 'I had to deliver a lot of home-made jams from Evie, and I couldn't resist having a sniff round the bookstall. There was an awful woman at the bazaar called Lorimer, she was with Grace Martyn watching the kids diving into the bran tub. The Lorimer woman said in a loud voice, "We are going to have to prepare our children for the next war, of course," and Grace said "Oh, they'll go to it with a will, sure to." She's pretty terrible, my boss, despite losing her son. I didn't like her when I was ten and I still don't.'

'You've known the family for a long time,' said Sorrel to change the subject.

'Yes, but only when they drove by or appeared at bazaars. My father was Methodist minister at the chapel in the village until 1938 when he and my mother emigrated. My sister and I grew up in Evendon.'

He drank the cider without noticing its sourness.

'Grace couldn't stick us. We hadn't any money and my sister Pauline and I didn't go to what she called decent schools. But my dad's sermons were the real trouble; the Martyns got to hear about them somehow. I used to wonder if it was from Evie, she came to our chapel now and then. Apparently my father's preaching drove the Martyns crazy. Of course they went to St Anselm's, the Norman church. They still do and George Martyn reads the lesson. They're everything they look, you know.'

'What do you mean?'

She shouldn't be listening. But there was something fair-minded in what he said. It hadn't a shred of malice.

'I mean they are rich and own a historic house and have a good hundred acres of first-class land and they're C of E and conservatives. They're not aristocracy but that's a minor point. It wasn't surprising my dad got on their nerves. His parish was small, only a few miles east and west of the village and made up of virtually all agricultural labourers, including a couple who worked for the Martyns at that time. Dad is a fire-eating preacher. Gentle as a a lamb until he gets into a pulpit. He'd have made a good actor.'

His father, he said, was shy, and skilled at escaping from gossipy parishioners if he wasn't really needed.

'People understood that. They were fond of him. What's the phrase from the *Boys' Own* paper tales about the army? "Capable of inspiring deep devotion in his men." That's my dad.'

'What about your mother?'

'I'm afraid she's a sort of saint; my sister and I think she is too good. She didn't want to leave England and begin a new life in Australia at fifty-five, but he was set on it so off she went. She's a little thing. Grey eyes.'

He was silent for a moment or two, then added that the new man who worked at his father's chapel was milk and water compared with John Fulford.

'Dad's line was always hellfire. The unspeakable state of the human soul. You'd never have thought, seeing him in the village, that he'd stand in the pulpit the next day frightening the congregation out of its wits. They liked it. Felt they were getting their money's worth.'

He chewed a piece of grass.

'There's always been a lot of tripe talked about the good old times on the land. They were very bad old times. The condition of farming before the war was sickening – over two million less acres cultivated than in 1914, and far fewer men and those doing the work paid a pittance. All of a sudden we're told the land is important again. Well, so it is. But let's not have the slop about the pastoral heart of England like a psalm.' He ran his teeth down the grass stem. 'My parents left in 1938 after Chamberlain made such a fool of himself.'

' "Out of this nettle, danger, we pluck this flower, safety?" '

Dion grimaced.

'My father was in the last war and didn't want to see me in the next. He scrammed.'

'Didn't your sister and you think of going, too?'

'Not really. Pauline was already married and I was working on our local paper, the *Echo*, and quite enjoying it. They didn't expect us to go. My father suggested it as a sort of joke. Knew we'd refuse. It was around that time that I had a dust-up with the Martyns. They wanted to get the house before the parents were ready to go. It belonged to George Martyn. Still does. I had a shouting match with Toby, I'm afraid. He never forgave me. We didn't like each other even as kids. We once had a tremendous fight behind the marquee at the Red Cross fete when we were both about twelve.'

'Who won?'

'An honourable draw. We keeled over at precisely the same time. Blood all over the place like a Jacobean tragedy.'

'*Blood!*'

'Only noses,' he said, laughing. 'Little boys' noses pour copiously. We terrified our parents which was rather satisfying, I remember.'

'But what did you fight *about*?'

'It was my fault. I called Toby a rude name because he was at a public school and he went mad.'

Sorrel could imagine that.

'Your sister doesn't seem to have played a very active part in the battles.'

'Pauline? She's worse than me. She couldn't stick Grace Martyn who'd been rude about our mother. It was a case of the Montagues and Capulets. Also my father, as it happens, fought in the last war, and George stayed at home and got filthy rich.'

'My father worked for him. I think he stayed behind too.'

'Sensible of him.'

There was a pause. Dion had taken off his socks and shoes and was dangling his large pale feet in the river.

'How I loathe this war,' he said after a while. 'Such waste. Such cruelty. Even today at the harvest when we're feeling so happy and satisfied, it's a brooding shadow . . . sorry, I won't talk about it. We'll quarrel if I do.'

'We could disagree without a row, I suppose.'

'There isn't a living soul who doesn't quarrel sooner or later with a pacifist.'

'Because we don't understand you. And we know you're wrong.'

'Yes. You're sure, aren't you?'

He took his dripping feet from the river and patted them dry with grass. He put on his socks and shoes.

'Has Grace been reciting any poems lately? This sceptr'd isle. That kind of thing.'

'I haven't seen her since I arrived,' said Sorrel, adding coldly, 'Why work for her if you dislike her?'

'My dear girl! Did you imagine I could choose? The call-up works for us as for everybody else. Agricultural workers do as they're told. I have digs in the village, and when the tribunal decided I wasn't to go to prison they simply looked through their papers, saw the Priory was crying out – well, Grace was crying out – for help and here I am. And here I stay. Don't look at me in that puzzled way. You're very sweet. And shouldn't be here with me which makes you sweeter. Forbidden fruit.'

They walked back through the garden and down the road. On either side were the woods, the air floating with thistledown. They came to the turn in the road. He stopped.

'You go first. I won't follow until you go through the gates. The Martyns wouldn't like seeing us together. They'd cut up rough.'

'With you?'

He really laughed.

'No, no, not with me, they cut up rough with me, well she does, every day of the week. It's funny. Grace needs me and shoves more and more jobs on my back which I enjoy, but she'd like to see me sizzle in hell. People are very contrary.'

'You're exaggerating.'

'Am I?'

He stood beside her, fair as a schoolboy, looking down at her in a friendly way. She suddenly said, 'I'm glad we met this evening.'

'I don't seem to have explained much.'

'No. You haven't. Shall we meet again?'

She hadn't meant to say that.

He said he often went to The Raven when he could get away from the farm in the evening, it was a break to sit by the river for a while and read. The worst – or best – of the harvesting would be done by tomorrow night. The kids were working well. Now and then, of course, they sang and danced and had fights, but they were a terrific help and the harvest wouldn't be the same without them.

'What about the day after tomorrow? Come if you dare.'

She knew *he* knew she couldn't resist that.

Apart from seeing Dion her days at the Priory were not a success. She had been invited for Toby's sake, and his parents were thinking about him all the time and scarcely talked of him. It was a strain. Sorrel thought of him too but could not share. She felt lonely in her heart.

During dinner on her first evening, the telephone rang. It was one of Grace Martyn's friends to say her son in submarines had been reported missing. Returning from the telephone Grace stood in the doorway to tell George Martyn what had happened, then with a muttered excuse said she would go to bed. She left the meal untouched.

George and Sorrel were by themselves. Evie served, and during dinner George made an attempt at conversation of the most banal kind, talking of the Wrens and making middle-aged jokes. Neither of them mentioned Grace's absence which, like the avoidance of Toby probably fighting in the desert, made it more noticeable. Sorrel was glad to escape and go to bed. Where she felt more lonely still.

The weather during the next two days grew hotter. Not a breath stirred the tops of the trees when she wandered round the farm. Once she caught a glimpse of Dion on the brow of the high field. The harvest was in full swing, there were men stripped to the waist and brown as mahogany. And Dion, surrounded by children, was like the Pied Piper. The air shimmered, the whole picture at a distance had brilliance, as if the sky and the corn had turned into one wavering golden vision.

Grace Martyn, recovered from another woman's tragedy, reappeared for luncheon, red with sunburn.

'I'm afraid I can't look after you, Sorrel. The farm simply swallows the time. And this is the crown of the year.'

It was Dion's phrase.

Grace was in an informative mood, describing loading the wagons and how each sheaf must be correctly placed otherwise it was impossible to make the load firm. The children kept asking for rides on the haycarts. That was quite out of the question – far too dangerous.

'George is organising something for you to do,' continued Grace as if Sorrel, too, had longed to go for a hay ride. 'There's an open-air play being performed this afternoon in the grounds of Turnbull House. *Tobias and the Angel.* George bought tickets for you and for himself, and lots of our friends will be there, either taking part or in the audience. It should be quite enjoyable,' she finished, sounding, this time, like Sorrel's English teacher.

But less than an hour before George Martyn and Sorrel were due to leave, he came out to find her on the terrace. He looked furious.

'I have to apologise, I can't take you out this afternoon. It is too bad. I had planned to spend the time with you, but the director of the Croxley Collection just rang to inform me, if you please, that another load is on its way. It was stored in cellars in Long Acre but now they've discovered the cellars are letting in water. I *told him.*' George Martyn's voice was uncannily like Toby's when angry. 'Months ago I offered him more space, told him to send me whatever was necessary. Now out of the blue I am to receive paintings, marbles and medal chests. There's no time for Evie to arrange a thing. It is too bad.'

'Can I help, Lord Martyn?'

'That's very kind, but no,' he said automatically.

He roused himself from annoyance.

'Now, my dear child, what can we do for you? Shall I ring Betty Lorimer? She is going to Turnbull I know: very keen on amateur dramatics, and used to go to London for all the shows before the war, so she's quite an expert. You'll like Betty.'

Sorrel said pleasantly that he was very kind but if she couldn't go with him, she'd prefer to stay in the garden and read. She had recognised the name Lorimer – the woman Dion detested – and privately thanked her stars for getting out of an afternoon with the lady. The artless compliment from the young girl pleased Martyn for a moment. But ill-temper returned and he marched indoors to look for Evie.

During the afternoon the van did not appear. George Martyn prowled about, once going down the drive as far as the entrance gates to see if there was any sign of it. The threatened arrival of more art treasures organised with such inefficiency had upset him. He liked things ordered and well arranged. He detested to be taken by surprise.

Sorrel wandered into the house to look for a book. She'd finished a romantic Irish novel lent to her by Margaret, and up in her room picked out *Bulldog Drummond* because Toby had once quoted it to her in a joke. And there on the flyleaf was his signature. Ronald Martyn. 1936. It was odd to see that he had written his real name. He wasn't a Ronald and whoever had given him the nickname had been right. I wonder if it was Edmund, she thought. His brother's influence was discernible now and then. In Evie's name. In Grace's stories.

Returning to the terrace she sat down facing a sea of cabbages and tried to read. But couldn't help turning back to look again at his handwriting. Her thoughts of him here at Evendon were almost all sexual and they upset her. Did all bereft women shy away from the thought of lovemaking because when you tried to recapture its joy you couldn't and your loss hurt you more? How quickly evaporated was that intense union. How lost. Thirsted for. Lost.

The afternoon dragged by, it was almost time to try and slip away to The Raven without being noticed. And then a dusty van came lumbering up the drive at last. George Martyn appeared immediately, he must have been on the lookout. The driver jumped down and he and a mate, an enormous man with a round bullet-head covered with thick short white hair, began to haul out a number of wooden crates. Martyn marched up to them.

'You are extremely late. Kindly take care. That one first, it is the smallest. *Careful.* No, not like that, you'll disturb the contents. No, not like that, you'll scratch the front door. To the left, please. Carry that crate *to the left*.'

He followed the two men, still barking instructions. Sorrel had time to walk swiftly down the drive and out into the road.

Tonight The Raven was bursting at the seams with American troops. They sat on the pub's low walls in the front garden, they lined up on the steps like debutantes at a coming-out ball, they draped themselves on the sills of open windows on the ground floor, they decorated the place like khaki-coloured flags. Formality, English reserve, were banished. As she came towards the pub there was a chorus of whistles and 'Oh Boys' and Sorrel burst out laughing.

Sitting with bare feet in the river again, Dion looked handsome, peaceful and utterly wrong. He did not hear her coming across the scorched grass and when she came up, he grinned and patted the river bank beside him.

'Going to take off your socks and dabble your toes? The water's surprisingly cold.'

'I don't think I will.'

'I never thought you would. I never thought you'd make this evening, either.'

'The Martyns are busy. Glad to be rid of me although they don't know where I am, of course. I saw you in the forty-acre field. It all seems to be going well.'

Like every farmer in the world, he looked up at the sky. 'If the weather holds. Weather has developed a capital W now I do this job. I listen to the wireless for weather reports, look at the clouds every five minutes. I swear I dream about it. Last year there was a storm bang in the middle of the harvest, one of the worst that people remember. We lost hundreds of pounds.'

'How did Lady Martyn take that?'

'Badly. It was pride rather than money. I'll say this for her, she enjoys success.'

They made a curious contrast, Dion in washed-out dusty overalls faded to the colour of wartime bread, a mixture of brown and grey. He was sunburnt and untidy and although he had scrubbed his hands, the fingernails were broken. Sorrel wore her only other civilian dress apart from the cotton checks. It was white crêpe-de-chine patterned with brilliant emerald-coloured leaves. They were startlingly unsuitable as a couple, as if a beauty from the manor were patronising a stable hand, a latter-day Lady Chatterley with her gamekeeper.

She had rather solemnly imagined that the talk would be all about conscientious objectors and Dion this time would try to make her understand his principles. Instead they sat idly as people do in the open. There was no emphasis in the conversation. When she mentioned the children at the harvest he laughed.

'Poor Grace. They play merry hell with her, pelting each other with the nation's food. She can't cope and gets so fussed, particularly when they line up to be paid. Once the worst young rascal in the village, Harry Jackson, managed to get paid twice. He dashed back to the end of the queue again and turned his cap round with the peak at the back to fool her. When I caught him, she couldn't get over it. But even Grace knows the children are part of the harvest. It isn't only that they're useful. They could no more resist the fields now than a bird could stop flying.'

He talked about farmers. Townspeople had got them wrong, just because they shouted at trespassers. They were neighbourly, even generous. 'Yesterday I was given an entire cartful of hedge cuttings, the thick thorny ones which are best for the bottoms of the ricks. The chap at Butterbox said, "take all you want." '

Soon the quarter of an hour was up. They both had to go.

'I wish we could do this again,' Dion said as they left the garden, 'but we'll be harvesting for the next three days until ten at night. And even now I must dash back.'

'And shouldn't waste your time on me.'

He ignored the flirtatious remark. She didn't know why she'd said it.

'You'll come to the Priory again.'

'I suppose so.'

'I shall hope so.'

The sun was still shining and it caught the leaves of the poplar trees at the edge of the wood, turning them white.

'I'm sorry I have to go, damn it,' Dion said.

'So am I. There's so much – '

'I haven't explained. I know. I didn't want to this evening.'

They had stopped walking, where the road curved towards the Priory. Sorrel looked up at him seriously. She so wanted to understand him just then. To do him justice. To accept as honourable the reason he wouldn't fight, as her beloved was doing, as all brave men must do. How could he stand here? And stand against the great surge and tide of war?

She murmured goodbye. Dion turned to her, he was so much taller and broader than Toby and he seemed to loom. Putting his hands on her shoulders, he gave her a passionate kiss.

7

By an unexpected stroke of luck Sorrel and Margaret Reilly were sent to Greenwich at the same time to get their commission. They greeted each other like sisters. Redheaded Moyra, lender of dresses, was also on the course looking more rakish than before and, although Margaret was at her nicest, she still disapproved and told Sorrel she knew Moyra was 'that awful thing, a good-time girl'.

Both Sorrel and Margaret were impressed by the magnificent place where they were to spend the next few weeks on what was called snobbishly the knife and fork course. 'To make sure we know which one's which,' said Sorrel. Margaret looked prim; perhaps she disliked Sorrel criticising authority.

It was while the Wrens were having dinner in the Painted Hall under the ceiling where Victory flew guided by trumpet-blowing angels that the news of El Alamein was heard.

'At last,' exclaimed Margaret fiercely, 'at last we're beginning to win!'

More and more details of the great Alamein battle came through, on the wireless and in the newspapers. The King sent a message to General Alexander and the Eighth Army congratulating them on the 'great victory'. There were messages from Australia, New Zealand, India, South Africa. The atmosphere was jubilant, excitement and enthusiasm everywhere. Sorrel couldn't share it. High Command had said the battles were decisive; in her ignorance she wondered what slaughter was in that word. She thought of the newsreels of the desert war, tanks in suffocating dust, the thunder of guns, thousands upon thousands of men in khaki. She imagined attacks, retreats, terrifying hand-to-hand combat, bleeding corpses. She could confide her unpatriotic terror to nobody. But time went by and no telegram arrived. And each day passing was one more towards his – and her own – safety.

The officers' course was intensive but unlike anything the girls had previously been taught; it had the quality of studying at a university. There were lectures on naval history, on the emergence of England as a sea power, on the character of the British seaman 'bred to tough weather and the challenge of the ocean'. They learned the story of legendary victories, St Vincent, Copenhagen, and inevitably Trafalgar. Sorrel thought Nelson ought to take his place on the rostrum. Slight and half-blind, vain and of superhuman courage. What was excluded from the lecture on Nelson was in every girl's mind as she listened – a destructive passion and a woman whose life ended in darkness and disgrace.

There were lectures on navigation and signals – worst of all there was squad drill. They spent half an hour each day in one of the quadrangles of Vanbrugh's noble buildings learning to give commands to a squad of girls. The petty officers who taught the drill were ferocious. They shouted if a Wren did not give her orders clearly and loudly, if the squad didn't move at once and in perfect unison. After these harrowing sessions, the future officers were marched back indoors for yet more lectures.

'The Discipline of Authority' was given by a sandy-haired young officer with an impressive row of medals. Another officer, a Wren this time, with a faint resemblance to Grace Martyn, lectured on 'Behaviour as an Officer'. Sorrel giggled when the lecture was over. Margaret looked stern.

'It's those knives and forks again,' said Sorrel.

Margaret sighed.

'My dear girl, the entire course is a test of whether a cadet has OLQ.'

'Officer-like qualities. I know. And *you* don't have to worry about *those*.'

Margaret did not disagree.

Both girls worked hard, there was no leave or time off except an hour or so in the evening. Uppermost in the mind of every Wren eating baked beans in the Painted Hall on a certain night early in November was – have I passed? And on the heels of that – where will I be posted? You could be sent packing up to Cape Wrath or down to the tip of Cornwall. You could land up in Wales in an earl's mansion, or be posted overseas to Ceylon, to Sydney. Adventurous girls thirsted to go abroad. Home-loving girls didn't. Sorrel and Margaret had discussed it.

'I know we have to agree to go anywhere, including overseas, but I hope to heaven I stay in England,' said Margaret, pouring ersatz custard on an ersatz canary pudding. 'You're okay. You don't mind where they send you.'

What she meant was – because you haven't a relation in the world. Margaret's tactlessness was funny sometimes.

After the meal the girls flocked into the common room. Somebody put on the gramophone. Margaret in a fit of expansiveness fetched some muddy coffee. She and Sorrel sat in a quiet corner while in the distance the girls listened to the music; a Wren who had been a dancer in peacetime jumped up to illustrate a new step, shaking her hands from the wrist and wriggling her bottom.

Margaret watched.

'That's the jitterbug. Byron does it marvellously.'

'Was he named after the poet?'

'It was his grandfather's name,' said Margaret as if that answered the question. 'Byron Schlegel. A big Jewish family, loads of brothers and sisters, just like us Irish. They live in New York. His father's quite rich, apparently.'

Sorrel had not met any of the Americans who had fascinated her friend in Sussex. She knew Margaret had had a good deal of success from the moment the Americans set foot on British soil; she'd made friends with dozens of them. Now the number had, it seemed, been reduced to two. She talked about them. Most of the Wrens whom Sorrel knew had strings of admirers, juggled their leaves and their dates, received passionate love letters from this one and that, and discussed the men languishing after them with laughing satisfaction. Scalps dried in front of their female tents. Margaret was not like that. She spoke of the two Americans with enthusiastic gravity. Sorrel supposed she was a little – or a lot – in love with one of them, and the other was simply a friend.

Absorbed in her own love affair, missing Toby at times so desperately that it was like a cut in her heart, Sorrel had not paid close attention to Margaret's friends. Margaret talked such a lot, about herself, her Americans, her family, herself. On this last evening before they were to part again, this time permanently, Sorrel was contrite.

'I wish I'd met your two American friends.'

'I asked you out with them loads of times.'

'I'm a fool. I should have come with you.'

Hearing the confession, Margaret showed Irish dimples. She was charming when she smiled.

'Tell me about them,' Sorrel said.

'Oh, I could go on about them till I'm blue in the face. What do you want to know?'

'Which one is which.'

'Surely you've sorted that out!'

'I know one's called Byron and the other Gareth,' said Sorrel hastily. Margaret was accustomed to enthralled male attention and looked put out.

'Byron's the one from New York who jitterbugs,' added Sorrel.

'He's a born dancer. You ought to see him. So light and rhythmic and loose-limbed. He's wonderful.'

'Have you a photograph of him? And one of Gareth?'

'Awful snaps.'

'Do show.'

Why didn't I listen instead of brooding all the time over Toby, thought Sorrel. Love makes you inhuman and that's a paradox.

Margaret fished out her wallet and produced photographs two inches square. Sorrel recognised them for the pictures, not unlike those on prisoners' record sheets, of men and women when they enlisted. She and Margaret had both taken photographs like that. She winced at the quality as she glimpsed the pictures and put out her hand to take them.

'One at a time,' said Margaret, in the voice of a mother with a too-eager child. She passed the first.

'That's Byron.'

The man who glared straight into an American service camera still managed to look sardonic; he had a goblin face.

'He looks amusing.'

'Of course. He is. And brilliantly clever, he was studying law before he enlisted. He only has two more years before qualifying. He's going to be one of those lawyers who work for the huge corporations. They earn a fortune. His mother has written to me . . . such a dear. And they live in a vast apartment on West 8th Street.'

She spoke as if she knew the city like the back of her hand. Taking the photograph from Sorrel, she smiled down at it.

'He just can't help doing things well. Whether it's soldiering or dancing or taking exams or organising a party at HQ or writing a skit on American slang. He's just, well, brilliant.'

'And your other American?'

The gramophone began an old Noël Coward song. 'Mary make-believe, dreams the whole day through,' sang the soft precise voice.

The second picture was of a totally different kind of man. He was fair and romantic, with high cheekbones. It was the face of an actor. He had lustrous eyes and was almost too handsome.

'That's Gareth van Doren. His family are in the diplomatic, surely you remember that?'

'Isn't he the one who introduced you to the American ambassador?'

'Mr Winant. Yes. Gareth took me to supper at the embassy. Only us three. What a thrill.'

'Golly.'

'Gareth's family are very grand. His grandfather was a Supreme Court justice, and his father's one of the senators in

Pennsylvania. Gareth will go into the diplomatic too when peace breaks out.'

It would have been easy enough to smile and look impressed, which was what was expected of her. But Sorrel felt a desire to get at the invulnerable young woman boasting away. The situation made no sense.

'And you'll be an ambassador's wife, will you?'

Margaret took the photograph at a snatch and put it in her wallet, separating it from the other with a scrap of paper torn from her diary.

'They're putting on that same record. It's so sentimental.'

Sorrel ignored the Keep Out signal.

'Margaret. Come on. We'll probably both be in the back of beyond tomorrow. We may not see each other for months. Even years. We've been quite friends, haven't we? You saw me through when my mother was killed, and you know about Toby. So – tell me about *you*.'

Margaret often asked direct questions, her manner was frank and friendly and people were very flattered by her bright interest. But Sorrel had never used the technique on Margaret herself, and it took her by surprise. The evening was late, the music was sad. Margaret knew she was going to miss Sorrel; she was fond of this girl so different from her own family. She wanted to confide in her just then.

'I suppose I haven't really talked. No wonder you can't remember which guy is which.'

She had talked. But said little.

'I don't think I quite understand how it is,' said Sorrel.

'Nor do I. Sometimes I think I'll go crazy. I see them both at different times and they don't know each other. I met Byron when we were at Littleport, Gareth was introduced to me in London at a party. I've been meeting him too, any time I can. First Byron. Then Gareth. Then Byron again. Sorrel, what am I doing?'

'It isn't your fault.'

'Of course it is. You can't love two men. At least you are not supposed to. It's immoral.'

My God, thought Sorrel, she's sleeping with both of them. A feeling of interest, curiosity, wonder and a sort of dreadful envy came over her. She imagined her friend in bed with the clever goblin, then on another night with the future ambassador.

'But you must prefer one of them. More than the other.'

'I keep thinking that. But I don't. Byron's a particular kind of man, Gareth another. They are different in every way.'

In sex, thought Sorrel. Sitting beside the goddess of chastity she said, 'Suppose both men were drowning, which one would you save?'

Margaret's face lightened at the question, it was ridiculous enough. It resembled questions children ask each other at school. 'Which would you prefer? To be blind, deaf or dumb? What are you going to have put on your tombstone? I've thought of mine.'

'You mean if I could only save one of them. And had to decide which one would be likely to be okay and swim to safety. I'd save Byron.'

'Are you sure? He looks just the sort of man who'd find a lump of wood and hang on and stay afloat. But Gareth – '

'No, no. Byron would drown.'

She hesitated and then continued. 'But just because I'd save him doesn't mean I like him more. Or not so much. Or whatever you're asking.'

'I'm asking about love.'

Margaret said nothing.

'So what is going to happen?' Sorrel asked.

Margaret sighed. 'I'm tired. Aren't you? We've been working harder than we realise. And we're strung up, too. Tomorrow we'll hear the postings and I dread that. I don't know what'll happen to me. Byron's in the army, he'll be sent off somewhere. Where, Sorrel? He may go any time. And Gareth's a flyer and you know what that means.'

'If one gets posted, you can concentrate on the other,' said Sorrel.

'But I'll miss the one who is gone more than I can bear.'

On the following morning every Wren at Greenwich was

pin-neat and nervous as a cat. Every black tie was perfectly knotted, every strand of hair in place, every button a bright gold. Sorrel and Margaret stood together not talking. Margaret had lost her roses, her face was pale. Sorrel gave her arm a squeeze.

'It may be all right. You know you've always been lucky.'

'Wren S. Scott. Wren S. Scott.'

Hearing her name called, Sorrel made a face at Margaret to get her to smile, but failed.

She marched smartly into the office for her interview with the chief officer.

It was the woman who had reminded Sorrel of Grace, fat, impressive, but without Grace's creamy serenity. She sketchily acknowledged Sorrel's salute, then leafed through some papers on the desk. Looking up, she gestured to an outsized map of the British Isles occupying most of the wall. It was scattered with coloured drawing pins.

'Well now, Scott,' she said, giving the girl a look as if detecting any tricks Sorrel was planning. 'Well. Where would you wish to be posted? Always provided,' a tinny laugh, 'you were allowed to choose.'

'I am not sure, Ma'am.'

The reply was given a cold smile.

'You must have some idea. Overseas?'

Love made her want to *be* Toby just then and Sorrel said, 'Yes, Ma'am. I'd like that very much.'

'Many of our Wrens wish for overseas posting,' said the Chief Officer in reproof. 'And if you remain in this country?'

Sorrel looked at the familiar map, her eye travelling to the tangled mass of its most northern outline.

'Scotland, Ma'am.'

The chief officer made a note.

Ramrod straight, Sorrel waited her destiny. I bet she won't send me abroad if she says everybody wants to go. If I'm posted to Scotland I shan't have to visit Evendon. Why am I thinking that?

'Yes,' said the officer as if talking to herself. She was writing, then gave Sorrel another probing look. 'Yes, I think - yes, Lee-on-Solent.'

Sorrel's eyes gleamed with amusement. So much for avoiding the Martyns.

'You take the news calmly, Scott.'

Sorrel wondered if she was imagining that the officer had hoped for some black despair.

With a respectful 'Ma'am' and a salute, Sorrel wheeled round and marched out.

Margaret was two Wrens behind her in the queue. Red-headed Moyra was next. She breathed 'wish me luck' as she marched away.

Tea, with the navy's habit of turning land into sea, was called Tea Boat and served in the canteen. Making her way through crowds of noisy girls, Sorrel found Margaret and saw her cheeks were pink again.

'Wizard!' cried Margaret, not asking about Sorrel's posting, 'Medmenham. Which means I can get to town and see Gareth. Wizard.'

'And Byron?'

'Him too,' said Margaret, blinking.

Moyra's usually piquant face was dark as she passed them, slopping tea in her saucer.

'Did you get Yeovilton?' asked Sorrel, 'That's where your parents live, isn't it?'

'Yes they do, and guess where that bitch has posted me? Inverness. She knew perfectly well I'm West Country and she bloody well shoved me up to the north of Scotland. I could kill her.'

'But she could have sent me there! I asked for Scotland.'

Moyra was derisive.

'Your name's Scott. She thought you wanted to be somewhere near your home just as I did. Why didn't I ask for Scotland, hell and damnation? All we do in the navy is jump to attention and say three bags full, Ma'am. I could kill her,' repeated Moyra, slopping more tea. 'Where are you going?'

'Hampshire.'

'Oh wonderful. I suppose your entire family lives there.'

With her commission, Sorrel's life changed. She left Somerset where she had never really settled despite a beautiful countryside and friendly but not very congenial company. She did not know until she became an officer how she needed this alteration of her life. With her new and becoming uniform, she put on authority. It was different. When she arrived at Lee-on-Solent the young Wren ratings saluted her. Girls called her Ma'am. The naval officers took to their new arrival, they liked her unselfconscious manner and were interested in her swimming eyes.

'I'm sure,' said a lieutenant, 'that one's a goer.'

It was noticed that she wore no ring. They heard that both parents were dead, her mother had been killed in a London raid. People called her 'that plucky little thing'. Officers invited her to their Mess – the Wrens' Mess and theirs were separate – and bought her drinks. Sorrel was as tall as some of the officers but they spoke of her as little.

When Sorrel first heard her job was to be torpedo assessing officer, she had a thrill of alarm.

'How's your trig?' asked her commanding officer on Sorrel's first morning at Lee. 'Trigonometry, Scott. Trigonometry. You took it at school, remember? By your face I take it you weren't a shining light at the subject. Never mind. Nose to the grindstone.'

To get rid of heartache and body ache, to stop dreaming you're being made love to so that you wake in tears, to stop remembering your lover suddenly with a sensation as if you'd been kicked in the stomach, the antidote is work. Sorrel knew it. And the navy put a pilgrim's burden of work on the shoulders of all its men and women. But in Littleport and Somerset she had enjoyed the photography, had a natural talent for it and a sense of form. She never had the faintest leaning towards mathematics which now, instead of being a tedious forgotten subject, became vital to her future. She was too eager, too keen, in a way too vain to think of failure. Toby affected her. She wanted to be like him, to take on, in her less martial way, his dedication.

The first lecture on her first day was given by a tall, precise lieutenant so much resembling a schoolmaster that her worst fears were realised. He started at the deep end.

'Trigonometry,' he announced, 'was founded by Hipparchus in the second century BC.' A faint smile. 'He was an astronomer. As a matter of fact he produced the first accurate map of over a thousand stars.'

No star shone for Sorrel, finding herself up to her neck in cyclic quantities.

There were eight Wren officers on the course and with no men around, the atmosphere was competitive for good reports. There wasn't a ripple of sex to disturb it. Sorrel saw that most of the girls were cleverer or better educated than she was. She gritted her teeth. She did not learn as fast as they during the first vital days when they were taught to master figures. She knew there was only one way to make a day longer and extend the time of study. She must work at night.

When the other girls, she supposed, were comfortably asleep, she sat in bed, toiling through a book as thick as the Bible, filled with diagrams containing every angle which existed and some, thought harassed Sorrel, which looked impossible. The diagrams and equations marched across the pages. They dazzled her with complexities and they dared her to understand them.

Propped up in bed, her head splitting from tiredness, she worked sometimes until the grey dawn when she heard the geese going by calling to each other on their way to flooded meadows where they fed and clustered.

There was no leave for the entire twelve weeks of the course.

One morning she received a letter. The handwriting was oddly familiar; the last time she had seen it had been on the piece of paper fished from her mother's handbag. It was from George Martyn. It was kindly, he always was with her, and it contained news which gave her a lift of the spirits.

'One thing I wanted to write to you about was Toby's non-existent letters. I take it you haven't heard either; I am sure you would have rung us if you had. Well, I thought I'd talk to a certain friend of mine in the War Office. No official secrets given away, naturally, but as we guessed, Toby's with the

Eighth Army. He is fine, but all the posts have been held up. We must just thank God all is well.'

The letter finished by saying he was her affectionate George. Quite out of herself with relief, Sorrel had time to be touched by his use of his first name.

Her only other contact with the outside world was a telephone call from Margaret Reilly, sounding so energetic and cheerful that Sorrel positively flinched. When, demanded Margaret, was she coming to town?

'I can manage it, why can't you? Stay at the CSC.'

'What's that?' asked Sorrel.

'Curzon Street officers' club, silly!'

Margaret added that Sorrel must join right away. It was the only place to stay and packed to the gills with the navy. 'I'll put you up for membership.' Always glad she could do Sorrel a favour Margaret chatted about herself, then with the demand that Sorrel should 'keep in touch, don't forget, now,' rang off.

It sounds as if going to bed with two men is keeping her happy, thought Sorrel uncharitably.

It was the early spring of 1943, over a year since her mother's death, when Sorrel completed the course and became an officer with a specialised skill. Captain Lyall who commanded the camp, a short fair man with blue eyes and the DSO, two attributes which made him irresistible to young women, sent for her to give her his congratulations. He had taken a fancy to the pretty, over-tired young woman.

'Your report is first-class.'

She smiled.

'That's better. We've been wearing you out and making Jill a dull girl. How do you feel?'

'Fine, thank you, sir.'

'You surprise me. However. I have some news. One of our permanent officers, Third Officer Forrest, has been posted overseas and we have a vacancy. You'll be remaining at Lee. How does that strike you?'

That evening, flirted with by two sub-lieutenants who plied her with pink gins, Sorrel was called from the Mess to see the commandant again. She was flushed and starry-eyed. Captain Lyall was amused.

'Well, young woman. Been celebrating? This is turning into a redletter day for you in more ways than one.'

He handed her a telegram.

'Due home in five days. Am getting special licence. Love. Toby.'

Before arriving at Evendon on a day of pouring rain, Sorrel was as sick as a girl in the first stages of pregnancy. She tottered down the train corridor, tripped over a kit bag and was saved from falling flat on her face by a large soldier. In the lavatory she was sick three times. She emerged looking almost green.

'You all right, Ma'am?'

'Yes, yes, of course.'

The soldier decided she was suffering from the worst hangover in Hampshire. He winked.

She felt so ill that she thought the journey would never end and when she climbed out of the train at Evendon her legs were shaking. The train puffed away and she stood in the soft rain, then picked her bag from a puddle and began to walk towards the station hut where the porter never took her ticket. Suddenly somebody came running. She was lifted right off her feet.

'Darlingest. Darlingest.'

It was a world where everybody rushed into each other's arms, where every human being meeting a beloved would kiss and kiss. Platforms, streets, gates, front doors, were filled with embracing couples saying goodbye or, for a rationed time of joy, greeting each other. But Toby looked round quickly to be sure they were alone before he embraced her. They kissed. She determined not to cry.

They were married by special licence at St Anselm's small Norman church three days later.

There was no peal of bells when they stood upon the steps and somebody threw rice. The bells which had called people to divine service for a thousand years, which had rung in happiness for weddings, in sorrow for funerals, were silent by government decree. They must only be rung if the enemy landed.

Toby and Sorrel had both been granted compassionate leave.

'Passionate leave,' said Toby.

8

Soldiers on active service never came home and never had leave and, when she knew Toby was returning to England, she had been convinced he was ill. Wounded, perhaps seriously. The explanation was different – and secret. He'd been sent back for some kind of special training about which he was deliberately vague. Sorrel and his parents were not allowed to know what it was or why he'd been chosen. And could not ask.

On the first night they were together and they were to be married the next morning, they made love for a long time, then lay together as they used to do, with curtains parted to let in the moonlight. Looking at him – she had been too blind with passion until now to see – she discovered a long crimson scar running down his forearm. The scar tissue was as thick as the beading round a cushion.

'You never said you'd been wounded!'

'A bullet fragment happened to zoom by. Nothing to fuss over. The medics made a neat job. You should have seen it when it was split open. Strawberry jam. There's another here beneath my shoulder, see?' He turned over like a man exhibiting a tattoo. 'It missed the shoulder, which is a mercy, otherwise I'd be in trouble. The MO said joints, shoulders, knees and so on, are complicated, there are all kinds of little tendons with their jobs to do. If the bullet had been an inch or two further up I could have had a crippled arm. There's a bit of shrapnel in my back, too. In a muscle. We were in a ditch at the time! The shrapnel shows up beautifully in the X-rays.'

He turned back and grinned at her.

'What a softy you are.'

She put up her hand and traced the raised livid scar on his arm.

'Am I not allowed to care what happens to you, then?'

'Just love me. Love me now.'

In silence, he never talked during lovemaking, he began to caress her again between her legs.

Lying together in the quiet old house away from his parents, alone and united, he told her about Alamein. Long ago in the Sussex hotel he had once described the fighting in France and she had listened in awe, as if it were a sort of history. Now it frightened her. He spoke of 'tactical surprise' and 'dog-fights reducing the enemy's strength'. But what Sorrel saw in her imagination was the glare of the desert, soldiers with rifles set with bayonets in their hands as they ran through dust clouds. She listened only for his part of the fighting and knew that at any time, while the masses of men and tanks and guns moved forward, any time while she had been in Sussex and Somerset and Greenwich, he could have been dead. As he talked in a low matter-of-fact voice he felt her tremble. He liked that.

The Martyns had not been surprised when their son, arriving in advance of Sorrel and in a state of elation, announced that he'd been to Caxton Hall before leaving London to get a special licence. He was marrying Sorrel Scott. They had been given time to get used to the idea of the Wren as their daughter-in-law, although Toby had asked them in the only letter from him they'd received not to discuss it with Sorrel.

'I don't want you talking it over with her yet. I know you understand. Of course I asked her and she agreed but I don't want to say any more until I get back. Nothing's worse than a war widow who didn't get her man, is there?' he wrote merrily. 'When I'm home we'll tie everything up and you'll be as pleased as Punch. I am.'

Wartime weddings could be very small and there were only a few local friends at the church. One glamorous woman, George's sister Dot, had travelled from London. After the ceremony everybody walked the five minutes back to the Priory. Sorrel remembered little. A glimpse of Toby's strong profile during the service. The efficient way he slipped the ring on her finger. And then he'd looked at her – and she'd felt she was falling in a fast lift.

After the reception they were driven to London in the Martyn's rarely used Daimler with some petrol George had obtained 'from a kind friend'. They spent their wedding night at the Dorchester and the next day Toby suggested they should return home.

'I know,' he tenderly said, 'you love Evendon as much as I do.'

Sorrel determined to be a real daughter-in-law to her new parents. When they arrived back at the Priory on the second day of bliss, Toby's father greeted her very warmly, kissing her and giving her a fatherly hug. But Grace looked tired, greeted the newly married pair with an absent smile and soon hurried away.

'She's worn out with her work on the farm,' said George.

But Sorrel saw during luncheon that Grace had changed towards her, for the worse. She competed for her son's attention by telling or recalling excluding jokes. Toby tried to cope with the problem at first by explaining the allusions to Sorrel; but he soon gave up. Jokes and stories went on right through the meal.

'Do you remember when you fell off the roof of the garden shed?' It was a favourite tale and they all laughed. Toby had built a cannon on the shed roof, made of bricks and with flower pots for the gun barrel. He'd spent hours firing at imaginary intruders and finally, stepping back to admire his cannon, fell over eight feet.

'I thought you were dead. But you opened your eyes and said "What's for lunch, Mummy?" '

When the talk turned to school, Sorrel mentioned her trouble with trigonometry. Grace sailed right through that.

'Toby, you were a terror. Nearly blowing up the lab with your chemistry experiments. Your house master took your father aside and said – '

'He's a danger to man and beast,' finished George.

Both men fairly gave Grace her head. George was indulgent. Toby, relaxed after lovemaking, had all the time in the world to listen. His mother's reminiscences were touched with poetry and he could not resist, just now, the pull of the old days. But sitting over coffee, with spring pouring in through the open windows, a sorceress claiming indoors as well as out as her kingdom, he began his old song. He attacked the government. In Toby's book the war was being fought by soldiers hampered by bungling inefficiency at home. Sorrel noticed that he did not praise the Germans any more. It seemed they were no longer the unbeatable troops, the perfectly disciplined war machine. In the Western Desert it was the Allies who pressed forward week by week and Rommel the desert fox who was in retreat. Toby turned to the other theatre of war. He had 'a good deal of time for the Russkies and their heroic victory in Stalingrad. They've proved the Germans can be beaten in the field, as we have,' he informed his parents.

They listened and nodded and Sorrel, for all her passionate love, marvelled at their meekness.

Toby's admiration for a country or a people was invariably followed by the reverse. England had become so vulgar. It made his flesh creep to listen to the wireless, hear the awful songs, read the newspapers.

'And food,' said Toby, unconscious of irony, 'is an obsession.'

But Sorrel's ripple of criticism for him could not last. She was in a state of nervous worship, sated with sex, trying to feel her feet like a swimmer whose toes explore deep water hoping to touch sand. She was not herself.

In a short space of time she was discovering the differences between lover and husband. Lovemaking in the past had the taste of being wrong; it had been like committing a sin, it felt wicked, with the excitement of possible shameful discovery. When he'd crept into her room at night, softly closed and locked the door, she'd felt her whole body grow moist. He wanted her now, not only in bed at night but during the day. He stood behind her, pushing against her, biting her neck gently and saying, 'Now. Now.' But often in the many times they made love he did not wait for her and she was confused and robbed and dared not show it. He was more urgent and more selfish. And after the night before they were married, when he told her of Alamein, he did not admit her again into his hidden thoughts.

On the afternoon of their second day – they were due to go back to their units the next morning – they went for a walk down the country road which passed The Raven. It was unbelievable to Sorrel to think she'd crept out of the house to meet Dion there. She could see the tops of trees which grew along the river bank, and her heart began to beat faster at the idea of meeting him on their walk, or in the farm. But she'd only seen him once at a distance, leading the horses down from the fields.

As the sunny evening began to fall, the rain had stopped and it was soft and warm with wild daffodils under the trees. Toby said he would give her another riding lesson.

He went to Butterbox for the pony, and when they rode together he was pleased with her progress.

'I'll make a fine rider of you, darlingest. And how good you look on a horse. Just right.'

They took the pony back to the neighbouring farm and then walked with The Chief back in the soft evening.

Just as they came in sight of the house Evie came running.

'There you are, Toby. Somebody wants you on the telephone.' She spoke as if to Montgomery.

'Right, Evie. Sorrel, will you take The Chief back to the barn?'

'Would you like me to do it?' said Evie.

Toby laughed.

'Don't spoon-feed her. She can manage a horse perfectly well. Take him back, Sorrel. The dear chap likes you.'

Evie and Toby returned to the house, Toby looking back to give an encouraging wave.

Sorrel thought the large horse did, indeed, seem to approve of her. He walked gently beside her back to the barn. She put him safely inside, shut the door and began to wander through what once had been the gardens. She was in an end-of-leave, end-of-joy mood, thinking neither of past nor future. You had to take what was given, and like an acrobat or a dancer, balance in the present, stand on a rope above a neck-breaking height, spring into the arms of your partner – your future – knowing he wouldn't drop you.

She put her hands in her pockets and walked slowly, letting the sun warm the back of her neck. And came face to face with Dion pushing a barrow of bulging sacks. He put the barrow down.

'I have to congratulate you. You look very happy.'

'Thank you. I am.'

'Good.'

He took the handles of the barrow again. She had a feeling of shame, her voice had been so graceless. She was like the favoured with the outcast, the freeman with the slave. She looked for something to say which would mend things, spoke in a rush. 'Didn't you once promise to tell me something about the Priory?'

He stopped, just as she'd hoped he would.

'Well. That's nice.'

'What is?'

'You remembering.'

'Why should I forget?'

'Very easily – with Toby back from the wars and your marriage. Two reasons for putting a bit of local colour out of your mind.'

'But I'm interested in the Priory.' She was glad she had asked and glad his face had changed.

'I know one or two things,' he said, sounding like the man she used to talk to. 'The house was a priory, of course, but a very small one. Dedicated, not to St Anselm like the church, but to a rhyming cousin, Aldhelm.'

'Who's he when he's at home?'

'A Saxon saint. They were rather proud of him, the first English scholar to make a mark. He was abbot of Malmesbury, a skilled architect, and actually went to visit the Pope in the 600s,' said Dion, standing by his barrow, the most unlikely historian in Hampshire. 'He was also a writer. Did a very long poem on virginity.'

'And impressed everybody,' said Sorrel, laughing.

'Not exactly. They maintained that Latin had quite gone to his head and they didn't understand what on earth he was telling them,' said Dion. 'Your family's house, Sorrel, had around fifteen monks living there, working and praying. Farming too. They chose to build on this site because it's near the river, so there was the usual monastery fishpond. You can see it in the kitchen garden; it's extremely deep and there are enormous carp in it – they glimmer up sometimes.'

He reflected for a moment. 'Odd to think the monks were here for nearly 250 years.'

'Until the Reformation?' Sorrel did know that piece of history.

'Sure. The poor old things were thrown out then. There's a local tradition that when the abbot locked the front door he pocketed the key, said a prayer to St Aldhelm, and then vowed: "Heaven will bring us back". A good exit line, but I'm afraid heaven never did.'

The deserted place simply fell to pieces over the years, he said, like many of the abandoned monasteries. The villagers stole most of the stones. But during the Restoration men with money began to buy up the wrecks of religious houses.

'A prosperous farmer called Elijah Cobb lived round here. Apparently he had friends in high places, and he bought what was left of the Priory from a baronet who'd gambled away all his cash. Cobb rebuilt the place – rather well, don't you agree? There are still traces of the original priory, apart from the fishpond and the barn. I haven't seen them, but Evie says there's a row of little Gothic windows in one passage and a stone crucifix in the wall.'

'I've noticed those!' explained Sorrel. Dion's eyes grew bright with interest; she literally forgot that a few minutes ago she'd thought this man an outcast. Just then, as can happen even to the most besotted, she forgot Toby.

'They're on the way to the drawing room – ' she began.

'*Sorrel*.'

At the far end of the stable yard, not coming towards her, was Toby. He simply stood and shouted.

Sorrel blushed crimson.

Dion raised his eyebrows.

'I'd better go. Goodbye. Good luck.'

He picked up the wheelbarrow and made his way, deliberately slowly, down the path.

Still hot and red, Sorrel went to Toby. She scarcely recognised him. His face was a witchlike mask, with a large nose and a gash for a mouth.

'How dare you talk to that creature.'

'I was only – '

'Don't excuse yourself. I told you months ago what I think of him. What everybody thinks. He's a bloody man. A coward. I'd like to bash his face in. Everybody feels like that about a conchie.'

'Toby!'

She was appalled at the male witch more than at her responsibility for calling him into existence. '*Please!*'

Grabbing her arm he frog-marched her away. She felt a fool. He took her across the rose garden where the potatoes were losing their white flowers. When they reached the far end of the terrace he let go of her and threw himself down on the bench against the wall of the house.

'Sit down.'

Her blush had faded. How ugly he looked staring out at nothing. The birds tweeted cheerfully. Sorrel stopped looking at the furious stranger she had married. She remembered Dion's expression and the 'good luck'. He had known Toby would behave like this.

'I know how you feel. Lots of people do.'

'Lots?' he repeated savagely. 'Every decent man and woman. You were being *pleasant to him*. I can't believe – '

'Oh Toby,' she interrupted to his astonishment. 'Do shut up. You're a brave man and a soldier and you don't understand people like Dion Fulford. He truly believes that war is wrong. In his conscience. He had to go before a tribunal and it was their decision that his case was genuine.'

'How do you know all that?'

'Because he told me so. He was round the farm when I was here in the summer and we talked a bit.'

She could no more have told her accuser that she'd met Dion Fulford by arrangement than she could wrench off her wedding ring and throw it in his face. She loved Toby. He shocked her.

He began to cross-question her. While he continued to be so furious, so accusing, so cruelly prejudiced, her determination hardened. She had never come up against a bully before and she saw her hero was just that. He wanted to force her to her knees. To crush her under the wheels of a gun carriage. To flatten her, thought Sorrel in bleak humour, like the creatures in Disney cartoons who were squashed into mere shapes of dogs or cats. But the Disney animals after lying on the ground like pastry cut-outs puffed themselves into life again.

'I'm ashamed of you,' he said with bitterness.

'I don't see why. It isn't like the Great War.'

'It should be.'

'Toby, you mustn't say things like that! The last war was terrible. Terrible. And conscientious objectors were pariahs, attacked in the street, jeered at, loathed. People have changed. Some artists and composers, important ones, say they'll work for the country but don't feel they can fight. They've been made exempt. Have some pity, Toby. Please.'

Forgetting right and wrong, she instinctively touched his hand. He caught hers and gripped it and put it to his face. Her eyes brimmed.

They sat in silence, clutching each other's hands as if facing a terrible danger.

When they stood up and went indoors both their faces had strangely cleared.

A grey-haired talkative colonel came to dine that evening. Toby was attentive and respectful, Grace all flowing interest and George Martyn warmly hospitable. The colonel gave Toby Martyn's bride a look of approval. Sorrel looked as ripe as an apricot on a wall. She and Toby had spent two hours before dinner making love. They'd loved with the violence that comes after quarrels, with the sharpness of approaching separation. When their climax came, they groaned. Now they drank champagne and did not bother to look in each other's direction . . .

Toby's course of training was to last for only three months and Sorrel as a special concession was given a weekend pass to go to Evendon again. Toby looked remarkable. Wherever he was stationed he must be working in the open; he was darkly tanned, the top of his hair turning slightly gold; he was radiant with health. Soon the short time of his stay in England was over. There was a forty-eight-hour leave before he embarked.

This time Sorrel met him in London. They had luncheon at the Ritz and did some shopping. He had been kitted out with two new sets of combat dress, and, swinging down Piccadilly on his way to Bond Street, complained about that.

'Do you realise combat is army issue, Sorrel? The navy have theirs made for them at Gieves. We can't. Most of the time we're not even allowed to wear the Sam Browne.'

He did buy some boots, spending an hour at an expensive bootmakers where he was charming to the old man who served them, and the floor was soon littered with twenty pairs, all discarded.

His astonishment at shortages amused her.

'As a mere soldier,' he said as they went into a sixth shop in search of razor blades, 'even I can spot things are damned badly organised.'

But youth and good looks and uniform finally produced the razor blades and – unheard of luxury – French scent for Sorrel.

They returned to Evendon in the afternoon.

It was their last day, and they did not once mention it. The strange happiness which had visited them the last time war tore them apart came again like a spirit, filling them, fooling them, turning them into people who did not know they were under a curse. And after they'd made love, he told her how his brother died. The story was so short. There had been some parachutists in a field ahead of the regiment on its way to Dunkirk, and somebody had to go ahead to reconnoitre. Edmund volunteered faster than Toby.

'I can't forget it,' Toby whispered, lying close to her. 'He wasn't a born soldier. When he joined the army things were different – it was a way of life, you know? Of course he had courage, but that night he volunteered from a sort of bravado. Edmund did things like that. I was the better soldier simply because the job suits me. It never suited Edmund, he just happened on it. Well – he was killed. The bastards shot him four times. He was dead when we found him.'

She put her arms round his neck but for a moment he had forgotten her.

His gear was packed, the staff car due to collect him at half past nine. Toby went on a tour of farewells. He went early and alone to see The Chief, and after breakfast with Sorrel asked her to come with him to say goodbye to 'the staff', as he called the three people who worked in the house.

Walker, the chauffeur, was often in a bad temper now he was forced to drive the pony and trap, but he beamed when Toby came into the tiny downstairs room near the kitchen where he cleaned the shoes. Toby wrung the old man's hand and gave him £10. It was the same with Ada, the housemaid Sorrel knew disliked her; Toby gave Ada a £5 note, a fortune to an old woman who was paid only three times that sum for a year of work.

'God bless you, Major, Sir,' said the maid, giving a sort of bob.

He left Evie until the last. He had bought her a bottle of real French scent when he and Sorrel had found some in London. He gave Evie her present and then put both arms round her. When he kissed her, Evie blushed. How attractive he is, thought Sorrel, with people in the position of his underlings; he's so affectionate and kind. He's irresistible. He behaves like the lord of the manor, of course, but I suppose that's what he is, really.

As they went into the hall she looked at the clock. Fifteen minutes left.

'The parents next.'

Toby looked at her. She knew he was testing her, and knew he didn't realise how exactly she understood that. Pain went through every part of her body, she was drenched in it. She grinned and he tucked her arm into his, like a comrade's.

'Come along. My father will be pouring us out a much-too-early sherry.'

'Good-oh.'

She had never been to her father-in-law's study before. It was the room into which he vanished to work undisturbed – his sanctum. Nobody, not even Grace, was allowed to interrupt him there. If he rang the bell, Evie was expected to answer it at once.

The room was very old-fashioned, thought Sorrel. The furniture was dark and heavy, a glass-fronted bookcase which looked as if it was never opened, and one or two eighteenth-century seascapes in which the waves were like corrugated paper.

'Well, my boy?' said George heartily as Toby and Sorrel entered, 'here's a glass to speed you on your way.'

'I wonder which way it is going to be,' said Grace roguishly. Something in the timbre of her voice reverberated in Sorrel's heart.

'Wherever we fetch up, I'll think about you at Evendon,' said Toby, sipping the sherry. 'Remember, I want all the news. I'm sure the farm will go from strength to strength, eh, Mother?'

'It's pretty good at the moment. I often think the cycle of nature is a miracle,' she said.

'You're the miracle,' said her son on cue. Despite having just finished breakfast, he tasted the sherry with enjoyment. 'Wonderful stuff. I notice you don't let on where you get it, Pop. I'm not sure we want to know, do we, Mother? Probably a smuggler's tale.'

'Whoever heard of such a thing!' said George.

Toby looked at Grace again.

'What a lot you've pulled off in the farm. Why, Evie tells me the Priory is producing four times more food than ever before.'

'Next time you're home we'll be baking bread with our own flour.'

He made admiring noises, and Grace said ruefully that there were always difficulties with the Agricultural Committee.

'Use that charm of yours. When you do that people fall like a ton of bricks.'

George glanced at his silent daughter-in-law.

'Your wife's looking remarkably pretty.'

'Of course she is,' declared Toby. 'And now I must love you and leave you. Well, Mother?'

He went to her and gave her a smacking kiss on each cheek; it appeared to be more a family joke than an embrace; when they separated, they were smiling.

'My boy,' said George.

He and Toby gripped hands. Why don't they hug each other, wondered Sorrel, since they want to. And Toby's the kind of man who should throw himself in his father's arms.

'We won't see you off, Sorrel will do that,' said Grace gaily.

'No, she won't. She can come to the front door and then march back for another sherry.'

Toby turned to give his smartest Sandhurst salute. 'Good luck,' they chorused.

In silence he and Sorrel went down the passage where the sun shone like a blessing. In the hall the stones of the quarry-tiled floor looked like warm grey silk. There was a scent from some early beech leaves Evie had put into the empty fireplace.

A staff car, the corporal driver standing by it, was in the drive, Toby's gear already stowed away. The man saluted. Toby turned to Sorrel, putting his hands on her shoulders. She gave him for a second time a mischievous smile.

'Take care,' they said at the same time and that made them laugh.

He did not kiss her. She knew he wouldn't.

The relief when what you dread is over, the relaxed nerves when the train steams out, came to Grace. Thank God, she thought, when Sorrel said goodbye two hours later. She had not relished the idea of her son's wife mooning about and, when Sorrel explained she must leave, Grace scarcely bothered to conceal her satisfaction.

Had anybody told her that Sorrel wanted to go even more eagerly than Grace wished her to, Grace would have refused to believe it. Just as she would have refused to accept that she had infected Sorrel with her own feelings.

Grace gave no quarter, admitted no fault, literally could not see another's point of view. It was her strength and weakness. Her husband, both her sons, Evie, her friends, all accepted that it was a waste of breath to argue with her. Her loves and her prejudices, her loyalties and her spites were constant. She was as unselfconscious about showing her nature as a child of six. She had felt an instinctive antagonism for Sorrel's mother, a sense that George had questionable reasons for befriending Lilian Scott. George had his secrets, and Grace was clever enough not to probe. But she'd never liked Lilian, and never taken to the young Wren. The arrival of Sorrel Scott at the Priory had been an unlucky day for the Martyns, thought Grace. She would have to put up with the girl, she supposed. And was shameless enough to wonder if the marriage would last.

Grace was a woman of strong character who liked to think and sometimes quote that she was the master of her fate and the captain of her soul. Her sureness had been the same when she was a slim girl in the early 1920s. It had been Grace more than George who had made the match. His wealth dazzled her parents, regular army people with good connections and no money. The fact that Martyn had been a war profiteer, the sort execrated by men in the trenches, was not mentioned in Grace's home when Martyn began to court the girl. Peace had changed a great many things, including moral judgements. And if Grace's family, with three generations of soldiers behind them, did think about profiteering, they kept it to themselves. The family from great-aunts downwards had a well-bred reverence for wealth, provided its owner used the right knives and forks.

George fell in love with Grace. He was a hard businessman who threw bachelor life to the wind, and embraced with relief the young girl's round body and soft cheek, and just as tenderly welcomed her idealism, patriotism, poetry. The couple suited each other. Impressed each other. He was older than she was, nearly nine years her senior, rich, sexually experienced and silent upon the subject; he laughed at her jokes and echoed her high-flown sentiments. He knew that despite her youth she was as hard as he was.

The marriage prospered. Grace grew fat. If George had one or two discreet love affairs with girls safely in London, she knew nothing about that. He respected her, and although she could be tedious, still admired her spirit and her beliefs.

Grace was happy. Even when war came, she was happy. Her patriotism, like the old-fashioned water-wings, kept her afloat in deep water. She had two sons in the regular army but she came from a family who knew the burden and danger of choosing to serve one's country. Even the black sorrow of Edmund's death with its excruciating constant pain was honourable. She could just about bear Edmund's loss.

It was not like this now. She did not struggle against her feelings about Toby's wife and did not know that her jealousy was as strong as a girl's for a lost lover. Her love for Toby was uncomplicated and hungry and sad. And to make things worse it wasn't even possible to bury herself up to the neck working for the farm. The presence of Dion Fulford poisoned that.

She had asked for help, and like an evil spell in a fairy story, had been granted what she asked and hated what she was given. It was true he was an excellent worker, physically strong and apparently tireless. Although he'd been a journalist and never worked on the land, he was quick and clever. He used a mixture of coaxing and authority with the two land-girls, he managed the cowman, who was stupid and slow and a bore. It was Fulford who planned the crops, led the great heavy horses for ploughing and muck-spreading, organised the haymaking and the harvest.

She couldn't fault him. He walked from the village in the vilest weather, was at work hours before the others. One morning she couldn't sleep, got up at some unearthly hour and went out into the farm. Seeing a hairline of light she went into the cowshed. A voice shouted: 'Mind the bloody blackout!'

Grace hastily slammed the door. Inside, a single 25-watt

electric bulb was rigged to hang from the ceiling. There wasn't a sound except the soft breath of cows, the ping of milk squirting into the pail. Bent on his stool, a cap on his fair hair, Dion was absorbed. He half-turned, muttered good morning, and went back to his task. She had come in to give him orders. To her mystified annoyance, she couldn't.

He was her farmworker. He also became the bailiff, took over the worst part of the job, the growing demands from the government for paperwork, documents to be read, regulations to be obeyed. He was even making Grace quite a lot of money.

With one beloved son dead in France, the other returned to the war, his wounds like a battle flag, the sight of a strong handsome man safe in the fields repelled her. Needing him, leaning on him, she could scarcely bring herself to talk to him.

In the past she and George had looked down on the Fulfords; John Fulford, minister of that gimcrack chapel at the other end of the village, preaching discontent among the agricultural workers. And that mouse of a wife with a saintly expression. The two children were shabby and pugnacious. Where did they get such clothes? And their manner was impertinent.

She tried to put the pack of them out of her mind.

Toby had been gone three hours now. The sun in its cruelty still shone on one of the worst days in her life, as Grace went round the farm, chatting to the land-girls and gracious with the cowman because he was feeding The Chief. Returning to the house, she heard the sound of George's car. After Toby had left, he hadn't gone to London but had driven into Portsmouth on one of those business appointments connected with supply. The demand for uniform was even greater since the desert victories.

As Grace came round the corner to the front of the house, she saw her husband getting out of the car, holding a parcel. He usually came home bringing something or other. He called his spoils 'My lucky dips'. As a *quid pro quo*, he sometimes took a small case packed with eggs to London. Or a few onions. 'They're as scarce and valuable as peaches,' he once told her.

'What have you brought me today?' called Grace.

'Guess.'

'I can't. Tell me.' She was comforted to see him.

'Dried figs. Four boxes in this little crate.'

Exclaiming over the prize, she did not ask where it came from. Her silk stockings, his razor blades, the sherry and smoked salmon, the boxes of baby food eaten in place of rationed breakfast cereals, the yards of woollen fabrics and a leather jacket lined with sheepskin, invaluable for Grace in winter, all the booty he brought home was welcomed with simple pleasure. As far as Grace was concerned, it proved how efficient and influential he was. She was convinced it was obtained honestly.

They went into the house and he asked her, a rare occurence, to come and talk to him in the study. In the room where only hours ago Toby had kissed her, Grace plumped down in an armchair. George poured some madeira. As he handed her the glass, for the first time in her life she thought, George looks old. She added to herself, he works too hard. She would not even think that it was Toby who had made him look like that.

He sipped the madeira, rolling it round his tongue.

'It's good stuff. It has body, comes from Funchal. Where's young Sorrel? I must give her a glass.'

'Yes, it's very good. Didn't you know Sorrel had to go? Her leave was up and she went hours ago.'

He was very taken aback.

'But she didn't say goodbye to me.'

'My dear man, I can't think that of much importance. We'll see her again. Rather more than we may want to.'

'Of course we'll see her, Grace. Don't be a – ' he swallowed the epithet. 'Don't be a possessive mother.'

'I'm certainly that.'

Looking down at her ill-treated hands, fat and dry, parched and seamed with earth which no scrubbing would remove, she saw that her wedding ring was growing too tight. Her fourth finger was slightly swollen.

'Where do you think he is going, George?'

'Not back to the Eighth Army. He won't be needed there now they're beginning to win.'

'Then where?'

He shook his head, murmuring God knows. And as she looked back at him, her big desolate face was a mask of suffering. Rachel mourning for her children.

PART TWO

9

You got used to it. To being married without a husband. To being in love without a lover. To questions in men's eyes when they saw a wedding ring, to being run after by some who thought a woman on her own fair game.

She knew he was alive simply because she was not told otherwise. Once she received a letter from him.

'How are you, darlingest?' He was fighting fit, he said. Sorrel was surprised the censor had not blacked out the first word of Toby's favourite description of himself.

Now and again she telephoned the Priory and she and George Martyn exchanged non-existent news. Grace never answered the telephone.

'We miss you, my dear child. Come and stay when you get some leave.'

He always said that.

At Lee she managed to make a life of her own. She was a fully fledged officer accustomed to the small unmistakable signs of authority. To the responsibility of being in charge of other young women. She learned that Wren officers found it easier to be more or less teetotal; there were continuous offers of drinks, the Navy's way either of being hospitable or indicating the man was attracted, or both. She became impervious to heavy-handed compliments, whistles from ratings and occasionally to obscene innuendo. She was dedicated to her job. And thank heaven, it was difficult.

At Lee-on-Solent there was a section of the Fleet Air Arm

which trained pilots in the tricky job of dropping torpedoes. Sorrel's new task was to be in charge of a glorified Link Trainer with the daunting name of the Torpedo Attack Teacher, affectionately known as TAT. The machine was in a dome where she sat high up in a control box, while the trainee pilot was in a model plane where various weathers were simulated: sun and rain, thick fog, dark night. When he pressed a button which would fire the torpedo, Sorrel could plot in her eyrie the angle of the shot, and tell if he would have hit or missed his target.

Her mechanic was a massive Canadian, over six foot four with shoulders like an ox, called Miller and known as Dusty. Never had a man suited his nickname less: everything about Dusty was scrubbed, from his enormous hands to his square gleaming teeth. Naval officers sent on the course, particularly those who'd seen active service, were not best pleased when they went to the TAT for the first time and saw a pretty young Wren at the controls. One officer, much decorated, who had been in action off Cape Matapan when the navy sank three Italian cruisers and two destroyers, took one look at Sorrel and walked out again. He'd be damned if a woman was going to tell him his business. He had to come back later and Sorrel, charitably, scarcely caught his eye.

The men in the navy had varying attitudes to her and her job. They were gallant and sexy or stonily resentful. A third attitude came mostly from the NCOs, and from Dusty. He was protective. There was nothing he wouldn't do for her. He loomed up if there was the mildest argument with a pilot, ready to speak for her, defend her, simply to be there, all fifteen stone of him. But there was only one thing from which Sorrel needed protection, and that was fate.

The war was changing. The Germans, victorious in 1942 when Toby sat at his parents' table lauding them and decrying the British, were in retreat. In May the desert war, after two years, was over at last. General von Arnim surrendered with 125,000 German troops. Almost as many Italians were taken prisoner. The war had cost the two enemy countries almost a million soldiers dead or imprisoned.

In England a sober but nervous hope had begun to rise and

in July the news broke. The Allies had invaded Sicily; British, American and Canadian troops under General Eisenhower, and masses of ships, were taking part. Everybody at the base, from the commander to ratings peeling bucketfuls of potatoes, talked about nothing else.

'Sicily's invaded. We'll be in Rome next!'

Sorrel telephoned the Priory that evening and George Martyn said at once, 'Are you thinking what I'm thinking, Sorrel?'

'I believe so.'

'Our boy must be there. The landings are going well, little opposition from the Italians along the coast.' George spoke with his usual optimism. 'Yes, I feel he's there. Sorrel?'

'Yes,' she said in a low voice. His vitality helped her. A little.

'Will you do us a favour? Of course Toby will write to you sooner than to us. If you hear from him, do you promise to let us know?'

'*Of course.*'

'I hope we see you soon. In the meantime, God bless and keep you.'

It did not sound like George.

But it was weeks before she heard from Toby. Montgomery's troops were past Catania, the Americans had reached Palermo and the town was a wreck from intensive bombing. She was inured to knowing and hearing nothing of her husband while Wren friends opened their letters, their faces pink from excitement, reading them too fast, talking and laughing at the good news. Sorrel accepted with a new hardness that her state of mind was what she'd taken on the day she married Toby. She did not lose her love, but she did not indulge it. She dared not. And perhaps it diminished a little or at least lost some of its awful power.

She wasn't ready when the letter came at last. It was on the usual single sheet, thin as India paper, and it was short enough.

Your wonderful letters come in little batches,
sometimes three at a time. It is like getting months of
pay all in one lump, and I know I mustn't spend them

too fast. I eke them out. I can't tell you the treat of reading them, imagining your life.

But you scarcely mention Evendon, and I wonder if maybe your leaves have been cancelled or perhaps you gave up some for a friend. It would be like you!! But do see the parents, darlingest, if you can.

You must be wondering how we are and the answer is we had a v. enjoyable sea voyage, got brown as berries and all look pretty fit. Do you remember a vac. my mother and I took during my Sandhurst time? She walked me nearly off my feet. It's just like that and I could do with my old riding boots.

Well, darlingest, Reveille has just sounded. Don't forget me. Your very loving husband.

Toby

Sorrel re-read the letter, puzzling over the reference to a holiday with Grace. It was unlike him to write about time spent with his mother. Sorrel knew that Grace's demand for his attention had embarrassed him; she had dug up the past when Toby was at home like an archaeologist convinced she could turn dry bones into warm flesh.

On the way to the Wrens' mess, by good luck Sorrel met a friend of hers. Anthony English was sandy, balding, a lieutenant too old for his rank, married and unambitious. He was a good officer, and she thought he must also be a good husband and father. He and Sorrel liked each other. Sometimes he invited her to the officers' mess for a drink; sometimes she returned the compliment and Anthony drank a sherry with her. The courtesy rule was strict – either way you had to be invited.

This time Anthony spoke first. 'Come and have a drink with me, Sorrel.'

The naval officers' mess had the atmosphere of a London club. It was painted a dark and dignified green, smelled of polish and cigarettes, and there were always half a dozen officers reading the papers or writing letters or quietly chatting. Anthony signed for the sherries.

'Cheers.'

'Tony, you do the censoring, don't you?'
'For my sins. Why do you ask?'
'Do people ever write in code?'
'My dear Sorrel, what are you saying? Have you discovered a nest of Quislings?'
'I don't mean real code. I mean in the letters you censor, do the ratings use allusions?'
'I'll say.'
'Now you think I'm talking about sex,' she said, laughing irritably. 'I'm not making myself clear. I have just had a letter from Toby. You know he's overseas. Well, his letter is about *boots*. He has never written to me about a boot before, it doesn't make sense. I'm sure it's code. Do you think he's referring to the map of Italy?'
Anthony shook his head.
'You think I'm dotty, I suppose,' she said.
'Of course I don't. I am disapproving of your husband. They shouldn't do it. And they constantly do.'
'You mean he *is* telling me where he is.'
'Of course. Every schoolboy knows Italy is shaped like a boot. He's in the invasion, Sorrel.'
She took it in.
'Let's drink to him,' said Anthony English.
She waited until after dinner when she had the chance to telephone the Priory. This time it was Grace who answered.
'Lady Martyn? It's me, Sorrel. I've had a letter from Toby.'
'So have we.'
Ignoring the competitive tone, Sorrel asked whether Grace and Toby had once spent a holiday together.
There was a metallic laugh.
'What on earth do you mean? We've spent hundreds of holidays together.'
'Did he write about one specific holiday in his letter?'
'One specific . . . I don't know what you're talking about.'
'In his letter to me he said did I remember a holiday you and he spent while he was still at Sandhurst and you nearly walked him off his feet. I don't understand what he means and I wonder if you do.'

The silence was so long that Sorrel thought she had been cut off.

'Lady Martyn, are you still there?'

'Of course I am. Toby and I had holidays in Cornwall and the Isle of Wight. He always said I walked him off his feet. It was a joke.'

'He wrote about something else. His old riding boots.'

'Does he want us to send them? How can we, when – '

Grace wasn't being her clever self.

'Lady Martyn, I think it's another hint. First the holiday. Then a boot. Italy is shaped like a boot.'

'*Taormina!* Of course. We went there in '37. Good God, why didn't the censor – '

'No, no, he wrote nothing that could be understood by anybody but you.'

The sentence went home. Grace agreed. Yes, they'd spent three weeks in Sicily and had a magnificent time . . . she went on for a while and Sorrel listened dutifully and then asked if Grace could tell Lord Martyn.

'I'll ring him at his office. Sicily!' said Grace, the triumph and remembering gone. She gave a shuddering sigh.

As the year dragged to its close, Sorrel felt a revulsion at spending her leave at Evendon. She would soon be due for her five days and knew where her duty lay. But she didn't want to sit in the beautiful old house where she would imagine him coming into the room, or constantly hear his stuttering laugh. She recoiled at the idea that Evie would give her the same bedroom, and she'd sleep in the bed where Toby had lain with her. On the last night he had made love to her differently, pushing her face downwards and mounting her as if he were riding The Chief. She didn't want to think about that either.

Dion Fulford came into her mind sometimes. But love and loyalty had hardened against him a second time and he no longer interested her. She would be free of the accident of meeting him if she could avoid Evendon.

Christmas at Lee went by merrily; it was prankish and noisy and officers lined up to kiss the Wrens under mistletoe drawing-pinned over the door of the mess. In chapel the voices of men singing Christmas hymns in unison was so beautiful. Sorrel wished they did not make her feel weak. Where was the Spartan wife Toby had left behind?

Her leave was due in the New Year and she was still trying to decide what to do with it and how to avoid an invitation from a fellow Wren, kindly and dull and somebody she scarcely knew, when she received an unexpected letter from Toby's aunt Dorothy in London.

> Have you quite forgotten your promise to come to town? Tons to do and lots of Yanks around. When's your next leave? Come and stay. Call me. Affectionately,
>
> Dot

Dorothea Martyn, twice divorced and now using her maiden name, lived in Mayfair. She had been one of the half dozen guests at the wedding, very few of the Martyns' friends and relatives could manage to come to Hampshire at short notice. Sorrel had been too dazed to remember much, the wedding reception had been a champagne-misted blur. But she did vaguely recall a pretty fair-haired woman called Aunt Dot who had told Sorrel she must stay with her when she was on leave; Toby had accepted on Sorrel's behalf. Later he'd said Sorrel must definitely visit her.

'Such good value. Much better than staying on your own at the Curzon Club if you want to go to town.'

'When you're not around, I can't exactly invite myself.'

'What's all this girlish hesitation? You usually go at things you want like a bull at a gate.'

'What a disgusting description, Toby Martyn.'

'Well, a very pretty *young* bull. But you do. Look how you charged into the Priory when you didn't know my father from Adam.'

'I thought about it a lot before I did.'

'I don't believe you. And I like you charging. It shows guts. Besides, Dot is my aunt, Pop's sister, so you are related to her now.'

To Toby the blood tie was a universal passport to hospitality and affection. Married, Sorrel now had two parents whereas before she had been an orphan. She also had an aunt waiting to be devoted to her. The Priory was Sorrel's home whenever she wished to go there and Dot Martyn's place in London was to be the same.

It had been during that evening, one of the two of their passionate leave, as Toby called it, that he'd talked about money.

'I've fixed for some cash to march into your little bank account, darlingest.'

'But you musn't give me any of your precious pay.'

'You misunderstand,' he said, laughing. 'I'm talking about the allowance Father used to give your mother, which he then transferred to you. Now he's paying it to me.'

'Why?'

'Because you're my wife, stupid. Haven't you learned that already?' An embrace. 'So,' he continued, loosening his arms, speaking tenderly, 'I've fixed with Coutts that you now get the monthly allowance from me. With your army wife's allowance as well. What's amusing you?'

'The idea of your father stopping my money and paying it into your bank. And then you paying it back to me. It's like Alice in Wonderland.'

'You're missing the point again,' he said indulgently. He wore a dark blue silk dressing gown and, freshly bathed, was doing his hair with two ivory backed brushes, almost polishing the hair he brushed so firmly. 'It's because you are my wife. My responsibility. A Martyn.'

She had sat admiring his straight soldier's back, handsome neck, the shorn hair which left a sheen like velvet on the back of his well-shaped head. She thought of the scar on his arm and the piece of shrapnel in his shoulder.

'Toby.'

'Darlingest?'

'Did you ever find out why your father gave my mother the money? She was quite secretive, poor Mother. She hated me asking things, and shut up like a clam if I tried to get her to tell.

When I asked your father, all he said was he and Mother were some kind of distant cousins.'

'I know. He mentioned it to me. A great-grandmother of yours married a Martyn. Or was it the other way round?'

He put the brushes meticulously back in the leather case. 'I can understand how he felt when your mother was widowed. As I said just now about Aunt Dot. It's a family thing.'

The letter to Sorrel from Aunt Dot proved him to be right. And it was timely. It gave her an alibi to herself, she need not go to Evendon after all. She knew Toby would have preferred her to go to his home, but Toby was far away and she had a kind of liberty.

When she telephoned Dorothea Martyn, a voice of lively youthfulness said what fun and asked for dates and times.

At Lee for days the country had been more or less submerged in a clean white mist. But when Sorrel arrived in London, it was fog as black as coal, and as stifling as breathing poisoned gas. As a Londoner she didn't mind, she knew the fogs of old. She made her way out of the gloomy veiled station to the Underground. How the town was changing, she thought. She hadn't noticed its transformation on the night and the day she had been here after her wedding. Being insanely happy did something to one's brains. She only recalled dancing in the Dorchester and making love afterwards. The rest of the time was blanked out as if she'd been under an anaesthetic.

Now in the crowded compartment of the Underground she saw that the London world she'd known with her mother, respectable, reserved and gloved, had vanished. This worn-out fog-bewitched city wasn't English any more. Polish soldiers talked to each other in their incomprehensible language, short dark-eyed Frenchmen stood beside South Africans as blond as Swedes, or thin serious Norwegians. Leaving the train at Green Park she travelled up the escalator behind a Czech soldier whose olive-skinned face was like an actor's. And everywhere, everywhere, the Americans. There couldn't have been so many Americans together in a country away from their own since the United States began.

Out in the street was obscurity, buses materialising and

disappearing, their lights only tiny crosses gleaming through paper glued to headlamps. She crossed Piccadilly expecting to be run over and walked on through the choking dark, by blackened houses sliced in half, and tanks marked Static Water. Once she saw a ragged coat hanging on a ruined wall – as if a man killed in the blitz had stayed unburied, still pressed against what had been his home.

She found her way to Curzon Street and passed an ivy-cloaked house, the Officers' Club. On an impulse, Sorrel went up the steps and through the swing doors. At the reception desk an old porter Sorrel knew, his name was Brierley, was being harassed by two handsome girls in Free French uniform. They demanded bedrooms. He assured them there were no rooms vacant. French persistence and English stubbornness had met head on. The girls looked furious. They turned away to talk to each other for a moment, and Sorrel took the chance to interrupt.

'Good afternoon, Brierley. My name is Martyn. I am a member but not staying at present, which must be a relief to you.'

She smiled with disgraceful English fellow feeling, sharing a smug disapproval of the greedy French. The old man looked at her gratefully.

'I only popped in to ask if you happen to have seen Third Officer Margaret Reilly at all? She stays here sometimes.'

He said, why yes, Third Officer Reilly was quite a regular and as a matter of fact was staying tonight. She was out at present. Did ma'am wish to leave a message?

Sorrel did. She was pleased at the thought of seeing Margaret again. For all her friendly nature, she had no close companions at Lee. Her senior officer was rather jealous of her, and the others were of the giggling kind. Sorrel, married, felt quite old when she listened to them.

While she scribbled a note she heard the Free French go into the attack.

'You found a room for '*er*!'

The poor porter denied it and they did not believe her. Adding Aunt Dot's telephone number to the letter, Sorrel thanked him and left, French arguments fading as she emerged into the fog. It was months since she and Margaret had taken their commissions at Greenwich. Margaret had not been able to come to the wedding; she had sent two presents. An electric iron and a copy of *The Forsyte Saga*.

Dot Martyn's small house, a few streets from the Curzon Club, was near Shepherd Market. Sorrel located a cobbled mews entered under an arch which had vanished into the gloom. With the help of her torch she discovered the house, a mews cottage which had once been a stable. Ringing the bell dubiously, she rather wished she had not come.

When the door opened, she could see nothing.

'I can just make out that naval hat,' said a voice. 'Don't fall over the mat. It's brought down more pilots than the German ack-ack.'

With the door safely shut, Dot Martyn switched on the lights and exclaimed, 'Welcome!'

Toby's aunt was small, slim, expensively dressed, and beautiful. She led the way up a steep stair into a room which ran the full length of what had been a loft storing hay and corn for carriage horses. The room suited its owner. It was full of elegance and soft colours, a marquetry chest of drawers inlaid with flower patterns, graceful Regency chairs, a yellow silk-covered easy chair, round mirrors to give sparkle and a divan heaped with taffeta cushions of French blue. The lights on this dark afternoon shone golden, but were blurred by traces of fog creeping through chinks in windows. A photograph Sorrel had never seen before was on a small table. Toby was looking at her. He'd been romanticised again.

'I had that one taken specially for me,' said Dot, slightly pushing it so that Sorrel could see it straight on. 'Lenare's the only photographer who can do soldiers. Doesn't Toby look fierce?'

She poured some drinks.

'He doesn't get that from us, you know, neither from his father nor me. But we did have a great-grandfather who fought bare-knuckled for enormous sums. The less said about *him* the better. Take that chair, it's the most comfortable. I can't tell you how glad I am you managed to come.'

Sorrel smiled and made polite replies.

'I adore your uniform,' continued Dot, sitting down and crossing thin silk-covered legs. 'Clever of the navy to make you girls look like a lot of Lady Nelsons. Admiral Parry was here last week and he said Wrens have a tremendous time, the officers falling like ninepins and the girls fending them off. What's that new joke, up with the lark and to bed with a Wren? I hope *you* are fending them off for darling Toby's sake. Are you a positive Penelope at her loom?'

'Of course. I spin and spin.'

Dot's chatter was interrupted every few minutes by the telephone. She sprang up, had a quick laughing conversation clearly with a man, and then returned to her guest. Dot, it seemed, was that enchanting insect, the social butterfly. Sorrel had rarely met one until now and never had one as a friend. She was impressed by a woman who looked and behaved as Dot Martyn did – who was slender and fair and younger than her brother in looks (one could not guess her age) and several stone lighter. But she resembled him just the same. She had the scent of charm and money.

Sorrel's spirits rose. After months of work and half-widowhood she was to be taken under the butterfly wing. Dot rang off from a third telephone call.

'Shall you wear uniform at the Bagatelle?'

It seemed they were going to dance at one of London's most famous places. Dot had provided some men, she said.

'Have you a dress you specially like? Or what about us going to Harrods to get something new? My present. I didn't give you a thing for your wedding.'

'An enormous cheque.'

'That doesn't count, and anyway, Toby got it.'

Sorrel said, sighing, that she had no clothing coupons.

'Pooh, don't worry about that. Friends keep showering them on me,' said Dot, scrabbling in a tiny embroidered handbag amd producing a bookful.

Taking a taxi in the fog, Dot and her visitor went to

Knightsbridge. Dot bought her two of the prettiest dresses Sorrel had ever seen, one black velvet, the other the colour of a pink orchid. The woman in the dress department knew Dot, and choosing the clothes was fun. Dot produced sixteen coupons and paid for the dresses which were packed in reverent tissue paper. Another taxi took them, at a crawl, back to the mews.

During the next few days Sorrel was swept into a new and exclusive world in which Dot was queen. It was a world of men in uniform. American officers arrived, bearing gifts as a matter of course. They came for morning coffee and then escorted the girls, as they called them, to luncheon at the Dorchester or the Ritz. This was followed by tea at Grosvenor House where the skating rink, an enormous space below ground, had been turned into a club for officers and there was now a dance floor resembling an enormous lake. Both Dot and Sorrel were claimed by one young man after another. Dot danced, as she did everything, perfectly.

Returning to the mews, the two bathed and changed.

'*Vogue* says "come in and have a bath" is the new social gesture,' said Dot. 'And it's better than gallons of gin. I hope you've noticed that the water is measured?'

In clear bold script, painted black on the inside of the jade green bath, were the words '*Five Inches!*'

'A camouflage guy did it for me, isn't it cute? If the King and Queen can bath in so little, we certainly can.'

In short wartime silk dresses, fur jackets (Dot lent Sorrel a white mink) and a good deal of unobtainable French scent they were collected by the same men or new relays. American. English. Sometimes Polish – Dot loved Poles for their formality and fierce sexual reputation.

On the second evening after a day when the fog had blessedly lifted, the wailing voice of the siren sounded while they were getting dressed.

'Botheration,' said Dot, coming into Sorrel's tiny bedroom, radiant in bluish green and greenish blue, 'We were booked for the Mirabelle but now we'll have to switch to Hatchettes. It's the *only* place in a raid. During the blitz we danced there every night, and the management provided eiderdowns. When it got to around five in the morning, we all slept on the dance floor.'

Putting her head on one side, she surveyed Sorrel who was wearing the orchid pink dress.

'That colour's just right. I've always had an eye for colour. You're not at all like your mother, are you? I've never talked to you about Lilian. Poor Sorrel, it was awful, wasn't it? I was shattered. But I can see you're over it now because you're married. It makes all the difference when one's in love.'

The front door bell rang. Dot heard it between the thunder of the guns. 'That must be Randy and Buzz. Let them them in, will you, darling? Tell them I have to alter the reservations. You and I will talk about your mother another time. She was a friend of mine when we were girls.'

Gunfire seemed to shake the ground when Sorrel opened the front door. Two young men, both large, came into the blacked-out hallway.

'Is that Dot? Can't see,' said one of the visitors, waving a pencil-light from a torch.

Sorrel shut the door, switched on the light and introduced herself. The young men, raising their voices above the gunfire, shouted that they had a cab waiting. And almost at once Dot tripped down the stairs, calling a welcome and filling the tiny house with her scent.

It was Sorrel's first raid. By chance and certainly not by choice, for Lilian Scott had been indifferent about the bombing, she had taken her daughter to Sussex in the late summer of 1940 just before the London blitz. One of Lilian's bridge-playing friends invited them to stay in her pretentious house in Aldwick. Sorrel remembered the months of the Battle of Britain as the most boring of her life, except for the afternoon when she had watched a dog-fight over the sea. It had been Aldwick which finally sent her to volunteer for the Wrens months before her call-up. Now here she was in a raid. In a famous restaurant underground.

Distant thuds shook the dance floor and the band played 'Moonlight becomes you, It goes with your hair.'

The two Americans were pleasant and rather shy. Randy

was a pilot in the American navy, he came from Texas and spoke like a cowboy in the movies. The other man, Buzz, was in the air force. Sorrel noticed that his accent was very different from his friend's, but that was all. She had no idea which accent belonged where in that huge foreign country.

'Randy sure hates the raids,' said Buzz, taking Sorrel in his arms. They began to dance. Across the crowded floor Sorrel saw Dot, her lovely face melting and smiling as she looked up at the handsome dark man with her.

'He doesn't look at all nervous.'

'He never shows it. But he's sick to his stomach when a siren goes. And when he flies it's worse, poor guy.'

'But how awful! That's *real* courage.'

He was touched.

'You nervous, Ma'am?'

'I don't know. I've never been in a raid before.'

'Then you're not,' he said steering her through the dancers. 'Nerves can be hell. I guess you don't have them.'

Sorrel's partner was an odd-looking man. His eyes were so narrow they could have been Japanese; his face pale and pudgy, he stood very straight, without the casual American grace. It was his voice which was alluring. He spoke in a soft drawl, exactly like the men and girls had spoken in the film of *Gone With The Wind*. His home, he said, was in Alabama. His manner matched the accent, it was a caricature of the Old South. When Sorrel spoke, he listened with courtly attention. If she made the weakest joke, he shook with laughter. Holding her in the dance, his hands scarcely seemed to touch her.

'I'm told you're married,' he said. 'That must break a lot of hearts.'

'Dot says I must be like Penelope at her loom.'

'Come again, Ma'am?'

Sorrel said Penelope, the wife of Ulysses. She was sure he remembered that while Ulysses was at the siege of Troy, Penelope was driven mad by suitors. All she did was spin. She told them when the web was finished she would choose one of the suitors, but every night she secretly undid it and started all over again the next day.

'Oh yes. Sure.' His big ugly face was respectful; he hadn't a notion what she was talking about.

The All Clear sounded at two in the morning, and a burst of laughter broke right through the restaurant like a wave. Everybody looked at everybody else, enjoying the shared courage. They were still alive, weren't they? And brave into the bargain.

Sorrel was unaccustomed to very late nights and was still deeply asleep when the telephone rang next morning. Dot, wrapped in a silk kimono, came yawning into her room.

'It's for you. A woman.'

'I'm so sorry it woke you, Dot!'

'Friend of yours?' said Dot with another yawn. Then, ever social, 'Ask her around.'

Margaret Reilly sounded as if she had just emerged glowing from a cold bath.

'Hi! Long time no see!'

'Hello, Margaret, it is nice to hear your voice.'

'I was over the moon when I got your message. There's somebody here who's dying to meet you. Shall we say coffee at the club in half an hour?'

When Sorrel weakly said she couldn't manage to get to Curzon Street until lunchtime, Margaret was as disappointed as a child.

'Make it 12.30 and not a minute later. You'll understand when you get here.'

Sorrel rang off and tottered back to bed. Dot had already disappeared. Silence fell on the little Mayfair house where two women worn out with enjoyment slept soundly. In other streets, other houses were still burning and civil defence workers dug for survivors.

Sorrel was over half an hour late for her appointment and when she left the mews she had to run. Through the swing doors she found the hall crowded with men and girls in the uniforms of the three services, the flashes on shoulders spelling everything from parachute corps to the names of countries – Norway, India. Sorrel looked hurriedly round, perhaps Margaret had not waited for her.

Then through a gap in the crowd she suddenly saw her friend. Margaret was in a corner by the staircase with a man in American air force uniform. She was looking up at him, he down at her. They were completely still. They had an intent, trance-like look as if they couldn't drag their eyes away from each other. They didn't say a word. The man was startlingly handsome, with the sort of looks which make women stare. As Sorrel watched he took Margaret by the shoulders – it was obvious even at a distance that he longed to kiss her. But he did not. There they stood, staring, until he turned and left her, passing close to Sorrel on his way out.

She pushed her way across the hall. Margaret had not seen her and when Sorrel touched her arm she started, her whole face blazing. Then she saw who it was and said with strained heartiness, 'Where did you get to? You've just missed Gareth. He waited as long as he could but he's had to go to the embassy now.'

'I think I saw him. Recognised him from your photograph. Fair and tall?'

'Very.'

'He looks nice, I do wish I hadn't been so late.'

'Yes, he is and you were. Come and have a drink.'

Margaret was visibly recovering. In a room humming with talk, the two girls sat down and Margaret repeated that it was a great pity Sorrel had missed him, 'I so wanted you to meet.' She began to describe Gareth all over again, forgetting she'd said much the same thing in Greenwich. She talked of his exalted connections, the family in Pennsylvania, and how she had been introduced to Mr Winant, the American ambassador.

'Mr Winant is so handsome. Much more than he looks in the papers. Dark and clean-cut; Gareth says he reminds him of a portrait of Abraham Lincoln. The same extraordinary eyes, brilliant under thick eyebrows.'

She had spent an evening with the ambassador, just Gareth and Winant and herself. 'It was so homey.' They'd eaten smoked salmon sent by a friend of his in Scotland, and sat in a study 'just bursting with books' listening to jazz. Late in the evening Donald Hagan, a three-star general recently arrived from the Pentagon, joined them for coffee.

Margaret's conversation was dazzling and dazzled. She appeared to have arrived where she felt she belonged, moving naturally in exalted circles. She did have the grace to say she had been sorry not to come to Sorrel's wedding and she asked briefly about Toby. But when Sorrel mentioned Alamein she frowned. 'Of course you know the battle would never have been won if it hadn't been for the Americans,' she said. 'The Germans kept back their best troops, they thought the Yanks would attack from the rear.'

When Sorrel and Margaret had been friends at Littleport, Margaret's passion had been her Irishness. She wore the shamrock and flew the green and gold flag in her conversation. Through the bathroom door, Sorrel used to hear her sing:

> Hail glorious Saint Patrick, dear saint of our Isle,
> On us thy poor children bestow a sweet smile,
> And now thou art high in the mansions above
> On Erin's green valleys look down in thy love.
> On Erin's green valleys. . .
> On Erin's green valleys. . .

Sorrel had liked the tune. Now the same partisan stood like the beautiful girl at the start of Columbia pictures, her figure wrapped in the Stars and Stripes.

'You've got to meet him, Sorrel, you'll love him. Everybody does. We'll take you to the embassy canteen. Canned turkey and cranberry sauce.'

Half an hour of her friend's lively company was enough for Sorrel, tired from lack of sleep. When Margaret said she must go, and that she had no time for luncheon, Sorrel was selfishly pleased.

She walked back slowly to Dot's house. It was that blank space of time, early London afternoon. She was thinking about Margaret. How talkative she was, nervous, too strong and more beautiful than ever. Sorrel had scarcely spoken a word during the time they'd been together. When she remembered the brief look she had had at Gareth van Doren, she understood Margaret. I suppose Byron's out of the picture now. Margaret's in love with somebody very grand and it suits her. She's settled to love only one man. High time too.

Sorrel's leave was almost totally American. Polish and English officers appeared sometimes, but it was the United States who monopolised Dot. She greeted them with open-hearted hospitality. She had a good deal of grace and a poise that nothing could shatter. Sorrel admired her. She admired Dot's energy, her trick of making the things she dealt with appear, perhaps they were, the acme of fashion. She was the centre of an exciting unmistakably wealthy world. She lived in style in a country where people queued for four ounces of chocolate. Her war work was at the mews house where the Americans could relax and feel at home in an alien country, returning – with admiration – Dot's own gifts. They crowned her queen, and she accepted that.

The last evening of leave was spent in the usual way. Two new Americans, both marines in smart uniform, came to collect the girls. The quartet went to a suitable Hollywood movie: *Yankee Doodle Dandy* starring James Cagney whose sexy eyes, dancing feet and pugnacious face were Dot's favourites of all. During the film an air raid warning sounded. The announcement was flashed on the screen. A few people in the audience left but Dot's party didn't budge. After the film the quartet walked to Grosvenor House in the dark, the men giving their arms to the girls.

'We're going to the new deep shelter restaurant,' Dot called out to Sorrel. '*Vogue* says it's all the rage and defies the sirens.'

During supper, while the band was playing 'Kiss Me Once and Kiss Me Twice and Kiss Me Once Again', the conductor somehow blended in the level bars of the All Clear.

Sorrel thought Dot looked rather white in the face when they collected their coats. Pulling on her sable jacket she said sharply, 'Hurry up. Or somebody will grab our taxi.'

Sorrel did not say that it was easy enough to walk round the corner to the mews. Dot never walked anywhere.

She did not invite her guests in for a final drink, and said goodnight to them repeating that if they didn't hurry they'd lose their taxi. But the marines stood like sheepdogs until the girls were safely indoors.

Sorrel heard the cab drive away. She wondered what the men talked about on their way back to their US club. Dot? Herself? Probably nothing about her; the wedding ring seemed to affect Americans.

Both Sorrel and Dot slept very late again and when Dot eventually woke her, coming in with coffee, she sat down on Sorrel's bed. Without make-up her face was the colour of paper. Her beautiful hair, clouded fair and worn in a circle like a halo, was a mess. She looked forty-five or more.

Sorrel sat up guiltily, saying that she should have made the coffee. She was wearing the nightdress Toby's coupons had bought for her two-day honeymoon, it was tied on each shoulder with enormous blue satin bows. Dot poured the coffee, which was too strong and too black.

'So you're off this morning.'

'Back to base, alas. I'm so grateful. I've had a wonderful time.'

Dot gave a shrug as if to say 'don't bother'. She put her hand flat under her chin, as if doing so removed the wrinkles in her neck.

'Something I've meant to ask you. Toby's money does come through all right. You are okay for cash, I hope?'

'Dot, you are kind. Of course I am. Wren officers are paid quite well, and there's the army allowance.'

'As the wife of a major,' said Dot mockingly. 'So you're pretty flush. You should save.'

'I've never thought of that. I suppose I should,' said Sorrel from politeness. It came into her mind that with money as the subject, at last there was a chance to find out something which perplexed her. George Martyn's sister would surely know the answer to an unimportant but annoying mystery.

'Could I ask you something? It's about money, as a matter of fact.'

'Ask away.'

'Did you know Lord Martyn used to give my mother a monthly allowance?'

'Oh, *did* he?'

Dot's eyes were slightly brighter. 'I often suspected as much but wasn't certain. So. What happened when poor Lilian was killed? I suppose the money stopped.'

'That's just it, your brother began to pay me instead. Not as much as he gave Mother, but quite a lot. He's so kind. But I never understood it. What's the money *about*?'

'Did you ask him?'

'Oh yes. He said he and Mother's family were vaguely related. Fourth cousins or something. And when my father died and Mother was left nearly penniless – father's firm paid no pension – he stepped into the breach.'

'Very generous of him.'

There *is* more, thought Sorrel.

'You don't believe we are related, do you?'

'I'm afraid not.'

'Somehow I didn't either. I don't know why it seemed a tall story.'

Dot looked at her sardonically.

'But nicely told by George, no doubt.'

Sorrel had the grace to look embarrassed and said hurriedly that she'd been astonished and grateful. But puzzled just the same.

'However,' Dot was still dry, 'you accepted the money and quite right too. You'd have been a fool to refuse. George likes to give and would have been offended if you hadn't let him. How amusing.'

'You're laughing at me.'

'Am I?'

'Dot. You know something. I wish you'd tell.'

'Perhaps I shouldn't,' said Dot. 'And perhaps I will. Not that my precious brother ever told me, and I'm certain he hasn't said a word to Toby or to Grace. He'd never tell them anything which wasn't to his credit. He knows when to brush things under the carpet and shove a heavy piece of furniture to keep the carpet good and down, if you see what I mean.'

'I don't think I do.'

Dot put down her cup. She looked at Sorrel, and turned

something over in her mind. Perhaps it was the cruel morning light showing the girl in all her youth, fresh as a rose or a daisy. Perhaps it was an old grudge against her brother, or maybe only the blue satin bows which made up her mind. She said suddenly, 'This room is cold. We need some heat.'

The gas fire made a comforting roar. She returned to the bed where Sorrel sat up, interested, expectant, innocent. To the girl it was a relief that the questions were going to be answered at last. The mystery dated from the time before she'd known Toby, from the very day when she'd been given the blackened handbag. It was old and stale now, that mystery, and belonged to her dead mother. But it had never quite stopped teasing her. Had the money been paid because of a love affair? Or some kind of debt which Lord Martyn owed her father? She wondered if her feeling for Lord Martyn had never been warm because she had not believed the first important answer he gave her, one winter afternoon.

'It isn't exactly a romance,' said Dot, lighting a Lucky Strike cigarette and snapping shut the silver lighter engraved with her name. 'You know your father used to work for George in the dim and distant?'

'Your brother said they were colleagues.'

'Polite of him. Your father was an accountant as you know, but I wonder if your mother told you how brilliant he was. Quite brilliant. He once said to me, aeons ago, that he could make figures do anything he liked. He said they were a team of dancers and he could line them up or set them jigging or make them form circles or separate into twos and threes. He said they were so entertaining. Did Toby tell you how my brother became rich and earned that title he's so proud of?'

'Toby said it was war work. Something to do with supply.'

Dot giggled. The lines on either side of her eyes made little fans.

'Didn't you ask anything else? How funny you are.'

She laughed at the awful disinterest of the young. They wore an impenetrable armour called indifference. The worst war ever waged in the history of the world had swept its glittering scythe through the grass, cutting down hundreds upon hundreds of young men, leaving them to rot in mud or hang turning to carrion on the rusting barbed wire. To this girl with the ribbons it was merely history. It was not even important to learn that her husband's father had profiteered from the slaughter. He'd made his fortune from the cotton mills he'd been clever enough to buy, God knows how or with what. His energy and foresight, his charm, oh George had charm all right, won him contracts; and George's mills and factories poured out the uniforms for soldiers in Palestine and Mesopotamia. They'd died wearing her brother's cotton khaki while he sat on his backside and became a lord. When she thought of it, which was rarely, she hated her brother for making money while her first, her real lover, lay among the corpses on the Somme.

'That's right,' she said, 'George manufactured uniforms by the million, made a packet and got Sir'd for it into the bargain. After the war in the early 1920s he went from strength to strength. A lot of money was being made exporting to the Empire *and* on the Stock Exchange. We all thought it was going on for ever. But my brother opened his mouth too wide. He was greedy, even as a boy, and I suppose success made him worse. There were some very fishy dealings in the City and apparently he sailed too close to the wind. A man I knew in Lloyd's warned me, and I managed to sell in time. But your father, Sorrel, sailed further than George. Maybe he'd caught my brother's gluttony because he'd been using the same spoon. I don't know. The unpleasant fact is he was mixed up in a very big swindle. George had employed him on and off for years and just saved him from prison. I suppose he didn't want to see him go down. Then Frank Scott died very suddenly, and apparently George began shelling out to Lilian. He is generous. One has to admit that.'

There was a pause.

She patted Sorrel's shoulder.

'I've upset you. But you did ask. And I always believe people should know the truth, it is so patronising to lie to them. There's nothing to look so woebegone about,' she continued.

'Lots of people narrowly escaped gaol. One of my friends last year had something worse happen. She had a crazy affair with a pilot, they used to stay at the Dorchester for weekends and she always paid. Told him she was rich. Secretly she'd been selling her sister's jewellery. The police traced some of the missing stuff and her sister tried to stop them arresting her but it was no good. The poor thing is in Holloway. Do have a bath and cheer up.'

10

It was after this when she returned to a Lee-on-Solent transformed by sparkling snow and sharp sun, like old post-cards of Switzerland, that Sorrel had a new kind of heartache. When she was not longing for Toby and wondering painfully about him, mute, anxious, she thought of what Dot had told her. She only realised how much she had treasured the memory of her father when she heard a story against him.

She had to believe it. Why should Dot bother to lie? But her father's memory and her own pride were in the mud. She hated to think he was guilty of a crime, her youth recoiled against the picture of her father, humorous and fond and human and self-mocking. It was all smeared now. His sordid crime had somehow become connected with Toby and herself. George Martyn paid them money because of the dirty past. It made her dirty too.

When she saw George Martyn again, heard the story from his own lips, she would throw the money back in his face.

But she had no more leave due. The diamond weeks went by, cold as charity. The milk froze into a white lump, the deserted stretches of the estuary sparkled, hot baths were rare as pearls. Walking to the base from her digs was a question of sliding, sometimes collapsing into snow drifts.

As she'd learned to do in that far-off time when her burden had been remorse over her mother, she worked. She was a teacher-instructor now and she knew she was good at her job. So did her senior officers. Sorrel had become sensitive to the slightest alteration in the sound of the TAT machine, she could detect every change of tune.

One particular conversation with her mechanic recurred.

'Dusty. It's got the wrong note again.'

'You sure?' Dusty never called her Ma'am when they were alone. His democratic Canadian soul rebelled.

'Certain. Could you pop up to the catwalk and look?'

Up would go Dusty, lean over the engine, fiddle, listen, fiddle again, then mutter 'jeepers' and admit that she was right. Sorrel had various duties now. Each pilot when training over the sea carried a camera in the place of torpedoes. A target ship was sent out with the task of taking avoiding action from the plane, zigzagging, doing everything possible while it steamed ahead at full speed. When the pilot pressed the button, a photograph recorded whether his shot would have hit the ship. With the pictures developed, Sorrel plotted the ship's course, the position of the plane, the trajectory of the torpedo. The job was finicky and fascinating, like a game. Often a pilot called to see her, saying gloomily, 'Don't tell me, let me guess. I bloody well missed again.'

Sometimes Sorrel went out to watch the planes, *her* planes, thundering overhead on their way to real assignments. They were Barracudas or Revengers, great lumbering things with torpedoes fixed underneath, looking so heavy and clumsy it seemed miraculous they could take off. Sorrel watched them disappear like a mother swan seeing her brood take flight.

At the end of January the war news was good, the Russians in advance, the Allies moving steadily forward in Italy. There was a sudden shock – a new blitz over London. Alarmed, Sorrel telephoned Aunt Dot.

'Yes, it's the good old bad old days again,' said Dot gaily. 'The first time since those hit and runs when you were here last, remember? This is bigger stuff. Bombs crashing about quite near, and the sky absolutely flashing with them and the guns. Mike and I couldn't resist going into Park Lane for a dekko.'

'You ought to be safe in Hatchettes.'

'Should I? We'll see. Mike and Guy are coming round this morning, we're off to see the crater near St James's Palace.

Apparently a bomb just missed the dear old place. All the windows broken and the clock skew-whiff. Then we shall pop into Fortnum's for luncheon.'

Two days later the news from London was worse. Sorrel rang again.

'What a pet you are. Yes, it was rather dramatic. The sky was a firework display and the shrapnel pelted round like hail. Buzz Alderman's in town. Remember him? He decided to take me to Hatchettes, you'll be relieved to hear. We danced. Then the old routine, eiderdowns on the floor. Nice to sleep next to the American air force!'

The new bombing of London was called the 'little blitz' but did not deserve a diminutive and the news came to Sorrel and her friends from various naval officers and Wrens who went to London that there had been enormous damage. Huge fires had not yet been extinguished because the water pressure was too low. The Luftwaffe destroyed parts of Willesden and Kilburn and nearer home a bomb fell outside the Albert Hall, and several outside the Treasury. In the papers there were photographs of Churchill interestedly studying a gutted building.

'The trouble with the chap is that they can't keep him away from any action,' said Anthony English to Sorrel. 'He shouldn't be given his head. We can't spare him.'

Dot remained up-to-the-minute.

'The crowds in the Underground are enormous. Buzz is helping me to organise cocoa parties for the Green Park lot. Did I tell you he produced a Yankee fleece-lined waterproof for me? Isn't it swell of him?' Even Dot had become slightly transatlantic. 'I look like an Eskimo, it has the most whiskery fur hood.'

In March the 'little blitz' finally ended. The snow had ended too and spring came slowly to the estuary. Sea lavender began to flower, and wading birds picked their way delicately across the mud. In both messes at Lee people talked about the Second Front, the great launch of the Allies into France. Surely it would be soon? Everybody spoke of it and nobody knew a thing.

It wasn't until April that Sorrel was finally given some leave, and then not the five days due to her. The commanding officer of the Wrens had never liked her. Chief Officer Hobson sent for her, to inform her that she must take some leave at once, 'it may be your last chance for the duration.'

There was an excited note in Hobson's voice and Sorrel looked at her questioningly.

'That will be all, Martyn. You can take forty-eight hours and no more.'

George Martyn when telephoned was urbane, apologised for not being able to send the trap, but the pony was needed on the farm. He wondered if she could arrange a train which arrived about the time of his own from London? He was sharing a lift from a local friend. No?

'Well, you'll have a sunny walk at any rate, it looks set fair,' he said. 'Grace will be delighted. It's much too long since we saw you.'

When she had rung off, Sorrel asked herself if she was about to make an enemy of this man. And what would Toby think if she did? He was devoted to his father. But resentment and shame still smouldered when she thought of her own father's dear, dead face.

She walked from the station on a day as lovely as can only happen in the freshest English April. Primroses grew in the overgrown ditches and thick celandines on the verges, their shiny petals like the rays of stars. The air was filled with chirpings and tweetings and an early swallow flew across the sky. But her thoughts were heavy and she did not notice the spring.

There lay the rambling old house, the colour of dark honey tinged with greenish grey. Some crows were cawing in a group of trees. The beds of vegetables spread further now; they were set about in front of the house where lawns had been. A familiar figure was bending over one of the beds. He straightened up as she came towards the house, waved, and began to pick his way across the earth towards her. He was muddier and browner than before.

'Hello, stranger. I thought you were never coming back.' He

held up a very small carrot. 'Pathetic, isn't it? I keep telling Grace they are not ready and need a good two more weeks.'

He might have been seeing her every week by his friendly manner. She was embarrassed and not herself.

'How's the farm going?'

'Oh, big news. We've been allotted some Italian prisoners. They arrive this week.'

'They ought to be a wonderful help.'

'Think so? I keep imagining them standing in the fields singing an aria. *Cavalleria Rusticana.* As for Grace, she's alarmed and believes every rumour.'

Sorrel had forgotten how much she liked him.

'What rumour?'

'Haven't you heard? No Englishwoman is safe within ten miles of an Italian. Do you think she believes they are going to leap on *her*? Sorry, that wasn't very polite.'

She couldn't help laughing.

'It's all right,' he added, discerning a certain nervousness. 'Grace is in the village and, as you know, your father-in-law isn't back until six. Evie won't split if she sees you talking to me. I suppose you wonder how Evie can be civil to me and still worship your husband. Fortunately women are not logical.'

'I wasn't wondering that at all. I do wish you wouldn't trail your coat, hoping I shall step on it. It's a bad habit.'

He stood looking down at her, narrowing his eyes against the sun. She was trim and neat and good-looking and official. A poster for recruiting.

'Now you sound like a Wren officer.'

'Of course I do. That's what I am.'

'And are we going to meet, by any chance?'

'I'm not sure.'

'Yes, you are. You made up your mind when you came into the drive. You're a sudden sort of girl. It's a bad habit.'

She smiled.

'See?' he said. 'I'm ploughing with our horses this afternoon. My favourite job. They seem to understand the work as if they'd known it since they were foals, but before the war they were hauling carts in the London streets. My friend at the

Agricultural Committee got them for us. I have to catch up with the paperwork tonight. What about The Raven tomorrow? Same time and place?'

'If I can.'

'Mm. I shall expect you.'

He went back to the carrot bed and Sorrel walked into the house. There was a patter of claws on stone and Scrap appeared, importantly ready to bark. He bounded up in delight.

'Down, Scrap, down,' said a voice.

Evie must have spied her from a window; but Dion was right, for she was all smiles and welcome.

'Leave at last! It's ages since you came to the Priory. You're getting very thin.' She looked at her in a nannyish way. 'Don't they feed you Wrens properly?'

'Baked beans. Toad in the hole.'

'Not good enough,' said Evie. They went upstairs but not to Sorrel's old room.

'I couldn't put you there this time. Lord Martyn is using it for more stuff from the Croxley. You never saw so many pictures. Piled against the walls and stacked on the bed, all sewn up in canvas bags. Every free inch of space taken. You're in Toby's room. You'll like that.'

Sorrel dreaded it and scarcely looked round when they went in, except at an enormous vase of bluebells on the windowsill.

'I picked them in the woods,' Evie said, going over to rearrange the tall flowers. She added shyly, 'Any more news of the major?'

'Nothing for three months, Evie.'

'His father says he's fighting in Italy.'

'Yes. We believe he is.'

Evie fidgeted with the bluebells.

'They ought to tell us. They ought to let the mail through – it's so dreadful not knowing.'

She sounded like a lover.

When Evie had gone and while Sorrel changed out of uniform she kept telling herself it was better to be in this room than in the one where she and Toby had made love. Surely there memory would be waiting for her like a demon. She supposed that nobody had slept here since Toby had gone; did that explain why she trembled to breathe the very air? The long country days of autumn had passed, the freezing silence of winter dawned and died, and all the time this room had been empty – she was sure of it. The sense of Toby was so strong. Her body ached, she wanted him, wanted him *now*. She was twenty years old and had known passion with only one man. Anywhere but in this room she could keep it at bay, by companions, by the blessed toughness of work, and by a new kind of hardness she had developed. A shell. But now it sprang up from the damped-down fire and burnt her. Her poor defences went up in smoke, crackling like dried paper. She longed for him, lusted for him, remembered him inside her, she let her yearning body suffer. Burn away, she thought, Toby is here.

Wandering round the room, she saw familiar things, all Toby's, all his. School photographs in which he sat, arms pompously folded, grinning among rows of boys. Cricket teams. Rugby fifteens. Gradually in the pictures he lost the boyishness; there were the first signs of the soldier. She looked at the prized pictures of Sandhurst and at the slender figure of the King. She touched the blade of the fencing foil which hung on its leather thong. And then she opened the wardrobe door.

All his clothes were there, cleaned and pressed, hanging in rows as straight as the soldiers in the Sandhurst picture. Fine tweed jackets. Tennis whites. Tails – she'd never seen him wear those. And at the back of the wardrobe was a pink coat for hunting, soft as velvet and thick as felt.

She stood looking at the clothes. At the rows of shoes shining with polish, waiting to be worn, taut with old-fashioned shoe-trees fixed into them. At a shelf full of hats, trilbys and two opera hats squashed into black silk circles, at riding hats, domes of velvet which hid the protecting steel . . . she looked, and looked, and slammed the wardrobe door.

George Martyn had arrived home earlier than usual. He was already in the drawing room, glass in hand, gazing out of the window when a beautiful girl in a pale dress came into the room. Out of uniform, she seemed a vision of peacetime.

'My dear child!'

He came over to kiss her, fussing over her in the way he had – which chair would she prefer? Did she like sherry, or would she perhaps have a glass of madeira?

'Grace is in the village, looking at a new room for one of our land-girls,' he said. 'Apparently the present landlady has decided to put four evacuees in our land-girl's room, and thereby earn four times the rent.'

He chuckled, as if slightly approving of a shrewd decision.

'So I'm afraid you're going to have to put up with me for a while,' he said, sitting down facing her. 'Well, how are you, Sorrel? You seem a little quiet. Was your journey worse than usual?'

'Not at all.'

Her cool reply had no effect. He still regarded her benevolently.

'And it wasn't too bad having to walk from the station?' he asked in a rallying tone.

Sorrel did not answer. She measured and disliked him. When his face was not softened by the deliberate charm he used with her, when it was in repose, he looked as hard as iron. His nose was strong and fleshy, his mouth noticeably thin, his cheeks furrowed with lines like the clefts made by water running down a mountain. His curiously coloured hair was brushed back, a steel helmet. Here was an opponent, not a friend.

'Lord Martyn.'

'My dear?'

'There is something I want to say.'

'So I see. What is the trouble?'

George Martyn leaned back in his chair, as relaxed as if he were with an employee. He was thinking how extremely pretty this girl was, admiring the freshness of her skin, the spring of her curling hair. What could Grace in any way have against the appealing creature? He approved of his son's choice, and they would have handsome children.

'It is about the money you used to pay my mother.'
He gave a slight laugh.
'That old story. What can you possibly want to know now?'
'You said you and Mother were related. You didn't tell me that when Father worked for you he got into bad trouble.'
If he was surprised, supposing anything could surprise him, he did not show it by a blink. He was bland.
'Aha,' he said.
She waited, tensed to throw back his money.
'So my dear sister has been raking about in the past, has she? I might have guessed. Dot has never been able to resist gossiping about a bit of scandal. Dot is a chatterbox. The past, my child, is dead and gone.'
'*So is my father.*'
'Now, Sorrel,' he calmly said.
'I refuse to believe it! I won't believe that – '
He interrupted, bearing down with all his weight of years and authority.
'Yes, yes, you are the soul of loyalty and there's every reason why you should be. I like that. I like a loyal heart. But you must listen to me. I don't want you upset, especially in times like these. Do you understand me?'
His kindness made her angrier, but before she could speak he went on, slightly raising his voice. 'What your father did or did not do is no concern of his young daughter. If Frank Scott was alive, he'd tell you that he agrees with me. The subject must be closed.'
'I refuse to take that allowance.'
'What are you talking about?'
'The money you pay to Toby, and he pays to me. Hush money.'
'What melodramatic nonsense.' He sipped his sherry. She was by now so painfully angry that her heart was thudding.
'I shall write and tell Toby what's happened. I don't want the money, and I don't want it paid into Toby's bank. We won't touch it with a bargepole.'
'He wouldn't know what this is all about.'
George Martyn was undisturbed by her accusing face.

'Toby believes you're a third or fourth cousin. The idea rather tickled him. He liked, he told me, the distant relationship. Your husband is on active service, do you intend to worry him about *money*?'

She said nothing.

After a long pause during which he watched her quizzically she spoke with difficulty.

'Very well. I won't write. But I shan't touch the money. I hate it.'

'Never be emotional about money, my dear. Money is nothing to do with anything but itself. It grows. It disappears. It is a thing, not a human being. You have to be its master. And besides,' he went on engagingly, 'in your allowance as a major's wife, in your Wren pay, how can you begin to sort out which money is mine? Do you plan to write to the War Office?'

'Of course not.'

'Then you're in for a pretty puzzle.'

How attractive she is, he thought. Those eyes swim even when she is cross. No wonder Toby wants her. But will my poor boy return to claim her again? And a pain went through his heart, piercing it again and again.

'Well. Are we friends?' he said in a rallying tone as the pain began to fade.

'I'm sorry. I suppose you are right. One should leave the past alone.' She just about managed to say it.

'That's right, Sorrel. Particularly now. Particularly now.'

Grace made an effort to be pleasant to her son's wife because George had told her, disagreeably, that it was her fault Sorrel had stayed away. But the burden of the hundred acres – as they became more successful they were more exhausting to organise – was wearing her out.

To be fat was tiring. Walking round the farm, riding in the trap, climbing the many flights of stairs, including a steep flight to the bedroom where she now slept alone – George had parted from her recently saying her snoring disturbed him – Grace was a vehicle of feminine flesh whose engine was too small. She was often so tired she could have sat down and wept.

But although she was polite to Toby's wife, she could not like her. She saw the girl was pretty – George said beautiful. Grace thought her pert. And unlike the dead Lilian to whom Grace had condescended, Sorrel had character.

But her dislike was losing its strength because she was so tired. Not only from the farm, but from a hidden grief over Toby. She seemed to be afraid all the time. She couldn't tell George how she felt, just as she could never *really* speak of losing Edmund, because once she had done so and seen the terrible sight of George in tears. It was another thing to try and forget. She was so tired. Even her claws were blunted, her catty tongue silenced, her spouting poetry, her capacity to gleam with spite or to take the stage, all were muffled. But she could not make a friend of Sorrel. Like another Martyn, but one whose grasping hands held on to a certain remnant of beauty, Grace resented Sorrel's youth.

On the morning after her arrival, it was Evie who took Sorrel round the farm, showing her four full-sized ricks in the yard, neatly thatched.

'Dion did them. He'd never thatched in his life but he had a lesson from his friends at Butterbox.'

One of the ricks was already sliced down like an enormous gingerbread cake. They walked to the duck pond to admire the flotilla of ducks, and to the cowshed where Sorrel saw unsteady soft-eyed calves. The farm thrived and Evie spoke of Lady Martyn's skill.

After the tour Sorrel's day was dull, and only enlivened in the late afternoon by the arrival of four officers from the local army camp. She was having a solitary tea on the terrace when she heard a car, followed by voices. The young men, pleased to see a pretty girl alone, crowded on to the terrace.

'Mrs Martyn!' exclaimed one.

'The Wren we have heard about,' said another.

'What have you heard?' asked Sorrel, laughing.

'We don't think we should tell you, Mrs Martyn!'

In well-fitting battle dress, bronzed from training in the Hampshire countryside, they were a hardy-looking group, and when they shook Sorrel's hand, they nearly broke her bones.

They stayed awhile, making jokes, and bringing with them that particular air which had been Toby's and his friends. Something strong, male, approving, innocent even. She was very glad to see them after a long afternoon in the company of a ghost.

The smallest and thinnest of the four was the commanding officer; he had a lined, tough-looking face and Sorrel thought – how Toby would like you. Looking at his watch, he tut-tutted and said, 'We must put on our skates,' and went to the front door. She heard him call, 'Evie!'

Evie came hurrying.

'Baths, Evie? Got to keep clean before we meet the enemy.'

'They're all ready, Captain. And towels. And some new soap.'

'You're a marvel. Told you that, didn't we?'

With assurances that 'we will be back tomorrow', the young men left Sorrel. The afternoon grew quiet again, distant bursts of laughter faded inside the house.

Sorrel hadn't meant to agree to see Dion Fulford again. It was two years since, unmarried and independent, she had deliberately gone to The Raven to meet a man who was a pacifist. It was different now. She was Toby's wife and owed him her happiness and loyalty. How could she make a friend of a man he loathed? If he knew he would be so angry. And he would never understand.

But the answer was simply to do with time. Months and empty months separated her from Toby, and although she yearned for him, she was no longer weakened by her love. Parts of her nature had begun to return like old friends who had left because she ordered them to go. Commonsense. Impulse. A sense of justice even. And there was an uneasy attraction for Dion which, of course, was not important; she merely liked the way he looked.

In the garden at the back of The Raven he was sitting with his back against a tree, reading. Glancing up, he gave her an extraordinarily sweet smile. He did not spring to his feet as officers did, as Toby used to do, but patted the grass.

'Remember when I put my feet in the river? If I did that now they'd fall off.'

'Is the water so cold, then?'

'Like ice. Try it.'

She dipped her hand into the river and drew it back with an 'Ouch!' She looked at the swirling water.

'Are there fish in the Test?'

'They teem. Trout and bream, perch, roach. The Test is famous for trout. You had some for dinner last night.'

'How do you know?'

'Because Evie asked me to catch them.'

She picked up the book he had been reading.

'*Cobbett's Rural Rides*. What is it like? I've vaguely heard about it.'

'Poor old Cobbett, that's what we all say. He rides about saying everything in England is wonderful and he's boring. Then he gets to the Fens and absolutely hates them. "Desolate gloomy land, Nature as man's enemy", that kind of thing. He's fun when he is not enjoying himself.'

'Not like us,' said Sorrel. She looked across at the pub and noticed an emptiness.

'Goodness. Where are the Americans? The landlord must miss them.'

'Yes. They've all gone and he can't get used to the empty saloon bar, let alone money slapped on the counter. The village misses them too. Very much so, particularly the kids. Even I miss them, as a matter of fact.'

'Why you?'

She couldn't imagine he was interested in the masses of American troops; he wasn't part of what was happening.

'All the time they were in camp near here, I was never once asked by an American why I wasn't in uniform.'

'But are you – '

'Asked? Oh yes. Sometimes I feel very cut off. As if I were the only sane person in an increasingly mad world. The isolation of the sane, somebody called it. *You* couldn't understand that.'

'Try me.'

'Try to explain, you mean?'

He looked puzzled, she had never seen him like that before.

'It's curious, but my resolve has begun to weaken. I didn't think that could happen. It's got nothing to do with what I think is right. Or with hostility from people. You get used to that. You get a tough skin and scarcely notice it after a while. It's the sense of being alone which gets stronger. Every man and woman in this country, and over half the globe, including *you*, Sorrel, spends every waking hour directed towards a single end. Victory. I am cut off.'

'But you're growing food.'

'Dig for Victory?' he said satirically.

'Food's as much part of the war effort as guns.'

'You talk like Grace. Or a ministry advertisement. Two kinds of men go into farming. The man with a true vocation, and the one who takes it on as a duty to society.'

'Which are you?'

'Guess,' he said annoyingly.

In spite of the first peaceful smile when she arrived, he was edgy. He did not look at her.

'You shouldn't be here anyway. Why do you bother?'

'I like you.'

'Oh thanks.'

'You once said I was rude, now it's your turn. What have I done, Dion? I am not against you. I respect you. I'm not like – '

She stopped herself in time.

He did look at her then. The soft pale dress, the cheeks in which a spot of colour burned, her curiously swimming eyes, too bright just now. The river chuckled by.

'I'm a bastard. I have no right to vent my ill-temper on you. Bad timing when I haven't seen you for so long. I feel depressed.'

He sprawled, bronzed, powerful, gentle, propped on his elbows in the grass. She did not think – this man's alive and perhaps Toby's dead. She never let herself think such things. They could drive you mad.

'Even if you are a fool, and I am not,' he said, 'it just isn't possible to be immune from what everybody else thinks. The government doesn't give a hoot about pacifists. We're a drop in an ocean of men. They shove us into some job or other and forget us. It's six years since conscription. A lot of water in the Test has run since then. And every day, every week, every month, there's been an incessant stream like that river yonder.'

'I don't understand.'

'Of course you do. A stream of exhortation, demands, advice, blackmail. Join the Home Guard. Fire Watch. Save Fuel. Salute the Soldier Week. It's your Britain, Fight for It Now. Buy War Bonds. Carry your identity card and gas mask. It's like being talked at inside your head.'

'They're only trying to help us.'

His sarcastic smile turned, after a moment, into a real one.

'You're very sweet. And you can't know how it feels. You obeyed the rules and were called up.'

'No I wasn't, I volunteered.'

'So you did. And meekly put on the regulation kit.'

'I did not. I have never worn regulation *underwear* since I joined! Do you know what we call the knickers issued to the Wrens? Blackouts. They are awful. Elastic in the leg. I wouldn't be seen dead in blackouts. I wear my own underclothes.'

'Oh Sorrel.'

He took her hand and squeezed it hard, then let it go.

They walked back down the deserted road until it turned towards the Priory.

'Wait a moment,' he said, stopping. 'I want to say goodbye before Grace hoves into view.'

'But we are sure to meet again.'

She had a feeling she'd said that before.

He looked at her with clear eyes.

'I can't make tomorrow. The Italian prisoners, poor things, will arrive in a fluster with one miserable corporal in charge of them. And if I know Grace, she'll mess things up. I have to stay and sort things out. Do you understand?'

'Of course.'

'No. You don't. The point is I daren't arrange to meet you. If we'd fixed something I'd want to be there, and wouldn't concentrate on work. It is best to say goodbye now. Sorrel?'

'Yes.'

She wondered if he would kiss her. She did not want him to.

'Will you do something for me?'

'Yes.'

'Before you know what it is?'

'Yes, Dion.'

'Do you ever get to London?'

'Yes, sometimes. Not often, though.'

She was curious to know what he wanted. More curious because he seemed to her a man who never asked for anything.

'My sister Pauline lives in London. If you get the chance, I wonder if you'd look her up. I'd be very grateful.'

'I'd be glad to.'

'You think it's an odd kind of favour. But I worry about her, particularly since the "little blitz". Chris, her husband, has been in the Far East for two years, and with our parents in Australia, she's on my mind. She has two small kids and it can't be easy. There's no telephone at my digs and in the local post office there are queues, poor things, and I can't wait that long. I certainly couldn't use the Priory telephone. Imagine Grace's expression. It would be good of you to see her. Tell her to write more often. You'd like her. She's nice.'

'I'll go on my next leave, *when* I get any. But you must warn her in advance that a strange Wren may turn up.'

He gave her a piece of paper on which he had written his sister's address and telephone number. He had been very sure of me, thought Sorrel.

A pause.

In the dappled evening, he loomed, a kind of fair-haired angel. He did not attempt to touch her.

'Thank you, Sorrel. And goodbye.'

'We'll meet again.'

'Don't know where, don't know when,' he quoted with a shrug. 'Maybe. Well. Goodbye.'

Without waiting for her to go, he walked away. He did not look back.

11

Like women everywhere, Sorrel had become practised at believing her husband was safe. What did 'safe' mean? It meant alive. In England in the early spring of 1944 people opened the newspapers to see thick black arrows pointing into the heart of Italy. But the Germans were fighting back, in villages and on beaches and on bridges and in rivers. It was the kind of war they had become used to. They held positions, then fell back, destroying as they retreated. For five months now the Allies had battered at them without success.

At Anzio it was the Allies who were besieged, and at the foot of the Benedictine monastery at Cassino the British infantry huddled in holes. The New Zealanders and Indians fought with heroism but failed to take the rubble which was all there was left of Cassino, where the Germans fought from cellars and bombed houses and alleyways and from behind ruined walls. By the end of March the two armies had fought each other to exhaustion.

Sorrel received no more letters and didn't expect any. She settled into the limbo of belonging to a lover fighting somewhere in a bitter unending war.

Fortunately her work was hard. The TAT was used over ten hours a day; she went to bed white with tiredness. Her fellow offices liked her, she was spoiled and at the monthly dance to a wheezy gramophone, she had ten partners to choose from. The commander of the base, the short and attractive Captain Lyall, was rather proud of her work and interested in her machine. It featured on the list of things demonstrated to visiting bigwigs.

'Martyn. I am bringing two captains and, don't blush, an admiral to see your pretty toy.'

'Sir.'

'You don't sound happy at the prospect of distinguished visitors, Martyn.'

'I'm afraid our machine has been getting the hiccups, sir.' Canadian Dusty had called it coarser names.

'Give it a glass of water, Martyn. I shall be with you at fourteen hundred hours. And your toy has got to work.'

There was a feeling of expectancy at the base. The two favourite words were Second Front. Whole areas of Hampshire had become an armed camp and at night when Sorrel was in bed she could hear the thunder of Sherman tanks travelling by for what seemed hours.

Now and then in her rare times off, when she was not with her navy friends, Sorrel thought of Dion Fulford and recalled her promise to meet his sister in London. She had said yes because it was always hard to refuse a favour. But the idea of going to seek out a stranger bored her. It was only when she was given an unexpected twenty-four-hour pass that she decided she must keep the promise.

She telephoned the London number. The voice which replied was light and matter-of-fact.

'Sorrel Martyn? Dion's talked about you. Are you coming to town? How about lunch?'

Sorrel booked a room at the Curzon Club, deciding she could scarcely explain Pauline to Aunt Dot who doubtless knew all about the Fulfords and all about conscientious objectors too. What had George Martyn said? 'Dot's a chatterbox.'

Her arrangements made, Sorrel suddenly remembered a letter she had received from Margaret, complaining that they never seemed to meet, and adding 'even if you only get twenty-four hours, do ring on the off-chance.' Sorrel telephoned Margaret's base and eventually managed to get her friend, whose reaction was enthusiastic.

'What luck! I'm going to be in town too. Curzon Club at midday? Perfect. Don't faint, I've put my two rings up. I'm a second officer now,' added Margaret, laughing.

A facetious lieutenant, Roger Maitland, who was rather too attentive to Sorrel and took her refusals with conceited chuckling heard she was going to London and offered her a lift.

Installed in a staff car with driver and a tankful of precious navy petrol, Maitland greeted her with 'Hop in. Hop in. You'll have to squeeze up, I'm afraid. Not much room in the back.'

On the journey he was talkative and more facetious than usual; double meanings spilled all over his conversation. Sorrel managed a feeble smile and hoped he would not pinch her knee. She found herself longing for a train corridor between rifle butts and kit bags.

They drove through a countryside teeming with troops, roads thundering with tanks, and when they reached the suburbs, saw gaps like broken teeth where there had been comfortable homes.

The Curzon Club as usual was filled with people in uniform. The porter gave her a key, and Sorrel, her mind on a bath, was halfway up the stairs when an unmistakable voice called her name. Margaret, glowing and beautiful, and with two gold rings on her sleeve.

'You're in good time. Wizard to see you. Don't dash away,' said Margaret cordially, beginning to steer her down the stairs towards the bar. Sorrel knew she must relinquish thoughts of a longed-for five-inch bath.

In a big, noisy, panelled room filled with the smell of cigarettes and alcohol Margaret took Sorrel over to a table where an American officer was sitting. Sorrel had been ready to meet the extraordinary, fair flyer she had seen so briefly. But no.

'Byron, look who I've found! Remember Sorrel Scott, my friend from way back? We volunteered and suffered together. Sorrel. This is Byron Schlegel.'

She recognised him from the postage-stamp photograph, knew the high forehead, crinkled, already receding hair, brilliant Jewish eyes and a general air of mischief and wickedness. Byron Schlegel, looking for trouble, knew how to welcome it and make it jump. He sprang up, taking her hand, saying it was a real pleasure and asking if Sorrel would have a highball. He'd succeeded in teaching the bar-waiter to shake one. As the two girls sat down and he offered the usual Lucky Strikes, he said hospitably to the visitor, 'I just love Margaret's tales about when you were both ratings. Particularly your underwear made of parachute silk. She still wears hers.'

A year ago Margaret would have blushed.

He was more than Sorrel had imagined, guessed from the photograph; funnier and flashier and far more clever. He was perceptive and when Sorrel, slightly shy from too much Jewish brilliance, trotted out a cliché or two he looked as if he was trying not to laugh. He called Margaret 'Duchess'. He wore uniform with style, as if he had never worn any other clothes in his life. She wondered if that was how Byron was with everyone and everything. He took them over. Took them on. Annexed them.

Sorrel had just spent three hours in the company of a facetious Englishman. Sitting with Byron Schegel she felt positively unpatriotic. He was warm and quick, attentive and flirtatious and there was not an innuendo in sight. He enjoyed being with them and took it for granted that they felt the same. He drank a good deal and smoked too much, lighting one cigarette from the butt of the other.

'The Duchess is set on my conversion,' he said to Sorrel.

'I only want to persuade you not to get high at twelve in the morning.'

'But I'm so attractive when I'm high. You daren't deny it.'

Turning to smile at Margaret, Sorrel saw an expression she'd never imagined on her face. Margaret looked helpless.

After a while Sorrel left them to telephone Dion's sister and arrange to call the following morning. When she came back to the bar, Byron asked her to join them for lunch. Somehow during the meal he discovered she was doing nothing for the rest of the day and demanded she should come to a movie with them, and afterwards to dinner.

She protested.

'I really can't. I don't like playing gooseberry.'

'Hell, what's that?'

'He doesn't know any English really,' said Margaret. 'Gooseberry, Byron, means you are unwanted. It originally meant the chaperone who spent her time picking gooseberries while engaged couples had a little chance for romance.'

'Tell me one darned thing that girl doesn't know. We can't bear too much info, Duchess.'

Despite pressing invitations, Sorrel escaped after the Rita Hayworth film, and returned to the club for a bath. Afterwards she sat gazing out of her window at the leaves of a plane tree. She wondered why Margaret and Byron had asked her out for the evening; didn't they prefer to be alone? She did not understand Americans, they had a kind of natural lavishness, a friendliness and hospitality which took for granted that it was reciprocated. The only word for them was spacious. She thought she understood why Margaret looked at him helplessly. He was fascinating and he had her at his mercy. But how did she feel about the godlike future diplomat? She had chosen, then? She had told Sorrel that if the two men were in danger, Gareth would manage to stay afloat, Byron would drown. Had that anything to do with love?

It was dusk when she joined them in the club bar and the trio went out into the evening street. The sky was clear and pricked with stars, and a thin moon hung low. A perfect night for bombers. Byron tucked Sorrel's arm under his left, Margaret's under his right, and swung along, walking fast.

'I like being with two dames at once. But who doesn't?'

Sorrel was amused and quiet at the start of the unlikely evening. She had tried to avoid it. But they had been determined to keep her with them. The Dorchester, like every expensive place providing food and music in the new cosmopolitan London, was overflowing, but Byron wore American uniform and was given a good table not too near the band. The meal was better than Sorrel expected and worse, said Byron, than he could imagine. He ordered champagne and sent a note to the bandleader who nodded in Byron's direction and struck up a crazy song much played on the wireless.

He says Murder he says every time we kiss
He says Murder he says at a time like this
He says Murder he says, is that the language of love?

'Come along, Duchess, and show Sorrel what I've taught you.'

A moment later they were on the dance floor, jitterbugging. Byron danced superbly, but what couldn't he do? He swung his ample companion about as if she weighed seven stone, threw her at arm's length and pulled her spinning back into his arms. They were the first couple on the floor and, at his most daring feat, sliding Margaret under his legs and catching her and bringing her up to face him, there was a scatter of laughter and applause. Then other couples, American servicemen and their girls, joined them and the floor was filled with writhing, jiving couples.

'Why, Mis' Martyn.'

It was Buzz Alderman looking down at her. 'What are you doing here alone?'

'I'm with those jitterbugs over there,' she said. He took her hand.

'I didn't know you and Byron Schlegel were acquainted.'

'We weren't until today. Thc Wren he is with is a friend of mine. I've known her since we volunteered.'

Why was she explaining this? It was because he appeared earnestly to wish to know. He asked permission to join her, and waved at a waiter to order 'the young lady a fresh ice, if you please'. He had noticed the ice was melted into pink-coloured water.

Buzz was pleased to see her. He asked her about her life in the Wrens, he recalled that her husband was a major in the Midhamptonshires. It was astonishing how much the ugly engaging American remembered about her, yet they had only met once before.

'Are you staying with your aunt?' he enquired.

Sorrel explained that she wasn't this time, as there was a friend she had to call on. She was slightly embarrassed, adding hastily that the friend was a girl with two young children.

Explanations again. It was odd that they seemed necessary. Buzz nodded with grave understanding.

He was courteous almost to reverence, he seemed to be saying that it was an honour to know an English lady, wife of an English officer. He was as formal as a Southern gentleman might have been fifty years ago, and Sorrel felt she would prefer to be less respected and more flirted with in a mild way. An impossible idea with Buzz.

'Why, Buzz Alderman, who said you could sit at my table?'

Byron came back hand in hand with a pink-cheeked Margaret. There were introductions and jokes. The quartet sat down and Byron ordered highballs.

Sorrel enjoyed the evening, although she saw little of Margaret who was dragged away for almost every dance. When they did return occasionally, Buzz's manner to Margaret was different, easier. Married women were apparently canonised in Alabama. Considering the highly sexed reputation of Yanks in Britain, she wondered if we had got it wrong; then looked at Byron and decided we hadn't.

While the other two danced, Sorrel and Buzz sat and talked. She had only once before known a flyer well – Tom Langton, her forgotten first lover. The Fleet Air Arm pilots she knew at Lee never spoke of that other life in the sky and Tom Langton hadn't either. But Buzz did. He described a raid he had been on over Hamburg the previous week and how heavy the flak had been. 'If you fly below it, it whizzes round on its way down. You have to be real smart and dodge.' He and his crew, he said, never took anything to eat but bars of chocolate. They sang over the intercom.

'What do you sing?'

' "This is a Lovely Way to Spend an Evening." '

It was bitterly cold in the plane, he said, and they wore electrically heated flying suits. But when they climbed out of the plane on their return, sometimes their breath froze. 'I had a beard of ice. I looked like old Father Christmas . . . I'm talking too much, Ma'am.'

'But I like it.'

'You listen so nicely,' he said.

When they danced she liked being in his arms. They returned for more drinks with a lively Byron and an excited Margaret. But quite suddenly Sorrel was tired. How did Buzz know? He stood up at once. Byron and Margaret were back on the floor, doing the rumba, and waved in their direction as Buzz led Sorrel from the ballroom.

'I'll walk you home.'

They went out into the unlit street.

'Sorrel. Is it okay to call you that?'

'Of course. Please do.'

'Sorrel. Take my arm, the pavement's rugged. What long steps you take. The girls back home take such little ones.'

Soon they were at the door of the club and stood for a moment. She could see nothing but the outline of his shoulders and the naval cap against the pale starry sky.

'Thank you, Ma'am,' he strangely said.

Setting off next morning Sorrel wondered what on earth she was doing, going to call on a girl she didn't know. Every time she enjoyed herself, every time she managed to put Toby out of her mind for a while, she had a subsequent wave of misery. This morning the news had come that Monte Cassino had fallen at last. Every victory, every battle, seemed to be Toby's. Where was he? Alive? In danger? The only answer to unhappiness was to go straight back to Lee and work. Her emotions were monotonous, painful and monotonous. She could scarcely bear to re-create her husband's face in her thoughts.

But she had promised Dion Fulford, so she took the bus to Kensington, looking out at the panorama of a city at war. Leaving the bus at South Kensington, she walked the rest of the way westward down the Brompton Road, finally turning into a parallel road and arriving at Thorley Court.

It was an ugly, once-modern block of flats built in the early 1930s, with double doors of plate glass and wrought iron plastered with paper strips and miraculously unshattered. The doors were propped open with a rough wooden wedge, and in a hall which had not been swept she saw the names of the flats' occupants on a board. There had been a similar smarter board lettered in gold in the hall of her mother's home at Coniston Mansions. Beside each name was a small movable notice. 'In' or 'Out'.

'Mr and Mrs C. J. Bell. Ground Floor. Flat 12. In.'

Going to the door at the far end of the hall, she rang the bell. A girl looked out.

'You're Sorrel. Instantly recognisable by the uniform. Come in. We're out in the garden.'

She led the way into a suite of rooms dark in comparison with a stretch of garden beyond open French windows. There was a square of grass, a few budding trees, and a pram pushed under one of them. It contained a small child who bounced up and down, making the pram rock.

'He thinks he's in a boat,' said Pauline Bell. 'Come and sit. I brought out the rug and some cushions. The sailor in the pram is Davy. Over there is Rose.'

A child dressed in white was playing with a ball.

'It's nice to meet you,' added Pauline as they sat down on a heap of worn cushions under a sycamore tree. 'Dion has often talked about you.'

She did not resemble her brother, being small and thin with indeterminate fuzzy brown hair and a narrow face. Her hazel eyes were slightly triangular, giving her face a touch of comedy. She had an energetic air. She was not pretty but lively, not clever-looking but quick, not remarkable, like Margaret, but practical and friendly. She looked strong. When Rose tripped over to loud and, according to Pauline, exaggerated cries, she picked up the child as if she were a feather. Rose clung, looking absurd, and Sorrel remembered a pre-war Madame Butterfly when the heroine had tottered across the stage carrying an enormous child supposed to be three, and singing 'I have named him Trouble'.

There was not much sign of being love's victim about Pauline.

'She's a pain,' said Pauline, as the little girl remained glued like a limpet.

'Bacon, bacon,' wailed the child.

'Oh, poor Rose,' exclaimed Sorrel, seeing the pouring tears.

'Poor nothing. She had bacon for breakfast and has been moaning for more ever since.'

'Could she have some for lunch?'

'She certainly couldn't. She ate all our rations for the week. Davy's. Mine. And her own. Rose. Want my bag?'

She unhooked herself, set the little girl on her feet and produced a handbag from under a cushion. Rose's tears stopped as if turned off by a tap; she emptied the contents of the bag on the grass.

'It's not my real one,' murmured Pauline. 'I've put in the things she can't swallow or lose. Children are so dangerous.'

The girls began to talk as strangers do, exchanging rather meaningless news. Pauline Bell looked appraisingly at her visitor, taking in the well-cut uniform, the groomed officer-look which made a chasm between women in the services and shabby young mothers.

'How was the journey to London?' she asked. People always said that.

'Luckily I had a lift, so I didn't need to come by train. But the trains are pretty awful, aren't they? Squashed against the window in the corridor and falling over rifles. It's the women nowadays who do some of the fighting,' said Sorrel and laughed.

'*Oh thanks*.'

At the sudden, angry voice Sorrel stared in astonishment. Her new acquaintance, glaring at her, burst out, 'I take it that was meant for my brother. Charming.'

'I'm sorry. I'm sorry! Of course I didn't mean Dion.'

Sorrel was as red as her companion was pale.

'I wouldn't dream of criticising him. I *like* him. That's why I'm here.'

Pauline's face changed.

'Oh lor. My turn to apologise. My skin's so thin about Dion, I blow up when people say the slightest thing. I'm stupid. Shall we start again? I really am sorry.'

The atmosphere settled down and they talked, more comfortably now, about Dion.

'I know he worries about me but we're quite okay,' Pauline said.

'What about the "little blitz"?'

'We're on the ground floor; practically in the basement. This garden's lower than ground level, and the flats are solid. It's better than going to a shelter,' said Pauline, adding, 'Everything sounds worse to people who are out of things in the country. Tell me about Dion and the Priory farm. A friend in the village says it's going well, to the surprise of other farmers.'

Pauline asked a number of questions to the point; she had lived in Evendon village all her girlhood. She listened to Sorrel's not-very-well-informed replies.

'It sounds as if Dion's running the show.'

'I'm sure he is.'

'And Grace Martyn will take the credit and be rude to him at the same time. Damn. I forgot she's your mother-in-law. I'm not the most tactful of women, I'm afraid.'

'Yes, she is my mother-in-law but what you say is doubtless true. I have never heard her say that Dion does a lot of the important work.'

'Ah. But he's a pacifist,' with a sharp smile.

Sorrel reflected.

'I don't think I know her very well.'

'She's a mixture. Like all of us. Before the war she painted some portraits which had real gumption. Including one of George Martyn which was exhibited at the RA. There was an exhibition of her work locally once, quite impressive. But I saw her painting of Edmund Martyn there and it was so sentimental.'

'I haven't seen that.'

'She presented it to Sandhurst, apparently. And did a copy which Evie told me she keeps in her room.'

'Oh.'

'See? A mixture. Hard, and all soft inside. She really did love Edmund, you know. Almost as much as she dotes on your husband. And then . . . she was proud, coming from an army family, having *two* sons who were regulars. She used to be so happy, going to the Sandhurst summer ball. She wore the sort of outfits that brides' mothers wore in those days. I remember Evie telling me that when Grace Martyn went to see the boys, she had a kind of glow.'

Pauline looked at Sorrel mockingly.

'Now I've made you feel all guilty. I don't see why. Because something tragic happens to a person doesn't turn them into a plaster saint. Why do you need to like her? I can see you don't . . . if she doesn't like you. Well. Does she?'

'No.'

'I thought not. It's the same when people die. Shakespeare got it wrong if he meant the good of men's *characters* is buried with them. When somebody dies people forget his faults. His vices, even. They erect altars and burn candles to the dead.'

'Perhaps it's better that way.'

Pauline eyed her.

'Of course it's not. It's false. And anyway Grace is alive and kicking, even if the poor thing did lose her elder son, so don't let's burn any candles to her. Come and keep me company in the kitchen.'

Sorrel shared the family meal. Bread, scrapings of margarine. Dried egg omelette and some carrots. There were jokes about the carrots.

'Pilots are supposed to get through entire fields of them in their diet, to make their night sight as sharp as an animal's,' said Pauline, feeding Rose. 'Which is why you have to be slippy if you meet a pilot in the dark.'

Rose ate little, and now and again the ominous word 'bacon' was heard. But after lunch Sorrel produced some chocolate from her gas mask case. Pauline protested.

'Your whole month's ration!'

But Sorrel assured her the chocolate was American, and Rose finished it before being carried away for her afternoon rest.

In between looking after her visitor and her daughter, Pauline fetched the baby, heated his milk, fed him and carried him, in turn, away to be changed. Sorrel heard her laughing with him. Then he was put back into his pram, pushed into a pattern of light and shade under the trees. The peace of two sleeping children descended upon the afternoon.

Pauline and Sorrel sat by the open French windows. The flat was comfortable, worn, smallish, crammed with family possessions. Cricket bats. Silver cups won at school. Rows of much-read books. A box of toys under the table. Pauline's sewing basket from which small socks trailed, and on the low windowsill that photograph which was in every home in England – a young man in uniform.

Chris Bell was a big, rather sleepy-looking young man. He had the face of a comedian, mouth and expression both about to laugh. Khaki did not suit him.

'He hates that one,' remarked Pauline, seeing Sorrel was looking at it. 'I think it's good; he has that sort of look, like a bear. He'd hit the roof if he heard me say that.'

It was an echo of another similar reaction.

'Toby can't bear his mother's portrait of him. *He* says she has made him look like Errol Flynn.'

'What's wrong with that?' said Pauline, laughing.

A faint breeze blew into the room, and there was an even fainter sigh of traffic. Sorrel looked at the girl sitting with her stockinged feet on the sofa. Like the butterfly Dot, here was the kind of woman Sorrel hadn't met before. The married women in the Wrens had husbands at sea; they were as groomed as racehorses, as bright as their gold buttons. Pauline wore her responsibilities, mother of two children, husband in the Far East, casually. She talked idly about the past.

'I never knew your husband well,' she said. 'But I did have a big crush on Edmund. He took me to the flicks. Of course he didn't let on to his parents. He was very handsome. It was marvellous, I thought, us being a secret. On our first evening out, he walked me home down the lane, there was a moon – well, there would be, it was August! – and he kissed me. My first kiss. Three, actually. I can still remember how thrilled I was. Poor fool.'

'You or him?'

'Me. He was a fascinating sort of chap. Fair and tall and I should guess rather a womaniser. Not as tough as your husband. He looked as if he gave himself treats, do you know what I mean? But golly, he was handsome. Much better-looking than Toby, sorry, but he was. Toby would agree. And Edmund was a big snob. Is Toby one?'

'I suppose he is, rather.'

'They all are in the regular army. They're like kids at public school. Full of brave *Boy's Own* ideas about the world. They admire romantic things like tradition and titles and wonderful old houses and history – the Thin Red Line, the North-West Frontier. Have you ever been to an army museum? Edmund once took me. It was all pictures of charging horses and flying flags. Romantic. Then, since the war we have all become snobs. We admire rank, you must have noticed. Rank and decorations. Pilots with their wings. MCs. DSOs. Ribbons.'

'That's true.'

Pauline studied her for a moment.

'Everybody thinks like that now. It is in the air. You can't help catching it.' She just hesitated and went on, 'You're thinking that I talk like Dion. So I do. Chris is away at the war, he was called up in 1940, four and a half years ago, *ages*. His regiment is now in the Far East which is all pretty horrible. I do feel patriotic at times. Churchill is a comfort. But there is another side of this war I loathe. We're so worked on. They've made us even willing to go hungry – just for the State. We've got humble. Cheerful about our miseries. Meekly queuing for three hours for a piece of fish which turns out to be bad. We scarcely get enough food for our children, and our clothes are mended until they're threadbare. We're in danger a lot of the time and we take that too. And shut up about it. Which is not what I'm doing now,' she finished, with a grin. 'I must stop. Dion calls me a revolutionary. Perhaps all mothers are.'

After a while the baby began to make a cooing noise like a pigeon, and Pauline went out into the garden, returning with him in her arms. Then into the bedroom to fetch Rose who appeared pushing a tiny wooden thing in the shape of a doll's pram. It was all the government would allow as a toy, a gimrack utility affair of plywood, the wheels mere circles of wood, the handle awry. She trotted about, stopping now and then to rearrange an ancient bear.

'Poor love,' said Pauline. 'The other day in Kensington Gardens she spotted a child with a real pre-war doll's pram. Coachwork and leather and a hood you put up and down, and a fat doll with yellow sausage curls and a red face. Rosy rushed over and seized the pram like a burglar. There was a fearful scene. Both children yelled and the fiercest person was an enormous nanny who pushed Rosy right over, and ran away as if afraid Rosy and I were going to attack them.'

'How disgusting.'

'Oh, it's like that. Rich and poor. Real toys and utility rubbish. You should see women in Harrods bribing the shop assistants. Five quid on the counter, and rice and semolina appear. All the stuff the children should get. It's like that. Isn't it, Davy?'

She kissed the baby's starfish hand. He looked up at her knowingly.

'Apart from when I bit off your head about him, you haven't mentioned Dion being a c.o.,' said Pauline. 'You surprised him, being nice to him.'

Sorrel remembered that she had sometimes been no such thing.

'Did Dion tell you much about himself?' asked his sister.

Sorrel looked at her rather solemnly, and Pauline thought, no wonder he likes you. I wonder if he has fallen for you. Poor Dion, if he has. The young Wren, engaging, slightly shy, took her fancy. And she wanted to talk about her brother, whom she sorely missed.

'Chris helped Dion write the statement for the tribunal, you know?' she said, rocking the baby as she talked. 'You have to prepare a pompous document and get references from friends if you can manage any. To prove your sincerity in your beliefs. I thought Dion's statement was a bit much. Awful stuff like "I respect the authority of the State", and "ethical basis for profound beliefs" and the sanctity of human life and all that. Of couse it's all true, but it was typical of Dion to say to me that he knew it was pompous but we had to use the right lingo. I was quite wrong. The tribunal was rather understanding, and he was just shunted to the Priory . . . did Dion tell you why he became a pacifist?'

'Because he thinks war is wrong.'

'Who doesn't? Ruining everything. Bombing cathedrals and universities. Burning books. Destroying places filled with the treasures of the past we can never replace. Who doesn't? My brother isn't any different from thousands and thousands of people, artists, writers, or ordinary chaps like Chris. I daresay Dion would have wandered into the army like everybody else. But my father made him solemnly swear never to fight.'

'*Why?*'

'Because he knew what it was like. Father joined up in 1914. How long was the life expectancy of a subaltern then? Three months. It was a marvel Dad survived. Over a million from this country alone didn't.'

Rocking the baby, stopping to go to Rose and try to refix the wheel of the pathetic imitation of a doll's pram, Pauline told the story. John Fulford had gone right through the war from 1914 to the beginning of 1919. He'd been in the battle of Arras, was nearly buried alive at Passchendaele, just escaped being gassed. At one time all his friends but two had been killed. Listening to Pauline was like seeing a film of that other war. But John Fulford didn't die. He married in 1916, returned to London 'for hectic, awful leaves', then went back to the hell he'd come from.

'When Armistice came and he was finally sent home, Mummy had the most dreadful, dreadful time with him. For three months he never said a word. He took no notice of her or of Dion and me. She knew he didn't sleep, he ate almost nothing, and if she put her arms round him, he sort of recoiled. She said the only creature he would touch was their cat, a stray tabby Mummy had adopted. The cat used to climb on his knee and sometimes drape itself round his neck. Mummy said it looked as if Daddy was wearing a mangy old fur collar. And the poor man just sat, staring. In the end he came out of it very slowly. And studied for Holy Orders and became a minister –

Dion gets his brains from him. Daddy was so pleased when he got the parish at Evendon.'

'Dion told me what a good preacher he was.'

'A fire-eater,' said Pauline, laughing. 'I daresay he also told you the Martyns couldn't bear him. Your father-in-law was coining it when Daddy was covered with lice in the trenches. My God, I'm rude.'

'Pauline, I am not offended.'

'Perhaps you should be. But George Martyn can do generous things. Dad's old chapel had a flood, damage to the roof, and it was George who paid to have it repaired. Embarrassing, gestures like that. It's simpler to hate people.'

During the 1930s her father had watched what was happening in Germany and in 1937 one evening he and Dion had an extraordinary talk.

'It was like H. G. Wells. Cities burned to ashes. The world in flames. *Things to Come*. Planes coming over London in non-stop waves, and all the disease and death. Mummy and I hated even listening, but Dion agreed. And it was then that Daddy made him swear a kind of vow. It was a sin to go to war, he said.'

She was silent for a moment.

'I didn't mean to tell you all that.'

'I'm glad you did.'

'Are you? I don't think our parents have any idea how much Dion's had to put up with because of that promise. Poor Dion . . . '

The afternoon, the time, had gone. Sorrel had to leave. Pauline, carrying the baby, Rose wheeling her wooden pram, came to see her off into the street.

'It was good of you to come. And nice to talk about Dion,' Pauline said. She laughed suddenly.

'There's something I want you to know. I bet Dion wouldn't want me to tell, but I can't resist it.'

'About your father?'

'Oh no, something else. My beloved brother has joined up.'

At Sorrel's incredulous start Pauline roared with laughter. 'You look just the way I felt. Yes, I saw him two days ago. He popped in just to say hello and goodbye. He was in uniform.'

'I can't believe it.'

'He's still kept the promise. And his principles, come to that. Typical of Dion to have found a way round. He's joined the non-combatant corps.'

'I've never heard of them,' said Sorrel, trying to rearrange every idea of Dion in her head.

'They're nothing important. Rather like the pacifist stretcher-bearers in France in the last war. A section of the army medical corps. They help repair railways or make roads or build hospitals. Navvy's work, mostly. There's no chance of promotion. They can't be in charge of men in case they have to lead troops in an attack or something. Dion's officers and NCOs aren't conscientious objectors. Only the men.'

'But why leave the farm? Why change his mind?'

'I can't imagine. My brother's a mystery. He seems cheerful enough. But you should see him in uniform. Dion in khaki is a contradiction. He looks quite awful!'

12

On a wet morning a week after Sorrel visited London, she was making her way towards the hangar where her TAT machine was installed when a young rating appeared, saluted in an inept manner, and said Chief Officer Hobson wished to see her.

Returning the salute, Sorrel groaned inwardly. Chief Officer Hobson had never liked her and never bothered to conceal it. Coping with her was a trial of patience and discipline, let alone good manners. Sorrel had mentioned this to her middle-aged friend Anthony English, who guffawed.

'Don't be naive. You must know why.'

'I haven't an idea.'

'Because of Captain Lyall, of course.'

Captain Lyall was the commander, the short blue-eyed heartbreaker languished after by every Wren in the base but Sorrel. And even she, if single, would not have been immune.

'But I scarcely see him except when you're kind enough to take me to your mess. He does tell funny stories, Tony, and he does make me laugh. But why should Hobson –'

'Mind? Because you laugh so charmingly and Jack Lyall likes that. Haven't you noticed Hobson's feeling for the camp commander?'

'Oh.'

'Exactly. She is human too.'

Sorrel remembered this when arriving at the lady's office. Hobson was a strong, horsy not unattractive young woman who loved masculine company. She coldly returned Sorrel's salute.

'You are to be sent on a course, Martyn.'

Sorrel looked perfectly blank.

'A course, Ma'am?'

'You look surprised.' The tone was sarcastic. 'Did you think you were a fixture? You are to go on a cyphers and signals course. Extra cypher officers may be needed in the next stage of the war. Brace up, brace up,' she added to the girl standing in front of her in the position so unsuited to the rounded female form, chin up and bosom thrust out. 'The course is at *HMS Caduceus*. You leave tomorrow.'

The *Caduceus*, said Anthony English later, was the wand carried by Mercury, twisted with snakes and used for the governing of ghosts. The navy had chosen the name for a house called Timber Tops built by a wealthy draper about sixty miles from Evendon. The draper had loved things Tudor, and crammed his house with inglenooks, carved newel posts, criss-crossed beams and four-posters. The beds had gone, but the teashop Tudor air remained. The house was in a lost part of Wiltshire. Around it spread rolling plains like a vast green carpet, the mysterious place where the most ancient of British people had lived. Now, casting their winged shadows on Stonehenge, armadas of aeroplanes flew out at dusk, bound for raids on Germany and France.

The group of Wren officers who arrived with Sorrel came from all corners of the British Isles. Nobody knew anybody. It was the same with the naval officers. The course was to be tough and would last a month. Young men and women with scarcely a bowing acquaintance with cyphers or signals must learn everything necessary and then be sent straight back to their bases 'to stand by for any emergency'.

Accustomed to work at what they were good at and in the company of friends, they found themselves back at school among strangers. They sat at desks taking notes. They learned to operate a teleprinter machine and to study code books and translate coded messages into what the instructor called 'clear language'. The code books gave Sorrel the same horror as trigonometry. The officers' course at Greenwich seemed a positive naval heaven in comparison. Everybody worked like dogs and had pale faces to show for it.

The Commanding Officer of *HMS Caduceus* was used to the signs of overwork. He gave a party.

Timber Tops had magnificent parquet floors. In the draper's day, young men and women had danced on the well-chalked floors to 'The Red Red Robin starts Bob-Bob-Bobbin'. Open sports cars had parked near the rhododendrons and couples kissed in peaceful moonlight. On the evening of the *Caduceus* party, when summer twilight began to fall and birds whistled, vehicles drove up to the big house. But these were army cars and jeeps and men in uniform streamed into the house.

Civilian clothes were not allowed, and the Wrens could only bath, wash their hair, put on their best uniforms and clean shirts. And whatever make-up they had hoarded. The lipstick praised in *Vogue* that month, the colour of a dark rose, was not allowed; they must settle for a sort of soft pink.

Seeing the girls trooping down the stairs, the captain reflected not for the first time that people wearing severe identical clothes always appear to be good-looking. Put them in civvies and it was another story.

The officers waiting in the two rooms chosen for the party looked at the girls in navy and white, black ties and black stockings, as if seeing so many shimmering, silken, kohl-enhanced and braceleted houris.

There were far more men than girls and the visitors epitomised the international flavour of the war. Sorrel danced with a Polish officer in the white eagle squadron. His English was flawless.

'Will you do me the honour?' And, taking her hand, 'I wish there could be some real dances. Would they play a mazurka, do you suppose?'

Later she was captured by a Canadian not unlike her mechanic Dusty.

'I've just finished my own course, glad to say,' said her large and rangy partner.

'Cyphers and signals too?'

He gave a rich chuckle.

'Not like that. Not like that at all, lady. We've been learning to use flame-throwers. I guess I needn't tell you why!'

My God, thought Sorrel, what would Dion say.

Pressing his face to hers in the transatlantic style, the Canadian said that the Second Front was on its way and about time too.

The phrase, the thought, was everywhere. Not only during the dance, or in the mess next day, but when the course was over. Sorrel did well enough, but with no particular brilliance. She had scraped through, she was told. For once, her competitive soul was not cast down. At least I passed, she thought. And they're going to need all of us when the Second Front comes.

In the air. In her thoughts. Even mentioned in the train, and not only by the Forces. Two elderly women were talking about it.

'Syd says the Second Front will be any day now.'

'How does he know?'

'Mor'n you think. Works in the War Office, doesn't he? Know what he said to us last week? When the Second Front comes, Mum, we'll show old Hitler!'

They burst out laughing.

It was sultry and clouded when Sorrel returned to the base, and went to see if a letter had come from Toby. She knew very well there would be nothing. A small harassed Wren called Williams came panting after her.

'Chief Officer Hobson wishes to see you, ma'am.'

'Why the hurry, Williams?'

'She said at the double, ma'am,' said the breathless child, all of eighteen years old.

Sitting at her desk, Hobson nodded at Sorrel with a chill that absence had apparently not warmed.

'You are now a cypher officer, Martyn.'

'But what about torpedo-assessing, Ma'am, if I'm also to work on cyphers . . .'

'There's to be no more TAT,' said Hobson shortly. 'Report to the cypher room, you are on the second watch.'

Accustomed to her dome of authority, to sitting as it were above the world while the pilots were training, Sorrel found the cypher room hot and claustrophobic. It was crammed with people, there were at least eight ratings and Wrens working there. When her watch was over, she looked for Anthony English.

'Your turn to have a sherry with me, Tony.'

Her tall, good-natured friend was pleased to see her. She was his favourite, and if it was possible to be platonic, Anthony was about Sorrel. They went to the Wren officers' mess.

'I daresay it was a shock, your TAT job ending,' he said, reading her face.

'Hobson never said that would happen.'

'Didn't you guess? The training days for Fleet Air Arm pilots are over, Sorrel.'

She had half-known it would be so. The smaller number of pilots. The waning interest from Captain Lyall's visitors.

'Aerial torpedoes haven't been very successful,' he said thoughtfully. 'Jack Lyall told me that far too many of them were lost without hitting a single enemy ship. Unless the entry's perfect, as you know only too well and have been slaving to teach, the torpedo just doesn't hit home. They've proved a costly waste.'

'So much for my job.'

'Don't look like that. You did your duty, and which of us can manage more than that? You're not head of the Fleet, Sorrel.'

He added, rallying her, 'Cheer up. Look at the news from Italy. That's enough to coax a smile, isn't it?'

Excitement over Italian victories was growing every day. General Alexander's offensive, with its huge international cast, was surging up the highway to Rome. On 4 June, Rome fell. Everybody at the base celebrated, and nobody said that the German army was still fighting in Italy. It was only Sorrel who did not stay up late, drinking and joining in. She walked home alone to her digs on a night of stars and went to bed, thinking about Toby. *He is alive. I know he is. I'd feel it if . . .* the rest of the thought was unthinkable.

Two mornings later she and a plump silent Wren called

Agnes were walking to the base together, and climbed a rise which gave a view of the estuary. They came to a gasping stop.

Every part of the water, every inlet, every broad or narrow stretch spreading towards the sea was crammed with ships. There were towering battleships, destroyers, patrol boats, flat, curiously shaped landing craft, motor boats racing to and fro leaving a wake of hurried water. The ships were moored so close that Sorrel felt she could jump from one ship's deck to the next. Above were what seemed like hundreds of droning planes.

The girls walked in an awed silence. In the guard room there was the sound of a wireless turned up to full pitch, and groups of officers and ratings crowded round it. Sorrel heard the BBC voice, loud, clear, almost dramatic . . . 'Airborne troops have landed at the mouth of the Seine.' The invasion had begun.

Within hours the armada in the estuary had vanished. The BBC announced that four thousand ships and many thousands of other craft were part of the landing. The atmosphere at Lee was at fever pitch; planes landed, took off, everything was in haste, everybody almost exalted. Sorrel worked decoding messages from nine until midnight; all she had to eat was tea and dry buns.

The news filled the days and penetrated the nights. It was on the wireless constantly, blazoned in the newspapers. The numbers of ships and aircraft ran into thousands. But the numbers of men were not given. How many, thought Sorrel, had run up those beaches bent against enemy fire, to fall and be abandoned? As a girl of twelve she had been struck and haunted by an old newsreel of the Great War; she had seen one of the soldiers hit, seen him fall. His death had been captured for ever on a piece of film.

After the euphoria of 6 June, and the news that the Normandy beaches were clear of the enemy and the Allies had linked up, the voices on the wireless were less uplifted. Churchill warned against too much optimism too soon. There was bitter fighting in Caen and later when the Americans stormed the beaches in Cherbourg. All day, all night, there was the noise of planes.

People at the base had a passion for the news, worked long hours, slept little, read any newspaper they could get and stood by the wireless in dead silence. The invasion was such an enormous thing. The hugest military operation in history.

When she talked to Anthony English he was grim.

'It's a land-based war now. Our job is pretty well over.'

'I see.'

'I'm not sure I do. I find it hard to accept that the navy's had its big moments and it's all up to the poor bloody infantry.'

And then Sorrel thought of Toby, who wasn't part of it, and knew how he'd be sorry.

Ten days after the invasion a new bombardment of London began, and this time there was no chance for RAF heroism, no glory for shooting planes down out of the English sky. In the House of Commons it was announced that pilotless planes had been launched over Britain.

'I can't help being fascinated,' said Anthony, meeting Sorrel in a corridor. 'What will we do? Jam the radio waves? Send them back to explode on the enemy sites. You'll admit it's intriguing.'

She stopped herself from saying that it wasn't for the people who were killed. He looked so cheerful. Anthony was very keen to spot one and told her he'd been popping out whenever he had a second, to look at the sky through his binoculars. But although the pilotless planes, soon called flying bombs, crossed Hampshire, Anthony had had no luck so far.

Sorrel was concerned at the bad news and telephoned Aunt Dot. The number rang and rang without reply. Where was she? She tried again later, still with no success. She had just come off duty, having worked right through the day – the cypher room could never be left empty – when little Williams trotted up. Ma'am was wanted on the telephone. Sorrel was scarlet with fright when she picked up the receiver.

'Sorrel?' said a man's voice. 'It's me.'

'Oh – Dion.'

'You sound peculiar. You okay?'

'Of course. I was in a hurry, I'm out of breath. Why have you rung?'

'To know how you are.'

'I don't believe that,' she said, recovered.

'Why not? I like to hear. It was kind of you to go and see Pauline. I gather she told you my news.'

'Yes. I was very surprised. It must have been so hard.'

'Why?' he said, laughing.

'To – to change your mind. Change course.'

'I haven't changed my mind at all,' he said annoyingly. 'I'll explain that sometime. Look, I've got another favour to ask. You can say no if you like.'

'I shan't say no.'

'Rash as ever. I might ask something outrageous.'

'Ask away.'

'It's my tiresome sister again. It's hell getting to a telephone, and don't ask where I am because of course I'm not allowed to say. I've tried her six times. Leave is non-existent and now those damned flying bombs. . . . Pauline *must* get out of London or I won't have a minute's peace of mind. She can go to Chris's uncle and aunt in Cumberland. They keep asking her and she keeps refusing. This time she can swallow her stinking pride and pack her traps.'

'What do you want me to do, Dion?'

'Something difficult. Will you try and see her? They flatly refuse to give me any leave and you're my only hope.'

'But I won't get leave either and I'm not a relation,' said Sorrel in some desperation.

'Then say you are. Hell. My time's up. I know I shouldn't ask you but – well – I am asking. Will you *try?* It wouldn't be any good ringing her as you don't really know her and anyway her telephone's packed up. Oh, *all right'* – very irritably to somebody else. 'Sorry. I must ring off. Goodbye, Sorrel. Thanks a million.'

Sorrel left the telephone and went to have tea, having caught a large dose of his irritability. She had said she would help him, and it turned out to be nearly impossible and a damned bore.

Oh, to hell with Pauline, thought Sorrel. What's she doing

still in London with two children and the flying bombs crashing round? And following on the heels of that thought – I hope to God she's all right. Dion's voice had brought back her uneasy affection for him. She'd thought he was in the past now. And why had Dion asked *her?* They must have dozens of friends and she'd only met Pauline once.

Commanding Officer Hobson was very busy, and the last person she wanted to deal with was the young woman whom Jack Lyall admired.

'Yes?' she said in a freezing voice.

'I wish to request compassionate leave, Ma'am.'

'Out of the question. I'm shocked to hear you ask for such a thing.'

Sorrel stood her ground. She had remembered Aunt Dot.

'It's my aunt, Ma'am.'

'Your *aunt,* Martyn?'

'A widow, living in London. I have rung her four times and there's no reply. I'm worried about her.'

'No doubt she is away.'

'She never goes away. I wonder if I might have a few hours' leave. I can be back this evening, Ma'am.'

Hobson paused. She knew all about the girl standing respectfully in front of her. The whole Mess knew Martyn's history: her mother had been killed two years ago, Martyn had no parents and her husband, who had an MC, was on active service. She had been described by Captain Lyall as 'that kid with guts'. It would scarcely put Hobson herself in an attractive light if Martyn's only remaining relative happened to get herself killed by a flying bomb, and she'd refused the girl less than a day's leave. She grudgingly granted it.

Sorrel saluted, left the room more surprised than pleased, and decided she had better try and see Dot as well. But it was the fate of Pauline and her children which had begun to disturb her. Aunt Dot's fate didn't give her a moment's pause. She'd be in Hatchette's, for sure.

When Sorrel's train arrived at Waterloo the alert had been on for six hours. Her taxi-driver, a Londoner born and bred, was up-to-date with the news.

'If the putt-putt-putt overhead cuts out, that'll be you and me for eternity, Miss, see? Did you know they've flattened Bourne & Hollingsworth's. *And* Barkers. Kensington's had it pretty bad all round.'

Sorrel felt a thrill of fear.

'When was Kensington bombed?'

'Last night. The raid was on for hours and they hit that Lyons on the corner of the Earl's Court Road. There was bodies lined up all along the High Street, saw 'em with my own eyes, all covered up with blankets. It's a terrible sight, that. People going along and bending over to see who's dead and crying something awful.'

It was a horrible journey. Sorrel's war had been a vicarious one, her only real experience the moment she'd stood at the edge of a bomb crater looking down to where her mother had lost her life. To Sorrel the war had been the awful gaps and silences of pilots who never came back, the sorrow in girls' faces once or twice, and more than any other pain, the agony of fear for Toby. But this was different. She was terrified of what she was going to find. She kept thinking of Pauline with the fat baby on her lap, the little girl trotting in with her wooden utility pram. Bodies all along the High Street. The taxi drove on, doing its duty, down quiet streets where the trees were in full leaf.

It made detours. Many roads were roped off.

'Let's see what we find round here,' shouted the taxi-driver, and turned into a road – and there in the distance Sorrel saw the block of flats. Still standing.

'You had the wind up, didn't you, Miss?' said the driver when she paid him. 'These are dangerous days. Well, we're in it together, aren't we?'

He drove away.

Sorrel ran into the hall, up to Pauline's door and shoved her finger on the bell, ringing and ringing. The door was opened by a scowling Pauline.

'What the hell – good lord! What are you doing here? Don't tell me. Dion sent you.'

'You're okay. Thank God for that.'

It was she, not Pauline, who was pale. As fear receded Sorrel saw that the flat was littered with luggage. Suitcases. Brown paper bags.

'Do sit down,' Pauline said. 'I must say I take it kindly, you appearing out of the blue. How did you get permission? Dion is the limit. He wants to know if we're clearing out, I suppose. Of course we are. The bloody things went on all night and this morning – listen; that's one now, quite far off – and honestly, Sorrel, I've never been so scared before. Real panic. Some of the things fell much too close. Did Dion suggest,' she added with a touch of her usual asperity, 'where we should go?'

'Your husband's uncle and aunt in Cumberland.'

'Oh sure. Any port in a storm. Chris's aunt is only slightly less anti-pacifist than Grace Martyn. She's quite awful about Dion, Chris had a fearful row with her at the beginning of the war. What a prospect. However, I've swallowed my pride and rung her. She was very nice, I give her that. We must all come up at once, she said, but you should have heard the note of triumph. I think the idea of London being blown to bits rather pleases her, she never liked southerners. I'm being ungrateful. Hell, I feel ungrateful. How did you get to town? Shouldn't you be doing your bit for the war effort?'

'I had compassionate – '

'Not for me!'

'Not really.'

'Good lord,' said Pauline again.

She sighed, picking up some breakfast things from a table and going out to wash up. People did that. They left things clean for the bombs. She dragged the suitcases to the front door.

'Refugees. We're going to be refugees. How I loathe running away.'

There was another distant thump and the ground shuddered.

'I'll come to the station,' said Sorrel.

Pauline buttoned on Rose's coat and the small girl gave Sorrel the radiant smile which remembered chocolate. The baby had been asleep on Pauline's bed. He was woken up and wrapped in a shawl. Locking the flat, weighted down with luggage, they staggered into the street.

'One good thing,' said Pauline. 'Loads of cabs now the bombs have started up.'

Sorrel, Pauline, a dozing baby and a talkative Rose travelled across London to the whirring sound of flying bombs. The taxi-driver shouted comments over his shoulder.

'Hear that? On its way to Hampstead, I should guess.'

The buzzing sound, a devil's sewing machine, went on overhead. Once they thought it had cut out and Pauline said, 'Oh, please God,' and grasped the baby so tightly that he screamed. But the steady stuttering continued, and the driver called out that the poor bastards in Acton would get that one. They were getting closer to King's Cross every minute that passed. The girls sat clutching hands. How curious it was to look from the window and see people walking by in the street. Not cowering or running, walking quite slowly. But everybody was listening.

'Any news of Dion?' said Sorrel determinedly.

'He's on a course,' said Pauline in the same tone. 'And loathes it. Being very bolshie.'

There was a pause. They listened. More buzzing.

'I wonder how Grace manages without him. I want her to miss him like hell,' said Pauline. 'Thank heaven – we're here.'

Accompanied by a porter who told them the train was in and ran as fast as they did while pushing the luggage in a handcart, they rushed down the platform. The train was so crowded that the girls exchanged looks of horror. But two sailors, seeing Sorrel's uniform, opened the door for them and shouted 'Okay!'

'It's my friend and her children,' cried Sorrel urgently. One of the sailors literally pulled Pauline and the baby into the train. The other grabbed Rose.

Sorrel had a final glimpse of all three being hustled into a compartment by the sailors. She stood on tiptoe peering through many heads to catch a glimpse of Pauline. No luck. One of the sailors elbowed his way back into the corridor, pulled down the window and put up both thumbs.

'Leave them to us. Cheerio!'

The train started to move.

It was odd. She walked out of the station into the sun feeling positively cheerful. A bomb was chugging overhead, but the possibility of her own immediate death did not come into her head. With a feeling of satisfaction at a job well done, she took a bus in the direction of the West End. Mayfair was deserted and when she went into that centre of gaiety, the Curzon Club, it was as quiet as a church. Soldiers and sailors and flyers were in Normandy and Rome, Burma and Ceylon. The old porter gave her a dim smile.

'Are you staying with us tonight, Ma'am?'

'Unfortunately no, Brierley. Only popping in.'

'A pity . . . you could have taken your pick of our rooms,' he said dryly. 'It doesn't signify, you know.'

'What doesn't?' asked Sorrel, smiling and still euphoric.

'Where one sleeps, Ma'am. The top floor or the ground floor will make no difference. If a buzz bomb lands, it flattens the whole street.'

'If I was staying, I think I'd prefer the top.'

'So you could watch 'em go by?' said the old man. 'Everybody stares at them, don't they? It was my day off yesterday, I was playing golf in Surrey, and one went slap over the course, right above our heads. We were rooted to the spot,' he added. 'Horrible thing, it was. Do you wish me to book a table for dinner, Ma'am?'

She heard a faint sad echo of the Royal Arundel Hotel. For both she and the porter knew the dining room would be empty.

Sorrel said unfortunately she only had an hour or so; she thanked him.

In the deserted ladies' room, she washed her face and did her hair, asking herself critically if she would do for Aunt Dot. When she came back into the entrance hall, it occurred to her that she was rather hungry. She hadn't eaten since breakfast before seven. She needed a sandwich before greeting Aunt Dot, who was certainly not a lady given to impulsive unplanned meals. Sorrel went into the coffee room, it was empty except for one girl in Wren uniform by a window open on to the courtyard, head bent, writing a letter on her lap. It was Margaret Reilly.

Sorrel laughed in surprise.

'Why, Margaret, hello! We always seem to meet here. How *are* you?'

In the second faster than light when the eye takes in what it sees before thought follows, Sorrel saw a stranger looking at her. It was Margaret. The same green eyes, the same dark hair curling at the edges, the handsome nose, the flawless skin. But the confidence and the know-all charm, the commanding air, the Irish beauty proudly worn, where were they? She looked old.

'Byron and Gareth are dead.'

'They can't be. They can't be. Not both!'

Sorrel sank down beside her, her eyes full of tears.

'It isn't true – oh Margaret, Margaret.'

'Byron was killed four days ago in the Cherbourg fighting. There were terrible casualties there. And Gareth was sent to Italy on a mission. They wouldn't tell me anything. Except his plane was shot down.'

'But it's possible that – '

'No. It exploded in the air.'

Speechless, Sorrel took her hand. It was freezing cold. Passionate with sympathy, suffering for her, she still had a sensation of bewildered wonder. Which of these men newly slain had Margaret's heart?

'I've been at Medmenham for the last ten days. I saw both of them only last week. Byron had leave. And later, so did Gareth. I saw them.'

Margaret was simply speaking aloud. She looked as if she would never cry again.

'It's funny,' she drearily said, 'sometimes when the boys were away, and I thought about them all the time, I could hear them in my head. Byron's jokes. Gareth's drawl. Do you know what I mean?'

'Yes. Yes.'

'Then, five days ago I just couldn't hear Gareth any more. And the next night it was Byron. The voices stopped. They've gone.'

She looked down at the unfinished letter, then tore it to pieces. 'It was to Mrs Schlegel. What do you say when somebody's killed? Nothing.'

'But you're a Catholic.'

Margaret looked out of the window. In the courtyard a blackbird was loudly singing. Drowning its music, came the putt-putt-putt of a bomb overhead. A little later the ground shuddered. But the explosion was miles away.

'You do believe, don't you?' Sorrel said.

'Believe what? That I'll see them again. I don't know. I don't know anything any more.'

A slender woman with frizzed brown hair came into the room accompanied by a man in Free French uniform.

'Oh, this'll do,' she said, 'almost nobody about. Let's have a lovely drink, Christian, and when the bomb lands we'll be blown to smithereens together. What's more *intime* than that?'

There was the noise again. The woman rang a bell. Nobody came.

'Where is everybody?' she complained, her upper-class voice loud and laughing. 'I should have thought providing drinks for our gallant Allies was a national duty. And not an anti-aircraft gun sounding off. They've stopped firing at the things.'

Unlike his companion, the Frenchman spoke in a soft voice. She laughed.

'Christian, what can you mean, how does it make things worse to shoot them down? They'll explode anyway either in Mayfair or Shepherd's Bush. You pays your money and you takes your choice. I say, a brainwave! Where do drinks come from? Answer, the bar. So off we go barwards to serve ourselves.'

Sorrel heard the classy voice receding down the corridor.

'Margaret. Have you eaten anything? I'll get some coffee and sandwiches.'

There was no answer and Sorrel went to find her friend the porter. When the sandwiches, Spam, and the coffee, ersatz, arrived, Margaret touched nothing. She sat smoothing her smooth skirt. Sorrel did not know what to do. Time was ticking by and she wouldn't be able to see Dot after all; soon she must go to catch her train. Was Margaret on leave? Did you get compassionate leave for the death of a man you hadn't married, let alone two? How awful she looked. But for whom? Byron with his balding dark head and bedroom eyes and malicious face? Or Gareth, radiant, belonging to an exalted world? You couldn't break your heart over the loss of two men. It turned grief into farce.

'We had such plans,' Margaret said, after a while. 'I don't think I was ever so happy in my whole life. When I remember that they're dead I want to die too.'

Sorrel's heart swelled. She hated to see the goddess stricken, she felt a shared grief. And a selfish fear that any day, tonight, tomorrow, it would be her turn to look so empty, so sleepless and so drained. There was death in Margaret's face.

'I'm so sorry, Margaret. It's so dreadful. Which of them do you love?'

The moment she'd said it she could have bitten off her tongue. But before she could try to make it right the trance of her friend's face slightly lifted. The look of sorrow which takes personality away faded. For a moment she was herself.

'I loved them both.'

Faintly, faintly, Sorrel heard the old patronising tone.

'I know. Of course. But – '

'But you think somebody can't be *in* love with two men at the same time.'

'I suppose I do.'

'It isn't true. Nothing about love is true. Nothing they taught us. Nothing we believed and nothing the Church says.'

'I'm not a Catholic.'

'No, you're not. It's different for us. The Church is so strong about not going to bed with a man until you're married. Virginity is a holy state. We were taught that. Once I asked a nun why virgins were holier than married women and she said I'd understand when I was older. And when I grew up I did. I did. I understood about love. That's funny, isn't it? Understanding about love.'

She smoothed her unwrinkled uniform skirt again.

'The war came and it started to change everything. What we knew were sins. Sex with a man. Giving yourself to him. The girls do that, they all do. *You* did. You slept with Toby before you were married, I could tell. When we were at Littleport and he came down one day. I thought – she's no better than a tart.'

'Don't.'

'Why not? That's how stupid I was, judging everybody. I felt superior because I kept men off. I knew *not* doing it was the right way to be. But then. Sex and war are so mixed together. Which is the more powerful? I only know we're at their mercy, it's like being in the tentacles of an octopus; you hack it and it winds more tightly till it kills you.' Scarcely conscious of Sorrel, Margaret talked on. Here was somebody to listen. Not her family who would look at her in horror and send her to confession.

'I fell in love with Gareth first. You can't imagine how wonderful he was, I believe he was the perfect man. And when we went to bed it made us both deliriously happy.'

There was a pause.

'And then I got to know Byron. They never knew each other. I was so careful about that. But I know Byron guessed. He was different from Gareth, he was instinctive and worldly, he knew everything about women. And he found out for certain because once after we'd made love he said, who's been having you since I've been away? It was terrible. It was because of something I did . . . that he and I didn't do. You know? I thought I'd lost him, I was desperate, but all he did was laugh. He said knowing about me being had by another man made me more exciting. Gareth never knew; I was on a pinnacle with him. He kept making plans about us marrying after the war and living in Washington.'

'Would you have done?'

'I don't know. Oh God, why did they get killed? Both of them. Both of them.'

But it was only Sorrel who began to cry.

They left the club together, Margaret was due back and

Sorrel, too, had to hurry. The raid was still on but nobody took shelter. If the noise stopped, you'd had it.

When Sorrel said goodbye, she thought how ill her friend looked. Ill and old. She put out her arms and kissed her. She had never done that before and Margaret didn't kiss her back.

13

The huge black darts which had arrowed across the newspapers up the map of Italy had changed course; they pointed like the tips of spears at the heart of France. Battles were reported daily, almost hourly. The Americans, after fierce fighting, were through Cherbourg; Sorrel wondered if Byron was buried there in some corner of a foreign field. There were counter-attacks from the Germans but, said the BBC with calm optimism, 'We continue to thrust forward.'

In London and southern England the flying bombs came over day and night, thousands of people were killed and injured and more thousands of homes destroyed. The end did not come. There was no astonishing victory. Toby once said, 'The Germans fight like hell. That's what they do best.'

'Don't we?'

'Some of us.'

Toby's letters began to arrive, sometimes in batches of two or three, sometimes a single letter in his scratchy writing. He was still the soldier whose letters did not need the censor: he never said a thing. She put them under her pillow at night, reread them searching for hidden meanings among the platitudes. She loved him for not being able to express his love. How would a soldier know the way to do that? Once it came into her thoughts that there had been soldier poets, men of genius as well as courage. She pushed the idea away. She loved him for his simplicities, loved the tongue-tied man who had entered her body with passion and authority. She wanted him as he was.

She was young and she believed she'd become used to being without him. She became proud of her own resolution, began to feel she was growing like him, was protected by the armour of fortitude. But now the war's drama was shaking the world and there was no sign of its end, the armour seemed to fall away. All she had was a thin packet of letters. Waiting, dreary waiting, became unbearable. Where was her brave past? Sometimes in small writing at the bottom of a letter were the words 'I love you'. Seen by a censor's bored eyes.

When she was tired out with hours in the cypher room, she had times of being unable to sleep, and couldn't stop thinking about Margaret Reilly. In the last five years, much of the world lay in ruins and millions of people had made love before death stole their lives away. Sorrel could not feel for the masses. The thought of a universe of sex and hideous grief was beyond her imagination. But Margaret was real. Margaret, chaste and proud and certain and Catholic, had broken every one of her own laws. She'd been possessed not by one man but two. How often? Where? How soon, one lover after the other? She had lain down with two men as if she were living two lives, and had lost both of them. When she was not thinking about Toby, it was Margaret who possessed Sorrel's thoughts.

Her friend became a superstition with her. Sorrel had seen that look in other people but never so terribly as it had marked Margaret's once-beautiful face. She had looked as if she was bleeding to death. Sorrel thought – I shall be the same one day.

December, the end of 1944 in which so many had believed the German war would be over, came in freezing fog. The news in Europe was of no sudden victory, the German war machine, as it was called, was still not destroyed. Sorrel remembered Toby's description of the Germans.

'They're natural fighters. They don't know the meaning of giving in.' In Italy they held on to the northern mountains, in Europe the Allies had not yet crossed the Rhine.

Out of the blue Sorrel received two letters from Toby – marked 'Yugoslavia'.

You'll be v. surprised to see where your husband is hanging out at present – a long way from Evendon! This is a wonderful country and they're pretty wonderful people. Yesterday we went past a castle just like one on a cigarette card. Do you remember the Three Castles cards? Father used to smoke that make and the cards were ripping! This one was like that, turrets and a moat and arrow slits. I'm feeling very fit. Hope you are in good form, darlingest . . .

The second letter had been written after an interval; it was like the first, undated, but was about his family and the Priory. He did hope she'd manage a visit soon; 'the parents miss you.' The chaps he was with were first class and he was her loving husband Toby.

She found Anthony English in the office, busy censoring a pile of letters. He greeted her with pleasure.

'You're a sight for sore eyes. You look as if you've had news,' he added, noticing her too-bright face.

'I've heard from Toby. He's in Yugoslavia.'

'*Is* he, then?' Anthony English whistled.

'Tony. What's happening there?'

'Nothing to worry about on that score. The Germans are losing Yugoslavia hand over fist, the partisans are over 20,000 strong and apparently the numbers are growing all the time. They've got an extraordinary leader, Tito, a communist, of course. Your husband must have been sent to give him a hand . . . a boot up the enemy's backside would be more accurate, I imagine.'

'But how? I don't understand.'

'He'll be a commando, that's for sure.'

Anthony English's voice was full of admiration. 'Blackened faces and night attacks. Fighting in the mountains. Good for Major Martyn.'

Sorrel relaxed, hearing the confident voice. She felt like a woman going to the Palace, sharing the glory of a decoration. A bar to Toby's MC, perhaps. She was on night watch, working from seven until eleven at night, and during her work, and afterwards when she went to bed, she thought, Toby's a commando. It had a brave sound. But then it began to frighten her. Why Toby? He couldn't speak a word of schoolboy French, let alone the languages of the Balkans. It must be because he's Toby, he was born to be a commando . . . blackened faces and night attacks, she thought.

She telephoned his parents and it was Grace who answered.

Hearing Sorrel's voice she gave her no chance to speak but burst out effusively:

'So you've heard too? Isn't it a thrill? We had two letters, both arrived this morning.'

The note of competition was never absent – don't think you are the only woman he loves.

'Yugoslavia, what a thrill!' repeated Grace. And then, doubtless prompted by Toby's letters, 'You're very naughty, not coming to Evendon. When is your next leave?'

The idea of staying at the Priory depressed Sorrel as usual, but she could not refuse since her husband had said his home was hers, which was precisely what it was not. While she was waiting on an ice-coated platform, huddled into her greatcoat and stamping her feet, she realised that the only remaining pleasure of Evendon – Dion's company – was gone too. And that she'd never see him again.

The wind was biting as she came out of the station after her long journey, to be met by a muffled Evie.

'You poor thing, you're frozen! How late all the trains are. In you get.'

The pony trap was waiting.

'It's so kind of you, Evie, I didn't expect you, I could easily have – '

'Thumbed a lift? What would Lord Martyn say? Take the blanket. We'll get home as fast as we can. The Chief's glad to be out, poor dear. A welcome change from the milk bottles,' said Evie. Sorrel saw Toby's beloved horse in the shafts.

'He'll give us a nice brisk trot.' Evie tucked a check rug closely round Sorrel, and the same for herself. Wrapped as in rolls of carpet, they set off. The Chief was glad to move, his hooves rang on the ground, his breath was a cloud of smoke.

Evie handled the horse expertly, held the whip upright and never used it.

'We're thrilled about the major,' she said, using Grace's word which grated on Sorrel's nerves. 'Typical of him to get himself a job like that. I had a letter too, Sorrel. Imagine him writing to me. Can you guess what it was about? This blessed animal.'

'The Chief looks fine.'

'Poor lad. He still hates the milk round. Don't you, old fellow?'

Evie sounded like Toby just then.

'And since Dion went, nobody knows how to ride him. Our land-girls ride like sacks of coal. The Chief despises the both of them. Dion was different. He managed to give The Chief a canter every day, no matter how busy he was. Once The Chief jumped a five-barred gate from a standstill. Didn't flick it with a hoof. Dion was so pleased. Did you know Dion's joined up?' she finished, turning a wind-bitten face to Sorrel as they bowled along under leafless trees.

'Has he? I thought he was a pacifist.'

If Sorrel's voice was teasing, Evie did not notice. Yes, she said, he'd had a change of heart and joined the non-combatant corps. 'They're only dogsbodies, don't do any fighting, but I take my hat off to him just the same. Lady Martyn was staggered.'

'But approved?'

'Well, she couldn't say anything, really. But there's no denying it, Sorrel, the farm is suffering now he's gone. We've got a new man who calls himself a bailiff and doesn't like work. He's a big mistake, but what can she do? There was a terrible storm just after Dion left and we lost almost all the oats. Dion would have saved some of them. He's done it before. Poor Lady Martyn was in tears.'

The horse knew where they were, slowed his pace to a walk, and turned in through the familiar wrought-iron gates. In the winter dusk the house seemed as much part of the landscape as a huddle of rocks or a group of low trees. Not a beam of light anywhere.

'There go the Italians. I wonder if they've done a hand's turn,' said Evie.

Half a dozen men, in a motley array of old coats and jackets, were strolling rather than walking through the grounds. They were short and dark, chatting to each other, and seeing Sorrel in the trap one of them blew her a kiss and began to laugh. A soldier in khaki shooed them along as if they were a flock of geese.

'Don't look in their direction,' said Evie, 'or they'll take liberties. Lady Martyn caught one hugging our young land-girl behind the stables and nearly had a fit. Eyties!'

She had been derisive about the thousands of Italians glad to surrender to a score of British soldiers in the desert.

'They wouldn't know a day's work if it came up and hit them.'

'Then why have them?'

Evie glanced round, detecting sarcasm, but Sorrel's face was merely enquiring.

'They fetch and carry round the farm, although if there's a drop of rain and they're in the fields they scuttle for the nearest hedge. You should have seen them during the harvest, singing bits of opera. It was just like a scene from Gilbert and Sullivan. You'd think one or two would have the gumption to try and escape, wouldn't you? Not likely. The corporal in charge of our dozen could manage fifty. They got on my nerves at first. But,' she added fairly, 'one can't help liking them. Marcello offered to share all his Red Cross biscuits with our cowman the other day.'

She swung down Sorrel's canvas bag, pushed open the front door and stepped back for Sorrel to go in first. Evie's gestures of respect made her the stronger and the senior. She then disappeared to unharness The Chief and put the trap away.

Indoors, the house seemed empty. No fire burned in the fireplace as it had done on that first day when Sorrel waited and George Martyn had come to her. She went down the passage into the main hall where Toby's romantic portrait stared at her as if she were a stranger. There was no fire here either. Not even a bed of ash. The Priory was cared for, spotless, but too quiet and too cold. It felt changed.

Perhaps it is me, she thought. Because I didn't want to come here. How powerful old houses are. They live in a spell of time woven by all the people who've lived and died in them and who've never left and are somewhere in the very walls. If you don't love a house like this, it can be your enemy. I am sorry, she said mutely to the silence round her. I don't know why I am like this. I met Toby here and we made love here and we were part of you then. She wondered if it was her anxiety that the house would not accept. Or was it telling her she simply did not belong?

Going slowly up the staircase, she found Evie had already been before her to Toby's room where she'd left Sorrel's bag. She had used the Evie-esque ruse of using a back staircase.

Here there was a semblance of welcome. The old oil stove burned blue and smelled of country houses in wintertime. On Toby's chest of drawers was a tankard of winter jasmine and in the warmth the green buds were beginning to open into yellow flowers. She stood looking at herself in Toby's mirror, seeing a girl in uniform with strain in her face. She knew it had been a mistake to come.

Whatever Toby had written, she was not part of the family. I am here because of duty, she thought. That word. We repeat it and bow to it and serve it and quote it. At school it had been a joke, picked up from a Tennyson poem. The girls used to chant 'Duty, Stern Daughter of the Voice of God'. They thought it very funny.

We are right to owe duty to our country, she thought, but how can there be a duty in love? Must I come to this house? The answer was that she must because it would hurt him if she did not, and because after the war, when their real marriage began, she would become a Martyn and find a way to bear Grace, and to believe in his father.

Leaving the bedroom, she felt very cold and went back to the main hall. She was standing by the empty fireplace when the telephone rang. She waited for Evie's brisk step, or the slower step of the old housemaid. Nobody came. The telephone continued to ring. Perhaps it will stop, she thought. It will only be the WVS for Grace, or something to do with the farm. But it went on, demanding an answer, splintering the quiet, and in the end she couldn't stand it and picked up the receiver, looking round for a pencil.

'Evendon Priory?' said a woman's voice. 'May I speak to Third Officer Martyn, please.'

'Ma'am!' Sorrel recognised Hobson's voice and a shaft of terror went through her.

'Martyn? I have some bad news for you. You must be brave.'

Sorrel couldn't speak.

'I am very sorry indeed. We all are. There's a telegram for you from the War Office. Your husband is reported missing. Believed killed.'

Silence.

'I am so very sorry,' repeated Hobson, her voice gentle. 'But you must remember it only says "believed". That means there's no real evidence that your husband is dead.'

'When will they know?' Sorrel managed to say.

'The fighting in the Balkans is so confused . . . the country's in a turmoil . . . you must still hope.'

'Yes.'

'I've put you in for extended leave. Ring me if there's anything I can do.'

'Thank you.'

Sorrel carefully replaced the receiver. She thought – I wish I'd died in your arms. I wish I'd died here in this house, in that bed upstairs. I wish I was dead now.

All the regrets that haunt the living like apparitions came rushing towards her. She had not written often enough. Had not thought of him all the time. Had not prayed. Not visited his parents and shown herself a real daughter. Had never suggested having his child.

I won't cry. What's the use? I won't cry.

She went to the window and looked out at the frost-locked garden, seeing nothing. She shook her head now and then as if an insect was buzzing across her eyes. She swallowed as grief tried to well up, and shoved it down again and stood, her breath a smoke in the icy air, clouding the windowpane. She heard Toby's stuttering laugh and his steps coming across the parquet floor towards her and spun round in terror – it was Lord Martyn. Wearing a thick dark coat, he was unwinding a long scarf from round his neck.

'My dear Sorrel, how long have you been here? What are you doing all alone, isn't Evie looking after you and why hasn't somebody lit the fire, it's icy in here – ' He threw down his coat. And then he saw.

'What's happened?'

'We've had bad news,' said Sorrel, using the same words. She went to him and, because in sorrow people touch, took his hands. He stared at her.

'A telegram just came. From the base. Toby is missing, believed killed.'

'No, no, no!' The words came out in a choking groan. 'It can't be, oh no – ' and while she still grasped his hands his face became distorted and every vestige of colour drained from it, it was not pale but a ghastly green. With a noise like a cough, he fell.

She threw herself on her knees beside him. He was heavy and had fallen, a dead weight on to the floor; he might have cracked his head or injured his spine. She tore off her jacket and covered him. She knelt beside him, not daring to leave him, believing nobody was in the house. Crawling over, she pulled his overcoat off the chair and covered him with that too. She shouted:

'Evie, Evie! *Help!*'

There was no reply.

'Help!' shouted Sorrel again, and, useless and terrified, chafed the hands of the unconscious man, now and again shouting with no hope that anybody would come. Suddenly there was the sound of running feet. It was Grace.

'George!'

She rushed across the room, knelt down beside him, pushing Sorrel away. She put her hand into his waistcoat pocket and brought out a tiny glass phial, broke it under his nose with two fingers. George Martyn stirred. She leaned over him, her large body tensed. She said without looking at Sorrel, 'Get the cushions off the sofa.'

Sorrel obeyed.

'Put one under his head. Not like that. Further down. How long has he been unconscious?'

'Three minutes. Perhaps more.'

Grace shifted him, continuing to hold the broken capsule so that he could inhale, intently watching his face. It began to lose the awful greenish tinge.

'He came in, and suddenly fell, is that what happened?'

'No. It was when I told him Toby is missing,' said Sorrel – and saw what she'd done.

Grace reeled back as if Sorrel had struck her in the mouth.

'*What?*'

'The navy rang me just now. There's a telegram from the War Office. Toby is missing. Believed killed.'

'Dear God.'

Grace shut her eyes. Her dry eyes. Then opened them.

'*And you told him that?*'

'I had only just heard. Of course I told him.'

Sorrel was appalled.

Grace looked as if she wanted to murder her.

'What kind of a woman are you? You get this terrible news and use it like a loaded gun. You could have killed George. My God! I said Toby was mad to marry you. Go and get Evie. And keep out of my sight!'

Sorrel ran from the room. She found Evie in the kitchen. When she heard what had happened Evie stood as if frozen. Sorrel gasped, 'Lord Martyn had an attack when I told him.'

'Another? Where is he?'

'On the floor in the hall. She's with him.'

'There's an Italian working in the stables. Marcello. He stays here late sometimes. Get him, he can help carry Lord Martyn upstairs.'

Grief took second place as Sorrel fetched the man, who was short and sturdy, and he and Evie managed to carry George Martyn up the stairs. Grace squeezed alongside, holding her husband's hand.

The doctor arrived surprisingly soon, and went straight up to the bedroom.

Sorrel stayed in the hall. Nobody joined her. And now she was alone she had time for sorrow. She put her hands across her stomach and rocked with the pain, letting it wound her through and through. She did not groan or cry. She simply suffered. I've lost him. I shall never see him again.

At last there were steps coming down the stairs and she saw the doctor.

'Mrs Martyn. You've had a dreadful shock. How are you?'

'How is *he*?'

'George will survive. It wasn't as bad as it might have been. Hearts are curious objects. They can give a man a nasty turn like that, and then recover and work efficiently for years. It was a mercy you were with him, and that Grace used the amyl nitrate. Sit down, you look all in.'

He sat beside her. He was old, and that was comforting.

'Don't worry about George. He's very emotional and keeps things bottled up and, when his heart needs to be strong, this happens. He's comfortable. I've prescribed the necessary things. I've told Grace he must slow down, he works himself too hard. As for young Toby, he's a survivor. Plenty of hope for Toby.'

'Do you think so?'

He thought she looked very ill.

'I've known your husband since he was at prep school,' he said with too easy a smile. 'There's a lot of hope still. You must keep going on that.'

It sounded as if he were prescribing Ovaltine.

He asked if she needed some sleeping tablets but Sorrel refused them. He stood up, pressing her hand, and said he must go. He would be back in the morning.

Sorrel remained where he left her. Fear about George Martyn had ebbed and sorrow flooded in like water in a lock.

'Sorrel, will you come into the drawing room? The fire's lit and I've made the tea. Lady Martyn's there.'

It was Evie, sounding calm.

'I saw the doctor.' Sorrel stood up, and then involuntarily, '*Oh Evie.*'

The housekeeper did not react, throw open her arms, do any comforting thing. She looked at the floor.

'Lady Martyn won't believe it. About the major. She keeps saying he's all right.'

'The doctor said the same. That we must hope.'

They stared at each other.

'Hope's a horrible thing. You're better without it,' Evie said.

'But – '

'But we got telegrams like that in the other war. *She* keeps saying he's alive. I can't bear it.'

The elaborate room, with its French screen and long rows of curtained windows, was lit with pools of light from lamps on little tables. There was Toby's photograph. And Edmund's. The fire sparkled, sending its wavering light on the heavy figure in a chair pulled close to the blaze. Tea was on a table beside Grace who did not move when Sorrel came in.

'Help yourself to tea if you wish.'

'Lady Martyn, I am so very sorry. Sorry I gave your husband such a shock when I broke the awful news – '

'It is not awful.'

'*I am sorry*,' repeated the girl, feeling, like Evie, that she couldn't bear it. 'I feel so guilty at being the cause. I had no idea his heart was bad.'

'That's a lie.'

'What do you mean? Of course I didn't know!'

'Toby told you. I told you.'

'Never. Never. I swear it!'

'You're lying,' repeated Grace, 'because you won't admit George could have died and it would have been your fault. If I hadn't come in he would be dead.'

'*Lady Martyn, I didn't know.*'

Grace made a noise of disgust. She looked at Sorrel with a face of iron.

'Listen to me. I telephoned the War Office and they are sending me a copy of this telegram you say was sent to you. I shall see it for myself. In the meantime I don't want a word about you thinking my son has been killed. Not a word. Do you understand?'

'But – '

'My God, do I have to spell it out? Do you want him dead? Is that it? I won't have it said. He is alive and that's all there is to it. While you are in this house, hold your tongue.'

Grace's face was terrible to see. It was so hard and so stricken, so angry and so sad. Christ, thought Sorrel, are we snarling like tigers over my poor Toby's dead body?

'I have already found it necessary to speak to Evie. She lost her husband in the trenches. Now she is venting it on me. I won't have it said,' continued Grace in a hard, flat voice. 'He is missing because he's in hiding. He's with the partisans. continuing the fight. Yes, that's what he's doing.'

She had been staring across the room and now she turned her eyes on Sorrel.

'I don't wish to talk to you any more. You – you affect me.'

Sorrel went up to her room and sat on the bed. What do you do when somebody's dead? Let them invade you? Or keep them away? Do you suffer or do you fight? She didn't know. She simply sat, as time crawled by like a snake, and Evie finally tapped on the door and said Lady Martyn had gone to the sickroom and Lord Martyn was slightly better. Evie had brought up a tray of food. Sorrel shook her head. Evie did not try to persuade her, but went away.

Sorrel spent the night without sleep; she did not once lose consciousness but bore the passing of the hours, and at five in the morning rose, dressed, packed her kit, scribbled a line to Evie and crept from the house. Walking down the road her night sight returned, and she saw the dim sky and the trees. It was freezing hard. She thought – grief doesn't kill. It should. Oh Toby, you were right to want a Stoic for a wife. But I'm not. I'm not.

She had tramped for above five miles when there was the noisy sound of a jeep. It ground to a halt, and an American voice said, 'Want a lift, beautiful?'

She called, 'Yes.'

'What are you doing by yourself in the middle of nowhere?

Some guy's crazy to let you loose with the US of A on the lookout for dames. Sit between us. You okay?'

The two Americans, a sergeant and a GI, were in high spirits and delighted to have found a pretty girl to keep them company. They were too cheerful to notice her silence. They laughed and smoked and made jokes and sang. The jeep was open to every breath of icy wind, but they were warm and young and bursting with life. Sorrel automatically answered their good-natured questions and now and again managed an actressy laugh. After a while they settled down to singing; they had an inexhaustible supply of songs from Hollywood musicals.

Sorrel sat thinking, not of her husband but of Grace. Why had she found her optimism unbearable? Grace could be right, nobody seemed to know what was happening in Yugoslavia, Anthony English had said so, the newspapers said so, the fighting was 'confused' as they called it. People got separated from their units and disappeared and turned up weeks later. It had been like that in Italy. But Evie was right. Hope was a terrible thing.

The Americans were on their way to camp outside Reading and offered to find her a second lift to get her to London, but she refused. She asked to be put down near Reading station. With still undimmed spirits and kindness, they did as she asked, shouting after her, 'You look out for yourself, beautiful. If you want help, ask a GI.'

Daylight was beginning and so was a winter fog. The train was packed and Sorrel stood looking out at the city as it spread across the dreary landscape. At rows of small houses where washing hung in the back gardens, looking as if it would never dry or be clean again. Here and there was a hole like a missing tooth, the house on either side supported by the familiar giant crutches. Further on she saw much larger spreads of ruin, there were whole streets which had been flattened by flying bombs.

When she arrived at Paddington she had to queue for over half an hour for a telephone, but the long wait simply did not affect her. She concentrated only on her misery. At last it was her turn, and she rang the base. Hobson spoke to her and when Sorrel asked for extended leave was over-kind and granted her two more days. She sounded like a schoolmistress whose pupil has tonsillitis.

The station was already submerged in a dark sulphurous fog, the people covered their faces with scarves or handkerchiefs which were soon filthy. Taxis crawled away in tiny glows of light. Sorrel took a taxi to Park Lane. All she could think about was seeing somebody who belonged to Toby. Innocently responsible for his father's heart attack, with his mother so cruelly set against her, she longed to see Dot. She had no family, and when she returned to Lee there would be nothing but empty comradeship. She was ill and more alone than ever in her life.

Over the arch of the mews the sculpted head of the horse had disappeared into the fog. The cobbles at her feet were almost invisible. She somehow found her way to Aunt Dot's door and rang the bell. Supposing she's out for the day, what shall I do? Where can I go? The thought of the club brought back a vision of Margaret Reilly's white face. My fear was right, thought Sorrel. I'm like that now.

She stood in the fog, not aware of the thick darkness pressing against her. She did not look up at the dim shapes of bedraggled pigeons huddled along the edge of the roof. The tears she'd kept away began to come. Toby was dead. Lying dead, God knew where. How cold Evendon had been. How ghastly his poor father had looked with that greenish face. How pathetic in her cruelty Grace was. Grace, more than anybody, seemed to rend her heart. Sorrel cried for the grief of a world where your mother's grave was a bomb crater and your husband's death a telephone call. Her girlhood had gone with Lilian, her future with Toby. She stood in excruciating pain in the fog by the locked door of the house. 'Oh Toby,' she kept saying aloud, 'Oh Toby.' Her eyes were blinded and she didn't see a figure loom out of the fog.

'Hey, surely that's Sorrel Martyn!'

It was Buzz Alderman.

She was too far gone to recover, too swept away in floods of misery and when he heard her crying he put out his arms and pulled her into them. He held her close, so close that she couldn't have got away, but she didn't want to. Pressed against him, she knew her heart was broken.

When she sobbingly told him what had happened he said nothing, but continued to press her in his arms. At last she quietened, making the shuddering gasps of somebody who has cried too long.

'Dot must be out,' he said gently. 'Come back to my club. You could use a drink. Come along, there's a good girl.'

He put his arm round her shoulders. Knowing the way in the black void, he led her down the street. His arm was warm.

He turned in through some gates and they walked down a path with grass on either side, into the dimly glowing porch of Claremont House.

The eighteenth-century mansion had been let, lock, stock, and the least valuable of its chandeliers, to the American air force. There was music coming down the hall, and as Sorrel and Buzz, dazzled by the light after the blackness, came indoors, there was a roar of laughter from somewhere. Big double doors opened on to a drawing room where there was a crowd of American servicemen and their girls. And a strong smell of cigarette smoke, alcohol and scent.

Buzz and Sorrel left their coats with an attendant who stood by a table piled with furs.

'We'll go to the ballroom,' Buzz said. He took her towards the music. The old ballroom was still used, as it had been in rich peacetime for dancing and meals and festivities. On a dais at the far end of the room a group of musicians in uniform were playing 'Stay as Sweet as You Are'.

Buzz ordered drinks. He did not talk to her until they arrived – glasses of neat rye whisky.

'Drink up. It'll do you good.'

He had always thought her a beautiful girl. He had been strongly attracted to her when they'd met months ago. But she had been happily married, and despite married women here in England not seeming to keep their vows and cheating on their absent husbands with all his friends and with Buzz too, he could see there was no hope of sex with the beguiling distant English Wren. He respected her. At home in Alabama you did respect girls of good family. Women were of two kinds, there was no half measure with Buzz. A woman was a whore or a lady, and the English Wren was a lady.

Now he felt differently. A surge of pity and sex filled him. She was so pretty, so pale, so foreign, so alluring, so sorrowful. He asked about her husband, and Sorrel, recovered a little and feeling the whisky warming her icy coldness, told him. She spoke about Grace.

'She refuses to accept it. People say where there's life . . . but I feel in every bit of me that he is dead.'

His curious face, puffy and colourless, with slanting eyes, had an ironic Eastern cast of features. He did not show his thoughts.

'It's tough to choose between hope and despair.'

'I daren't hope.'

'Maybe that's the brave way.'

'Oh, but I'm not. I'm a coward. Such a coward.'

He was an utter stranger and she told him things she'd never spoken of to other people. Was it because he was American and she sensed that he was emotional under that quiet calm? Perhaps people talk to priests like this, she thought, and poured out the story of the pathetic brief marriage, the parents-in-law she did not understand, her own rootless present.

'I belong nowhere. To no one.'

The whisky, the warm room, the music, the small created world of youth and America affected her. She felt dazed and she felt better.

'I absolutely mustn't have another drink,' she said.

'And I absolutely think we must eat. I'll call up Dot first. I'll say you're here and would like to stay with her tonight. Is that what you want?'

'Oh yes. Do you really think she'll be home?'

'She's always in around now or slightly later. Dot's pleasures are pretty routine,' he said. He looked at her protectively.

'Don't move an inch. I'll be right back.'

When he had gone she sat looking at the dancers, but she did not see them. It was as if, standing in front of them, Toby's ghost appeared. She saw him as he'd been on the morning they had said goodbye, thin, tired after making love to her all night long. She heard his laugh. The ghost vanished as Buzz's tall figure threaded his way between the tables, stopping for a moment to talk to another pilot who sat at a table with three girls.

Buzz sat down beside Sorrel.

'She was back. And she'd heard the news, her brother called her up. Sounds as if he's made a good recovery. She asked if she could speak to you, but he said you'd left. She's eager to see you – just the right person to be with. She'll see you don't grieve.'

'But I ought to.'

'That's just nonsense. You do. You are. But I won't have you getting sick. I am going to look after you.'

'Are you?'

'What do you think?'

They went out into the fog again to walk to the mews, and she put her hand through his arm. A quivering sensation came over her. She almost tripped on the invisible pavement and he caught her in his arms. A longing went through her, did he know that? As they turned into the almost invisible mews, he suddenly pulled her over to a corner and pressed her against a wall. In a black obscurity like blindness or the smoke of death, he began to kiss her. Gentle, Southern-born, tender, enigmatic, he forced her mouth open and thrust his tongue into it, grasped her to him; she could feel his want against her, he was violently trembling. She answered the embrace as fiercely, holding him against her as if she were drowning. He gasped, 'I want you. I want to throw you on a bed and rape you.'

'It wouldn't be rape, I want you too.'

'Do you? Do you?'

They kissed again. He pressed her, moving and thrusting, against the wall.

'Oh God – what – how – I must have you – I shall go mad.'

'But how can we? You said Aunt Dot – '

'We've got time. I – I must – '

She said nothing. They walked in silence back through the fog which tasted like sulphur. When they re-entered the house their faces were grimed with it. Buzz fetched his key and still in silence they went up a graceful stair and along a passageway lined with the spaces where paintings had hung, ghost works of art, white on silk-covered yellow walls. He fitted his key into the lock of the door.

And Sorrel never once remembered that she had been to a man's bedroom before, and he, too, had put the key into the lock and turned it and led her into a room in an empty hotel by the cold winter sea. She did not remember Toby's face or body when she and Buzz, the door safely locked, the room strangely warm, threw off their clothes and stood for a moment, lit by desire to a sort of madness, looking at each other's nakedness.

Then he walked towards her and, as he'd wanted to do, took her almost before she had time to open her legs and her arms.

She had made love with only two men before this. The forgotten pilot who had taken her virginity, and Toby whose lovemaking was intense and excited and sometimes too fast. Even when that had left her unsatisfied, love had glowed in every part of her. This was frighteningly different. It was savage and exciting and somehow it was connected with death. What did she or he know of whether they would survive? She was shivering with excitement and he made her come at once, and then again, and later again. Tender Southerner that he was, he treated her as a whore and a slave. He thrust into her so long and so strongly that she reached her climax without wanting to and lay helpless under him. He was heavy on her and she could scarcely breathe, he seemed unconscious of crushing her, he lay taking her like a starving man. At last, after the third time, he separated from her in silence and leaned, stretching out an arm of strong muscle and fine dark hair, to pick up his watch.

They had not spoken a word.

'We must go.'

She lay naked on the bed. The room's American warmth made it possible to lie without even a sheet. She closed her eyes. All the sensual aftermath of sex, the certainty that she'd never want it again, that this satiety would last, that she could sleep and forget her sorrow . . . suddenly left her. Toby was dead. She would never know him again. The pain was so sharp that she almost groaned. Buzz, beside her, didn't move for a while. She felt him reach for a cigarette and heard the snap of the lighter. As the pain began to recede she thought – this man does not love me. I don't care. Is it a sin to let him do all he did just now? I don't care. It keeps this away. *This.*

'You'll want a shower,' Buzz said, climbing out of bed, 'I need one too.'

He had not returned to the courtly American who had looked after her with gentle concern. He was still a sexual stranger, a marauder who'd used her body until he'd finished with it. And who now ruled that they should wash away what was left of sex. To make them clean. Is it dirty, then? thought Sorrel. But the pain had come back and she forgot the question.

She went into the bathroom. The Americans, who could not give their fighting men enough luxuries to repay them for their risked lives, had fitted showers to the old-fashioned baths in all the bathrooms. The soap was too highly scented for a man. She tried to make her mind blank, concentrating on washing, then wrapped herself in a large white towel and came out to find Buzz still smoking, wearing a dressing gown.

'How is it?' he said.

And she saw the other man had come back.

Sorrel spent the brief leave with Dot. Toby's aunt was sympathetic but not sentimental, her very practicality helped. And she was rich and that was a kind of balm. Had Dot been home when Sorrel rang the bell in the fog, had Buzz not appeared when she stood sobbing in the dark, Dot would have comforted her as much as any human can comfort another. But it had not been like that. It was Buzz who kept speechless misery at bay with sex. He was on leave after missions over Germany and until he found Sorrel had been spending his time with the bright hungry girls who surrounded Americans.

To Sorrel Buzz was the drug prescribed. The strong drug to alleviate pain. When she saw him her body reacted, she wanted him because it stopped her from feeling. She wanted him from excitement and desperation. She simply wanted him.

Buzz's own emotions for her alarmed him. He did not understand them. In sex he had always been a man without love, his deep feelings were for his parents, his sister, his home and the strange beautiful State where he was born. This English girl, pale with sorrow, got him in the guts. In the balls. She was like the best of the Alabaman girls back home, the sweetest and the liveliest, even now there were signs of the girl she really was despite her mourning. He called to see Dot and Sorrel, to spend time with other Yanks in Dot's small drawing room, and then, sooner or later, he and Sorrel would walk to Claremont House. And fall on the bed and make love as if they had never done it before in their lives and could not stop.

During the hours of sex neither spoke a word of love. Used no endearments. They merely stripped naked and claimed each other's bodies. 'Use me,' was all he said as she put her hands on him. 'Use me.' And she did.

When he was with Dot he reverted to the Alabaman gentleman, gallant, attentive. Sorrel only had two nights with Dot, and when they were dressing for dinner on the second night before Sorrel must go back, Dot wandered into Sorrel's bedroom where the girl, in black taffeta, was doing her face with make-up supplied by Buzz. She also wore a pair of the curious, newly-invented nylon stockings, black and transparent.

Dot sat down on the bed. She was in gold, her hair a soft halo, her own face painted. She studied Sorrel in silence.

'Are you sleeping?' she finally asked.

'I wake a lot. But I do sleep.'

'How are you? Really?'

'It comes in waves. Goes. Then come back.'

'I remember.'

Sorrel put down the comb and turned to look at her. She wanted to ask about the sorrow of Dot's own past. But meeting her eyes, couldn't and only said, 'I'm worried about Lord Martyn. I should have rung.'

Dot lit a Lucky Strike.

'What would you say if you did?'

Sorrel was rubbing scent on her wrist. She noticed nothing in the question.

'Ask how he is, naturally.'

'You would annoy Grace.'

Then Sorrel did glance up to be met with a dazzling smile.

'You don't have to worry about George, he's on the mend, I've been ringing a good deal. I think it might be better if you didn't. As you told me, Grace refuses to accept it about darling Toby. She's like that. It was the same with Edmund. Yes, I *know* Toby's only been reported missing, Sorrel, and he may easily be still alive. I still hope too. But Grace won't take bad news of any kind. It wasn't until Edmund's CO went to see her and described the thing and said how he'd taken the poor boy's burial service that Grace accepted it.'

Sorrel listened painfully. Forgetting herself for a moment.

'And when she did she started making plans about having his body moved after the war and buried in Evendon churchyard and what she'd have engraved on the stone.'

Dot drew on her cigarette.

'We all thought she was an odd choice for my brother.'

'He seems devoted,' said Sorrel listlessly.

'People are all "devoted" to Grace as you call it. We're slightly afraid of her in actual fact. Her standards are too hideously high. Coming from generations of soldiers. One of those families who can reel off battles everybody had forgotten. It explains her mania about her country. Of course I love old England,' said Dot, gesturing at the silk box of the bedroom, 'but half an hour of Grace and I feel like a Fifth Columnist. Anyway, don't call them up. Do it later when you're back at the base and when,' she added, looking straight at Sorrel, 'you feel better.'

Sorrel wanted to say, 'I never shall feel better.' She couldn't imagine a time when she would not be in pain for part, for most of her waking life. She still wished she was dead.

'George is bearing up. Like you,' said Dot. 'Anyway, to more cheerful things. What about Buzz bringing you that gigantic bottle of Chanel? He's fallen for you. Better beware.'

'It's only his American generosity.'

'Funny joke,' said Dot with a wink. She looked calmly at Sorrel across the bars of cigarette smoke and Sorrel had a sudden, sharp fear. She knows. How can she know?

Dot was going to a party at the Ritz that evening and when Buzz called she was just leaving. Buzz kissed her, setting the velvet ribbons in her hair awry.

'Now look what you've done!' cried Dot, laughing. Sorrel stood on the stairs, watching the embracing couple, and Dot called over his shoulder, 'Jealous?'

She tripped away on exaggerated heels to a waiting taxi.

Sorrel and Buzz went up the narrow stair to a drawing room which smelled of Dot's tangy scent. She had arranged drinks for them, set out on a side table. She always did things like that.

'Well?' he said, as they came into the room.

'Well, Buzz?'

'What do you want to do this evening?'

She poured him some rye, thinking how smart American uniform was; too smart. There was something exaggerated in the cut; it was like fancy dress. He sat down, looking absurd among the silk cushions.

'Like to go to a Crosby movie? Something to make you laugh?'

Just for a moment it was the Alabaman gentleman who spoke. But as he took the glass he looked her up and down with heavy eyes and her stomach turned over. She swallowed a dozen pills of the drug he always brought with him.

He would not go into her bedroom but made her lie down on the floor. The air-raid warning sounded again as he plunged into her with that now familiar violence she wanted and would have begged for. In the distance somewhere was the dull thud as a bomb landed, but they never heard it. They struggled like enemies, Buzz's weight pressing her to the floor so that she could scarcely breathe.

A week later Dot rang her at the base to say Buzz had been killed in a raid over the Ardennes.

PART THREE

14

In a sunlit May in 1945 the war in Europe was over and London went mad with joy, the lights blazing in Piccadilly and people swarming like bees round the Palace to shout for the King. Bonfires sparkled in Green Park; they were made from doors of air raid shelters. Everybody in the world seemed to be kissing everybody else. There were flags. Church bells. And Britain was drunk not with alcohol as much as with joy.

A week after the celebrations Commanding Officer Hobson sent for Sorrel and said without preliminary, 'Well, Martyn. Good news. You're to go on indefinite leave until the navy decides what to do with you. And with a good many more of us, I might add.' A slight laugh ended the sentence.

'Ma'am?'

'Don't look so flabbergasted,' said Hobson in good-natured tones. 'You're scarcely wanted to do your old job any more, now are you? Torpedoes are extinct, and what kind of decoding will we need?'

Another laugh. Hobson actually looked quite pretty. She had finally succeeded in getting the irresistible Captain Lyall to propose.

'The sea, thank God, is free again,' was her next pious remark. 'So off home with you.'

The girl was silent. Hobson put her own happiness aside for a moment. Responsibility dies hard.

'You're not brooding, are you, Martyn?'

'No, Ma'am.'

'Good. You've borne up well. Very well. A number of people have remarked upon it.'

Sorrel thanked her. Hobson tried without success to imagine herself in the shoes of the young woman facing her. But happiness blurred the thoughts, and for the first time since she had met Sorrel, sexual resentment had melted. She saw a pale good-looking girl who had been wounded, perhaps fatally, by the war. A girl to whom peace must be a mockery. I suppose there are women all over the country in the same boat, thought Hobson. They'll cope. We're a bulldog breed.

'You're young and have your life before you,' she said, reaching for the cliché. 'You'll make a new life for yourself. Our war is over. We've got to get used to that, haven't we?'

Two days later, having said goodbye to many acquaintances and her only real friend, Anthony English, who had kissed her, Sorrel left Lee-on-Solent for the last time.

She was on her way to Evendon.

She'd written to her parents-in-law a number of times and had received two short replies from George Martyn. They read like duty letters. Since the news of Toby, since George Martyn's heart attack, Sorrel had kept away. She felt responsible for George's illness, and she dreaded seeing Grace again.

There was another graver reason why Sorrel avoided going to see them. Her duties in the Wrens, her friendships, never intimate, her daily existence with its blessed routines and disciplines had kept her going since she had lost her husband. She accepted that Toby was dead. The intervals between the pain grew longer, though the pain itself when it came was still so bad that she felt ill. But recently there had been something else in her thoughts; she had begun to have a feeling that she'd done something dreadfully wrong. That sexual interlude with Buzz was heavy on her conscience. She'd been unfaithful to the husband she passionately loved and for whom that time in London she hadn't even begun to mourn. What had she done instead? Lain with a man she scarcely knew and did not love and behaved like an animal on heat. It was degrading. Although Buzz's death hit her like a piece of shrapnel, as the weeks and months extended she forgot her addiction to sex with him completely. She only remembered his Southern accent so soft and lazy, his courtesy and his ugly, appealing face.

It was Toby who returned to her imagination and to her body, and it was Toby on VE Day and afterwards who made her conscious of all that she had lost.

Before leaving Lee she telephoned the Priory. There was no reply. She rang later in the evening and heard the bell ring and ring but no answer came. She supposed Evie, the heart of the house, must be out and perhaps George and Grace too. Everything had changed, even the idea of the family and their lives at the Priory.

Travelling to Evendon still in uniform, she didn't feel changed at all. Peacetime did not seem to have arrived. The idea of being a civilian depressed her, it was such an anti-climax. Life had been simple because the navy made it so. She would no longer have a set pattern, no longer have reason for doing things, no longer be in comforting masculine company a good part of every day. She made a plan. She would do what looked most natural, turn up at the Priory to have a drink with her parents-in-law. Drink, as it were, to peace. And make her own peace with them. She would not stay unless – which seemed unlikely – they pressed her to do so. She would take a train back to London and stay at the Curzon Club. With luck she might see Aunt Dot who must be in the thick of peacetime parties. It was unfamiliar to think of Dot without war as her background. She seemed essentially a lady who valiantly ignored air raids, had stores of unobtainable things like drink and scent from countless American friends, whose entire life was based somehow on the war. But Dot would adapt, it was in her nature to match the times. And Dot would give Sorrel what she sorely needed, advice on her own blank future.

How beautiful Hampshire is, she thought, coming out of the familiar station where no car or pony trap awaited her. Over the wooden-built entrance a flag hung, not stirring in the still air. It was a perfect day, fresh, with a pure blue sky and in the distance the faint haze of coming warmth. Everything was sweet-smelling and quiet, and when she set off to walk the few miles to the Priory, the birdsong was loud, a large untrained choir, every bird competing with its neighbour in shrill sweetness or monotonous merry chirps.

Walking down the road she was suddenly eager to see Toby's home again, to go up to his room, to see the portrait of him in the hall, even to talk to Grace. She felt impelled towards the old house, which she'd never done when Toby was alive. What pushed her and made her quicken her steps was the unfamiliar force of peace. Soon she saw the lanky poplars at the corner, the trees putting out small leaves silver on their undersides; when a breeze shook them, they sounded like the sea. A stirring like hope came to Sorrel. She arrived at the gates.

They were shut.

She'd never seen them closed before and noticed the wrought-iron tracery, patterns of leaves and formalised flowers.

She turned one of the gate's enormous black handles; it did not yield. The gates were not shut, they were locked.

Sorrel couldn't believe it. She stood looking through the twisted iron flowers towards the house – was that, too, locked? But it was not possible, the Priory was a farm and you never went away and left a farm.

I suppose they've had no visitors for a long time and have decided they prefer to lock the gates, she thought. There must be somebody there. The sight of the distant house drew her on. The Priory grounds rose a little, they were surrounded by a low brick wall, below which was a ditch brimming with recent rains. Sorrel jumped over it, scrambled up the bank and climbed easily over the wall.

There lay the house, its old familiar rambling self. She had not seen it for many months and thought, with surprise, that it was beautiful. She started at a sudden burst of noise. A flock of rooks landed on a tree nearby and began to caw harshly one after the other, then in croaking unison.

Sorrel went into the porch and rang the bell. She waited. She rang again, hearing the bell jangling in the distance in Evie's kitchen. Nobody answered but the rooks. Nobody opened the door or looked from a window. She bent and stared through a low window into the hall; she could make out the carved oak chest and the brass-bound umbrella stand. Nothing was changed. Nothing was alive either.

In the next half hour she wandered round the grounds and into the farm buildings without meeting a soul. All the livestock was gone, not a horse, a cow, a duck, even. Everything was empty. Beyond the house she could see the rise of the forty-acre field; it had been planted with young corn and as she looked a wind raced across it, exactly as if it were green water turning, moment by moment, into waves. There was no sign of a land-girl or an Italian prisoner. The rooks flapped away. Most silent of all was the cherry orchard in full and ravishing flower, the beautiful trees covered in bridal, heart-rending white. Sorrel looked at them. She was alone in the world. The last survivor of the long, long war.

She went across the yard where she and Toby had led the horses on the day he'd taught her to ride, and where they'd met Dion and Toby had been so angry. She peered into windows, some of which were barred, and made out a table, a vase. She picked an early flowering rose. She was a ghost.

What had happened? Where had the Martyns gone? Why hadn't Aunt Dot written or telephoned? On VE Day when the church bells pealed and everybody embraced, Sorrel had felt lonely. But not like this. Not a visitant from a previous life, haunting the place where she had been happy. This was – is – Toby's home. He and I fell in love here. Why didn't I come back after he died? It's true Grace was angry but only from worry about George and misery over Toby. They needed me. And all I did was sleep with Buzz and go into my shell and try to feel nothing, while they were suffering as much as I was. She saw too clearly what she had done. She had thrown away the parents of the man who loved her. And they'd gone without thinking it necessary to tell her why.

The sun flooded down on the one dark-clad figure in a scene of Maytime gaiety. The old house, it own secrets locked inside it, was asleep.

She bent and picked up a stone, a jagged fragment from one of the corners of the terrace. She put it in her pocket and went down the drive between the vegetable gardens and the flowering weeds, over the wall across the brimming ditch.

She did not return towards the station, but took the road she used to walk with Dion Fulford at a time that seemed a century ago.

The Raven was hung with strings of faded flags draped from the inn-sign of the knowing black bird and tied to a tree by the front door. All the windows were open and Sorrel half expected to see American soldiers squatting on windowsills and sitting on the steps. The only people about were two old men standing by the open door, sunning themselves like a couple of grey-muzzled retrievers; they were holding tankards and talking, each giving the other thoughtful nods.

Sorrel was greeted with the kind of look she was used to, the 'there's a brave lass' which girls in the services accepted and expected. The bar was dark after the bright day, and smelled of beer. The barman and a small tweed-jacketed man with the air of an ostler were deep in conversation, but turned to give her good morning.

'I am sorry to bother you,' said Sorrel politely, 'but I wonder if you could help me. It's about the Priory. Are the family away? The house seems to be shut up.'

'Aren't you the Major's wife, Madam?' said the barman with considerable interest, and the short man with him gave a grin. 'Of course she is. Met you once, didn't I, Mrs Martyn? Gave you a lift to the Priory.'

It was Jack Bishop whose van had brought her to meet the Martyns on one momentous winter day.

'Thought I recognised you,' chimed the barman, who had white hair and sharp grey eyes. 'Saw you at the church, day of your wedding.'

'Condolences on your sad loss,' put in Jack Bishop. 'The wife and I were deeply shocked. Deeply shocked.'

'Same as all the village,' agreed the barman, polishing a glass. 'Sorry to presume, Madam, but didn't you know the family is selling up.'

She blushed with shock.

'*Selling up?*'

'Why yes,' put in Bishop. 'Left about five or six weeks ago, wasn't it the day the Yanks entered Hanover and the Russians were in Vienna?'

The barman consulted a calendar on the wall. It had pencilled notes scrawled under each day.

'Makes four weeks to the day, Jack. Not as long ago as you think. Yes. That's when they moved.'

'Beg your pardon, Mrs Martyn,' said Jack Bishop, standing with his legs apart and looking at her curiously, 'but you must have come from overseas, not knowing about the family.'

'My letters haven't caught up with me yet,' said Sorrel, by now ready with that simple explanation. 'It was very stupid of me, just getting on to a train.'

'It's what we all do. Want to come home,' said Bishop. The barman offered her some sherry. Sorrel accepted. She was on her guard, but her visit was not yet finished.

'I suppose you don't happen to know where my husband's family has gone?' she said, sitting on a bar stool and speaking in a relaxed voice, while she hoped the question did not sound as preposterous to them as it did to her. The two men were intrigued by the visitor and her unexpected appearance, let alone the fact that she'd gone red as a peony when she'd heard the news. They said the post office would have a forwarding address, sure to, but they'd heard the Martyns had gone to London; apparently it had been her Ladyship who wished to leave.

'Perhaps she couldn't bear the place because it reminded her too much of my husband. And her other son as well.'

They stared at the ground, embarrassed. Jack Bishop muttered, yes, something like that.

'They haven't moved their stuff out yet and lots of it's valuable, as you know, Mrs Martyn. They had bars put up.'

'What about the farm? All the animals?'

'Sold to Mr Longstaffe at Butterbox. He snapped 'em up, every last duck and pig, and the horses, though I heard the major's old hunter was found a good home with Mrs Lorimer. She hunts, as you know. There's that land. Longstaffe doesn't want it and nor does anybody else. But the land'll go with the house.'

Sorrel had learned all there was. She did not like to leave at once and the two men made an effort to talk to her, speaking admiringly of her father-in-law and how he would be missed in the village. Did she know his lordship used to call in at The Raven sometimes? He was like that; he'd stand drinks for any troops that happened to be about. Generous to a fault.

Faintly, a thought from another life, Sorrel imagined George Martyn drinking here in this very bar . . . glancing from a window, and seeing her on the river bank with Dion.

She was glad to leave, and having thanked them, agreed that it would be best to make enquiries at the local post office. She walked out.

When she had gone the two men exchanged looks.

'There's more in this than meets the eye,' said the landlord. 'His lordship never done that by mistake. Not informing her.'

'She's been overseas. Didn't get his letters.'

'Stuff and nonsense. Everybody gets their letters,' said the landlord, expert in such things.

Sorrel walked down the road in the sun and shadow. She felt stunned. It was cruel of her parents-in-law to throw her off in this way. They had deliberately concealed the news, they did not want to see her again. She supposed it must be because she'd been an uncaring kind of daughter. It was her own fault, she had been in the wrong. They had lost their second son and they had adored him. She remembered the way they used to sit at the dining table, eyes fixed on him while he ranted about the lower classes or extravagantly praised the enemy. Sorrel thought of George's kindness to her mother, his slightly false paternal way to her. But always generous. The shock of the locked house darkened the day. In her thoughts the Priory had existed the way she had known it when she was happy, with its well-tended and busy farm, Dion leading the great horses, the steady pulse of life – and Toby. As she walked back and passed the house again, it chilled her. It was the tomb of her marriage.

Suddenly she remembered Dot. Of course! Dot would supply the answers, she might even say Toby's parents had genuinely meant her to know and that a letter had genuinely not reached her. Quickening her step and slightly recovered, slightly hopeful, Sorrel arrived again at the station. There were two telephone boxes outside the station, the sun pouring through their closed glass doors. When Sorrel went into one of them, there was that particular smell, a mixture of old telephone books and dust and cigarettes.

She put her loose change on top of the money box and dialled Dot's number. It was early afternoon. Would she be back yet from one of her lunches, probably yet another Victory celebration? The number rang. No reply. Sorrel felt miserably disappointed and was now convinced Dot would explain everything. She stood letting the number ring boringly, while she imagined the mews house . . . the number rang on. Just as she was going to hang up an instantly recognisable voice, youthful and spirited, said:

'Mayfair 6070.'

Sorrel pushed her money in and pressed the button.

'Aunt Dot?'

'Who is that, please?'

'Aunt Dot, it's Sorrel!'

'Of course. Stupid of me. How are you? Still beavering away in Hampshire? I daresay you've got the universal hangover we're all suffering from. Did you celebrate until dawn?'

'Yes. Well. There have been some quite nice dances.'

Dot said good but did not sound herself.

Sorrel burst out, 'I'm at Evendon. I went to the Priory just now and it is all shut up. They told me locally it is to be sold. Is that true?'

The pause was too long.

'What on earth made you trek all the way down there?'

'I telephoned yesterday and there was no reply and I thought the family must be out, so I just came. I wanted to see Toby's parents.'

'Did you now?'

Warm Dot, impulsive Dot, where was she?

'Yes, Aunt Dot, I did. I've been feeling very guilty at not being in touch,' said Sorrel, suddenly angry at the tone of Dot's voice. 'I daresay it's been my fault. But Toby's parents haven't been in touch with me much either. And now the war in Europe's over and everything's going to be different, I very much want to see them. It's been too long.'

Silence.

'Are you there?'

'Yes, I'm here.'

'What's happened, please?'

'Nothing dramatic. My brother's sick of the country and Grace is depressed. It's finally become clear to her that your husband won't come back. They're staying in town awhile and deciding things. A lot of things.'

'I understand.'

'I don't expect you do.'

'If you mean I haven't realised that they don't want to see me, of course I have. I'm not mad. I just wish I understood. Dot – ' Sorrel was suddenly aware of the image of Toby's aunt, her frivolous face, radiant smile, her warmth and gaiety. 'It can't be that I didn't write, surely? When your brother was taken ill, Toby's mother was so furious with me. It was embarrassing. I thought once he was better she would cool down and we could meet, but I've been too miserable to see them. I just tried to push everything out of my mind. Was it that? My not coming to see them?'

'Of course it wasn't.'

'Then I don't understand.'

'Don't you, Sorrel? Think about it. I must go. That's the doorbell. 'Bye.'

Dot rang off.

Sorrel replaced the receiver. Her heart was pounding. She had never met such antipathy, such a change of face.

She went into the station.

Indefinite leave. The words meant home. When they were spoken, people thought of cottages or castles, cramped houses back to back or manors like Evendon. Of what was left in the dockland slums, or comfortable suburban houses pretending to be Tudor. It was because of that pull, that power in an idea, that she'd come here. The Priory had been a sort of home, often as she had denied it. She had a niche there. And there was a photograph of Toby and herself on their wedding day in the drawing room.

The old porter she had known by sight for nearly four years was busy watering lettuces growing in a bed by the platform. She had the idiotic desire to be recognised when she spoke to him, but he looked at her as if she were a stranger. She asked the time of the next London train. A good half hour, he said.

'There's one on the down line,' he added, putting down his watering can as a plume of smoke rose far off down the line, and the train appeared, growing larger and noisier each second until it drew up with a steamy sigh. She watched the passengers getting out. A soldier. Two sailors who saluted her. We're your mates, said the salute. A woman with a basketful of books. A middle-aged man in a raincoat, despite the sunny day. And then, a young woman. She was short and thin, wore a pinafore dress and a checked shirt like a cowboy's. She walked with a springing step towards the barrier.

It was Pauline.

She saw Sorrel at the same moment and ran up to her.

'By all that's wonderful! I've been thinking of you every day, I was going to pop into the Priory for news of you, I *completely* lost your address – what luck finding you! I suppose you've just come from the Priory.'

Sorrel shook her head, but couldn't speak. Why did Pauline's kind voice make her cry?

'My *dear* girl, what's happened?'

'Toby is dead.'

Pauline was aghast. The old porter, exasperated by two passengers who were neither coming nor going, returned to his garden.

'Oh, my poor Sorrel, poor poor girl. When? Where?'

'In Yugoslavia months ago. Missing, believed killed – he was a commando. I'm sorry for being an idiot. It's just that – that I went to the Priory and nobody was there.'

'You mean they're away?'

'It's locked up. It's going to be sold.'

Pauline took it in. She looked with concern at the forlorn

figure. She said briefly, 'Are you in a hurry, Sorrel? When are you due back?'

'I'm not.'

'But surely – '

'I'm on indefinite leave.'

Pauline took that in too. She said after a moment, 'Why not come with me? I'm here to look at Dion's old digs. Couldn't we have some tea and talk?'

Sorrel mopped her eyes.

'Do come,' said Pauline. 'It would be nice to talk, surely? It's so good to see you after all this time.'

She waved her ticket at the porter who ignored her.

They began to walk away in the direction of the village.

'Chris is okay, is he?' Sorrel said in a normal voice.

'He's had a fever and last time he wrote he was chockfull of pills. Yes, he's okay but sometimes I daren't even think it, let alone say it. With the war out there still on. Sorrel . . . '

'Yes?'

'You said missing believed killed. Have you given up hoping then?'

'It's been too long. I know he is dead.'

Pauline was silent for a while. They walked along.

'I bet he died in glory. He was a brave man.'

There was another silence as if at a graveside. But there was nobody to say the prayers.

In the village the high street was narrow and here and there bicycles were propped. The shop fronts were blistered and peeling and in the window of the haberdashers were rolls of mauve and white gingham marked 'Export Reject. Spend your coupons on a bargain'. The squared check patterns of the gingham had slipped, they were blurred as if out of focus.

Beyond the shops were a few cottages, one of which was set back at a distance from the road with a path between rough grass and an unpatriotic mass of dark red wallflowers. A board, now almost illegible, bore the ghostly message 'Teas served'.

'Dion and I often came here,' Pauline said. 'I wonder if Miss Banning is still in the land of the living.'

She rang the bell.

A woman of about sixty, with a mop of white hair and the face of a handsome man, came to the door. She exclaimed at seeing Pauline. There were introductions and Sorrel's hand was firmly grasped.

'I suppose there's no hope of tea, Miss Banning?' said Pauline.

The lady said she would see what could be done, and ushered them into a front room.

It was hot and airless, the room looked as if it was sealed, and the only sound was the dreary buzz of a fly. Miss Banning threw open the windows, and the smell of wallflowers poured in. She told them to sit down, gave them a schoolmaster's smile and left them.

'This place looks as if she hasn't used it for the duration,' remarked Pauline, sitting in a chair covered with crumbling brown leather. There was a handmade rag mat in front of an empty fireplace and polished fireirons. On a table was a large photograph of a soldier in the uniform of the Great War. He smiled in immortal embarrassment, twenty years old.

'Miss Banning knows who you are,' remarked Pauline. 'I daresay she saw the picture of your wedding in our local paper.'

'Did she know Toby and Edmund?'

'Yes and no. Like us, at bazaars. She used to be a teacher at the infant school, you know. She taught Dion and me. Strict but fair. Oh goody, tea.'

The tray brought in by their hostess might have been prepared in The Blue Parrot in 1942. Sorrel noticed the thin and yellowish victory sponge. There were slices of bread and margarine and a dab of plum jam. When Miss Banning had gone, Pauline poured out, and cut the cake. She smiled at Sorrel with her odd-shaped triangular eyes.

'The last time I saw you was at King's Cross and I was shaking like a jelly.'

'I thought you were magnificent.'

'Oh Sorrel, you are funny.'

'But I did.'

Pauline shook her head.

'If it hadn't been for you they'd never have crammed us into the train. Those sailors thought I was related to a Wren. They really looked after us, bounced Davy up and down and made a pet of Rose. I never wrote and told you how grateful I was. I meant to. Well, I'm saying it now. But – let's talk about the Priory. What's happened?'

Sorrel said she had come to Evendon convinced the family were merely out when she had telephoned. She described what she had found. Pauline frowned.

'How *very* odd. Surely somebody in the village will know. Let's ask Miss Banning.'

'I went to The Raven. They said the farmer in Butterbox bought all the stock. And the Martyns have gone to London.'

Pauline discussed the mystery but did not take up the most glaring point of the story – that the Martyns had not told Sorrel. For the moment Sorrel hadn't the spirit to mention it. Pauline was knowledgeable about George Martyn.

'You can bet your bottom dollar there's a reason why he's left.'

'The landlord said my mother-in-law couldn't bear the house any more.'

'That sounds like Grace. Poor thing. Both sons gone. But there'll be something else in it, and that'll be money.'

'Why?' said Sorrel drearily.

There was nothing dreary about Pauline whose face sharpened and shone.

'You must know your father-in-law by now. Dion says anybody who wants to make money can do it. I believe Bernard Shaw said it first. That's George Martyn. Money fascinates him, he respects it, he opens the door and gives it a big welcome. The boys always surprised our parents, both being so unlike their father, with not a business thought between them. Edmund went into the regular army because he couldn't think of anything else. And your Toby was a born soldier.'

Yes, thought Sorrel. And loved the army more than he loved me.

'Your father-in-law is up to something.'

But Pauline still did not ask the key question.

Sorrel answered it.

'I didn't know they'd gone because I haven't heard from them for months. Or written to them either.'

She tried to be fair. It was her fault. She had never been fond of them. She added the story of her conversation with Aunt Dot.

Pauline considered.

'You want to make up with them, don't you? For Toby's sake. Take no notice of Dot Martyn being nasty, she was only repeating their tune. Anyway, she's not always so nice, Sorrel. I remember her in my teens, she could be jolly cold. Ring her again, crack your way through the ice and ask outright where they've got to.'

Pauline studied her for a moment.

'You're too thin. What have you been eating in the navy?'

'All kinds of nourishing things.'

'Well, you don't look as if you have.'

'Perhaps it's being on indefinite leave.'

'Perhaps it is,' agreed Pauline.

'Pauline – I know I made a fool of myself on the station but I don't feel quite so bad, you know, about Toby. I think I must be getting used to it. And I don't want to.'

Pauline did not hesitate.

'You must,' she said. 'Human life is like the seasons. Things grow and ripen and sometimes die too soon. We have to go on, you know.'

'I don't know. I wish I did.'

'You know in your heart, Sorrel.'

Miss Banning's strong sculpted face looked round the door. She came in carrying an old-fashioned silver kettle of the kind which, warmed by a spirit lamp, used to stand on lacy pre-war tea tables.

'You want the pot filled?'

She looked at the victory sponge, saw it had been half-eaten, and retired from the room, satisfied.

When she had gone, the mood changed. Pauline talked about her stay in Cumberland and Chris's uncle and aunt.

'They're very kind, I have to admit, but try as I might I couldn't see the least, the smallest reflection of Chris in Aunt

May. Chris's parents died years ago, you see, and Aunt May's his only relative. She and his uncle looked after Chris, paid for his school; they were surrogate parents, really. But they persuaded him to go into a bank when he was thirsting to be an engineer. The trouble at Keswick was that when you are middle-aged you are so tidy. Kids make a mess and you can't get used to it. Poor Aunt. She kept picking up toys which landed back on the floor thirty seconds later. It was a blessing she's a fanatical member of the WVS so she was out a lot. Without her, Uncle Jim came out of his hiding place and was rather fun, he was even an elephant and gave Rose rides. But when Aunt came back he looked like a naughty schoolboy. It's glorious to be home. Not to have to ask permission when you have a bath.'

She stopped talking. Then said almost to herself, 'Isn't it strange. No war in Europe. And maybe soon – '

'Soon Chris will be home.'

'Mm. Sometimes when I think about him my mind goes numb. All I remember is the photograph, the one he hates. It's as if I'd made him up. And he's a character in a book.'

'What about his letters?'

'Were Toby's letters any good?'

Pauline spoke of the dead with perfect naturalness.

'No.'

'Nor are Chris's. How can he write about anything worth telling? Besides, he's a natural comedian, he's so *funny*, Sorrel. But hasn't the knack of putting that down either. His letters are so dull and I so love them.'

Pauline went to find Miss Banning and Sorrel heard voices in a conversation apparently satisfying to both, since the old woman chuckled. Pauline returned, looking disapproving.

'She won't let me pay for our tea. She's naughty, I absolutely begged. No go. All she wants is a promise that Dion will come and see her. She's practically the only person in the village who was half decent to him.'

Walking down the road, they came to a group of old-fashioned houses, weathered and worn. Pauline rang the bell of a house with a green door and an over-polished knocker. A plump, still-pretty woman answered. She had dyed ash-blonde hair, naturally pink cheeks, an air of health and eyes like pebbles. She greeted Pauline brusquely and gave her a key.

'Step up and take a look. Nothing's bin touched.'

'Help,' whispered Pauline as she and Sorrel went up a narrow stair. 'She thinks *I* think it has.'

'How will you know?' whispered Sorrel in return.

'Shan't bother to check. She's the sort who uses honesty like a boxing glove.'

A faint curiosity stirred in Sorrel as they went into what had been Dion's room. This was where he had lived, probably given a grudging breakfast by that female whom they had met at The Raven.

The room did not belong in a house of glittering stair-rods and, where doors were open, ugly furniture which looked as hard as its owner. Dion had painted the bed and the wardrobe a deep sea blue. The bedcover was patchwork and all over the walls were pictures, now beginning to curl and yellow, from magazines. Country scenes. Botanical drawings. Birds. Some maps. The shelves were filled with books. Pauline roamed about, opening and shutting drawers. She found a large dead moth.

'Poor thing. How did it get in there?'

She threw the weightless brown shape like a dried flower out of the window.

She put her hand flat on the bed. 'Damp as a pond. He'll have to move. I wonder if Miss Banning would put him up.'

'Surely he's not coming back to Evendon!'

'Didn't I tell you? Back to his old *Echo* job and quite looking forward to it. Sorrel, will you do me a favour? Find a tatty old volume called *A Bird Book for the Pocket* by somebody called Sandars published about fifteen years ago. He needs it for something he's writing. I'd better go down and beard the dragon. That bed's the limit, and I'm giving her two weeks' notice.'

When Pauline had gone, Sorrel looked dubiously at the shelves. The books were so tightly packed together that it was difficult to pull one out. But she noticed that they were arranged in subject order. Geography. History. Politics. Natural History. Fiction. In alphabetical order too. The bird book wasn't easy to find, its spine was split and the title nearly unreadable, but there it was. Under 'S'.

As she had once done before, a long time ago with a book of Toby's, she opened it and turned to the flyleaf. In Dion's neat handwriting was his name, the date – Summer 1943, and beneath it, 'Bought at a Red Cross sale. Price 2d.'

Pauline reappeared.

'*Not* best pleased. When I gave notice she started saying she had undercharged him the entire time he was here because she was sorry for him. What a beast. She was dead set on avoiding having evacuees planted on her because they were so much work. She positively jumped at the chance of Dion – and then when he lived here used to dig at him all the time about being a c.o. I don't know how he stood her. I only came once and I wanted to strangle her.'

The landlady did not see them out, and the moment they were back in the street it became noticeably warmer. They returned to the station.

'I'm glad to get him out of that damp hole.' Pauline glanced at her and added with a gleam, 'You think I mother him.'

'Lucky Dion.'

Pauline gave a snort. 'One couldn't mother Dion if one tried for fifty years. Mummy never succeeded and nor can I. He's like a cat who sits on the mat when he wants to, never when you invite him. The only time I had the least sisterly effect was when he got a hacking cough (obviously from the damp) and I forced him to accept *two* hot water bottles, and swear to put them in his bed all during the day. Come on. If we run we'll catch the 6.15. My dear old Irish helper is minding the kids and she'll want to get home.'

When they were settled in the carriage and the train had started, Pauline said, 'I've been thinking. Directly we get to London, I think you should go straight round to see Dot Martyn. It's always better to do things like that at once. Like making up after a quarrel, the longer you leave it the worse it gets. If Dot Martyn's nice and asks you to stay, that's okay. If for some reason she doesn't, then here's my telephone number.'

She extravagantly tore a cheque from her chequebook and scribbled on it. Later she fell asleep, looking young.

Sorrel put her hand in her pocket and brought out the stone she had picked up at the Priory. She looked down at it. It was greyish, greenish, there was a round yellow circle of lichen. She wondered how old it might be. Had she thought to keep it as a memory of a place where she had been so happy and so stricken? Its edges were sharp and scratched her fingers.

She threw it out of the window.

15

The horse over the archway had survived the war and looked down at her in a melancholy way; one of its ears was chipped. And as she walked down the mews on the uneven cobbles, Sorrel suddenly, intensely remembered Buzz. She could see his big broad-shouldered figure, the pale fattish face and narrow eyes, and for a piercing instant remembered how they had made love. They had lain in a room which was hot against the bitter English cold and faintly before sex deafened them had heard music coming from downstairs. The music of the time. Haunting and sexy and sometimes sad. And men and women had danced to it, excited because the sweet hours were short, pressed so close that uniform buttons bruised soft breasts. Sorrel thought she had forgotten Buzz, that his physical presence in her was gone for ever. She'd become in her imagination the war widow in uniform not dark enough for sorrow. The hours she and Buzz had spent making love in the overheated room before they washed away the trace of sex had been too avid, too desperate, too impersonal to last. Enjoy'd no sooner but despisèd straight.

Why, then, did she think of him now with a pang of the heart?

The mews was unkempt and in the spring light of evening the houses were as well. They had not been painted for nearly seven years. She walked up to Dot's door.

She knew the answer before she touched the bell. There was a big oak tub on the left of the door. Dot, laughing at herself, liked to plant it with herbs. 'It's my allotment,' she said, watering it with a minute hand-painted watering can. Everything in the tub was dead, the leaves so dry and yellow they looked mummified. But Sorrel rang. Knocked. Rang again. The only sound was the clack of wings as two pigeons flew overhead.

Badly needing to hear a friendly voice, she rang Pauline from a telephone box on the corner.

'Is she there?' said Pauline at once.

'Not a sign. I looked through the letter box. Letters on the floor.'

'But you only spoke to her yesterday.'

'She sounded in a hurry. Perhaps she was leaving town.'

'Hop on a 73.'

'Pauline – I can't possibly land my problems on you.'

'I don't see why not. Hurry up or you'll miss a whole convoy of 73s.'

Travelling to Kensington, she chided herself for needing comfort. But to whom else in this blank of peace could she turn? Pauline's door opened almost before she rang, and there was her friend hand-in-hand with a Rose who seemed to have grown inches taller and whose hair from Cumberland sunshine was the colour of flax. There was a good deal of kissing.

'Welcome to the old place again. I've laid on supper. And we've got a surprise for you, haven't we, Rosy?'

'A big, big, surprise,' said Rose.

Pauline led the way down the passage.

'Go on. You first,' she said as they reached the sitting-room door.

A tall man stood up. He was in battle dress, his hair, fair as Rose's, was shaved very short, there were parachute wings on his shoulder flash. He was a soldier in a world full of soldiers – they had streamed across the maps of Europe and Asia, thundered into Rome in tanks, cut their way through jungles, been pelted with flowers in the liberation of Paris. But it was Dion.

'Doesn't he look awful?' said Pauline taking his arm. 'I don't know what it is about him but he can't wear a uniform. Chris wears his with real panache, it actually suits him. The moment Dion puts on khaki he ruins it.'

'It's a special talent of mine,' he said, taking Sorrel's hand and pressing it warmly.

'He's hopeless at foot drill without arms,' said Pauline with a touch of pride.

'Only from lack of concentration. Any fool can drill if he puts his mind to it.'

'Oh, can he? What if he's incapable of putting his mind to it?'

'Stop making me look incompetent in front of your friend,' complained Dion, smiling at Sorrel. 'I don't believe either of you would have concentrated when there were so many other more interesting things going on.'

'What, for instance?' challenged his sister.

'Well. The ducks migrating north. Nobody's shooting them any more, and there are the most enormous flocks. And in France I saw a hoopoe.'

'*France!*' exclaimed Sorrel.

Brother and sister exchanged looks.

'I think we'd all better sit down. Sorrel's shattered,' Pauline said.

'Yes,' he agreed, 'I believe she is. And yes, Sorrel, I was in France.'

'In one of the divisions which parachuted into Normandy,' added Pauline. 'I wasn't allowed to tell you, he's been looking forward to seeing your face.'

Sorrel had sat down rather suddenly. She felt indignant. Where was the man whose noble and disputed sentiments she had listened to in Hampshire? Who had forced her to accept that he was in earnest in his brave stand against millions of his countrymen?

'You're thinking I swore I wouldn't fight,' he said dryly. 'I didn't. Our non-combatant lot carry no arms. We're given various jobs and one happens to be looking after the wounded, which is reasonably useful.'

'But the parachute corps – '

'Don't be taken in, Sorrel. I can't make out why the paras have acquired such glamour; the only difference between us and other troops is we have to do that nasty jump. Training for that wasn't too much fun, I admit. I was always thinking – I'm not sure I trust my parachute. Supposing the girl who packed it was like me and didn't concentrate. I'm a devout coward. But happily the 'chute opened perfectly and the floating down was good. An excellent view of the countryside.'

Davy trotted in to sit on Dion's knee. Rose with a furious face demanded to do the same, and the children perched on him, tickling him and giggling. Late in the evening, when they had been put to bed, Pauline made tea and sat on the floor.

'Now, Dion, tell Sorrel about the German officer.'

'Oh Pauline.'

'*What* about the German officer?' asked Sorrel.

Dion protested that she couldn't possibly want to hear yet another invasion story, they were boring.

'He's so bloody-minded,' said his sister, 'he only tells when he decides to. Very well. I shall tell her.'

She began, but Dion interrupted and contradicted and in the end it was he who told the story which was what she'd meant him to do.

He had been among thousands of British paratroopers who had tumbled through the air over France during the first month of the invasion. His own group had landed in an enormous apple orchard on the banks of the Muance. They'd been warned that there were a number of German troops still about, although the main battle for Caen was over.

Dion and three companions went through the orchard where they found some wounded men, including two Germans; they managed to carry them to a deserted farm. They bandaged their wounds, gave them the drugs non-combatants were allowed to carry, and tried to make them comfortable on the few mattresses they could find. But it was desperately cold. It had been raining steadily, the air was damp and chill, the wounded men trembled and there were not enough blankets to go round. Dion set off to see what he could forage. Perhaps he could locate a Red Cross post or find an inhabited house. He knew from his map there was a village on the far side of the orchard, and began to hurry between the trees. A man suddenly appeared from behind a large apple tree.

'Imagine. He shot at me,' complained Dion. 'I know shooting with a revolver is famously inaccurate, his certainly was, blasting off all over the place, but the bullets whined past and I fell flat on my face, and one hit the trunk of a tree behind me. It actually ricocheted and zoomed by again like those fireworks on Guy Fawkes which keep exploding round one's feet. I shouted at him in German.'

'Dion learned it at school,' from Pauline.

'Rather sketchily. But I managed "Herr Officer, have you blankets?" Pretty silly question when you come to think of it. He positively glared, his mouth open and the revolver, he'd used up all the cartridges, hanging in his hand.'

'Then he got hopping mad,' said Pauline.

'He certainly did. He started yelling at me "what is all this rubbish?" "*Unsinn*", that's the word he used about four times. So I explained that I was a conscientious objector. I did know that word, I looked it up before we flew to France. *Kriegsdienstverweigerer*. How about that? He said *Gott in Himmel*, what are you doing here? I told him again. I was looking for blankets for the wounded, and had he any or did he know where I could find some. I added that two of his countrymen were among my wounded. He wasn't listening. He didn't have any blasted blankets.'

'Did you let him *go*?'

'My dear Sorrel, I could scarcely stop him. Do you imagine I'd take him prisoner? He seemed quite off his head with rage and after a final glare, and calling on his Maker, he vanished like the demon king. I heard him shouting to some invisible chaps somewhere among the apple trees. I got my blankets in the end in a sort of café. But one of my Germans died, I'm sorry to say.'

Sorrel stayed the night at Thorley Court. And the following day as well. Dion also stayed, sleeping in the sitting room. The time that followed for Sorrel was taken over by the Fulfords who seemed to have a pact to look after her. They were souls of hospitality. The war, or what he had seen of it in France, had changed Dion back to the man she'd first met; the brooding sullen look was gone.

They went for walks to Kensington Gardens and sat on grass bleached straw-colour under the huge old elms. Sorrel thought him attractive. He didn't affect her with the fever she'd had with Buzz, there was no lust in action in a waste of shame. But she was drawn to him physically and knew he felt the same, although he never even touched her hand. But his large grey eyes spoke.

During one long afternoon she talked about Buzz. She hadn't meant to, but he asked how she was recovering from Toby's loss. He said, looking at her in enquiry, 'Have you fallen in love since?'

'No – I – I did have an affair. Just after I heard.'

It was a confession. She waited, and all he said was, 'That can happen.'

'The man was killed. Poor Buzz.'

'Poor Sorrel, really,' was the answer. She found she could talk in release about Buzz then, and the few days they'd had, and how soon he had been killed afterwards. She tried to be truthful, and added that she'd felt miserable and guilty about him.

'Because of Toby. *Don't* feel that. Never feel that.' Sorrel found herself telling him, too, about Margaret Reilly. He listened in silence, and all he said when she finished was, 'Love can be hell.' She didn't know why his voice made her cry.

On another afternoon she asked him about Pauline's husband. 'Tell me what he's like, Dion. Her descriptions are hopeless.'

'She's shy of sounding excessive. She loves him such a lot,' he said. A wave of envy went through her; the world was full of lovers, and she wasn't among them.

'What's Chris like? Rather shambling. There's something fascinating about him. It's the way he sees things, he's funny and unexpected. You know he worked in a bank? I'm certain when he gets home he'll throw it over and train to be an engineer. You must get Pauline to show you his drawings of machinery – they're beautiful. So. There he is. A born draughtsman. A strong, comic, dependable, loveable man. You'll like him, he already likes you. He's also irritable and there'll be some ructions when they eventually settle to real life. That's what we all have to get used to. A future. Being able to do what we want and not what they make us do.'

'You've always done what you wanted.'

'Now that's nonsense. I toed the line as you did, as every living soul was made to do. I was shoved into the Priory, wasn't I? No,' he went on, thinking aloud, 'I forget the exceptions. Some musicians managed to go on writing music. Britten's a pacifist. And there were painters who were given the job of recording the war. So they still painted. Victor Passmore wasn't so lucky. He was court-martialled and went to prison for four months. Guess what? While he was in jug they put on an exhibition of his work, called Artists of Fame and Promise.'

'People can admire a man's work and dislike his principles.'

'Much too simple. If they, whoever they were, had known he was in gaol they wouldn't have put on the exhibition at all. It's the sort of idiotic accident people like me enjoy.'

'You're so contrary.'

'Am I? What are we talking about me for? What will you do when you take off that uniform I used to be so rude about?'

She looked pretty and young and sad.

'I think I dread becoming a civilian. What a responsibility. Having to choose how to lead one's life.'

'Instead of jumping to attention.'

'I just feel it's such an anticlimax.'

His lazy expression changed.

'I never imagined you of all people would regret the war.'

The words made her start.

'I didn't mean that! How could I when Toby – it's horrible of you to believe I did.'

'I'm sorry.'

'No you're not. You're being the holy conscientious objector again.'

'How angry you get. Have I offended you?'

'Yes.'

'I take it back. Yes, I do, I am sorry. I just didn't like the word anticlimax. Pauline, by the way, asked me to talk to you about an idea of hers; the poor idiot imagines I'm more persuasive than she is. Now all I do is put my foot in it. Am I forgiven?'

On their homeward walk through the sunny streets, they passed crowds of American troops mustering at corners, shouted at by their NCOs, moved about, shifted, and climbing into jeeps and trucks. They looked cheerful. And still after years in Europe draped themselves against railings or sat on the ground. Toby would have thought them a ragged lot of soldiers, but since Buzz, Sorrel had a fellow-feeling. Through sex she had become a little American, and when she looked at them they whistled.

Dion said the great masses of men reminded him of the flocks of starlings which came to London every autumn from across the North Sea. 'Only they're bound in the opposite direction.' He added, 'And now, Sorrel. I must tell you Pauline's idea. Are you ready?'

She looked up at him, laughing, and when he returned the look, for some reason, she didn't know why, she blushed.

Pauline, he said, wanted Sorrel to come and live at Thorley Court with her. Dion agreed that it was a first-rate plan. Sorrel, touched and embarrassed, protested. There was no reason on earth why Pauline should be saddled with her.

'What has that got to do with anything? She'd be glad of a lodger. And you said you want to live in town and learn whatever it is.'

'Shorthand typing. I read in the papers there's already a shortage of secretaries.'

'Good idea.' He didn't press the point about where she was going to live. He continued to walk beside her peacefully. Sorrel risked a little pride.

'I'm not quite penniless, Dion. I have two months' resettlement leave with pay and I shall get my army widow's pension when it's official about Toby.'

He stopped walking, turned round and kissed her.

An army captain approaching on the same side of the street looked furious. A mere corporal, parachute corps or no parachute corps, putting his arms round a Wren officer. It was a disgrace. Both the Wren and the corporal would have been in serious trouble a month ago. But the captain passed them with only a look of angry disgust. He decided not to pursue the matter. Peace was here indeed; and he knew his protests bored them at HQ.

Dion's kiss was light. He repeated it.

'What was that for?'

'Because you called yourself a widow, I expect.'

Sorrel never meant to live with Pauline; it was hard to become a charity. But she reckoned without her friend. Pauline knew that the certainties of wartime had been Sorrel's lifebelt and without them she had not yet learned how to swim. The girl still mourned. Pauline had energy and a warm heart; like Kipling's Kim she was the friend of all the world. She adopted Sorrel, using arguments it was difficult to refute.

'It's impossible to get a flat at present.'

That was true.

'I *need* company.'

That wasn't.

Many friends came to the flat during the first weeks of peace. Thorley Court was still a kind of club. There were schoolfriends, mothers with children who lived nearby, foreign troops she picked up in the bus, exiles who became friends. She opened the front door and in they poured, usually with presents of food welcomed with, 'Golly. I was down to carrots and that rind of cheese.'

Knowing Sorrel was settled with Pauline after her demobilisation, Dion felt satisfied. He himself was demobilised soon afterwards, and between them he and Pauline had arranged digs with Miss Banning. He telephoned Pauline with enthusiasm. A warm bed and endless cups of tea. What more could one ask?

He was back at his pre-war job on the *Echo*, the small paper covering part of Hampshire. The editor was glad to see him, gave him a desk and an elderly typewriter and – Dion really knew he was back now – a list of flower shows and meetings of the Conservative Party. A few days later Dion telephoned Pauline again.

'Guess what's happened?'

'*What*!'

'You're getting very jumpy now peace has broken out. Did you think I'd lost the job already?'

'I thought you mightn't like it.'

'After the thrill of muck spreading for Grace Martyn and being a para? My dear sister, a desk and a typewriter are time off. No, it's something else. Remember the proprietor of the *Echo*?'

'You pointed him out to me once. Tall, grey hair, sideburns, aristocratic and portly.'

'Got him to a T. He rang. My boss nearly had a fit, he didn't know James Tarrant had ever heard of me. Actually Tarrant had my name from George Martyn.'

'From *who*?'

He laughed. Pauline had an inexhaustible supply of amazement, indignation, derision, partisanship. But the story was worth telling. James Tarrant was a local man of some importance who owned six newspapers in Dorset and Hampshire, was rich and much respected. He had heard rumours that the Priory was for sale.

'I imagine he sniffed a bargain. It seems Martyn's rather over-keen to sell, and Tarrant happens to have become interested in farming. His newspapers run themselves.'

'So he found out you'd been in charge at the Priory.'

'He heard I was the farmhand and asked me to his house for a drink. Impressive place and one of those gracious wives who look as if they're permanently opening garden fêtes. He positively grilled me about the farm. The stock. Crops. Even our modest little profit. I told him all I could remember. When I started, I was surprised how much I still knew.'

'You didn't ring me to tell me all that,' said Pauline.

'You're too sharp and no, I didn't. Do you remember my notion for starting a country magazine? Tarrant was looking pleased with so much gen I'd given him, and I also offered to write up the main points if they'd be any help. I don't think he's used to getting things for nothing. You know how rich people are.'

'Of course I don't.'

'Nor do I, but I bet I'm right. They like a *quid pro quo*. When we finished he asked about my job, was I settled in, had I any new ideas for the *Echo* and so on. So I risked it. I told him my idea. What do you think, Pauline, he was quite interested! In a cautious way, of course. I've got to do him a plan. I hope it'll be good, it's only in my head so far.'

'Of course it'll be good. Use those brains Daddy used to say were better than his.'

'They're not as good, and no better than yours.'

'Don't be a fool, Dion Fulford.'

Pauline reported the news to Sorrel.

'Has he ever talked to you about it? I thought not. He's modest in an imperious sort of way. Perhaps it's more accurate to say he's modest about himself and pretty critical about everybody else except you and me. Even we don't escape sometimes.'

She told Sorrel that the idea of a country magazine had been in Dion's mind since he was a boy of fourteen. He'd made one, once, with pictures from *The Times* and articles by her and himself. 'Mine was pathetic. A sort of swanky school essay. Doesn't it seem extraordinary? To think it may come off.'

'Is he excited?'

'He wouldn't show it. But he is.'

In the following week Dion spent his lunchtime and early evenings looking for inexpensive offices, finally discovering two rooms over a bicycle shop. He asked his old friend, the *Echo*'s accountant, to have supper; they worked out some figures. The magazine was to aim at the West Country, its circulation would not be large. At last he sat down to write the plan.

Looking out of Miss Banning's window, he thought of the new life beginning in Britain now. The ploughed-up land would be returfed, girls in white dresses would play tennis again in the long afternoons. Cabbages would be replaced by roses. It was a time of return, of people to their land and the gardens, of the art of planting, the place of the village in history, of country walks and rare birds and forgotten flowers. He chose a title – *Country Matters*.

'I like it,' said Pauline on the telephone.

'Are you sure? Hamlet did use it in rather a different sense in Ophelia.'

'Dion! Nobody buying your mag will think *that*!'

When he'd got the plan together to his satisfaction, he telephoned James Tarrant who asked him to bring it round that evening.

Dion cycled to the Georgian house. The bazaar-opening wife was absent and Tarrant received him in a room full of bronze busts, globes, ancient books and red leather. Gentlemen with waxed moustaches, girls with half-opened fans, gazed down from the walls. How soon, thought Dion, men of business turn themselves into aristocracy. Tarrant looked as if he were a fifth duke at least. He was hospitable, gave Dion a glass of sherry and sat down to read the plan. Dion noticed that he didn't start at the opening page, but turned to the last where the finances were set out.

He read in silence. Right through. Then studied the last page again.

'I'm not unenthusiastic,' he said. 'I quite like the look of it. I think – ' a pause, 'I might be willing to underwrite it for a year.'

'It will need eighteen months, Sir.'

Tarrant took that as if expecting it. Definitely the fifth duke.

'Eighteen months it shall be. One thing, however.'

Dion waited.

'I can't see my way to keeping open your position on the *Echo*, suppose, unhappily, your magazine does not succeed.'

'I realise that.'

Tarrant rubbed his chin. Dion, who had been wondering ever since the first interview who it was that the proprietor reminded him of, now remembered. It was Gladstone.

'You are willing to take the risk?' said Tarrant.

'Yes, Sir.'

'Good. Then so am I.'

Brother and sister and ex-Wren lodger were adapting to the months of peace. Sorrel began a course in shorthand typing at a school in the Strand, learned to wear civilian clothes all the time, and conquered the automatic reflex of saluting when she saw a naval officer. In the country Dion was still working on the *Echo,* but his plans were making progress. In London Pauline bought an antique sewing machine, and she and Sorrel taught themselves dressmaking. More letters than usual arrived from Chris. And then August came, and awesome news. Hiroshima. Japan surrendered, and peace came back to all the world.

On the morning of VJ Day Dion arrived at the flat while Sorrel, Pauline and the children were having breakfast.

'I got up very early, caught the first train and walked all the way from Waterloo. It was fun,' he said. 'London is going mad again.'

Both children shouted when they saw Dion who knelt down to hug them, before kissing Pauline and Sorrel impartially. She felt a little shy.

'I see you're still in the paras,' said Pauline, regarding his khaki jersey. It had huge darns in both the elbows.

'I'm fond of it. It's the one the German officer didn't manage to shoot a hole in. Well? What's the plan? Are we going to junket tonight?'

'Pauline's been invited to a big party in the West End. I said I'd babysit, she won't agree and we're arguing,' said Sorrel.

'Of course she must go. Then I'll have you to myself,' he said. 'We'll celebrate when the kids are in bed.'

'No, no, no!' shouted Rose, joined by Davy.

'Oh, all right, we'll celebrate while you're up. Look what I've brought.' He produced a bottle from his suitcase. 'Pre-war Veuve Clicquot. Miss Banning has been keeping it for the peace, and wouldn't let me refuse it *or* open it.'

Rose sat on her uncle's lap and Davy undid his shoe laces. Pauline went to the kitchen to make fresh tea. Sorrel merely stayed. He smiled across at her.

'Did Pauline tell you your old home is to be sold?'

'To your newspaper proprietor? Yes. Has he decided?'

'Definitely. He's always wanted to run a farm and, as his

son's getting married, Tarrant is giving him their very grand house as a wedding present. Imagine. The talk locally, by the way, is that Tarrant got the Priory at a bargain price.'

'That surprises me,' said Sorrel in a thin voice.

'Because your father-in-law doesn't sell things cheaply? True. But I gather he wants to be rid of the Priory. Tarrant's keen to get the place going, hates to see an empty house and locked stables, let alone *his* fields being farmed by somebody else for the time being. He and I went all round yesterday. My God, Sorrel, it's quiet.'

'I know.'

'You went there, I remember. Did it depress you?'

'Not particularly. But I'm glad it's coming to life again.'

She could not tell him what it had felt like to haunt the place where she had been happy.

VJ Day rang and sang over London that high summer day. Pauline was collected by a unity of nations – American friends, Polish admirers, Frenchmen ready with compliments and her own countrymen with jokes. She vanished into a sea of uniforms, with everybody waving from two taxis.

Sorrel and Dion walked back to a flat littered with glasses and bottles of rye whisky and Jamaican rum. Sorrel could see both children were worn out with excitement. Rose's round, usually pink face was pale, and Davy was sucking his thumb and twisting one ear with the other hand, 'as if,' remarked Dion, 'he's telephoning.' It was decided to put them to bed early, and the children were coaxed towards beds they protested against and longed for. Soon they were deeply asleep.

Sorrel listened at their door for a while, then crept back to the sitting room and began to clear up. He sat on the sofa.

She tried not to be conscious of him, but after going in and out of the kitchen two or three times, said, 'You are the limit. Why aren't you helping?'

'I've decided not to.'

'Oh, have you? Well – '

'Come here.'

'Certainly not, I really must finish – '

'Come here, Sorrel.'
'Why?'
'I don't know.'
He held out a large hand. Making a face at him, she put down the tray and took the proffered hand. He pulled her down beside him. When she was about to jump up again he said, 'Shall we make love?'
Sorrel went scarlet.
'My dear girl,' he said in a matter-of-fact voice, 'you can't pretend you don't know how I've been feeling. Wanting to kiss you properly since I arrived. Now . . .'
He began to kiss her. She shut her eyes, tasting the kiss, feeling the heavy arm circling her, slipping and sliding into the excitement which waited for her. It was such a long time since Buzz, since any man, had touched her, his hand against the place of love. She felt the tingling overtures of desire and stayed, embracing and embraced.
When they separated she looked as if her whole body was melting. But he was unchanged. He wasn't already lost in sex, something which had always happened to the other men before they possessed her. He said, in a detached voice, studying her face, 'You're very beautiful. And sometimes sad. And I'd be a bastard to try and make you do it.'
She said nothing.
'You decide,' he said, teasing her.
'I – I can't.'
'Do you want to, Sorrel? To make love, I mean.'
Why did he ask, what did he want her to say?
She shook her head, not in denial but because in a gentle way he was tormenting her. He laughed and pushed her back against the cushions, and she put up her hands and gripped him, wanting him inside her, waiting to be possessed by this enigmatic, alluring man. She wanted – she almost loved him just then, if it were not for the thorns that pressed against her heart when Toby returned there.
Understanding what she didn't say, he pulled down the shoulder of her dress and began to kiss her naked breasts.
He left London the following day for Evendon, kissing each

one of the family in turn, and mocking his sister for her 'father and mother of a hangover'. There wasn't a single trace in his manner to Sorrel that was changed. At the front door he gave the family an inept salute.

But after that whenever he telephoned Pauline he always asked to speak to Sorrel as well. The conversations were facetious, he made her laugh. He didn't say a thing that could be taken seriously, that had a special meaning. But she looked forward to talking to him.

I can't be falling in love, she thought.

She felt a kind of unrest, she was happy and uneasy. His lovemaking had been exciting, passionate, experienced – wonderful, in a way. Yet he'd never been lost, as she had been. And how could you know a man deeply when you and he had shared that hot, mysterious act only once? But Toby's claim on her had begun to fade. It was like music going into the distance and there were times when she could scarcely hear the chords that had once broken her heart. In their place was a music so different that listening to it seemed wrong.

He was as strong as Toby, but his was an utterly different vision of the world. Everything about him was unfamiliar. The strong, graceful body which had taken hers, his thick fair hair, his ironic face, his unnerving habit of reading her thoughts. His idealism. His lack of it. His mocking of himself as well as her. Autumn was beginning to come to London. With the first yellowing of leaves, and bonfires where once there had been burning houses, hope came like a spirit into the shabby flat.

As a painter might offer a picture in payment to a friend, Sorrel liked to clean the flat on Saturdays. Dion called his sister's untidiness 'wondrous'. She agreed and made resolves as drunkards do who swear not to touch another drop. The rooms were full of toys given to the children by kind American friends who'd actually written to the States to get them. Unobtainable bears and expensively dressed dolls all lay on the floor. The sleeves of jerseys protruded from drawers. Dust collected on furniture and books toppled off windowsills. Sorrel shooed mother and children from the house on a fine Saturday afternoon, and tied on an apron.

'Aunty Sorrel's so fierce,' said Rose, and then, 'Can I ride in the pram?'

'You're much too big and rather old, poppet.'

'Davy rides all the time. It isn't fair.'

Pauline surveyed her daughter, who wore the expression of wily lawyer with weakening judge.

'Mum?'

'Oh, all right.'

She dumped her into the other end of the pram. Rose, triumphant and absurd, dangled long legs over the edge. Davy was a philosopher, and moved over.

Satisfactorily alone, Sorrel swept and cleaned and started on the usual pile of ironing. In two hours the flat was transformed. With an artist's pleasure at a finished picture, Sorrel went from room to room, then sat down with a cup of tea to think about Dion. Perhaps he would ring. Perhaps come to London again. And the sweet wordless conversation of sex might happen. How she wanted that.

Sipping her tea, she opened the *Daily Mail.* There was a leader: 'Tory astonishment. Our new Socialist government is actually beginning to behave like Socialists.'

She idly turned to another page.

Staring out, his arms round his mother, haggard, emaciated, an eagle indeed, was Toby.

16

It wasn't Toby. She was imagining the man resembled him. She tried to focus on the print, but couldn't. She kept staring at the worn, laughing face. It isn't. It can't be. Sorrel, stop it, *Toby is dead.*

At last she managed to read what was printed below.

Back from the Dead

The Hon. Major Ronald Martyn, MC, of the 6th Middlehamptonshire Regt., missing believed killed in Yugoslavia in December 1944, dramatically returned to life today when he landed at Southampton. Major Martyn, seconded as an observer with the Titoist guerrillas in the Balkans, was taken seriously ill during the campaign. Cut off by the troubles that have afflicted the region, he had no choice but to walk several hundred miles into Greece. He finally managed to gain passage on a cargo steamer bound for England. He was reunited yesterday with his family.

Lord Martyn, owner of the Martyn mills in the North, is a well-known industrialist, created a peer in 1920. He recently left his historic home in Evendon, Hampshire, and has moved to London.

Major Martyn, speaking of the Balkan partisans, said, 'I have never known such courageous men. They fight like lions. It was a privilege to be accepted by them.'

Ice-cold, her teeth chattering, Sorrel rushed out of the flat, slamming the door. As she came into the street Pauline appeared with the pram.

'My God! What's happened?'

Unable to speak, Sorrel thrust the newspaper into her hands. Pauline read it in a moment, threw it down and flung out her arms.

'How wonderful. How wonderful. Oh Sorrel, it is unbelievable.'

'I can't find him. I don't know where he is.'

'Let's go indoors.' Pauline gave her a final hug. But Sorrel was beyond joy. They went into the sitting room. The children, impressed, sat on the floor, large-eyed and watching the grown-ups. Sorrel sat down and Pauline knelt beside her.

'Now. Are we *certain* we don't know where they are? You wrote to Lord Martyn, didn't you? To be forwarded. And no reply?'

'No reply.'

'What about the landlord at The Raven? He knew something.'

'All he said was he thought they'd gone to London.'

'And Dot Martyn still isn't back?'

'I've rung three times. She's not there.'

Pauline chewed her thumb. Sorrel was looking at the newspaper again. She gave something like a groan.

'Look! He's alive. I'll die if I don't see him . . .'

'Hey, wait a bit. Let's look at that again,' said Pauline, and springing up fetched her magnifying glass from the desk. She looked closely at the picture.

'Fascinating. Look, Sorrel.'

She hadn't placed the glass on the figures, but was enlarging a wall above their heads.

'Doesn't that say "Piccadilly"? Just on the left.'

'Does it?' Sorrel stupidly asked.

'You're not concentrating. Yes . . . I can make out . . . A - l - d - e - *I know where that is!* It's Aldenham House. The smart building facing Green Park on the other side from the

Ritz but further down. Just the sort of place George Martyn would choose – oh look, Sorrel!'

Sorrel took the glass. And put it on Toby's face.

Pauline regarded her with concern.

'You're white as a sheet. I'll make some tea. No, kids, leave Aunty Sorrel alone, come into the kitchen, I've got some bikkies.'

But if tea, strong and sweet, was supposed to have recuperative powers, they were not apparent.

'You don't look any better. I'm not sure you're strong enough to go to Aldenham House alone.'

'Is that really where he is?'

'I'm sure of it. Perhaps we'd better come with you.'

'No. I can manage. It's just that – just that – '

'That he's alive and you are afraid to believe it.'

'Perhaps it isn't Aldenham House.'

'Yes it is. If he isn't there, I mean if he's out, there's only one thing to do.'

'What?'

'Sit on the doorstep.'

Coaxing and petting her, helping her do her hair, giving her some money – Sorrel had lost her purse – Pauline, with the children, went to the bus stop. Rose was curious.

'You are coming back, aren't you?'

'Of course she is,' said Pauline. 'She's just going to see her husband.'

'But he's dead.'

'No he isn't. He's in the newspapers.'

As Sorrel was about to board the bus, Pauline took her arm and shook it. 'Remember. He'll be as shattered as you are. *And as happy.*'

On the journey Sorrel wondered why she had not taken a taxi. But what was the point, since she didn't believe she was going to the right place. Exhausting questions poured into her head. She felt frightened and shaken. The sun lit Piccadilly, and an American jeep went by, driven by police with white helmets whom the GIs named Snowdrops. In the park people lay on the grass; there was a holiday air. She left the bus and walked back from the stop towards Aldenham House. There was no doorman, the smart building was deserted and when she entered a thickly carpeted hall, she had a sensation of despair. He wasn't there, it was a crazy idea of Pauline's. She'd have to go to the War Office and it could be days before she traced him. She stood looking up at the board which gave the names of the occupants.

And then she saw a visiting card had been pushed into the space of Flat 57. It said 'Lord Martyn', and next to it the wooden slide said 'Out'.

If he isn't there, you must sit on the doorstep, Pauline had said. I wish I could stop shivering. Pull yourself together, Toby will hate it if you're in a state. Toby! She was thinking of him in the present.

It was deathly quiet on the fifth floor. The traffic noise had faded to nothing although the windows on the landing were open on to the summer sky. The sun poured in. The door of Flat 57 was at the Piccadilly end. She went to it.

Nobody will answer. I'll sit on that chair.

She rang.

The pause was filled with silence.

Suddenly the door opened and framed there, thin, haggard – alive – was Toby.

Sorrel fainted.

When she came to, she was lying on a bed and somebody was bathing her forehead. A voice at a distance said, 'She's coming round. Stop fussing, she only passed out. Girls in the village used to drop like flies during morning service. It was praying on an empty stomach. Perhaps she's had nothing to eat.'

Slowly, dizzily, Sorrel opened her eyes. Toby was bending over her. She couldn't bear to look and shut her eyes again.

Grace put the flannel on her forehead; it was too wet and dripped down her face.

'You're drenching her, Mother. She's coming to. She's all right.'

'Of course she is. I'll leave you to it.'

There was the sound of a door closing.

And then Sorrel opened her eyes and somehow lifted herself upon her elbows and the next minute was in his arms.

He climbed on to the bed and scooped her up and held her tightly, tightly, saying nothing, hugging and kissing her, rocking her like a baby. She wanted to cry and didn't dare. Already at this moment of union she must keep his rules again. She abandoned herself to the feel of Toby, the body like iron or steel, the smell of his clothes, of himself, the cheek against hers. So thin. When he pressed his face close she could feel his cheekbones.

There was no sex in the long embrace as he rocked her in his arms. No room for desire, it was too full of other things. Of months of sorrow, of hardships suffered, of the ravages and revenges of war. They simply lay touching each other, hands and arms and cheeks and shoulders, occasionally kissing. They said nothing until in the end they had to part.

He pushed some more pillows under her head and sat up.

'*Where have you been?* I was out of my wits with worry.'

'Oh Toby.'

'I should be angry with you for disappearing like that. Why weren't you with the parents? What happened? No, you must tell me later. Let me just look at you. You're beautiful. More beautiful. . . . I was so furious with them, poor old things, when I found you weren't here. I yelled at them.'

'It wasn't their fault. It was mine.'

She saw that for whatever reasons they'd rejected her they had told Toby nothing. There must be gaps and she did not know how to fill them. They hadn't said anything because they loved him too much.

Now she was no longer dizzy, she really saw him for the first time. He was a man she scarcely recognised. He was skeleton-thin, the skin drawn tight across his face, and the lines, so attractive when she had first met him, running from cheekbone to jaw, were now as deep as if they'd been dug by a sculptor's knife. His eyes were startlingly blue, the skin under them blackened. He seemed – the word came unbidden – ferocious.

But his eyes were not. He took her left hand and began to play with her wedding ring.

'Why did you do it, darlingest? Stop seeing my parents?'

'I was so unhappy. So stupid. I don't know why I did anything.'

The answer seemed to satisfy him and it was the truth. She said, as if it were a litany, 'Oh Toby. Oh Toby.'

She told him brokenly how she had seen his picture and had guessed – that was not true – the name of this place. He was not listening or did not seem to be. He looked as if he couldn't drag his eyes away from her. When she stopped speaking he said again, 'I was out of my wits. I had a crazy idea I had lost you . . .'

Suddenly he sprang up with energy like a released spring.

'And now we must go to the parents who are feeling very guilty about us, darlingest. Can you get up? Are you quite better? Do your hair . . .'

While she tried to comb it, he came up behind her, thrust his haggard face over her shoulder and gently bit the lobe of her ear.

The Martyns were sitting on a low divan in a rich characterless room with windows high up over Piccadilly and the trees of the park. Neither of them smiled when Toby came in bringing Sorrel like a captive.

'Here she is. Full of apologies for being so naughty.'

He pulled up a chair for Sorrel, and sat beside her on its arm.

Nothing was stranger than the manner in which the Martyns accepted her. Grace gave a slight incline of the head, reminiscent of royalty seen through the window of a car. George Martyn regarded her without a smile. His mouth was thin. Their son looked at them with amusement.

'I wish you could see yourselves. Two wet weeks. What you *don't* look like is parents whose son has returned from the tomb. You were all smiles last night until I lost my rag about my missing wife. Now here we are. Happy endings all round. Perk up, Mother. Guess how Sorrel discovered my whereabouts?'

'I have no idea,' Grace managed with a smile.

'She worked out the name of the flats in the newspaper picture. Wasn't that brilliant of her?'

‘I didn’t know there was a name.’

‘Only the first six letters, A - l - d - e - n - h - ’ Sorrel said.

Toby laughed in the excited hysterical way she remembered, the laugh like the rattle of machine-gun fire. He turned first to his mother, then his father, demanding they should see the joke. The joke that he was here, alive, not three words on a telegram.

George Martyn glanced towards Sorrel as if trying to think of something pleasant to say and not finding it.

‘You seem well.’

‘She’s horribly pale,’ said Toby. ‘I’m not used to white-faced girls. The Yugoslavs are brown as gypsies, with huge melting black eyes. And you’re very quiet, Sorrel. Haven’t you got over the shock of your husband’s resurrection?’

He began to laugh again and this time they did as he wanted and joined him.

Although the miracle had happened, and their son was with them, noisy, restless, exhausting, although they must be stunned with happiness, Sorrel knew his parents were mutely refusing to reinstate her. She had caused George Martyn’s illness. She had kept away. Toby had been missing and they had no longer felt any kind of duty to her, she had simply been amputated. Toby’s return set them the impossible task of sewing Sorrel on again.

The quartet had only been together a short while when the telephone rang and Toby sprang up like a jack-in-the-box to answer it and carry on a loud conversation with somebody called Andrew, punctuated with laughter. He arranged to meet him the following day at the Cavalry Club. Then rang off.

‘Andrew’s a funny chap,’ he said. ‘Last time I saw him was at Dunkirk, walking round the place talking to the men and wearing a jockey cap to make them laugh so they’d forget the shells popping.’

He went to the window and stood looking out.

‘Haven’t they any work to do?’ he said, of the crowds sunning themselves.

He walked round the colourless room, reminding Sorrel of

an animal in a cage, finally returning to sit on the arm of her chair and talk to his parents.

Watching them, Sorrel saw them differently. Grace's expression when she spoke to Toby melted with love; it seemed wrong to be looking at such naked emotion. But even while Sorrel's eyes were on her, Grace looked in her direction and Sorrel saw the face of a gaoler. George Martyn was less crude. Courtesy was cold, paternal charm gone. He talked excludingly to his son.

Sorrel remained silent. The paralysing effect of what had happened was beginning to wear off. There had been an unspeakable joy, a belief that such bliss would never leave her, a gratefulness to heaven, and the shock of sight – had Lazarus's sisters felt like that? Toby was real again, at times too real. Once, meeting Grace Martyn's eyes, she saw something near to hatred and longed for Pauline's goodness and good sense. She did not want to remember that a few days ago Pauline's brother had made love to her. And she'd told him – how could she have said such a thing? – that it was the best lovemaking she'd ever known. Had it been true? Even then she had obscurely felt she was doing wrong.

During the rest of the day, during a long dinner at the Dorchester, lingering over coffee, once interrupted by a colonel in the Black Watch who came over to wring his hand, Toby described what had happened to him. He'd already told part of the story to his parents; George Martyn asked for more.

'Start at the beginning, my dear chap. In detail.'

'You're letting yourself in for a long harangue, Pop. Are you strong enough? And you, Mother?'

He did not ask Sorrel.

He and a small picked team were sent on a special course when he'd been in England. They had been trained for a different form of war than the great pushes across the desert or later in Italy. They learned mountain warfare, fighting with bare hands and with knives, learned to use lariats. One of the instructors had owned a ranch in South America and could trip a running man with a lariat at forty feet. His use of ropes was uncanny. Lariats were not only for capturing an enemy or for road traps, they were used for crossing unbridged rivers, scaling walls, climbing mountains. The team learned to exist – 'God, we were hungry!' – on rations near to starvation. He was told that when the time was right he would be sent to Yugoslavia.

'I knew what we were in for before I embarked. But couldn't tell you, of course. The high-ups were very against our thinking it was a suicide mission. We were not expendable, that kind of talk was frowned on. Our job would be to get to certain places in Yugoslavia, contact the partisans and give a hand. But that was in the future . . .'

He sipped his brandy. His parents and Sorrel were silent.

'Of course you gathered I was in the Italian shindig. We landed in Sicily in July and it was brisk going but messy most of the time. My lot landed up near Brindisi. There was a Yugoslav, Milo, brought in by the patrols. He'd got across the Adriatic somehow and wanted arms for his guerrillas. He was what the high-ups were banking on and, frankly, I think it was set up by some of those secret chaps we know nothing about. Poor old Milo.' An abrupt laugh. 'He was under the delusion he'd only got to ask and he'd be given a suitcaseful of tommy guns and grenades. But I liked him. I trusted him. His English was perfectly awful but it was enough and we understood each other. Until I had to send him on to Allied Command, he didn't understand that! He was purple in the face with rage.'

Toby laughed again.

Sorrel sat with George and Grace Martyn, and music played; people danced, while she heard of Toby's life all the time she had believed him dead. He had been chosen to command a boat crossing the Adriatic, there'd be only five of them, Toby, Milo, and three of Toby's men. It was decided not to drop them by parachute, they should go by sea and on foot, it was safer and more secret. They carried a good many arms, so Milo got his suitcasesful after all.

Milo knew the mountains like a Londoner knows the City, and during the following days groups of partisans appeared at intervals, materialising out of nowhere to claim their helpings of guns and ammunition.

The country was wild, empty, mountainous and thickly forested. There were German troops somewhere there, and German troops somewhere in the sky, once or twice the forest silences were broken by the sound of planes. But the journey was interrupted only by having to ford rushing rivers, camp in ice-cold caves. Sometimes they were escorted by groups of wild-looking men, 'savage as tigers until you got to know them. There was a girl . . . God, she was beautiful. She'd cut off all her hair, but her face . . . and what do you think? All round her belt she hung our hand grenades. I said to Milo, suppose you kissed her and one of the pins came out.'

The story hadn't any kind of poetry but it turned Toby into the unknown and ominous character, a true hero. She had thought that was what he was when she first met him, but the saga now filled her with awe. He and his companions quickened their pace at times, riding horses stolen by the partisans from the German camps. Riding, climbing, sleeping on pine needles, hungry, in danger, they lived on dry black bread and pink vanilla brandy. They hid in ruined castles on the tops of rocky promontories. They were fighting against a race who claimed the Nordic myths, but it was they who were Sigmunds and Siegfrieds, without the magical help of the Valkyrie.

The partisans had fought alone since 1941. They were, said Toby, 'wonderful fellows'. He described their pure communist ruthlessness. Nothing made them afraid. Nothing stopped them. German reprisals on their own people did not make them hesitate, *their* lives were of no account and neither were those of civilians captured and killed. The civilians were Yugoslavs, weren't they? They died for their country and that was that. The more civilians shot, the more villages burned, the more enemy convoys would be ambushed. And if they were lucky enough to capture some Germans, the more throats would be cut.

After weeks of success, one evening Toby and Milo and their men emerged from the woods to a place where there were traces of terrible fighting. In stony fields were the burnt skeletons of tanks, cars in blackened messes, bodies lying where men and women had fallen. The sun was setting as they crossed the street of a ruined village. And were ambushed.

In the bloody fighting which followed only Toby, Milo and three partisans escaped. The rest were butchered.

Toby stopped talking and gestured to a passing waiter for another brandy.

'Major,' said the waiter smartly.

'You haven't told us about when you were ill,' prompted Grace. 'Who looked after you? All you said last night was you couldn't get any message through to let the army know you were alive.'

Toby picked up the glass between his fingers and shrugged. Yes, he'd developed some kind of fever which had been a damned nuisance and at times he'd been off his head.

'Don't look so pained, Mother! Milo said with that bug you always go mad. They gave me a disgusting brew of God knows what and nothing to eat and when I was at my craziest they got me drunk. I believe I lived on rajika. We were back in the mountains, and then there was news that the Germans were running like rabbits and revolution had broken out. I was just one delirious Brit as far as the partisans were concerned. They'd have finished me off to get rid of a minor problem, if it hadn't been for Milo. He drew a knife on them I learned later. As I said, they're ruthless. One respects that.'

'*I* don't.'

'Of course you don't, Mother, you don't know them. What matters is they fought to liberate their country. They could see what they call the crown of victory. They're magnificent. They keep vows without having to make 'em. And what was the point of keeping one Englishman talking bosh and off his head in the corner of a cave? I wouldn't have blamed them if they'd cut my throat. As it was, thanks to old Milo, I'm here to tell the tale.'

He went on talking. And they listened, how the Martyns listened. Nobody mentioned the enormous war won in Europe at terrible cost since Toby had gone to his destiny. He spoke of his companions. Violent in what he despised, he was passionate in what he admired. His heart burst with the thought of his fellow-fighters. He exulted in the men who'd been beside him, his imagination enfolded them.

'The only argument I could ever use which worked – they're stubborn as mules – was to say something they planned was against Yugoslav honour. Do you realise – ' he turned from Sorrel to his parents, 'do you realise they are the only people in the entire war who freed themselves?'

When he left Yugoslavia his story took on the character of an odyssey. He recovered from his illness and was strong enough to travel; he foot-marched towards Greece from one country in turmoil to the next. There was chaos in Greece during *their* revolution, 'and the communists there don't like the Allies so I kept out of sight.' At last he landed up in a 'tiny godforsaken port called Preveza'. He learned from the locals by gestures and broken French that there was a British tramp steamer anchored in the harbour; it had come from Alexandria with a cargo of raw cotton and been driven to take shelter from a sudden bad storm.

The captain of the steamer agreed to take him back to England.

'He wasn't at all pleased. I looked like a scarecrow and I heard him say he was fed up with damned refugees. I swallowed my pride and kept my mouth shut. That was a leaky old bucket of a ship! It heaved about even in calm seas. I was as sick as a dog.'

'But why didn't you radio Gibraltar?' asked his father quietly. 'It would have been less of a shock.'

Toby laughed.

'You should have seen the wireless; it worked about once a week. And in any case the captain had no intention of putting in at Gib either, the storm had made him desperately behind schedule. He just pressed on regardless. His crew couldn't stand him, actually. They disliked him about as much as he disliked having a refugee on board.'

'It does not sound to me,' said Grace, 'as if you were treated as your rank deserved.'

'Oh Mother!'

The evening ended with the solemn 'God Save the King'

played by the band. The Martyns stood to attention. Afterwards the dancers went by, girls in pale dresses, wearing flowers in their hair. Young men still in uniform.

When the quartet took a taxi to Aldenham House, Sorrel had the sudden absurd thought – I haven't a nightdress, even a toothbrush. It seemed a year since she had left Pauline at the bus stop. She and Grace were sitting on the main seat, Toby and his father on small folding seats opposite. Toby's knees touched Sorrel's. Grace leaned forward and put her hand, plump, weather-beaten and winking with diamonds, on her son's.

'Grand to have you back, my dear.'

The lighting in the streets brightened and obscured the faces of the two men opposite her. Sorrel felt very nervous. Something in the way Toby had helped her into the cab, something self-conscious, tender, embarrassed, told her very well what they were going to do. She thought – oh God, don't I *want* him? What's happened to me? Don't I love him any more? He is my husband, my beloved, my dear dear Toby back from the dead. He is the man I lay in bed sweating for, the one whose body owns mine. Why do I feel like this?

The answer came too soon. Dion. Last week she and Dion had made love and she had responded to his passion with a flare of her own. She'd wanted him and he had strongly and surely wanted her and in sex they had matched, given and taken, seemed . . . that sad longing . . . to become each other. Yes, it had been like that.

The taxi drew up at Aldenham House, and the quartet went through the doors and into the lift. When they were standing together, Toby, in a rare gesture in public, put his arm round her shoulders. Sorrel by mistake looked up at his mother. She had to look away.

'Well, darlingest?' Toby said when they were alone in his room which was strewn with uniform, battered canvas bag, Sam Browne, a pair of binoculars, its leather strap mended with string, and piles of tattered maps. 'Well, darlingest?'

He held out his arms and she ran to him.

'Mmm.' He smelled her hair. 'Who's been buying you scent, bad girl?'

'The entire American army.'

He gave her a pinch which became a hug. They kissed for a long time. When he drew away, he was breathing fast.

'Do you know, I haven't had a woman since I last made love to you? Never once. I have been as faithful as you have been. Thank God.'

The next morning while Sorrel, worn out with emotion and lovemaking, slept late, Toby bathed and dressed and breakfasted with his parents. Sorrel woke to find herself alone. She thought about their lovemaking of the night. And wondered, and wondered, and found no answers in her body.

When Toby came into the room he smiled.

'You're awake and I have a surprise. I've just rung the Savoy. We're moving there for a week or two.'

'*The Savoy!*'

'Yes, it's the lap of luxury for my pretty. Do you realise that your dear husband is rich?'

'Has your father – '

'Of course not, silly girl. It's my pay, it's been pumping into my bank for so long that it is now bursting out and begging to be spent. Father was rather shocked when I told him where we're going. He doesn't splash money about the way I do.'

Smiling at his lordly manner, Sorrel was filled with an almost hysterical relief at the thought of being away from his parents. She didn't understand the Martyns' antagonism and the more she saw it in their faces, the more worried she became – even rather frightened. Yet when she thought about them, there were times when she felt an unreasoning pity. She couldn't understand that either.

She lay watching Toby, who stood looking out of the window.

'God, I miss Tibbits,' he said.

'Who was he, Toby? One of your friends in the regiment?'

'Of course he wasn't, he was my orderly. I told you about him.'

He had not.

'Mother's helping me pack, but the person I need now is Tibbits. Nobody else knows how to do things the way I like. He was killed at Salerno. I told you.'

He had not.

'I'm so very sorry,' she murmured, out of her depth.

'It was different in Yugoslavia, there would have been no place for Tibbits there. It's now that I miss him. He was only a half pint of a chap, with one of those pale Cockney faces. But he kept going with the best of them. On the march, three days of it, during one bombardment when we were on our faces in the nearest ditch, Tibbits was hit by a shell fragment. He just tied the wound in his arm up with a rag and went on marching. When we finally reached the trucks I looked for him, and saw the arm soaked in blood. "It's nothing, Major," he said. How he stayed on his feet, God in heaven knows. Back in England we got him straight to hospital but it was touch and go whether he'd lose the arm. He did have two fingers amputated. Dear chap . . . he was in Italy with me too. And it was there, after all he'd been through, that he bought it.'

Toby stood silent. Then with a visible effort turned round to Sorrel with a grin.

'How will you like the Savoy?'

'You're so extravagant, I shall love it.'

'You must get your stuff. You did say you'd been demobbed, didn't you? I'm afraid I didn't take in anything last night – except you.'

'I was the same. Yes, I'm a civilian now. I haven't much to fetch, Toby, only a few boring clothes.'

'Then I shall buy you a trunkful.'

'Will you? How gorgeous. I've been lodging in Kensington. Shall I get my things while you're packing?'

While she had been in bed alone that morning, searching her heart about Toby, she realised she could tell him little about her life. Nothing about Buzz. Nor about Pauline who was a Fulford. Last of all could she speak of Dion. She saw that Toby would never understand her past. He might even stop loving her – no, that was impossible. But she was sure of one thing: that he would never be able to grasp what had happened between men and women during the war that had just ended. *Virtus semper viridias*. His creed was honour, and it hurt like hell.

While he was with his mother, Sorrel took the chance of telephoning Pauline.

'Sorrel! I've been thinking about you all the time. Are you all right? Is *he* all right?'

'Everything's fine. May I come round?'

'Of course. Now?'

When she saw Pauline and the children sitting in the garden at Thorley Court, Sorrel had a funny feeling that she was returning to real life. Rose wore a dress Sorrel had made for her, green and blue cotton patterned with leaves and flowers. Sorrel was sure Pauline had chosen it today on purpose. Davy was building a brick house and, as usual, knocking it down again.

'There you are!' cried Pauline. '*What happened* when you rang the bell?'

'Toby opened the door. I'm such a fool. I fainted.'

Pauline couldn't help laughing.

'Poor Toby, that was rather dramatic of you. But what an entrance. How is he in himself? Men who've been prisoners can arrive home pretty ill.'

Sorrel explained that Toby had not been taken prisoner, he'd been with the partisans all the time 'hiding but fighting'. It was true though, he'd been very ill.

She told the story in the barest outline and Pauline sat listening with her arms clasped round her knees, absorbed and dreaming, looking just like the child in the painting of *The Boyhood of Raleigh*. It was the face of a girl who could put herself into other people's lives, suffer and rejoice with them. Sorrel wondered if she herself sounded happy enough. There was something missing in her voice. Pauline did not seem to notice . . . now and then she sighed, as if she, too, were living on pink brandy and black bread.

'Such a happy end,' she said finally.

Sorrel said in a rush, 'Not with the Martyns. They're so

cold. I think they still blame me for George Martyn's heart attack and haven't forgiven me.'

'Oh, they're just odd. Dion always says so, specially Grace. You haven't seen them for months, you've forgotten what they're like. I'm sure they haven't changed towards you.'

Sorrel, who knew it was not true, agreed.

'Shall we lunch? The usual Spam and bread but I've got some tomatoes and we can have it out here.'

'I wish I could, but I have to get back. Toby and I are moving to the Savoy.'

The remark was greeted with a hoot of laughter.

'You mean he's taking you to a glamorous lunch.'

'No. We're going to stay there.'

She said it with perfect seriousness and Pauline went on laughing.

'I suppose it does sound rather funny.'

'Oh Sorrel,' said Pauline, wiping her eyes. 'Come on, I'll help you pack for your apotheosis.'

They shoved Sorrel's few clothes into an ancient much-labelled leather suitcase which Pauline's father had used in the 1920s when the family visited Honfleur. Pauline and the children trooped out once again to see Sorrel off. Rose looked tearful.

'I don't want you to go.'

Sorrel kissed her.

'I s'pose you'd better kiss Davy too,' said Rose grudgingly.

Pauline gave Sorrel one of her hugs. 'You have to learn to be happy, you know. Start all over again, as if you and Toby had only just got married. So much has happened to you both. To all of us. You must jump over that, as if you're crossing a stream.'

'It's difficult.'

'Yes. But jump now and you'll land safely on the other side. It's all to do with time, Sorrel. The old gent with the hourglass is a damned nuisance.'

'I won't let him be,' Sorrel said and kissed her.

Getting into a taxi, she set off for the glory of the Savoy.

17

Her new life had a certain unreality. Uniforms were seen everywhere, rationing and shortages continued or were rather worse than they had been, and a bitter winter was forecast. She found herself in shining bowed-to luxury. She couldn't get used to it. Toby had decided they would remain at the Savoy for a least a month; he was spending his arrears of pay as if he were a millionaire.

What Toby now took on, with the energy of a soldier who did nothing badly, was to renew his army friendships. Sitting at a desk in their bedroom – from its high windows he could see the grey Thames – he was on the telephone for hours. And the days and nights of his return became a series of reunions, bad jokes and bright faces. People were happy that autumn. Real life was starting all over again.

Toby bought her some remarkable clothes, he had wallets full of coupons given him by his father, and liked to go with her to choose dresses, suits, shoes – he loved buying her shoes. He bought her a balldress designed by Norman Hartnell, of white satin sweeping to the ground. And took her into the Savoy restaurant to show her off to his friends. Sorrel enjoyed meeting the men Toby invited to lunch or to dine with them. Alec and David, seasoned soldiers now. Older officers. Colonels. Brigadiers. She admired them and felt admired in return.

And then Toby would go upstairs with her to a room with gleaming curtains and a gold telephone, modestly undress in the bathroom before getting into bed with her and turning off the light. His way in sex seemed different; this wasn't the man who'd made love to her in the bath. Such an orgy of sex, of passion, was unthinkable now. He took her without preliminaries, the only indication he was going to make love was a doting self-conscious look. He never said a word, never embraced her in any way with caresses, but only with his hard body penetrating her, never waited for her to have her climax and, because he was very quick, she did not. He finished, trembling, and rolled away from her. Sorrel lay awake. She looked at the light shining in bands where the curtains were closed. She listened to the traffic and sometimes to the gentle sound of rain upon the roofs. She thought of the man asleep beside her. She loved him. Yes, she did love him. But he was changed, and so was she.

He did not talk to her again about Yugoslavia although, now and then, when she came up to join him and his friends, she caught the name 'Milo' or the word 'partisans'. He stopped when she approached, and smiled at her artlessly. She thirsted to hear more and somehow to share the unshareable part of his life. Naively she had believed that after the first night when he'd told his stories to his parents and to her, much more would emerge when they were alone in each other's arms. He'd tell her – what wouldn't he tell her? Of his brave friends, of forays with the enemy, of more journeys, more risks and victories. She had believed that like Desdemona she would give a world of sighs, would love him for the dangers he had passed, and he love her for she did pity them.

It was not like that. She was no part of what had happened to him; it was another, secret, treasured life which duty had made him tell but once. And just as he kept her away and would not share, so he lacked any curiosity about her own life without him. He never said 'did you miss me?' or asked how it had felt to believe herself a widow. If she talked about the Wrens he looked approving, and once said it was sad not to see her in uniform.

The Savoy honeymoon could not last, but somehow in her role of mistress, companion, presider at dinners for his friends, she was not expected to ask when it would end. Once when she did he said, 'Aren't you happy? I thought it just suited us.'

It certainly suited Toby. He liked the service and the respect, the commissionaires called him 'Major. Sir!' He was in excellent spirits, and left her alone a good deal. 'I'm meeting Alec.' Or Jim, or Josh, or his colonel. He went to see his parents. 'Don't bother to come with me, darlingest. You know Mother natters on about the past.' It was an order although it was said with a kiss. When she asked about Aunt Dot, he laughed.

'Staying with some very grand people in Northamptonshire. Typical Dot. No sign of her in town yet.'

There was another subject she was not allowed to talk about – Evendon. Even The Chief. On her first day with him her old impulsiveness made her exclaim over the loss of his home. Toby's face had closed.

'Oh, that's all over now. My father's right. Change is the order of the day.'

That was all. She knew he minded bitterly, and her heart swelled. She dared not say any more.

Every morning he rose an hour before Sorrel, and sat by her bed to eat his breakfast, dressed in a uniform pressed to perfection, handsome and thin as a rake. His nervous energy never abated. Would he suddenly tell her he'd put in to go overseas again? She could not guess. The barriers he'd made meant she could not ask either. It astonished her that weeks in this rich place satisfied him. He used his time to gather friends, talk and laugh for hours on the telephone, to go shopping with Sorrel and dance with her at night sometimes. Make love to her at night sometimes. He went to visit Evie who was staying in London with relatives, but he went alone. He took his mother out to luncheon but did not ask Sorrel to come with him. 'You understand, darlingest? She likes a fellow to herself occasionally.' He went to his club and met the friends who did not dine with them at the Savoy.

Without him, she was left to her own devices. She went to rich, often empty shops and bought clothes. She walked by the river where the fog seemed about to claim the city like an enemy. At the hotel there was music in the afternoon, and men in uniform with pretty women in Paris dresses, unfamiliar in their extravagant femininity. Now and then she saw an American soldier or airman. But every day the sight grew more rare.

She tried to enjoy the expensive limbo in which Toby had imprisoned her, but she was lonely. She telephoned Pauline once or twice, always hearing her friend's teasing voice with relief. They chatted for a while, but neither of them suggested a meeting. It would mean telling lies, and wasn't Sorrel at the start of her marriage?

She was lonely. When she talked to Toby about the Wrens occasionally, Margaret came into the conversation, and Sorrel had a feeling of sadness that she had lost her other wartime friend. Since the day she'd seen Margaret and learned that Gareth and Byron were dead, Sorrel had not seen her. The girls had written to each other intermittently; once Sorrel had telephoned from Lee. Her friend had sounded recovered, but without any of the old sparkle. That had been months ago.

One dark afternoon, Sorrel wrote to Margaret at the WRNS address where she'd been stationed when she last heard from her. Without much hope, she put on the envelope 'Please forward if necessary'. There had been no reply, and she wasn't surprised.

It seemed as if winter was on its way. The weather was cold when, with Toby out and not due back for hours, she went for a walk. She passed the Palace; the great building looked deserted, scarcely a single room shone through the foggy dusk. Wandering through St James's Park, she saw a shape floating ahead of her. It vanished into the trees – it was an owl. Dion had said you saw them in London occasionally. She often remembered things he'd told her. Thought about him. Was it possible to keep him, and Pauline, as her friends? She knew it was not.

Returning to the hotel, she was saluted by the head commissionaire. The salute made her smile inwardly, it still brought the automatic reaction of wanting to lift her own hand in reply.

There was music in the lounge, people were having tea. As Sorrel sat down, a voice cried, 'There you are!'

Standing in front of her, wearing a dark dress and a velvet hat with a little veil, dimpled and rosy-cheeked, was Margaret.

'But how extraordinary – ' began Sorrel. Before she could finish Margaret had sat down beside her.

'No, it isn't, I got your letter this morning. It's been chasing me all over the place! I rang reception here, and they told me you were always back by tea-time. So I thought I'd surprise you!' She turned to Sorrel with the familiar, very Irish grin, adding it was odd to see her in civvies. She appeared to have forgotten her own dress and perky velvet hat.

'Have you noticed? No? Wait for my bombshell. I'm married!'

She spread out her hand to show a gold ring above which shone a small diamond solitaire.

Yes, said Margaret interrupting Sorrel's congratulations, she had been married abroad. She'd put in for overseas service and had been posted – it was so romantic! – to Naples. That was where she and Paul had met. It was two months after VE Day; he'd been in the army 'kicking his heels, as we all were, until he was sent home. Weren't we lucky to be in Italy? Of course there's a lot of damage but it . . . well . . . it's no good telling you about Italy, you have to go there yourself.'

They had become engaged and her father pulled some ecclesiastical strings and arranged for them to be married in a private chapel at the Vatican.

'Is Paul a Catholic?'

'Of course he is, Sorrel! How could he not be?'

They had been given a special blessing by His Holiness and Margaret had a medal also blessed by the Pope. She fished out some photographs and showed Sorrel a twinkling bride in white lace with a bouquet of enormous lilies on the arm of a fresh-faced young officer, slightly shorter than his bride. Eating an éclair, Margaret talked, just as Toby had talked. It was a time for epics. She described her romance in Italy, the twilight in Rome, the flower shops full of white violets, the fountains, the holy water font in St Peter's 'big enough to bath a baby in'. She spoke of the Bay of Naples, of the way Italians sang; 'they're like the Irish, they sing as birds do.' She lamented that her sisters were not allowed to come to Rome to be bridesmaids. 'Sheila was so disappointed, she cried!' Margaret was radiant and fatter and talked for an hour. Sorrel wondered at the power of humans to recover. Where was the girl, ghost-faced, weeping over the two men who had taken her to bed? Whose heart was broken when they were killed? She envied her for being – what? For being Margaret Reilly.

When her friend finally ran out of steam, Sorrel managed to tell her about Toby. Margaret was stunned.

'Missing, believed killed – *why* didn't you tell me when you wrote?'

'I don't know. I suppose I couldn't bear to.'

Margaret said nothing for a moment or two. Just for that time, no more, her face changed. Yes, she said, she understood. But then she leaned over to pat Sorrel's hand.

'It's a miracle, Toby coming back. Miracles do happen, you know, I *truly* believe in them. And now you're as happy as I am.'

She smiled, showing her dimples. She looked charming.

'It was a sort of miracle that I met Paul. It was on board *Ceres*. I almost didn't go, but changed my mind at the last minute and then we met – and that was it! Next day he took me to Vesuvius, do you know, the ashes on the mountain are literally hot? Another day we went to Capri, there was a tree covered with huge scented lilies . . . Italy . . . ' She spoke dreamily. Then, 'Is that the time? Oh bother, I must fly. It's been so good to see you, Sorrel, here's my new address in Manchester. Paul's demobbed and he's going to work for his father's firm. This is our new house. Do come and stay, I'd love it and so would Paul. Oh, I've saved the best till the last. I'm *just* preggers.' She waited, blissfully, for the compliments, agreeing that it was wonderful and adding that her parents were over the moon. She stood up, stately, large, noble, the goddess returned. And sailed away through the lounge.

Sorrel watched her go. How happy people can be again, she thought with a feeling of desolation. And her thoughts turned, as they always did when she was alone, to Toby.

She did not understand what had happened to them. Had his life in the forests altered something in Toby, or perhaps brought out a dormant quality like a chord at first indistinguishable in a symphony, then played again, then repeated and growing stronger until its strength was almost unbearable? His nature was masculine in its most cxaggerated form; look as she might, she never discerned a single feminine trait. He was hard as his muscles were. But when they had been in love in a past she couldn't bear to recall, there had been in him a most particular, most tender indulgence. Where had it gone? He made love to her now. But sex never opened the gates of his hidden self as it used to do. What he had feared and suffered, what terrible things he may have seen – or done – he never told her. And as the nights went by they lay in each other's arms and grew less close.

He never asked her about the time when she'd believed him dead. He seemed to have no interest in her life without him. It was as if from the moment he'd left her at Evendon one spring morning, not kissing her because the corporal was there with the staff car, she became frozen in his memory. Like Hermione in *The Winter's Tale* she was a statue which *he* made warm, which *he* miraculously restored to life. They had been tested in spirit and in body. God knew what tests Toby had passed which she was not allowed to know; for Sorrel, the test on her body had been how she could bear a wracking sorrow. She'd chosen a desperate mating, violent and short-lived, with poor short-lived Buzz. As for her spirit, she'd tried to be alone. Now she had been sent spinning back to be the statue-come-to-life. The chaste bride.

Yes, she thought, I do, I must love him. But suppose he will not let me any more? Is he afraid I will touch some part of him which is wounded more deeply than those old scars can show? Are there secret wounds he has to hide from me? He wants, and doesn't want me. There are times when he almost despises me, because I never waded across the rivers or starved in Dalmatian caves. Never wore grenades strung round my belt.

She thought of Dion and Pauline, her only real friends. Life in the Wrens had been full of day-to-day comrades, easily met and now disappeared. And when you were in love, you had no friends. It had been like that with her and Toby once. It should be now and she was desolate because it was not.

The war. It was the war which had turned Toby into a haggard stranger whom she *must* love, using loyalty and not her instincts and her heart. She was lonely for how it used to be.

She knew Dion shouldn't come into her thoughts; since he had made love to her she had not heard from him, and hadn't asked Pauline about him – nor had Pauline mentioned him. It had seemed a mutual decision.

Making up her mind, wanting to escape from the sombre thoughts, Sorrel left the lounge and went to one of a series of telephone boxes on the ground floor.

'Oh good!' said Pauline. 'I've been wondering how you are. Back at Aldenham House, I expect.'

'No. We haven't left the Savoy yet.'

'How grand.'

'Not really. Toby just wanted to stay on a bit. He's blowing all the pay that was in his bank when he got home. I haven't lived in a hotel since Mother was alive and we stayed in one before the war. It's quite odd.'

'A lovely kind of oddness, though?'

'I often wish I was at Thorley Court.'

'Dried egg omelette. I know exactly what you mean. Sorrel?'

'Yes.'

'Do you want to bring Toby round? I can't think he'd like it very much.'

'I suppose he wouldn't.'

'Did you tell him about us?'

'I'm afraid not. Have I offended you?'

'Don't be an idiot. You agree with me. There's no earthly reason to tell him if he hasn't asked.'

She did not, kind Pauline, sound surprised at Toby's lack of curiosity. She chatted instead about various friends who had called. Rose and Davy were well and Rose was learning the words of a new French record.

'I'd like to hear her.'

A pause.

'I keep getting letters from Chris but not a hope of him coming home yet,' Pauline said. 'Sometimes when I think about *the* day when he walks in through the door, I get scared. I don't think I'm the Pauline he said goodbye to. I'm bossier, not half as nice. Maybe he'll be changed too. Dion says why do I think everything has to be the same. Nothing ever is.'

'No. It isn't.'

'Tell you what. I'll arrange to faint, like you did.'

It was after that, when Pauline had mentioned her brother, Sorrel asked for Dion's Evendon number.

'But he's in London today; he can tell you the number in person. Want to talk to him?'

A voice, taking its time, said, 'Hello.'

'It's me. Sorrel.'

'I gathered. How are you? Where are you?'

'The Savoy.'

'Still? You're kidding.'

'No, I – Pauline will explain.'

'I must ask her.'

Silence.

'Dion. I was wondering if we could meet. As you happen to be in London?'

Another silence.

'Why?'

With her back to a corridor where people went by, invisible to the man speaking to her, hidden from the man to whom she was married, she blushed deeply.

'I'd like to see you.'

'Are you sure?'

'Yes.'

'Mm,' he said. She knew that noise.

'Do you know the National Portrait Gallery?' was his surreal question. She stammered that she did.

'Meet me there around eleven. There's a room on the second floor where there's a portrait of Charles Edward.'

'Charles who?'

'Bonnie Prince Charlie, come on, you've heard of him.'

She knew it was wrong to agree. And wrong the next morning to fudge an excuse to Toby, eternally on the telephone, and leave the hotel at quarter to eleven.

The morning was cold; autumn was gone and she hadn't noticed. She hurried down the Strand, past gaps where shops had been. On a corner was an old woman selling bunches of soft feathery yellow stuff, and she had a moment to look at it in wonder. She hadn't seen mimosa for seven years.

Crossing Trafalgar Square, she passed a great mass of pigeons, pinkish and bluish grey, cooing and fluttering, and quite suddenly a picture came into her mind of pigeons huddled along the edge of Aunt Dot's roof. Where *was* Dot? She had asked Toby two or three times; he always said his aunt was away. Sorrel wished she could see her again. She wouldn't let herself think of Dot's icy voice during their last conversation; she remembered her as merry and beautiful, hospitable and youthful. Buzz's name for her had been the Wartime Belle.

My heart's like post-war London, thought Sorrel, a mess. She went in through old-fashioned doors to a museum miraculously survived, marbled and dark with rich wood, and many of its pictures reinstated.

Up a staircase covered in red Turkish carpet she made her way along the second floor, down a passage where there was a series of small rooms hung with paintings. She looked into two or three, but there was no sign of Bonnie Prince Charlie. Then, in a fourth room, she found herself gazing straight at the portrait of a man in Scots finery with a fair bland face. Below him sat a man as fair but not bland at all, and shabbier. Dion was alone, his back against a wall, reading. He stood up.

'Hello.'

'I thought I'd never find His Royal Highness,' said Sorrel, in the kind of bright and joking voice the army people used to her.

He looked at her curiously. She wore a suit with a little jacket, a yellowish pink blouse enhancing the skin which always reminded him of an apricot. A small girlish hat was set on her curling hair, and American nylon stockings clung to long English legs. She had expensive shoes. This wasn't the woman he'd made love to in his sister's flat.

'I'm here, but I don't think I quite know why,' he said after a moment.

'I wanted to see you.'

They stood facing each other.

'Shall we sit down?' Dion said, as if to a stranger at a party. Sorrel sat on the bench at a slight distance from him. They were alone in the company of Charles Edward.

'What's been happening to you?' he asked.

'Toby came back.'

'I know, Sorrel, and that is not what I meant.'

She searched round for a way of explaining why she'd wanted him to come and finally said, thinking it pathetically inadequate, 'I've been thinking about you.'

'Oh good.'

'Don't be unkind when things are so difficult.'

He raised his eyebrows. He was large and fair and relaxed and not friendly. He made her nervous.

' I don't want to lose you,' she blurted out next.

'My dear girl, spare me the cliché.'

'Don't be horrible. I hate it when you talk like that. Why won't you listen?'

'Why indeed. Very well, I will, for all the good it'll do me.'

She still could not think what to say, except to mutter lamely, 'I wish I could see you sometimes.'

He directly challenged that.

'And what about your husband?'

'He has nothing to do with it.'

Dion looked at her in exasperation.

'That is simply not true.'

'Why? Because – I – I – want to be your friend.'

Even as she brought out the threadbare words she knew they were rubbish. She did not want him as a friend at all. She wanted *him*. Wanted the powerful man she felt she understood and who understood her. She melted when she saw him. Wanted to put her arms round him. She did not face up to her motives, she simply wanted him.

He turned round, pulled her close and kissed her. The

moment that happened she scarcely knew where she was, was conscious of nothing but him, his mouth, his tongue, his body, his soul, even. She let herself go, returning kiss for kiss, clutching at his coat, and wished that they were naked. It was Dion who ended the embrace. His face showed nothing. His eyes were not heavy. They shone.

'Well?'

'What do you mean?' Sorrel managed to say, her heart pounding still.

'I mean which of us is it to be? Toby? Me? Choose. It is perfectly straightforward. Choose now.'

She hadn't thought of that. Had gone to him from instinct and embraced him with thwarted passion; she had been too eager, too impulsive, too rash, too thick-headed to see what *he'd* seen at once. She told herself lies. He never did.

'I can't,' she said, struck and trembling.

'Of course you can. Your husband has come back from the war. Your lover, at present, is with you. You can't have two men, like that friend you once told me about. Were you thinking you could be another Margaret Reilly?'

His voice was brutal. She'd forgotten she had told him that story. How could he use it against her?

'I never thought – never meant – '

'Oh b— stuff,' he said roughly. 'What you don't seem able to do, and Christ I don't think you ever have, is to see *yourself*. Don't you know what you're doing? Does Toby know about me? Of course he bloody well doesn't. Does he know about Buzz Alderman – did you dare tell him that? Sorrel, I met you this morning because I wanted to and not, I may tell you, because you asked. I came here to say this. Choose. You can't.'

'You mean I can't leave Toby.'

Her eyes filled.

'Of course you can't. He's had a hellish war and it's extraordinary he's even alive. I hate what he represents and I never liked him when we were young. But you can't smash him in the face because I won't let you. I shan't see you again.'

He stood up and a moment later was gone.

At the end of the week Toby, eating his breakfast by Sorrel who was still in bed, picked up the morning's copy of *The Times*, looked at the headlines and exclaimed in disgust that the country was turning into a shambles. He spoke with a note of accusation.

'Do you realise there's a *Labour* government. The new ministers have a pretty ludicrous record as fighting men, I may add.'

He was working himself up.

'And I suppose you didn't happen to notice the lack of applause in the cinema last night when Churchill was on the news? They practically didn't clap at all.'

'That doesn't mean anything.'

'It means too much. I've met a lot of friends from the regiment who can't wait to get the hell out of all this. David – Alec - both of them are leaving. People have had it. There's something wrong with England now. It's dirty. It should be sent to the cleaners. The Americans over here don't feel too cheerful either. A marines colonel I met at the club said the GIs left in London have a new expression: they say people are "gloomy as victory".'

With another malevolent look at the newspaper, he threw it down. Sorrel waited for a further tirade, as somebody braces themselves against the cold. But his voice surprisingly changed.

'I've got some news.'

'What, Toby?'

'Don't look so nervous. Good news. The parents are going to America.'

'For a holiday, you mean?'

'No, no, for good, silly. That made you jump! Father's really pleased at the prospect. New worlds to conquer and all that.'

She didn't know what he was talking about, and he grinned as he explained. His father had made up his mind to leave Evendon and sell up long before VE Day. He was so far-sighted, said Toby with admiration. He always knew the direction the wind was blowing, and he and a lot of high-ups realised there'd soon be a Labour government in power. They could sense it.

'Father says the country is going to be ruined,' said Toby briskly. 'There'll be vote-catching budgets with heavy taxes, and the talk is it'll be impossible to have a net income of over £6,000 a year. That will simply encourage the worst kind of dishonesty and Father isn't prepared to put up with it.'

He spoke with warmth and approval. Sorrel often heard that tone when he talked about George Martyn. And she saw that he, too, was bitterly opposed to socialism. It was the old Toby detesting the 'lower classes'.

'Father says the Yanks look on socialism as no better than communism in fancy dress,' he said. 'And who knows, they may be damned right.'

George Martyn had apparently begun his negotiations to go to the United States; he wanted to set up a business there as soon as things could be arranged.

'I salute him for it. He's sold the Priory now to some local chap with money, and now he's all set to sell the mills and factories. He's got courage, hasn't he? He isn't going to get a good price, I'm afraid, which only proves what he expected is going to happen. However, he did well during the war, so he's not too worried. In first-rate form when I saw him yesterday.'

'But your mother, surely she won't – '

'Be willing to leave the old country? Well, she's sad about it. Quite upset though she's putting a brave face on it, naturally. But she said something to me recently which is so like her. That where *he* goes, she must go too. Bloody marvellous, isn't she?'

'Yes.'

'And you, darlingest?' he said, bending forward. 'Are you going to be the same?'

His voice was tender. His haggard face had softened.

'What do you mean?'

'You know perfectly well,' he said, starting to laugh excitedly. 'We're going with them. Think of getting out of England. Hang on to that!'

He began to describe a country she scarcely recognised. For

a man who'd spent months in the forests in the Balkans, who'd been back in England a few weeks, and who before Yugoslavia had been on active service overseas or at home training as a soldier, Toby talked as glibly as a Tory member of parliament. He listed to his silent wife the reasons for quitting the country. Rising taxes. Scarcity of labour, and so of servants. The privilege of bureaucrats. Mutinies in the Indian navy and, most recently, the way Attlee was weakening the country. The new government was gearing itself up to pull the Empire to pieces bit by bit. He was withering about the rudeness of post office clerks, waiters, commissionaires, all of whom to Sorrel's certain knowledge were over-polite and called him Major. Rhetoric was something Toby enjoyed and he was derisive and inaccurate and full of feeling. He gestured with his coffee cup, fortunately empty.

'We'll turn our backs on it all,' he said.

'But that means you giving up the army. What about your promotion?' Sorrel asked, aghast. She couldn't take it in.

Toby was ready for that. 'What do you suppose the Labour johnnies want with the army? Colonel Harrison told me they're already making cuts and more cuts, there won't be more than a token force. Do I want to be a part of *that*? And what kind of a life will an Englishman have under these people? A life with no power to make other nations respect us. Because our strength is gone. I don't want to live in a country which will soon be tenth rate. No,' he finished, coming out of his anger as quickly as he'd jumped into it, 'you and I will be American citizens.'

'If they'll have us.'

'Of course they'll have us! We'll learn their lingo and live outside New York. Mother has some cousins with a house in White Plains. I've seen photographs of it, it's twice the size of Evendon.'

He leaned over to kiss her startled face, adding that his parents were giving a farewell party for friends before leaving, and his father had suggested that Toby and Sorrel might like to take over at Aldenham House afterwards. Then Toby, of course, would have to relinquish his commission and make all kinds of arrangements.

‘So we’ve got a home to tide us over,’ he said.

They left the Savoy on the day before the party. Sorrel had a good deal more luggage than when she had arrived; it was piled into an ancient taxi, and Toby bustled about, lavishly tipping the commissionaires and porters about whom he’d been so unkind. He was saluted and thanked and was in his element.

‘That chief commissionaire is a first-rater,’ he said, jumping into the cab and sitting beside her, ‘an ex-guardsman and doesn’t he look it. Wounded at Caen. We were hard-pressed there, there was some real fighting. Chaps like that are the salt of the earth.’

As the taxi ground away from the costly place which had been their temporary home, he was in high fettle. Change, things happenings, challenge and novelty were like raw alcohol. He was humming with life.

‘You’re being a mouse today, darlingest. Don’t you like the idea of queening it at Aldenham House?’

‘Of course I do. It’s very kind of your parents to let us stay there.’

‘Well . . . my father has paid the rent for the next three months, he wasn’t sure when he’d manage to get a passage for Mother and himself. But he’s done it. Two berths in one of the troop ships sailing next week. All rather a rush, but it’s nearly impossible to get across if you aren’t a Yank. Trust Father to get a first-class cabin . . . Mother wanted us to travel with them, but I told her it’s out of the question. Leaving the army takes time, I haven’t even seen my colonel yet . . .’

He turned to her, adding with a smile, ‘All I’ve been doing lately is wasting my time on you.’

‘Everything’s very sudden, Toby.’

Her thin voice, her anxious face, did not affect him. ‘You can’t tell me you’ll feel homesick for *that*,’ he said, pointing out of the window at the street. It had begun to rain. There was that film of dirt, that poverty-stricken and sombre look of bombed cities all over Europe. Something collapsed and sad and permanent, like a ruined civilisation.

‘Know what you’re going to be, darlingest? The English version of the GI bride!’

Neither George nor Grace Martyn was at home when Toby unlocked the door of the flat with his newly acquired key. There was a note on the silver salver in the hall.

'Sorry not to be here but all kinds of things to settle including seeing dentist!! Your father may be home before me. In any case, a big welcome.'

It was signed 'Mummy' and there was no mention of Sorrel.

They took the suitcases into the second bedroom which was dark and did not overlook the park. It was the room to which they'd carried Sorrel when she had fainted. They piled luggage in corners and on chairs and Sorrel put the largest case on the bed and opened it. The Hartnell balldress positively sprang out, the rich full satin shimmering like pearls.

Toby roamed in and out of the rooms, opening and shutting cupboards, opening and shutting windows. He was like a dog circling before it settles in its basket. The telephone rang. He called out, 'I'll answer.'

The bedroom door was open, the telephone in the hall, and Sorrel heard him say, 'Hello. Oh, *hello!*' in a delighted voice. He listened for a while. Then briefly, 'Yes, I'll do that. In ten minutes? Nothing simpler.'

He stood at the door.

'That was Aunt Dot. Finally back from her junketing in that rich place in Northampton she told Mother about.'

'Oh, she's home! I'm so glad, it has been months – '

'She wants me to go round.'

'It'll be lovely to see her again, Toby, I've missed her so much,' exclaimed Sorrel, delighted that here was the one member of the family who was her friend, the one she liked, almost loved. She'd put out of her mind the strained telephone call of months ago.

Toby fastened on his Sam Browne.

'Actually, she's asked me to go by myself. You don't mind, do you? I haven't as much as clapped eyes on her since the day we were married. Dot and I need a real chin-wag, and you don't want to listen to my boring stories all over again. You can see her later. Shan't be long. Can you cope?'

It was his army phrase. 'Can you cope' covered everything from unpacking a case to staying cool when your husband left to fight a war. She smiled and said, of course, and would he be sure to give Aunt Dot her best love and say how much she wanted to see her?

Toby gave her a ghost of a salute. A joke between them. He left the flat, slamming the front door. That was Toby. Doors were shudderingly slammed. Lift gates, she heard them now, clanged shut.

Alone, she stood looking at the suitcase full of satin. She picked the dress up, smoothing its pale surface. There was a tang of scent. She stood, then, looking at Toby's leather luggage. He'd brought nothing back with him, and it was brand new. As her clothes were. As their marriage was. She looked round the rich, meaningless room filled with pre-war painted furniture and too many mirrors, and through the open door into the passage. She turned to stare again at her husband's luggage. The only things he'd taken out of his case were the shoes in which he'd returned from Yugoslavia. Laughing at himself, he had kept them. They were made of rough leather, hard as iron, blackened and stained and misshapen.

And a premonition came over her. She had never experienced such a thing before save once when she'd been afraid – sure – that Margaret Reilly's tragedy would be her own. Now a cold shiver went down her back. I am never going to live here, she thought. I can feel it. Smell it. I am not even going to sleep here tonight. Oh God. What's happening?

Unable even to unpack, she went into the drawing room and sat by the window. She looked out at the misty trees of the winter park and watched the twilight begin to fall. An hour went by. Nobody came into the flat. Not her mother-in-law. Not Lord Martyn. Not Toby. She thought – I am being absurd. I must bustle about and do things. But the ominous feeling held her in its clammy grip and she felt unable to stir . . .

At last there was the sound of a key in the lock, perhaps it was George Martyn. She stood up eagerly.

Toby came into the room, switching on every light, which blazed and dazzled her.

'How was Dot? What ages you've been, I've been missing . . .' she began. The words died on her lips.

The face she had seen sometimes in repose, haggard, ruthless, a killer even, was looking at her.

'You're a whore.'

The colour drained out of her cheeks. But she wasn't afraid of the figure standing like Nemesis.

'What did your aunt tell you?'

'My God, you're cool. You're bloody cool. What do you suppose she told me? That you went to bed with every Tom, Dick and Harry in London while I was fighting for *your* country. That you couldn't wait. That you – it's disgusting. I can't talk about it.'

'What she said is not true.'

'Not true? That's fine. That's magnificent,' he burst out in a high, hysterical voice. He began to walk up and down the room, avoiding her and staying by the wall. She watched him, thinking – I deserve this. But *he* doesn't. Why did Dot tell him? How could she?

'Why did she tell you? What did she tell you?' she said.

'The truth. Dot never lies. She's incapable of a lie. I've known that since I was a child. She doesn't wrap things up. My parents do. *They knew*, Dot told them. But they didn't tell me because they thought I'd be upset. Upset!' His voice rose and cracked. 'No wonder I couldn't understand how peculiar they were with you. I thought my mother was jealous. That's a good one, jealous! She was ashamed of the tart her son had married. Oh, get out of my sight, I can't bear to be in the same room with you. When I think . . .' His voice broke and she thought – I can't bear it if Toby cries.

'Toby. Listen to me.'

'*No.*'

'I beg you. Yes, I'll go, of course I'll go. I won't ask you to forgive me, I don't think you ever will. And your parents were right not to tell you I'd been unfaithful because they didn't want you to suffer. Dot was wrong.'

'*Wrong!*'

'Don't talk like that. Look like that. Toby, when I slept with Buzz who was killed only a month later I truly believed you were dead.'

He did not answer. He rushed out of the room into the bedroom and when she followed him swung round and for one terrible moment looked as if he was going to kill her. It was the only time she quailed.

'*Just go*,' he said. 'Looking at you makes me sick.'

18

Her home, then, was a small bedroom at Thorley Court, overlooking the grassy garden. Her family, as Pauline had said the day an ashen-faced Sorrel appeared out of the blue, was Pauline herself and the children. That evening Sorrel had run out of Aldenham House, taking nothing with her. Only by chance had she found sixpence in her pocket to pay the bus fare. She'd rung Pauline's bell and, when the door opened, hadn't needed to speak a word.

'You want a drink,' was all Pauline said. 'Richard and Bob are here. Richard, here's Sorrel who is not feeling too good.'

And Sorrel was taken into a room where two Americans sprang to their feet, poured her a drink and greeted her as if the white-faced, speechless girl were the most usual visitor in the world.

Nobody asked what had happened, and after a while she pulled herself together. When, at the end of the evening, the two men left, Sorrel told Pauline what had happened.

Pauline sighed.

'Poor man. Poor man. A lot of them are going to hear things like that. Do you think he'll get over it? It's such a hideous shock for him, after he'd made you into a kind of saint. It was natural and unnatural, if one comes to think of it. Do you think he'll – well – '

'Forgive me? I'm certain he won't.'

'You can't be certain of anything when it's about love.'

'With Toby I can.'

Pauline said, 'Of course you must come back here. This time for keeps.'

'What about Chris?'

'He'll love you. He's written to me about you. He's under the impression that you saved his entire family from being blown to bits.'

'Pauline, that's mad, you didn't – ?'

'I told him you rescued us during the buzz bombs. He'd never forget that. In any case there isn't a hope we'll see him yet. He wrote last week and the situation in the Dutch East Indies is chaos. Freed prisoners. Rubber planters pouring back. Absolutely chaotic. Chris says we must grin and bear it and it's going to be months, not weeks. Think what a favour you're doing me. Keeping me company while I gnaw my fingernails.'

'I wish I'd been like you.'

'Of course you don't. You're a girl who rushes at life, finds out things, experiences, risks, wrestles. You match the times. That's why you volunteered so quickly and fell in love and married so quickly.'

'And ruined everything so quickly.'

'I didn't say or mean that. What I *do* say is I'm eternally grateful to have you.'

The morning after Sorrel's blind escape from Piccadilly, Paulinc waited until she'd gone out for a walk with the children, and then telephoned the Aldenham House flat. To her relief a man answered who said, 'The catering manager speaking. Is it in connection with the party, Madam?'

No, said Pauline. She wished to leave an address for Major Martyn. She gavc the Thornley Court address and rang off. Sorrel's luggage appeared in a taxi within the hour. There was no letter.

Sorrel had been too miserable and self-absorbed to wonder how her husband knew where she was. Pauline unpacked. She reflected that all her friend had to show for her pathetic marriage was a lot of clothes.

In her soul Sorrel knew Toby wouldn't forgive her. He was a man with unbreakable laws and kept every one of them. How could he accept a wife who'd slept with some unknown

American? When she and Toby fell in love, the weight of his knowing she wasn't a virgin had been heavy on her. She'd made up the story of a fiancé killed before they could marry. The lie was instinctive, for even then she already saw what Toby was. *Virtus semper viridias* said the motto on his regimental arms. But *virtus* did not only mean virtue. It meant everything Toby represented – manhood and courage, prowess, heroism and strength.

She couldn't understand why Dot had made her into the whore Toby now believed her to be. He'd said Dot was the soul of truth. When she thought painfully about it, Sorrel realised that Dot had thought it *was* true. It hadn't been – but it could have been. Sex in wartime was so powerful, so indiscriminate. Men and women did the act of darkness, and were as much part of the conflict as bloody hand-to-hand battles, cities on fire, partisans creeping through the night to cut the enemy's throats. Sex was the other opponent in the game with that black enemy. Yes, Dot truly believed her wanton, and behaved to her nephew like a surgeon cutting out a cancer. She had despised the lies on which poor Toby had started to build his marriage.

It was strange how shocked Sorrel was at being found out. Before Toby knew, her conscience was easy enough. Her feeling for Dion must be put aside, her duty was with her husband. She had never seen her faithlessness from Toby's point of view and now, when she remembered the murderous face, she did. And thought of something he had told her on their first night together. They had finished, or he had, making love and were lying quietly. It was the only time he was to speak of Yugoslavia when they were alone. He said in the dark, 'Living with the partisans was like being with my brother all over again. We understood each other. We had a bond. They were proud of all they'd suffered and, because I was one of them, proud of me. They had such discipline. They never looted, however hungry or desperate they were. They took nothing from the villages but what was given them. They scarcely drank when we were fighting. And they had no women.'

Sorrel started. 'But surely – '

'No. They never did. It was against their beliefs. As if they'd taken a vow of chastity. A blood brotherhood nothing and nobody must touch. They were excitable and loud and crazy and difficult at times. And so pure.'

She was desolate now, but it was a desolation of remorse and not of love. She began to see that she had not been in love with Toby for a long time. Not since the delirious days when they'd first been lovers in Sussex in the empty hotel, at Evendon when he'd crept through the house into her bed, when he had been the hero who had married her, who walked with her in the grounds of Evendon, and they had trembled with desire. The man who was in her imagination, when she let him be, was Dion. She knew she had refused anything they might have because she had not chosen him. He hadn't wanted her to. But there had been that single chance to be ruthless in love and she hadn't taken it. Her love for Dion, her misery at having made Toby suffer, were a crown of thorns. It's my own doing that I've lost them both, she thought.

But she refused herself the indulgence of picking through the past, and she had the distraction and blessing of living in a house of children. In the early morning Davy sang his speciality, an interminable song, a kind of saga of the day's expectations. Rose erupted into Sorrel's room, bringing books. Rose was pretty and wilful, quick as her mother was, and loud in her demand that everything, as in the Judgement of Solomon, should be sawn in half. Pauline said she had an over-developed sense of justice. Davy was his sister's shadow, but more thoughtful, more serious. The children came rushing home from school, giving Sorrel no time to brood, and if her thoughts ached, she only allowed them to do so after seven at night.

Chris's letters came from the Far East more often now, and Pauline tore them open so fast that she sometimes tore them in pieces, and had to read them like a paper jigsaw.

'Not yet,' she would announce. 'Damn, damn, damn.'

'Damn, damn,' chanted the children. Knowing their mother could scarcely scold. Pauline told Sorrel that waiting was much worse now peace had arrived.

'It's exactly like being pregnant. You get through nine months as contented as a cow, and the last three days are insupportable.'

It made things worse for Pauline that by the end of the year thousands upon thousands of men and women were flooding back home and her friends often rang in a state of trembling excitement.

'Oh Pauline! Pauline! He'll be home in two days!'

As the weeks of winter went by, Pauline grew nervous.

'He doesn't know the kids at all, Sorrel.'

'He knows Rose.'

'She wasn't even Davy's age when he left. Do you realise how *long* it's been?'

Pauline frowned at her husband's photograph.

'Suppose they don't like him. It can happen.'

'Pauline, that really is ludicrous.'

'I know. I am ludicrous. Let's have a glass of that filthy Algerian wine Jack brought, shall we?'

She busied herself pouring the wine, and as Sorrel looked at her she saw, for a moment, a resemblance to Dion. Her heart hurt for a moment as a tooth might give a sharp unexpected stab.

Pauline gave her a glass and they drank to each other.

'While we're on the subject of Chris coming home, I know I'm going on about it, but suppose he doesn't like *me*?'

She went to the mirror over the fireplace and said after a moment, to her reflection, 'God. You're plain.'

'I think you're beautiful.'

'Oh, *you,*' said Pauline, laughing.

When Sorrel first came back to live at Thorley Court she blurted out to Pauline one evening that if Dion rang she would rather not talk to him.

It's just that he might ask – ' she stammered, miserably conscious of trying to explain the unexplainable. Pauline was unsurprised.

'Might ask a lot of questions. He's like that. Does it with me sometimes. I agree. Don't talk to him until you're stronger. My brother has a kind heart and doesn't know he's quite alarming.'

And so when he rang his sister, only Pauline talked to him. Sorrel and Dion kept apart by a sort of mutual silence.

The other part of her life was silent too. The only sign of Toby since the night she ran away and the luggage arrived by taxi the next day was a letter a month later from the Martyns' solicitors. This informed her that Major Martyn was willing to give her an allowance of £5 a week.

'Princely,' scoffed Pauline in a burst of indignation.

The letter added that money previously paid by Lord Martyn, plus her army allowance, would be discontinued.

'They can't do that. You're his wife and the allowance belongs to you!' Pauline exclaimed. Sorrel didn't answer. She did not want to talk about it. Pauline fumed inwardly, and what she could not guess was that Sorrel wrote the same day saying she wanted nothing. There was no reply. All the money stopped.

Her refusal to take anything from Toby was instinctive. How could she take money from a man who hated her and had told her to get out of his sight? He did not think of her as a wife but as a whore. It was very strange. She'd loved him and mourned him and only when she believed death had cut him from her had she lain with another man. She saw a kind of justice in his casting her off. Because they were no longer the man and girl who had embraced and gasped in sexual joy in the dawns at Evendon. They had altered for the worse. Innocence was gone. And a kind of safety.

The first peacetime Christmas was only festive because of Pauline; there was no tinsel or bright glass baubles, so she decorated her tree with coloured ribbons. Dion, much taken up with *Country Matters*, the first issue not yet ready for publication, rang to say he couldn't spend the holiday with them. Sorrel knew that was not the only reason.

Pauline and Sorrel took the children to Trafalgar Square to see the famous, giant-sized green spruce just arrived by ship, a gift from the Norwegian people. Londoners stood round it in its Christmas glory and sang hymns in the cold afternoon.

When she returned to live with Pauline, Sorrel had begun

the secretarial course again, and in the new year of 1946 she completed it and had the chance of getting a job. She had recovered from the distraught girl who'd turned up at Pauline's door one late autumn night. Her beauty had come back, in a way. Setting off for an employment agency in Mayfair, wearing one of the expensive suits Toby had bought her, a pale chocolate brown, Sorrel looked cool and self-possessed. And was not. The agency was on the first floor of a house in Bruton Street, nothing more than two rooms which had been somebody's double drawing room once upon a time. A thin woman in a blouse which needed ironing gave her three addresses.

'Messrs Varley and Varley in the Temple offer ten shillings more than the other two firms. But they are solicitors, and you would have to use a brief machine. Are you prepared to do that?'

Sorrel reflected that for an extra ten shillings she'd cook the solicitors' lunch. She set off for the Temple. Poor for the first time in her life, she detested it and was eager and anxious to get work. It had been different having little money in the navy with Margaret Reilly. Both girls had had allowances from their parents and in any case there was nothing to spend money on except to go to the local café, or once in Sorrel's case to buy a handkerchief edged with real lace. Lack of money now was like being hobbled. There had been just enough left in the bank to last two more weeks, but she couldn't afford a bunch of violets for Pauline.

It was need of money which took her to an ancient square where she climbed creaking stairs, knocked at an antique door and was received by a man who looked like a parson in an Edwardian farce. He wore striped trousers, a black jacket and a starched wing collar which must have been painful. He regarded her over the top of his glasses.

'Miss Scott?'

Sorrel had become unmarried again, and had put her wedding ring into her dressing-table drawer where it shone in a circle of broken vows.

'Miss Scott, I see from your details that this would be your first post. Wren officer. Yes. Yes.'

He studied her shorthand and typing speed and set her a test. Sorrel was given a desk in a corner and faced, for the first time, the typewriter which would mean extra cash. The carriage was heavy as lead and as each line was completed rang as loudly as a bicycle bell.

She sat down to work, as meek as a handmaiden to some forgotten Knight Templar when the world and London were young. The man in the starched collar looked through the finished work with an inscrutable face. Then –

'Can you start after luncheon?' was the astonishing question. 'We will pay you for a half day. My name is Redfern. Like the gallery.'

'Yes. I can begin work this afternoon, Mr Redfern.'

'Eight pounds ten shillings a week. Hours, nine until quarter to six. We are very punctual. And every other Saturday is free.'

Life settled down as the 1946 spring advanced. She was earning enough to pay Pauline for her keep, to buy flowers and toys and sometimes, via a young woman in the office with mysterious connections, black-market nylon stockings. Pauline and Sorrel could not get used to the illegal sheen on their legs.

Pauline still awaited her husband's return and pounced on letters from Java, reading them at a raking glance.

'No good. Still chaotic, poor old Chris. He says the planters are cutting up rusty, and there are US troops, Dutch troops *and* the Indians. Hell. It may be months.'

'It'll be sooner than that.'

'It might be. And "poor me" are the two stupidest words in the English language.'

Then the telephone rang as it always did, and friends wanted to come round. The flat filled up with people and Pauline was the most slapdash and beloved of hostesses.

Sorrel knew that sooner or later she would see Dion. She didn't want to. Of course Pauline had told him Sorrel and Toby had parted, and Sorrel was now at Thorley Court. He had known since the day after it happened and had made no sign and Sorrel was glad. Would Dion, knowing her unattached, rush to London to claim her? What a ridiculous idea.

Claim her? He did not love her. It was true he had made love to her and it had been passionate and beautiful and she did not want to think about it. But all he'd said in the empty room in the National Portrait Gallery had been 'choose'. He had meant 'choose which of us is to be your lover'. Not 'which of us is to be your life'.

She'd chosen Toby from a sense of right. A paradox since, she supposed, to stay with a man you did not love was wrong. Oh, she thought, I'm like Margaret Reilly when Gareth and Byron were killed. I don't know anything any more. Perhaps she should be grateful to Aunt Dot; perhaps you couldn't base your life on a lie, however much you kept it up to protect somebody. It must be what thousands of women were doing now.

The ecstasy of VE and VJ Days, the kissing and the dancing, were gone. Where were the pipes of peace? Basic rations hadn't grown larger, there was still only one egg a fortnight and two ounces of butter a week. It was somehow much harder to put up with now the war was over. Sorrel and Pauline consulted about food and, when Sorrel was at work, she took a bus to Soho in the lunch hours and hunted or queued. On lucky days she found a tin of salmon, doubtless from the black market. Once she flirted with a Greek shopkeeper and was given some spices. And on one glorious winter lunchtime managed to buy six eggs and a tiny bottle of olive oil.

Now and again Pauline's friend, Irish Kathleen, a mountainous old body with hair in earphones on either side of her face, came in the evening to mind the children who adored her. Pauline and Sorrel had the chance to go out to supper with whichever of Pauline's many friends were in London. Most were officers waiting for demob, and Pauline discovered an inexpensive restaurant in South Kensington where the long trestle tables were set with candles and you could have a passable meal and a dance to the gramophone.

> Love is funny, or it's sad,
> It is quiet, or it's mad,

It's a good thing, or it's bad,
But beautiful.

'*You're* beautiful,' said the man dancing with Sorrel. He was an old flame of Pauline's, wore the kilt and his name was Frazer. 'Pauline tells me I'm not to make a pass. Is she right?'

He looked into her swimming eyes, and his hand on her waist tightened.

Sorrel didn't take up the offer, she was pleasant, elusive and glad when she and Pauline were home. Pauline guessed Ian had been attracted to Sorrel; he was attractive himself, and undoubtedly heartfree. But it did not surprise her that Sorrel reacted as she did.

Pauline knew there had been something between her brother and her friend; she wasn't sure what it had been, serious? temporary? merely two people drawn to each other for a while? She often wondered how Sorrel felt about him now she was, to all intents and purposes, free. But what about him? When he telephoned he didn't ask to speak to Sorrel these days, and spoke mostly of work.

'James Tarrant's a tough cookie; we've got to succeed with this thing.'

'Oh, you will.'

'You're not prejudiced by any chance? He's moved into the Priory, by the way. I was asked to dinner last night. A bit of a change from being in the cowshed. I felt quite nostalgic.'

He was coming to London the following week to meet a writer, and would call in at Thorley Court. 'I want to see you and the kids.'

'And Sorrel,' said Pauline.

'Naturally.'

Spring had come. The parks were full of daffodils and on her way to work Sorrel saw a girl in a straw hat with an enormous striped bow. Even in the antique offices of Varley and Varley, among the deed boxes and files and daunting masses of paper, Mr Redfern had placed a pygmy-sized pot of tulips. He said he'd grown them at home in Streatham.

Sometimes when the sun was out Sorrel did not eat her

sandwiches in the office but went down Middle Temple Lane, out through the gateway and across Fleet Street. She walked as far as Gray's Inn, a new discovery. All the time she had lived in London with her mother, she hadn't known these parts of the City. They were so old. They made her own life seem small, as if she were a child sitting on the floor at the feet of great-grandparents. There was bomb damage, of course, but the atmosphere of the Inn was there, and some of the old and lovely buildings were intact, and the trees were budding.

One lunchtime she sat on a bench, admiring the red tulips and enjoying the sun on her face. And the almond blossom in full bloom. Like a patient waking one day to know the fever is gone, she looked round, smiled, and sighed.

As she watched the passers-by she saw a woman walking towards her, a sturdy figure in grey tweed, spotless white blouse and a black pudding-basin hat pulled down on her forehead.

'*Why, Evie!*'

Sorrel sprang up. But Evie, stopping, merely said, 'If it isn't Mrs Martyn.'

'How nice to see you, I've thought about you so much!' exclaimed Sorrel with her old impulsiveness, refusing to accept a snub. She liked Evie.

At the eager voice and open smile, the housekeeper's face softened. She said quite kindly, 'Excuse me for not mentioning it at once. I heard about you and the major, Mrs . . . Sorrel. I was very sorry.'

'Thank you, Evie. Yes. It's sad.'

They might have been speaking of a death.

'But why are you in London?' Sorrel went on. 'I've had no news of . . . well . . . you understand that.'

Evie had sat down beside her and Sorrel wondered if she now felt that she must. Did I make a mistake? I rush up to people because I'm pleased to see them, I never think – are they pleased to see me? Perhaps Evie didn't want to talk and I've forced her to.

'I've just been to an employment agency,' Evie said, after a moment. 'I've been offered a very interesting new post.

Housekeeper to the Earl of Shering. He has a very large estate – Brixton Place in Lincolnshire, I daresay you've heard of it. The Royal Family stay there occasionally. Of course there's Shering House in Park Lane, too.'

'But Evie, how wonderful!'

Sorrel was ignorant of earls or great houses, the Priory having been the only one, on a minor scale, she'd ever known. 'You must be excited.'

'I was surprised to be offered it,' admitted Evie. 'It will be a big responsibility. Lord Shering says I am to be in charge of the female staff. We have to build up the establishment again. Employ the maids and cookery staff and so on. There ought to be some good people about, now everybody is coming out of the services.'

'The earl is lucky to have you.'

Evie looked diffident.

'I suppose you decided you didn't want to go to America, but I don't know how the Martyns could lose you . . . they went some time ago, didn't they?'

'Yes. They sailed in November.'

'And Toby's gone too?'

That was a strange question.

'He's still in England for the time being,' said Evie awkwardly. 'When he leaves the army – he stayed on for a bit – he will go and join them.'

'Will he *like* that?'

'I don't expect so.'

Sorrel heard the old affection in Evie's voice.

'I still don't know how the Martyns could bear to part with you. I bet they tried hard to make you change your mind,' Sorrel said.

Evie looked at the toes of her black shoes, cleaned in the way Toby's were, to a starry glitter.

'When they left the Priory and went to live in that awful Piccadilly flat, Lord Martyn asked me to go to my sister in Putney. So I'd be ready to help when they finally sold and everything was moved out of the Priory. He never told me what they were planning to do later.'

'I don't understand.'

'They never said about going to America.'

'But when you did hear, they asked you to go too.'

'They did not,' Evie said. She looked at her shoes again. 'I'll admit I was upset. They didn't say one word. Well, Lord Martyn didn't, and *she* kept out of the way so as not to take the responsibility. He told me nothing until I'd done the move. It was a big job, took me over two weeks. I stayed there, it was cold as ice, and had to get all the inventories done and checked, sort out what they wanted to keep, and what was to be sold. *He* came down, of course. So did experts from Sotheby's and that. There was all the Croxton Collection to be moved back to London, I kept thinking suppose something valuable gets stolen or broken; I thought my head would split sometimes. Mrs Lorimer came over, she's taken The Chief *and* Scrap. Seemed delighted to do it, but I'm sure Toby was upset over that horse of his . . . well . . . there it was. Then Longstaffe from Butterbox got under my feet, he took all the stock. So, I did it. Everything's gone. Stored at Harrods or sent to sale rooms, and the farm broken up, all the stock gone, the cowman paid off. And the house cleaned from attics to cellars. It was a real treat to see it when we'd finished,' added Evie with the glow of an artist. 'And after Ada and Hooper had gone, both retired, you know, Lord Martyn asked me to come to that London flat.'

She paused.

'Said they were off to America and my job was finished. He gave me a year's pay.'

'Evie.'

'Not very nice, was it? After all the years with the family. I admit I was upset. Oh well. Toby took me out to dinner, he always was a kind boy. To the Ritz. He went on in that way of his about England being finished and the army wouldn't be worth twopence but it's all hot air. The army's his life and his father's talked him into leaving it. Toby dotes on his father, admires him too much, I used to think. Lady Martyn's favourite was always Toby but *his* favourite is his father. He'll do anything he wants.'

'One could see he's fond of him.'

'It's more than that. Giving up the army. What'll Toby do in America, well, I'll tell you. He'll not be happy. I don't know much about Americans, we met a few at the Priory, of course, but he isn't like them. His ideas are so – he isn't like them at all.'

She looked uncertainly at Sorrel.

'Perhaps I shouldn't be talking. Perhaps you and he will make it up.'

She pulled herself together. The bitter tone which Sorrel hadn't heard before had left her voice. She looked at Sorrel from under the brim of the pudding-basin hat, much as the old Evie did when sitting in the pony trap.

'I'm afraid it's too late to be mended between Toby and me, Evie.'

Evie glanced at her for a moment with the nannyish expression Sorrel used to see when she first married Toby. It was a proprietary look.

'It's a shame when a marriage breaks up,' she said. But she didn't use a nanny's direct attack and ask more; instead she said thoughtfully, 'We've never talked about your mother and father, have we? *She* asked me not to. Said Lord Martyn didn't want to upset you by raking over the past, so I didn't speak to you about them, which seemed a pity. You were only little, of course. I don't remember seeing you, though I knew Mr and Mrs Scott had a daughter. But I thought you'd like to know I remembered your parents very well.'

'Oh, I do!'

'I wasn't friendly with them, of course. I mean, we only passed the time of day. Your mother was such a pretty woman when she was young, we used to see each other in the village sometimes when I was shopping and we might have a little chat. She was shy. But they were nice people and your father behaved so well during all the trouble. I did admire him.'

'I never knew anything about it. I was too young.'

'But your mother explained to you later – '

'No, Evie. She never told me what had happened.'

'I daresay she wanted to put it out of her mind,' said Evie, nodding. 'It wasn't a happy time.' But she looked searchingly at her, and Sorrel felt she must explain that she was not entirely ignorant of her father's dingy old secrets.

'Actually, it was Aunt Dot who told me.'

'Oh. Did she?'

What did that ironic tone mean? Sorrel thought – my parents' story is as dead as they are, it doesn't matter any more. And for an inexplicable reason she remembered Buzz, and Byron, and the godlike figure of Gareth van Doren. Their tragedies were recent. And mattered still.

'Dot said Lord Martyn had saved my father from prison. She didn't go into detail, all she told me was there were some fishy things he had to hush up for Father. I suppose I should be grateful. I suppose my parents were.'

Evie smoothed one of her gloves. Everything about her was expensive. Her shoes. Her suit. Her handbag. The silky leather gloves.

'Your poor father got himself into a mess, that's true. And it wasn't an honest mess, a lot of money is a terrible temptation. But there's more to it than that.'

Sorrel waited. She thought – what am I going to hear *at last*?

'It was Lord Martyn who put him up to it,' Evie said without emphasis. 'You might say the big swindle was his inspiration. It was just before 1914 and when it looked as if it had been discovered the two men were plain scared. I remember Lord Martyn – he was Mister Martyn then – coming home one day chalk-white and he told *her* he was ill. She fussed over him, wanted him to go to bed, but he shouted at her to leave him alone. Lady Martyn never knew anything about it, never found out. Just sailed through it.'

'But surely – '

'No, it's true, she didn't know. You'll ask how I did. Well, staff hear things, pick things up. Once when he was talking to your father in his study the door was open and I had an earful. But *she* was innocent as a babe unborn. She's always been straight. I'm afraid I don't like her, Sorrel, but she's as straight as a die.'

'What *happened*, Evie?'

'Lord Martyn managed to pull out and make things look right, I should think he greased some palms, wouldn't you? Your father was given the push from working for him, and later the war came and Lord Martyn got his millions. He was a big man during the war, *and* a profiteer. He wasn't friendly with your parents after the swindle was hushed up. He dropped them, and he and the family and me, I was nanny then, all moved to Evendon. But I had an idea he paid your father money. Funny. I never thought of it till now but he got rid of your father just like he got rid of me. Not useful any more.'

She looked at her watch.

'I'm an old gossip, telling you all that stuff. Sorry. I've made up my mind now, working for Lord Shering, that I'm going to put the past right out of my mind and try to forget the Martyns. Not Toby, of course. But even he will forget me soon enough and that hurts a bit. We all have our troubles, don't we?'

She stood up.

'It was kind of you to listen. And kind to say hello. After all, I never got in touch when I heard you and Toby had separated.'

Sorrel put her arms round Evie and kissed her. Evie gave a smile as shy as a child's and walked quickly away.

On her way back to the office, Sorrel thought about the truth Evie had given her. She knew this time that it was the truth. The quality in George Martyn that had affected her, something blank, something she couldn't catch hold of, a lack of heart? a lack of reality? came into her mind. She had often told herself she was imagining it, but what she had sensed was the wrong he'd done her father. Her father had suffered while George Martyn flowered, and the money had been conscience money.

She marvelled at the thought of Grace knowing nothing about it. The world was as simple to Grace as to her son; she had a rich and titled husband of spotless integrity, a patriotism in which the enemy had not a single virtue, a daughter-in-law thrown out because she was a whore. Sorrel thought of George Martyn's generosity and dishonesty, of Grace's principles and the ranting jingoism which set the teeth on edge. Dot's warmth and betrayals. And Toby, the noble knight, the Parsifal and the bird of prey.

She sighed as she went through the gates of the Temple.

Dion was due at Thorley Court that week; he had telephoned to say he would stay the night if his sister would lend him the sitting-room sofa. Sorrel no longer dreaded the idea of seeing him again.

Her love hadn't melted as she had believed it was sure to do. It had grown rather than diminished and she told herself the pathetic lies of lovers. 'At least I'll see him,' adding the bigger lie, 'and we can be friends.' On the morning Pauline told her Dion was due that day, Sorrel received a letter. The post arrived just before she left for work, and she did not open it until she was on top of a bus rumbling its way to the Strand.

The letter had an official look; it was very like the letters she herself typed every day for Mr Redfern. At the top of the paper were the words 'Mason & Carew, Solicitors', names she recognised. The letter was brief. Major Martyn would soon be leaving the country and wished to arrange a meeting for 'both parties'. Would Mrs Martyn be good enough to give a choice of dates and suggest a meeting place? They were her faithful servants.

She stared from the bus window at the crowds of people on their way to work. Bright dresses. Straw hats, even. What does he want? A divorce, I suppose. He is going to America and he can't leave things as they are. One thing was certain, he would never take her back supposing she wanted it. She had been like a queen unfaithful to a monarch in medieval times, a Guinevere. When you broke your marriage vow you were better dead.

During the lunch hour when the office was empty Sorrel telephoned the solicitors.

'May I speak to Mr Lewis Mason? This is Mrs Ronald Martyn.'

'Hold on please, I will ascertain,' was the reply. The woman and the voice were patronising.

When Lewis Mason came to the telephone he sounded

worse. Drawling and confident and apparently set on putting her in her place.

'I gather my husband wishes us to meet, Mr Mason.'

'That is the general idea. Have you decided upon a venue?'

'A what?'

'A venue. A place suitable for the meeting.'

Sorrel frowned.

'Is my husband staying in London at present?'

'Why do you ask?'

The question was impertinent.

'I ask, Mr Mason, for the simple reason that it is *he* who wishes to see *me* and I think his home, if he has one, would be the best place.'

'I'm afraid that is out of the question.'

'You mean he isn't at Aldenham House any more?'

'He is not in London.'

'What about his club?'

'Not quite suitable, surely?'

Sorrel was beginning to become angry.

'If my husband wants to see me he can decide where is suitable, as you put it. Tell him that.'

She was about to ring off but Mason, rather hurriedly, spoke again.

'I am sorry if I seem to have upset you. I believe, Mrs Martyn, you now have employment in the Temple?'

How in heaven did he know that? Before she had time to take in the implications, he continued, 'Do you think it might be possible for the major to call at your offices? At some time convenient to you, when you would be undisturbed?'

Sorrel said she supposed it could.

'At the luncheon hour, perhaps,' suggested Mason, who added a few more persuasive words. Sorrel found herself agreeing that she would see Toby tomorrow at lunchtime. She knew, while she was speaking, that the offices would be empty. She often had her sandwiches in solitude between one and two. Lewis Mason with surprising charm then thanked her, they confirmed the time of the meeting and he finished, 'We really are most grateful.'

Sorrel put down the receiver. She was going to see Toby tomorrow. She dreaded the idea and could scarcely bear to guess what the interview was going to be like. She supposed that Toby, seasoned and accustomed to other kinds of pain, would carry it off; he would never show her a second time how much she had wounded him. Perhaps he hated her now, and perhaps it would be better if he did. For herself, she felt a kind of desolation. He'll be businesslike, the way soldiers are. I must try to be the same.

She decided not to tell Pauline until afterwards. Coming out into the still bright evening when work was over, she bought her a large, expensive bunch of flowers.

The moment she went into the flat she heard the sound of Dion laughing. He and the children were in the garden, there was a litter of toys and a tray of tea on the grass. Seeing her, he stood up, smiling.

'Irises,' he said. 'Do you know they grow up as far as the Arctic Circle.'

'Listen to him,' said Pauline, appearing from the kitchen and taking the flowers, exclaiming over their glassy blue. 'He's the walking expert on everything if it flowers or flies or blooms or snuffles in the woods. You'd think he was the Creator.'

'Pauline detests information,' said Dion.

'Pauline detests an encyclopaedia for a brother. Want to see the first issue of his mag, Sorrel?'

'Don't force it on the poor girl.'

'Of course I will.'

Pauline went to fetch the magazine. It positively shone with newness. The cover showed the painting of a garden, across the sky was lettered *Country Matters. First Issue. June 1946*. The painting was evocative, of trees in summer leaf, a grassy path bordered with lilies and lupins and yellow roses, and a stone house in the distance. Crouched in front of the house on a flagged terrace, busily weeding a flower bed, was a man in a rakish old felt hat.

'Do you like the pic?' asked Dion. 'I discovered the artist by luck. She's a protegée of Miss Banning's and sells her stuff in the West Country. She's doing us twelve paintings for the twelve months of the year. Our sainted proprietor has bought that one which we think a good sign.'

He was as easy as the young man who'd first sat with her on the banks of the Test. He has got over me, she thought. No, that isn't right. We made love like people did in wartime, I mean nothing to him.

'You're not to read it now,' Dion said. 'I shall only keep asking if you like things and arguing if you don't. I've forbidden Pauline to read it either. Pick it to pieces when I've gone.'

'Oh, the false modesty,' scoffed his sister.

During the evening he told them about his work, and amused them, and Sorrel felt inhibited. Sitting on the sofa where people had slept in the first blitz, and afterwards right through the war to save travelling in the blackout, he was relaxed and funny and himself. The children hung round him, and both climbed on his knee at the same time. Pauline put on her new French record.

'*Je tire ma révérence, Et m'en vais au hazard*,' she sang.

That's Dion, thought Sorrel. She was sitting at the end of the sofa and in the way of sexual memories which come suddenly when most unwelcomed she remembered he had lain upon her, on these cushions, and they'd made love. They hadn't undressed. 'If we do, somebody's bound to call in and we'll be slap in the middle of a French farce,' he'd said, caressing her. She remembered his weight, the shape and feel of him, the way he'd looked at her when he took her, intent, masterful, yet a look which said – what could it possibly have said? That thrusting into her was pleasure to be enjoyed, and more enjoyed. But afterwards, when rapture had gone through her, a rapture she'd believed would never be hers again, for him there had been nothing.

When the evening was over, he made up his bed with blankets on the sofa, and looked up at her as she said goodnight. His fair hair fell in a crescent on his forehead. He looked handsome and she was sure he was laughing at her.

'Sleep well, Sorrel.'

The next morning when the family were having a cramped breakfast in the cramped kitchen, he said, 'You work in the Temple, don't you, Sorrel?'

'Dion, I told you, she works for classy solicitors, established 1825, and she uses a machine which weighs more than a Sherman tank.'

'The firm isn't classy, it's dusty. Pauline always makes things better than they are.'

'That's her gift, thank God,' said Dion. 'I'm going to Fleet Street to see a journalist I know. Shall we travel together?'

'Yes. Of course.'

There was a sound, a slithering noise from the hall, envelopes shooting across the mat. Pauline put down the coffee pot and sprang up.

'The post!' shouted Rose.

'Post!' echoed Davy.

She rushed out.

'One of these days . . .' said Dion to Sorrel. They heard Pauline call out, 'There's one from Chris. I must just . . . '

Silence. Then, 'Oh God. Oh God!'

Starting up in alarm, Dion got to his feet as his sister came into the kitchen holding a letter. She tried to speak, stopped, and gave something like a sob.

'Oh Dion. Sorrel. Children. He's coming home . . . in four weeks . . . he's coming home. Hell. I'm going to be sick.'

And everybody burst out laughing.

Dion and Sorrel travelled to Fleet Street on the top deck of the bus, her favourite seat. They left a still dazed Pauline telephoning friends, hugging the children and making what Dion said were lunatic plans.

'You're going to have your hands full with my sister until the momentous day,' he remarked. Sorrel murmured something about Pauline bcing worried that she had changed.

'Sure, she has changed. Chris won't mind. He's as strong as she is,' Dion comfortably said. 'They'll shake down again, you'll see.'

He looked up at the clouded sky and remarked that it was going to rain.

'Are you a weather expert too?' said Sorrel, attempting a light tone.

'I learned a bit about it when I was at Evendon. Farmers have a mania about the weather. Farming doesn't get out of one's system; I often find myself thinking what jobs are most urgent, how are the oats germinating, what happens if it rains? In a way I miss the awful anxiety.'

The bus seat was narrow and she could feel his body against hers. She wanted to move away.

'You're very quiet this morning.'

'I'm sorry if I'm bad company.'

'Don't be *silly*,' he said, as if talking to Rose. 'You couldn't be if you tried. There's something on your mind.'

'Not really.'

'Oh yes, there is. Tell me.'

She wanted not to.

'It's my husband.'

'Ah. You miss him. And when Pauline – '

'No, I, that is – ' The words wouldn't come.

'I haven't asked you what has been happening to you, Sorrel. Pauline said it would be better not.'

'She explained to you why I left.'

'Well. Yes.'

'It was an American. You know . . . Buzz Alderman.'

'I remember.'

'Dot told Toby.'

'But what has happened now?' said Dion. He sounded like a priest or a doctor.

'I had a letter from his solicitor. It's been arranged for him to come to the office today.'

She wondered why she was telling him.

'*Your* solicitor to see his, you mean?'

'No, no, I haven't got one. Toby is coming to see me.'

'But why at your office? Was that your idea?'

'His solicitor wouldn't agree to Toby and me meeting at Toby's club, or wherever he is staying at present.'

'Why on earth not?'

'I suppose Toby didn't want it. In the end the solicitor suggested my office and I agreed. Toby's coming in the lunch hour. Nobody's around then.'

'I see.'

'Do you?'

'It's nothing to worry about, Sorrel. Much better for you both to meet. Clear things up. Perhaps make up.'

'Never. He never will.'

'Do you want him to?' He still sounded like a doctor. She couldn't answer. Had she expected him to be kind? He gave her nothing.

'Pauline told me you're not getting a cent from him. And if I know you, Sorrel, I imagine he'll offer and you'll still refuse. That would be very stupid and quixotic of you. I wouldn't approve.'

'*You* wouldn't take anything.'

'You can't know that,' he said dryly.

'I don't want Toby's money,' she whispered tensely, afraid other passengers might hear. He looked amused.

'He won't force the cash on you, I am quite sure husbands don't. But he'll feel better in himself if you accept. Army people do like things to be tidy. If you're right and he doesn't want to be reconciled, are you prepared for him to ask for a divorce?'

This was not the man who'd taken her into his arms. There was a thick pane of glass between them, and it wasn't the kind anybody could smash.

'I suppose so.'

'Cheer up. When you dread something it often turns out not too bad. It's the bolt from the blue which strikes you dead. Look, this is where I get off. I may go back to the country tonight, so – good luck.'

He patted her shoulder, and stood up.

Mr Redfern had a number of appointments and left the Temple long before midday. He gave Sorrel so much work to do that she could never finish it by the evening and had the gall to add that if she ran out, his partner Mr Varley would 'give you something to occupy those busy fingers'. Putting on his bowler hat, checking through the documents in a satchel like a child's music case, he bustled from the office.

Dion was right, it had begun to rain. The day grew dark and the rain beat against the ancient windows like little whips. Sorrel worked. She put the papers in a careful pile on her right, the finished work on her left. Typing, correcting, checking, she tried not to look at the clock. But it wasn't possible, and every time she looked, the hands of the clock had moved less than she hoped. She wanted the ordeal to be over. She thought the morning would never end. And felt as if her body were made of the strings of a violin, and some idiot, herself, had screwed them tighter and tighter until the slightest touch would make them sing hideously.

Why had Toby insisted on coming to see her here? Why had he got in touch with her through that rude solicitor? Toby, the brave one, was he afraid to speak to her himself? It was obvious he wasn't going to ask her to come back to him. But he would loathe a divorce. She remembered he had once said how déclassé it was to be divorced. It was vulgar. Once at Evendon he'd told her about an officer in the regiment who had actually considered divorcing his wife.

'Our colonel had something to say about that, I can tell you. It would have been degrading. How could a man think of such a thing?'

She had laughed and called him Sir Galahad and said perhaps his mother's portrait of him was true after all.

At last the hands of the clock crawled to ten to one; Mrs Pritchett who worked in the adjoining office put her head round the door.

'I'm off to get some lunch. Are you staying in? Answer my phone if it rings, would you? Mr Varley's gone, and your boss won't be back for hours so you'll have a bit of peace. I'll be back just after two. 'Bye.'

Sorrel returned to her work. But she couldn't concentrate and was straining to hear a knock. Yet when it came she jumped violently.

She went to the door and opened it. Toby was there, so close that she had to back away. He seemed to occupy the entire doorway built for shorter men in past centuries, and stood as if in a picture frame. He wore civilian clothes, fine thin tweeds, his regimental tie. He was carrying a green pork-pie hat and she thought – surely you'd never wear that.

'Hello, Toby. Come in.'

'Thank you.'

She drew up a chair for him, but he went to the window and looked out at the cobbled yard, the old trees and lawns and ancient buildings, the grey river in the distance. He had turned his back, and it gave her a pang to see it was no longer as straight as it used to be. It was very faintly bent, like a bird with wings folded.

She sat down at her desk.

He turned round and looked straight at her.

'I've come to say there must be a divorce.'

'I thought perhaps that was why.'

Something in the drawn face moved her.

'Are you sure, Toby? I know you were so shocked and angry at what Dot told you. I only wish I'd had the guts to tell you myself. Somehow I couldn't bear to.'

He gave a slight shudder.

'I don't wish to discuss anything like that, please. Just the practical matter of the divorce.'

'But are you sure? I feel so bad. I never had the chance to tell you – '

'*Be quiet,*' he burst out. 'Will you be quiet? I could have done all this through the solicitors but I came because I feel it is right to say this in person. I have decided to divorce you.'

'To divorce *me*? How can you possibly do that? Hasn't it to be arranged between us? Poor Buzz Alderman was killed over a year ago. You can't cite him. What you suggest can't be done.'

'I think so.'

He turned to the window again and she spoke to the hunched back.

'I suppose we must end our marriage. It clearly makes you

very unhappy, and as for me, I don't know where I am. It will have to be tidied up somehow. But you can't cite a poor dead American airman.'

He spun round. 'I'm not talking about what you committed when I was overseas. I'm speaking of now. I've told Mason to cite Fulford.'

'Dion!'

'Your conchie friend. I know what's going on. When I found out – what you did – I had you watched. You're living with his sister. Seeing him . . . you saw him this morning.'

'Toby, what are you talking about? Yes, I'm living with Pauline and she's very kind to me. I had nobody to go to, I have no family, the Fulfords have been wonderful. I *love* them. Yes, I do, and don't laugh in that horrible way. You have absolutely no evidence against Dion Fulford,' she went on recklessly, realising he could not possibly know of the one passionate interlude in Pauline's flat. 'I won't allow it. I won't let you involve him in our miserable affairs. If you want a divorce you must give me the evidence. It will have to be trumped up, it often is. Then we can forget we ever knew each other.'

'*I!*' shouted Toby, so angry that for the second time since she'd known him she quailed. 'I pretend to sleep with some tart to give you your freedom? How dare you ask such a thing!'

'How dare *you* want to drag Dion Fulford into all this? I am sorry, Toby. I am sorry I've hurt you, sorry I slept with somebody when I thought you were dead. *I am sorry!*' she shouted, as angry as he. 'But I won't have Dion involved. It is nothing, nothing, nothing to do with him.'

Now that she was furious, her cheeks scarlet, her eyes flashing, he grew quite calm. He looked at her with a pitiless face. Finally he said, 'My mother's right. There's something dishonest in you. You're loose, and you're not straight either. Your family was the same. If it hadn't been for Father, he'd have gone to prison. You're no better, are you?'

She felt winded. She had tried to put out of her mind the sordid truths Evie had told her, the miserable tale of George Martyn and her father and their criminal dealings – and how

Martyn had grown rich and her father just escaped gaol. Now she was filled with passionate indignation. She thought vengefully – My God, he'll be shattered, how can he believe that stuff? It's time he knew the truth about his father as I know it about mine. She literally opened her mouth to tell him everything.

But just then, as if not being able to bear looking at her, he turned away again and stood staring from the window. She saw his familiar back, soldierly, square-shouldered, and thought how under the fine cloth there was a long jagged scar. And her revenge left her. It was as if a devil had been expelled, writhing, from her body; she literally put her hands across her stomach. She looked at Toby's back, with its faint bend, its hunch as if he were prematurely old. She felt her heart was breaking.

'*Oh Toby.*'

At the broken sound he turned round and to her horror she saw that his eyes were full of tears.

With something like a sob he rushed from the room.

She put her head down on the typewriter and began to cry. The tears flowed so fast and she could not stop them. She wept because old sins still had the power to hurt the young and because she and Margaret Reilly and millions of other women had been changed and spoiled by the awful game of sex and war. She cried because she and Toby had made love in the bath one summer night, and because he had taught her to ride, and because Buzz was dead. She did not know why she cried but it was for sorrow and loss and the end of love. She stopped sobbing at last, and washed her face in cold water and started to work again.

The only thing she remembered was the hunch of Toby's back.

The working day ended, and Mr Redfern returned, looking at her curiously over his glasses and remarking that she must not work late.

'You look somewhat tired, Miss Scott. I trust we are not overworking you.' He gave his neigh of a laugh.

Sorrel covered her typewriter with the macintosh cover and

picked up her hat and gloves. She didn't put on the hat but went bareheaded out into the rain.

As she crossed the cobblestones she saw a man sheltering under a plane tree. It was Dion.

She looked at him, not believing her eyes, and then ran towards him and he opened his arms and caught her. Leaning against him while the rain pattered noisily on the leaves above them, she began to cry all over again.

He let her weep, holding her close and murmuring something and nothing.

'It was so horrible. It was so sad, Dion.'

'It always is. When people don't love each other any more. The saddest thing in the world, worse than if they die.'

'Is it? Is it?'

'Oh yes,' he said, wiping the tears from her wet face. 'It's the worst. What did he want?'

'A divorce.'

'Sensible, surely.'

'But he wanted – '

'What?'

'To cite you.'

'I think that's an excellent idea,' he said and laughed.

She thought he was laughing at her and pulled away from him but he held her more tightly.

'Oh Sorrel. Why shouldn't he cite me? I'd *like* that. You're so sweet and beautiful, don't you know how crazy I am about you? I'm so in love with you I sometimes – hell – how could I tell you when I didn't damned well know how you felt about him? When you saw Toby, mightn't you have wanted to be his wife again? Mightn't he have begged you to come back? That's what I thought – that it was fair to keep away. My God, it's been a long afternoon. I didn't dare budge in case you took it into your head to leave early. I saw Toby arrive. And go. He wasn't with you long.'

'You don't mean you waited?'

'Of course I did. How could I not?'

He put up his hand again and wiped, or rather smeared, the tears across her face.

'Do you love me? Is it right what I suddenly feel in my bones? In my guts, to be exact. Let's walk, my dearest girl. The rain's nearly stopped and if we go down to the river we might see one of those black-winged gulls. They're predators. All the other birds fear them.'